Sabrina Jeffries is the *New York Times* bestselling author of 36 novels and 9 works of short fiction (some written under the pseudonyms Deborah Martin and Deborah Nicholas). Whatever time not spent writing in a coffee-fueled haze of dreams and madness is spent traveling with her husband and adult autistic son or indulging in one of her passions – jigsaw puzzles, chocolate, and music. With over 7 million books in print in 18 different languages, the North Carolina author never regrets tossing aside a budding career in academics for the sheer joy of writing fun fiction, and hopes that one day a book of hers will end up saving the world. She always dreams big.

For more information, visit her at www.sabrinajeffries.com, on Facebook at www.facebook.com/SabrinaJeffriesAuthor or on Twitter @SabrinaJeffries.

Praise for Sabrina Jeffries, queen of the sexy regency romance:

'Anyone who loves romance must read Sabrina Jeffries!' Lisa Kleypas, *New York Times* bestselling author

'Irresistible ... Larger-than-life characters, sprightly dialogue, and a steamy romance will draw you into this delicious captive/captor tale' *Romantic Times* (Top Pick)

'Another excellent series of books which will alternatively have you laughing, crying and running the gamut of emotions . . . I guarantee you will have a tear in your eye' *Romance Reviews Today*

'The sexual tension crackles across the pages of this witty, deliciously sensual, secret-laden story' *Library Journal*

'Exceptionally entertaining and splendidly sexy' *Booklist*

'An enchanting story brimming with sincere emotions and compelling scenarios . . . an outstanding love story of emotional di   ghtful touch of

By Sabrina Jeffries

SABRINA
JEFFRIES
THE ART OF
SINNING

headline
ETERNAL

Published by arrangement with Pocket Books,
a division of Simon & Schuster, Inc.

First published in Great Britain in 2015
by HEADLINE ETERNAL
An imprint of HEADLINE PUBLISHING GROUP

1

Cataloguing in Publication Data is available from the British Library

ISBN 978 1 4722 3213 7

Offset in 11.6/14 pt Berling LT Std by Jouve (UK)

Printed and bound in Great Britain by CPI Group (UK) Ltd, Croydon, CR0 4YY

Headline's policy is to use papers that are natural, renewable and recyclable
products and made from wood grown in well-managed forests and other controlled
sources. The logging and manufacturing processes are expected to conform to the
environmental regulations of the country of origin.

HEADLINE PUBLISHING GROUP
An Hachette UK Company
Carmelite House
50 Victoria Embankment
London EC4Y 0DZ

www.headlineeternal.com
www.headline.co.uk
www.hachette.co.uk

To Kimberly Rozzell Miller,
for all your hard work on my behalf. You rock!

Acknowledgments

Thanks to artist, author, and friend Ursula Vernon for her invaluable information about painting portraits and painting in general. May crows bring you gifts, and squirrels stop flashing you!

One

London, England
Late August 1829

London's loftiest lords and ladies packed the ballroom in the duke's mansion for the wedding breakfast of Dominick Manton and his new bride, Jane. But despite the number of pretty women among them, Jeremy Keane, American artist and rumored rakehell, wanted only to flee.

He shouldn't have attended. He should have stayed upstairs in his guest bedchamber doing preliminary sketches for his painting, even though inspiration eluded him and he still hadn't found the right model. Anything would be better than enduring this paean to domestic bliss.

Thunderation. He hadn't expected it to unsettle him so. Seeing a bride and groom smile adoringly at each other shouldn't continue to bring back the past, to plague him with the guilt of knowing—

Muttering a curse, he snatched a glass off a tray held by a passing footman and downed champagne, wishing for something stronger. He couldn't take much more of this.

With purposeful steps, he headed across the ballroom toward the entrance. He had to escape before he said or did something he regretted.

Then the woman of his imagination entered, and he stopped breathing. She was magnificent. She wore a dress of emerald silk that shimmered in a shaft of sunlight as if the heavens had opened to show her to him.

He couldn't believe it. She was exactly the model he required for his latest work.

As he watched, the brunette glanced about her. Tall and luxuriously figured, she towered over the delicate Englishwomen simpering their way through the crowd. With her strong features, jewel-green eyes, and generous mouth, she was the very image of the Juno in Gavin Hamilton's *Juno and Jupiter*. She even carried herself like that majestic Roman goddess.

She was absolutely perfect. It was not only in her looks, but her stance, at once self-effacing and imbued with drama. It was in the wariness lurking in her eyes.

He must have her. After months of looking for the right model, he *deserved* to have her.

That was, assuming she would agree to his proposition. She looked old enough to be her own woman, but he couldn't tell from the cut of her ball gown if she was unattached, widowed, or married. He hoped it was one of the latter two. Because if she were a rank innocent, he'd have a devil of a time convincing her family to allow her to sit for him.

He started toward her.

"Jeremy!" cried a female voice behind him. "There you are!"

He turned to find Zoe, his distant cousin as well as the pregnant sister-in-law of the groom, waddling toward him. Damn. He was trapped. Worse yet, when he glanced back for his goddess in green, she'd vanished. Of all the blasted bad luck. In a mansion like the Duke of Lyons's, there was no telling where she'd gone.

Stifling a curse, he faced Zoe. "Good evening, coz. Nice to see you again."

After bussing him on each cheek, she pulled back to glare at him. "I haven't laid eyes on you in three months and *that's* the insipid welcome you give me?"

"I'm still tired from the trip," he lied. "I just arrived from Calais yesterday evening, you know."

"I'm so sorry you and your apprentice had to stay with Max and Lisette last night, instead of at our house. But what with the wedding—"

"You had too many other guests to juggle. I know. And there was more room here, anyway."

That seemed to relieve her. "Thank you for understanding. But everyone is leaving this afternoon, so I do hope you're coming back to the town house with us as planned."

"If I can hold out until you're ready to leave," he said dryly.

She flashed him a veiled glance. "I'm sure wedding celebrations aren't your favorite."

His heart dropped into his stomach. Was she referring to Hannah? He hadn't thought any of Zoe's family knew about that part of his life. "What makes you say that?" he asked hoarsely.

"Well, I assume any bachelor would find weddings dull, but especially *you*." She laughed gaily.

No. She didn't know about Hannah.

Relief flooding him, he forced a sardonic smile. "Weddings are more exhausting than dull. Between fleecing all the lords in the card room and comforting all the disappointed young lovelies who missed out on snagging the groom, I'm fairly worn out."

"*Comforting*? Is that what they're calling it now?" She shook her head. "I see that your travels haven't changed you one whit. You're as incorrigible as ever."

"You know me." He somehow managed a light tone. "What's the fun in being corrigible?"

Thank God she hadn't guessed at the truth: that he hated weddings because they reminded him of his own over a decade ago. Which had been followed six months later by a funeral with two coffins—one for his wife and one for his stillborn son.

Regret and anger roiled in his gut. Damn it, he'd suppressed the image of those coffins for a while now. Must it rise again every time he attended some fool's wedding?

Fortunately, Zoe didn't seem to notice his consternation. "Anyway," she said breezily, "I thought I should tell you that your sister and your mother are on their way to London."

God help him. That was the last thing he needed. "I suppose they think to fetch me back home to Montague."

Situated on the banks of the Brandywine River a few hours from Philadelphia, his family homestead held the largest of the textile mills that were the source of his family's fortune. And now that his late, unlamented father was dead, his sister Amanda was running them all, since she possessed a half interest in the properties. He held the other half, although he'd toss it into the sea before he'd set foot on Montague land again.

The better choice, of course, was to sell Amanda his half. She wanted it, and he wanted to give it to her. But since the properties had all come from his mother's family, Father's will demanded that Mother agree to the sale. And so far she had refused, confound her.

She ought to know better than to think he would return to run the mills. He loved his mother and sister dearly, but Father's death hadn't changed a damned thing about his feelings for Montague. He would rather cut his own throat than carry on Father's legacy. And the sooner Mother realized it, the better off everyone would be.

"When do they leave for England?" Jeremy asked. How much time did he have to prepare?

"When *did* they leave for England, you mean. They should arrive within a few weeks." She ducked her gaze. "No doubt they departed as soon as they got my letter."

"Your *letter*?"

Zoe stuck out her chin, though she still wouldn't meet his eyes. "You can't blame me for taking pity on them. You don't keep them informed about where you're headed."

"Because it's none of their concern!" When she flinched, he moderated his tone. "And because I rarely know where I'm going next. I could write and say, 'I'm sailing the Danube with an Austrian prince and his consort,' but by the time they receive the letter, I'm likely to have befriended some monk with an Alpine refuge full of sculptures that I'm off to view."

"Precisely," she said hotly. "As you're so fond of saying, you blow with the wind. That makes it hard for them to keep up with you."

"They don't need to." He crossed his arms over his chest. "The point of this trip across the Atlantic was that I got to travel the British Isles and the Continent to see works of art I'd never experienced." And to make a life for himself well away from home. "They know that."

"Yes, but Amanda is desperate to speak to you about your father's estate. So when she wrote asking after you, I told her that you were returning to London to view the British Institution's annual summer exhibition before it closes at the end of the month. I thought your family might get the letter in time to be here for that, but I gather that the crossings have been rough recently, so my letter and their ship were probably delayed."

Scrubbing a hand over his face, Jeremy muttered a series of oaths under his breath. "You shouldn't have interfered."

Zoe laid her hand on his arm. "You're the closest thing I have to a brother. I hate to see you at odds with your family."

"I'm not at odds with anyone. But there's no point in talking to them. They have their minds made up about—" Catching himself before he could reveal too much, he pasted a bland smile to his lips. "It doesn't matter. What's done is done. I'll deal with them." Somehow.

She cocked her head. "You won't run off again, will you? You'll wait for them to arrive?"

"I came for the exhibition, remember?" he said irritably. "I haven't yet had a chance to view it."

He thrust aside the possibility that his sister might have an urgent reason for needing him. If it had been so blamed important, she could have included that information in a letter to Zoe. And clearly she hadn't.

Zoe arched an eyebrow. "I wouldn't put it past you to flee as soon as my back is turned. You have a bad habit of avoiding your American family."

It was more a case of avoiding what they wanted of him, though he couldn't say that. Instead, he donned the role that had become natural around Zoe. "You know me," he said genially. "Never met a responsibility I couldn't shirk."

She looked as if she were about to speak, when someone hailed her from across the room. "Oh, dear, I'm being summoned. I believe we're starting the wedding toasts." She hurried off as fast as she could with a babe in her belly.

Wonderful. Now he had to endure a series of sentimental pronouncements about the marital future of the happy couple.

His gut knotted, and he frowned. He refused to sit through that. And it wasn't as if he could wander the crowd, looking for his Juno during the toasts, anyway. That would draw too much attention.

So he'd just escape until the wedding party was done with their maudlin speeches. Thank God he'd thought to tuck his cigar case into his pocket. Pausing only to snag a lit taper, he fled through some French doors onto the empty terrace.

But not empty for long. Hot on his heels came another man, apparently thinking to escape the toasts as well. Jeremy didn't mind. He hated smoking alone.

The fellow stopped short at the sight of Jeremy and glanced back into the crowded room. Then, with a look of grim purpose, he shut the door behind him and evidently resigned himself to having company.

Jeremy took pity on the chap. "Cigar?"

"God, yes."

Lighting both off the taper, Jeremy offered one to his new companion. He watched as the dark-haired man in perfectly tailored attire puffed on it with what looked like satisfaction.

"These are good," the man said, as if surprised.

"They ought to be. Brought them from America myself." Jeremy drew on his.

The fellow shot him a hard glance. "You're American?"

He nodded. "The name is Keane. I'm a distant cousin of the groom's sister-in-law."

"You're the artist whom the papers criticize so much."

Jeremy grimaced. "Indeed I am."

The man gazed back into the room. "I'm Blakeborough. A . . . er . . . friend of the bride's family. Of sorts."

The bitterness in the man's tone gave Jeremy pause. He'd heard that name somewhere. Ah, yes. *Lord* Blakeborough. Or more precisely, Edwin Barlow, the Earl of Blakeborough. "Rumor has it that you were jilted by the bride," Jeremy said with a bluntness equal to the earl's.

Blakeborough scowled at him. "Rumor has it that you're an arse."

"Rumor is correct." Jeremy took a puff of his cigar. Might as well live down to his reputation.

The earl hesitated, then smiled. "You can't be all bad if you carry around cigars of this caliber."

"I believe in being prepared for the rare occasion when one must wait out the excruciating boredom of wedding toasts given by people whom one barely knows."

"Or people one knows too well," Blakeborough said morosely.

Jeremy almost felt sorry for the chap.

Almost. The earl was lucky not to have ended up married. Having a wife was a burden when a man was ill equipped to be a husband. "What we really need to salvage the evening is some good brandy."

"Ah! Excellent idea." Blakeborough fished around in his coat pocket. "I brought a flask." As he offered it to Jeremy, he added ruefully, "One must also come prepared for when the wedding of one's former fiancée becomes interminable."

Jeremy swigged from the flask and handed it back. "I'm surprised you came at all."

"Jane and I were never really romantic. Besides, I wanted her to know there were no hard feelings." His voice held an edge that belied his words.

"And that your pride wasn't damaged in the least."

Blakeborough smiled stiffly. "That played some small part in it, yes."

They smoked a moment in silence, the muted

sounds of sonorous voices barely penetrating their refuge. Then a burst of laughter made them both glance through the glass doors.

That's when Jeremy saw her again—his Juno, in the flesh. Thank God.

"Speaking of beautiful women," Jeremy said to Blakeborough, "can you tell me the name of that one there in the emerald silk?"

The fellow looked over and blanched. "Why do you want to know?"

"I want to paint her."

The earl glared at him. "That won't ever happen."

"Why not?" Then the man's curt tone registered. "Don't tell me—you've fixed on her as your future countess."

"Hardly. She's my sister."

God rot it, that was worse. Sisters were sacrosanct.

But Jeremy wasn't ready to give up. The earl appreciated good cigars, which showed him to be sensible. Maybe he could be made to see reason. "Since I have a sister myself, I understand. I would strangle any unworthy fellow who went after mine. But my interest in yours is purely professional."

"Forgive my candor, sir, but I've seen your paintings. There's no way in hell I'd let you paint my sister as one of your hopeless lunatics or seedy whores or whatever else you're thinking to make her."

Damn. Admittedly, his work had turned rather bleak of late, but only because he'd come to prefer depicting the raw drama of the real world rather than prettified history or wealthy ladies and gentlemen in fine attire.

And his latest painting would not only be dark but violent. Not that he meant to tell the earl that. "I can always disguise her features, change her hair color—"

"That won't work. In case you haven't noticed, Yvette is rather distinctive in appearance."

Yvette. Even her name was exotic, which made him want her even more. For the painting. That's all. "Exactly. She's arresting, and that makes for a good image."

"Yes, but to change her enough for her identity to be kept secret, you'd have to turn her into another woman entirely. So you might as well go *choose* another woman."

"I don't want another woman. I want her."

Blakeborough drank some brandy. "Well, you can't have her. Between her argumentative nature and her 'arresting' looks, she's had enough trouble finding suitors as it is. You paint her in one of your provocative scenes, and she'll die a spinster for certain."

Incredulous, Jeremy stared through the window at her. "A spinster! Are all the men in England mad?"

"Yes." Blakeborough sighed. "Not to mention wary of the scandals that dog our family wherever we go."

Suddenly Jeremy remembered the other bit of gossip he'd heard. Blakeborough's brother had been convicted of kidnapping the bride's cousin. That must be quite a tale. He'd have to get the earl to tell him sometime. *After* he arranged to have the impressive Yvette model for his latest work.

The first ones he'd exhibited in London—depictions of a lunatic asylum, a butcher shop, a carriage accident, and other "genre paintings," as some called them—had received mixed reviews. Some critics had lauded his new direction. Others had complained that he no longer created the grand historical paintings for which he'd become known.

But his new work, an allegory, would give to everyday struggles the same weight as great events in history or mythology. It would be his masterpiece. With any luck, it would gain him a place in London's Royal Academy of Arts.

With any luck, it would also launch him as an artist of equal caliber to Géricault or Delacroix, not just one more painter of the same old historical scenes. But for that, he needed a woman with a striking appearance to play the primary role. A woman like Blakeborough's sister.

"As it happens, I'm quite a popular fellow in society right now," Jeremy said. Even if not lauded by his peers to the extent he wanted. "So a fine painting of your sister by me might increase *her* popularity, too."

The earl pondered that a moment, then narrowed his gray gaze on Jeremy. "That's an excellent notion."

"You see? I wouldn't robe her in anything outrageous—"

"No, not that. What I mean is, you could paint her portrait, a formal one that shows off her attractions. That would surely help her in society."

Jeremy cursed under his breath. "I don't do portraits."

"Why the devil not?"

"Because the sitters always want false representations. They think they should be depicted as more beautiful or clever or rich than they are. And since

I refuse to cater to such hypocrisy, they're never happy with the results."

Blakeborough looked him over as if assessing his worth. "What if I paid you handsomely for the painting?"

"Fortunately, I don't need the money."

The earl snorted, clearly unfamiliar with *that* sentiment, especially coming from a lowly American artist. "Well, that's the only way I'll allow it. It's a portrait or nothing, sir."

Stubborn ass. "I will not paint a formal portrait of Yvette—"

"*Lady* Yvette," Blakeborough corrected him.

"And even if I did, I would paint her as she is. I would never agree to a portrait that 'shows off her attractions,' whatever that means. Might as well ask me to dress her up like a whore to entice customers."

"If that would work, I might consider it," the earl grumbled. When Jeremy lifted an eyebrow, he added, "I'm joking. Mostly."

"Why is it so all-fired important that she marry?"

Blakeborough stared into the ballroom at his sister. "I want her to be happy. And the longer she lives alone with me, the more likely that she will be dragged down by my cynical temperament."

"Ah. Now that, I understand." He wanted Amanda to be happy, too. He just didn't want to sacrifice his own happiness for it.

"You said you have a sister as well?" the earl asked.

"Yes. And if you think it's hard to get *your* sister married off, you should try it with mine."

"Unattractive, is she?"

"No, her looks aren't the problem. Amanda runs four textile mills in America as competently as any man, which doesn't exactly endear her to the male populace."

"Yes, but does she have a tart tongue like *my* sister?"

Jeremy snorted. "Despite being a little slip of a thing, she cows fellows twice her size."

"But surely she can't be as suspicious of men as Yvette."

"Only of every chap she meets. And though Amanda is quite pretty, she has a horrible sense of fashion. At least *your* sister knows how to dress well."

"When she chooses. You should see her wearing her most ragged gown and her permanently ink-stained gloves, poring over dog-eared manuscripts with a pencil behind one ear. Half the time, that damned pencil looses her hair from its pins to fall down about her shoulders."

Jeremy would love to see Lady Yvette with her hair down. Not that he'd mention that to her brother. "That can't compare to Amanda at the mills. She wears *trousers* beneath her skirts. Says they're necessary to her modesty when she has to climb the ladders."

"Climbs ladders, does she?" Blakeborough chuckled. "She and Yvette will get along famously. A pity that I need a wife willing to live in England. I'd marry her myself." He paused. "Does your sister even *want* to marry?"

"Who knows? Though I suspect she'd like to have children."

Or maybe not, given the tragic deaths of Hannah

and baby Theodore. That had made quite an impression on Amanda in her youth.

Shoving that painful memory to the back of his mind, he took a puff on his cigar. "But whether Amanda wants a husband or not, I'm selfish enough to want her to have one. Then she might stop plaguing me to return home and help her run the confounded mills. She could get her spouse to help her instead."

Blakeborough laughed. "You should coax her to come here to gain a husband. I can think of any number of younger sons with fine educations, good characters, and sterling connections who have no chance of making something of themselves while their families limit them to the few opportunities that are open to respectable gentlemen in the clergy, law, or the military. They would welcome the chance to start anew somewhere abroad."

Jeremy gaped at him. "What a brilliant idea! She's actually on her way here and should arrive within the month with my mother in tow. If you'd be willing to introduce her to decent gentlemen who might not mind moving to the countryside of Pennsylvania—"

"I'd be perfectly willing . . . as long as *you* are willing to paint my sister's portrait." The earl cast him a calculating stare. "What do you say? Is that a trade you would consider?"

Hmm. Much as he hated doing portraits, he hated even more the idea of arguing with Amanda continually about his refusal to return home. Maybe if he could gain her a husband, he'd finally get some peace.

He glanced back into the ballroom. And who was to say that in the course of meeting his obligation, he couldn't also convince Lady Yvette to model for the other work that had seized his imagination so thoroughly? He had a knack for charming women. Especially ones he wanted to paint.

"All right." He thrust out his hand. "It's a trade."

Blakeborough brightened as he shook it vigorously. "You won't regret it, I swear. We'll get our sisters married off yet."

And Jeremy would get his masterpiece at last.

Two

Lady Yvette Barlow had just left the retiring room, headed for the ballroom, when she practically knocked over the bride.

"Yvette!" Jane cried. "You came!"

"Of course I came." Yvette kissed her friend on the cheek. "I wouldn't have missed it for the world. I'm so very happy for you." She meant that most sincerely.

Her friend's pleasure shifted to embarrassment. "I know you were probably disappointed that I broke with Edwin."

"I confess I would have enjoyed having you for a sister-in-law. But *I* would never marry a bullheaded curmudgeon like my eldest brother, so I could hardly expect you to." She took Jane's hands in hers. "Besides, I wanted you to marry whomever made you happy, and clearly Lord Rathmoor does."

A blush stained Jane's cheeks. "It's true. I daresay you got an awful impression of him when we were younger, but—"

"That's all past. He seems quite nice now." Yvette forced a smile. "He said such sweet things in his toast to you that it made me positively green with envy." She meant *that*, too.

As if Jane realized just how deep Yvette's envy ran, she patted her hand. "Your time will come soon, my dear. There's plenty of fish in the sea."

"But I don't particularly like fish," Yvette said lightly. "Perhaps that's my problem."

Jane chuckled. "Your problem is your refusal to take men seriously. Even when men do want to marry you, you laugh them out of countenance."

"There are men interested in marrying me?" She surveyed the ballroom beyond Jane. "Do point them out. I haven't met these mythical creatures."

"Yvette—"

"I'm joking," Yvette said with a faint smile. "Though it does seem as if the vast majority of eligible gentlemen are only interested in my fortune. And the rest are simply too short for my liking."

"You see?" Jane shook her head. "You won't be serious about it."

"Oh, I'm quite serious about the height issue. You've never had to dance with anyone shorter than you. It's disconcerting to have a man staring into your bosom for an entire dance."

"Any fellow who does that is no gentleman, and you wouldn't want him anyway."

"Then that eliminates a great many chaps." Yvette sobered. "You have no idea how rare true gentlemen are. Most men can't even be trusted to do what they promise. Just look at my father. And Samuel."

Not to mention Samuel's friend from the navy,

Lieutenant Ruston—though Jane knew nothing of Yvette's history with that blackguard.

Suddenly Yvette noticed Jane's face clouding over, and she groaned. "I'm so sorry I forgot entirely about how Samuel wronged you."

"It's fine."

"It's *not* fine," Yvette protested. "My brother behaved abominably toward you and poor Nancy. You must have been terrified the whole time he had your cousin in his clutches. How awful for you!"

"I just kept clinging to the hope that he would refrain from harming a woman he'd known since childhood. That he would come to his senses." Jane gave a wry smile. "And when that didn't work, I shot him in the leg."

"He's lucky you didn't shoot him elsewhere." Yvette shook her head. "You do realize that the rest of the family washed their hands of him long ago, right?"

"Even you?" Jane asked softly.

Yvette sighed. "I keep trying. Even with his sentence of transportation, I find myself remembering—" She broke off with a pained smile. "It doesn't matter. He's headed to New South Wales now. We won't see him for quite some time, if ever."

Thank the good Lord. After what her brother had dropped in her lap the last time she'd seen him, she could have throttled him. *Just post the letter for me, and don't ask any questions, all right?*

Didn't the fool know her at all? Of *course* she'd demanded answers. And of *course* the little he'd said had merely alarmed her and incited her to make things right.

Unfortunately, she couldn't do that without help. And who would aid her in cleaning up another of Samuel's messes? Certainly no one here, given what he'd done to Lord Rathmoor's family. Even her eldest brother had refused, skeptical of whether they could even believe Samuel's claims.

Of course, Edwin didn't know what Samuel had done to protect her in her youth. He didn't know about the kernel of good that lay deep, albeit very deep, inside their brother.

"Don't let Samuel's fecklessness keep you from finding a gentleman of your own," Jane cautioned. "Not all men are like him and your father. Edwin is perfectly trustworthy. There must be more of his ilk around."

"Ah, but therein lies my problem. Trustworthy gentlemen frown on my lively speech and manners, and wish I weren't quite so tall. It's only the rogues who like me, precisely because I laugh at them and make them feel free to flirt shamelessly. They must sense the enjoyment I take in sparring with them." And the foolish attraction she sometimes felt for them.

When Jane's eyes narrowed, Yvette softened her arch tone. "It's a conundrum, to be sure."

"Gentlemen come in more than two flavors, Yvette. Some trustworthy gentlemen actually do flirt. Some are tall. And some even have a sense of humor and enjoy lively speech, Edwin notwithstanding."

"I have yet to meet one. But I'm willing to keep looking, if only to prove you wrong."

Jane uttered an exasperated laugh. "Don't you *want* to marry?"

"Not badly enough to settle for any dull gentleman willing to ask me."

Oh, how she hoped to avoid that trap. Perhaps after the scandal about Samuel's perfidy died down, things would be better. At twenty-four, she wasn't getting any younger. Still, she refused to simper and hold her tongue to gain a husband. She was liable to burst into laughter if she even attempted it.

But Jane, who'd always been the perfect lady, wouldn't understand that.

Yvette forced a shrug. "Besides, I've got a lovely fortune of my own and plenty to keep me busy. Why would I want a man underfoot?"

"Because life is more than charity work and dabbling in dictionaries."

"Dabbling!" she said. "I'm not dabbling. Aside from attempting to add to Francis Grose's deplorably out-of-date slang lexicon, I'm also compiling a list of new boxing words for Pierce Egan. He's expanding his *Boxiana*, and I've already found several terms for him." Something occurred to her. "I don't suppose your new husband would spend some time with me, adding to my store of general street cant."

"Today?" Jane said incredulously.

"Not at your wedding, silly. But soon. I'm sure he could give me dozens of new words."

"Hundreds, more like, though I doubt he knows any boxing slang specifically." Jane smiled. "I'll ask him. But it will be some time before we return from our honeymoon."

Their hostess, the duchess, appeared at Jane's side. "You must come, Jane. We need you and Dom to lead the first dance."

"I'll be there straightaway," Jane said. "First I simply *have* to go to the retiring room."

"Of course," the duchess said. "I'll tell the musicians to wait a few more minutes."

As Jane hurried off, Yvette's spirits drooped. Jane was one of the last of her friends to marry. And though Yvette truly *was* happy for her and understood perfectly why Jane had jilted Edwin, she'd been looking forward to having a female friend in the household.

Now it was just her and Edwin again. And sometimes the thought of knocking about Stoke Towers with her gloomy eldest brother until they both died was more than she could bear.

As if her frustration had somehow conjured him up, Edwin spoke from behind her. "Yvette, there's someone I'd like you to meet."

Good Lord. He'd been trying to cheer her up ever since they'd arrived, and he was very bad at it. Heaven only knew whom he thought might serve the purpose.

Forcing a smile to her lips, she faced him and his companion—and her heart dropped into her stomach.

Standing beside Edwin was the most attractive man she'd ever seen: a golden-haired Adonis with eyes as deep a blue as the estate's prize delphiniums. The man stared at her with an intensity that quite sucked the air from her lungs.

Heavenly day. He was tall, too, and dressed on the daring end of fashionable—in a brown tailcoat, a waistcoat of black cut velvet, and tattersall trousers, topped off with a bloodred pongee cravat. Interesting. And a decided improvement over the gentlemen Edwin usually foisted on her.

"May I introduce my new friend, Mr. Jeremy Keane?" Edwin said.

The man bowed. "I'm delighted to make your acquaintance, Lady Yvette."

His deep voice resonated through her like delicious music. Even his accent was compelling. American, perhaps? Oh, she did like Americans. They were so refreshingly forthright. And used such fascinating slang, too.

She dipped her head. "The pleasure is mine, Mr. Keane." But even as she said it, she put together the accent and the name. Oh, dear, he had to be *that* Mr. Keane.

As if to confirm her realization, the man raked her in a blatantly admiring glance. A *rogue's* glance.

Not again. Why must she always attract scoundrels? And be attracted to them in turn? Hadn't she learned her lesson with Lieutenant Ruston?

Apparently not, for Mr. Keane's glance was warming her most scandalously. Curse him.

Edwin went on. "Keane is an artist from—"

"I know all about Mr. Keane." When Edwin scowled, she caught herself. "From the exhibit of his works, of course."

Mr. Keane's warm gaze poured over her like honey. "I don't recall ever seeing *you* at my exhibit. Trust me, I would have remembered."

A shiver danced down her spine before she could steel herself against reacting. Very nicely done. She'd have to be on her toes with this one. "We attended it in the morning. I daresay you were still lying foxed in some gaming hell or nunnery."

"Good God, here we go," Edwin muttered under

his breath, recognizing the vulgar slang for bawdy house.

"I am rarely foxed and never in a nunnery," Mr. Keane retorted, "for fear that it might tempt the 'nuns' to bite me."

"I should love to know what you consider 'rarely,'" Yvette said. "That you even know that 'bite' means 'cheat' in street cant shows how you must spend your days."

"And how you must spend yours," he said with a gleam in his eye. "After all, you know the terms, too."

She stifled a laugh. Mustn't encourage the fellow. Still, she was impressed. Rogues always fancied themselves wits, but seldom did she meet one who really was.

"Mr. Keane has kindly agreed to paint your portrait, Yvette," Edwin cut in. "Assuming that your tart words haven't changed his mind."

The scoundrel had the audacity to wink at her. "Actually, I like a little tart with my sweet."

"More than a little, I would say, having seen your paintings," she shot back.

Suddenly he was all seriousness. "And what did you think?"

The question caught her off guard. "Are you fishing for compliments, sir?"

"No. Just truthful opinions."

"That's what everyone always says, though they never mean it."

"Are you calling me a liar, Lady Yvette?" he said in that deadly tone men use when their honor is questioned.

"Of course not," she said hastily. A man's honor

was nothing to be trifled with. "As for your work, I would say that your idea of 'tart' borders on the 'acidic.'"

"It does indeed," he drawled. "I prefer to call it 'real life.'"

"Then it's no surprise you've taken up with Edwin. He considers real life to be acidic, too."

"Oh no, don't drag *me* into this," Edwin put in.

Mr. Keane's gaze searched her face. "And you, Lady Yvette? Do *you* consider real life acidic?"

My, my. Quite the persistent fellow, wasn't he? "It can be, I suppose. If one wants to dwell on that part. I'd rather dwell on happier aspects."

A sudden disappointment swept his handsome features. "So you prefer paintings of bucolic cows in a field."

"I suppose. Or market scenes. Or children."

The mention of children sparked something bleak in the depths of his eyes. "Art should challenge viewers, not soothe them."

"I'll try to remember that when confronted at my breakfast table by a picture of vultures devouring a dead deer. That *is* one of yours, isn't it?"

Mr. Keane blinked, then burst into laughter. "Blakeborough, you forgot to tell me that your sister is a wit."

"If I'd thought it would get you to agree to our transaction sooner," Edwin said wearily, "I would have mentioned it."

"'Transaction'?" She stared at her brother. "What transaction?"

Edwin turned wary. "I told you. Mr. Keane is going to paint your portrait. I figured that a well-done piece of art showing what a lovely woman you are . . . might . . . well . . ."

"Oh, Lord." So *that* was his reasoning. A pox on Edwin. And a pox on Mr. Keane, too, for agreeing to her brother's idiocy. Clearly, the artist had been coerced. Mr. Keane was well-known for *not* doing formal portraits. Ever.

She fought to act nonchalant, though inside she was bleeding. Did Edwin really think her so unsightly that she needed a famous artist to make her look appealing?

"Forgive my brother, sir," she told Mr. Keane with a bland smile. "He's set on gaining me a husband, no matter what the cost. But I've read the interview where you said you'd rather cut off your hands than paint another portrait, and I'd hate to be the cause of such a loss to the world."

Mr. Keane gazed steadily at her. "I sometimes exaggerate when speaking with the press, madam. But this particular portrait is one I am more than willing to execute, I assure you."

"Eager for the challenge, are you?" Such raw anger boiled up in her that it fairly choked her. "Eager to try your hand at painting me attractive enough to convince some hapless fellow in search of a wife to ignore the evidence of his eyes?"

Belatedly, her brother seemed to realize how she'd taken his words. "Yvette, that's not what I was saying."

She ignored him. "Or perhaps it's the money that entices you. How much did my brother offer in order to gain your compliance in such an onerous task? It must have been a great deal."

"I didn't offer him money," Edwin protested. "You misunderstand what I—"

"I *want* to paint you," Mr. Keane snapped even as he glared Edwin into silence.

With betrayal stinging her, she gathered the remnants of her dignity about her. "Thank you, but I am not yet so . . . so desperate as to require your services."

She turned to leave, but Mr. Keane caught her by the arm. When she scowled at him, he released her . . . only to offer her his hand. "May I have this dance, Lady Yvette?"

That took her by surprise. Only then did she notice the strains of a waltz being struck. She had half a mind to stalk off in a huff, but that would be childish.

Besides, other people had begun to notice their exchange, and she could *not* endure the idea of people gossiping about her making a scene at the wedding breakfast of her friend . . . who happened to have jilted her brother.

"Lady Yvette?" Mr. Keane prompted in a steely voice.

She cast him the coolest smile she could muster. "Yes, of course, Mr. Keane. I would be delighted."

Then she took his hand and let him sweep her into a waltz.

As soon as they were moving, he said, "You have every right to be angry with your brother."

"My feelings toward my brother are none of your concern."

"I was telling the truth about wanting to paint you."

She snorted. "I don't know how much money—"

"But not for a portrait." He bent close enough to whisper in her ear, "Though he doesn't know that."

That caught her so off guard that when Mr. Keane pulled back to fix her with a serious gaze, she couldn't at first summon a single answer.

"I see I finally have your attention," he said.

"Oh, you always had my attention," she said testily. "Just not the sort of fawning attention you probably prefer."

A faint smile crossed his lips. "Tell me, Lady Yvette, do you have something against artists in general? Or is it just I who rub you the wrong way?"

"I don't trust charming rogues, sir. I've encountered enough of your kind to know all your tricks."

He arched one eyebrow. "I seriously doubt that."

When he then twirled her in a turn, she realized with a start that they'd been waltzing effortlessly all this time. That almost never happened with her. Few men knew how to deal with an ungainly Amazon like her on the dance floor.

That softened her toward him a little. A very little. "So what exactly *do* you want to paint me for, anyway?"

"An entirely different work. And agreeing to your brother's request seemed the only way to get close enough to you to arrange that."

She eyed him skeptically.

"Ask Blakeborough if you don't believe me. Before I knew who he was, who *you* were, I wanted you to sit for me. I decided it the moment I saw you enter the room. I asked your brother who you were; he asked why I wanted to know, and I told him."

His gaze locked with hers, as sincere a one as she'd ever seen. But then, Lieutenant Ruston had seemed sincere at first, too. "Why on earth would you want to paint *me*?"

"No clue. I never know why particular models intrigue me; just that they do. And I always follow my instincts."

Yvette blinked. He *could* have claimed it had something to do with her looks. The fact that he hadn't lent more credence to his assertion. "That's the most ridiculous thing I've ever heard." And rather flattering.

"It *is* ridiculous, isn't it? But true, I swear."

"So what exactly are the terms of your 'transaction' with my brother?"

He flinched. "Your brother is an ass."

"Not really. Just rather oblivious to other people's feelings sometimes." She cast him a hard stare. "Answer the question."

With a long-suffering sigh, he tightened his grip on her hand. "I am to paint your portrait. In exchange, he is to drum up some gentlemen who might be interested in courting my sister."

She gaped at him. "What a pair of nodcocks you are! Has it occurred to either of you that your sisters are perfectly capable of finding husbands on their own if they so choose? That perhaps we— Wait a minute. I thought your sister lived in America."

"She's on her way here. She means to drag me home to help her with the family mills." He cracked a smile. "I mean to fob some other fellow off on her who can go in my stead."

His look of boyish mischief seduced her. Until she

put herself in his sister's shoes. "First you abandon her to go flitting about Europe. And now that she has tired of waiting for your return, you think to get rid of her by marrying her off." She shook her head. "Your poor sister."

"Trust me, there is nothing 'poor' about my sister. Amanda can take care of herself." His smile smoldered. "As, it appears, can you. Which is probably what made me want you for my painting in the first place."

She fought not to be intrigued. "What is this painting about, anyway?"

"It's allegorical, about the sacrifice of Art to Commerce."

That took her by surprise. "Something like Delacroix's paintings?"

"You're familiar with Delacroix?"

His voice held such astonishment that it scraped her nerves. "I do read books, you know. And attend exhibits and operas with my brother when I can drag him to town."

"Operas, eh? Better you than me. I can't imagine anything more tedious than an evening of screeching."

"My point is that I'm not some ninnyhammer society chit who only keeps abreast of fashions."

"I didn't think you were." He bent close enough to say in a husky tone, "Unlike your brother, I am fully aware of your attractions."

The words melted over her skin like butter. And when he then tugged her slightly closer in the turn, she let him.

Not because of his devastating attractiveness, no.

Or his deft ability to dance. Or the glint of aware-
ness in his startling blue eyes. None of that had any
effect on her. Certainly not.

Fighting to keep her mind off the breathlessness that suddenly assailed her, she said, "So, which
character would I play in this allegorical painting of
yours?"

One corner of his mouth tipped up. "Does that
mean you agree to sit for it?"

"Perhaps. It depends on your answers to certain
questions."

The music was ending. Oh, dear, and just when
the conversation was getting interesting. Unfortunately, it would be highly improper of him to ask her
for another.

But apparently he'd thought of that, for he
waltzed her toward a pair of doors that opened to
reveal steps descending into the sunlit garden. And
as the music ended, he offered her his arm.

Curiosity prompted her to take it and she let him
lead her outside, relieved to see that they weren't
the only people strolling about. At least she needn't
worry about rousing further gossip.

Besides, she was ready to be out of the stuffy ballroom. Here she could breathe at last.

"Now, then, madam," he said. "Ask me whatever
you wish."

"Who am I to play in your painting? What am I to
wear? Will sitting for your picture ruin me for life?
Is that why Edwin would only agree to a respectable
portrait?"

"That's quite a lot of questions," he said dryly.
"Let's start with the last. Your brother and I didn't

get as far as my describing the concept of my work. The minute I said I wished for you to model for me, he flat-out refused to let you be part of any painting that wasn't dull as dirt, even though I told him you wouldn't be recognized."

"Won't I?" She felt a stab of disappointment at the thought that he didn't really want to paint *her* as she was. And why did she care, anyway? "So I'm to be wearing a mask or a cloak or something?"

"No, indeed. But you will be in a Greek costume quite different from your normal attire. I can even change your hair color if you wish. And you'll only be in profile, anyway. I doubt anyone will realize it is you."

She gave a harsh laugh. "Right. Because no one will notice that the woman in your painting happens to have my ungainly proportions."

"Ungainly!" He shook his head. "More like queenly. Majestic."

The compliment came so unexpectedly that it startled her. She was used to being teased for her height, not praised. She had to turn her head so he wouldn't see how very much the words pleased her.

She'd swear that he meant every word. Then again, she'd also believed Lieutenant Ruston's compliments, though they'd been far less original and far more dubious. At least Mr. Keane wasn't calling her "a great beauty" and "a delicate flower." She couldn't believe she'd fallen for that last one. She'd never been delicate a day in her life.

"But your proportions are unlikely to signify, anyway," he went on. "You'll be lying down."

That arrested her. How had she forgotten he was a rogue? "Why would I be lying down?"

He gazed at her as if she were witless. "Art sacrificed to Commerce? Were you even listening? Damn, woman, I can hardly show a sacrifice without laying you across an altar."

Stunned by his matter-of-fact tone, as if it were perfectly obvious to anyone with sense, she mumbled, "Oh, right, of course. I don't know what I was thinking."

Actually, she did know. She thought him quite mad. When he spoke of his art, there was no trace of the rakehell in him. Was it by design? Was he *trying* to rattle her?

Because he was certainly succeeding.

"Will you do it?" he asked. "Assuming we can manage it?"

"Managing it isn't a problem," she said, thinking aloud. "Artists doing portraits generally reside with the family during the process. So if you come to our estate for the portrait, we can arrange some way to meet for the painting you wish to do for yourself." She slanted a glance at him. "If you're willing to leave London for a bit, that is."

"Oh, I don't know." He stopped beside a marble fountain to smile teasingly at her. "It would take me away from all those gaming hells and nunneries. However will I survive?"

"I'm sure you can find a sympathetic tavern maid or two nearby to tide you over."

"So, no nunneries in your neck of the woods?"

"Believe me, if there had been, my other brother would have found them ages ago."

When he looked at her oddly, a blush rose in her cheeks. She didn't know why she'd mentioned Samuel's proclivities. She couldn't seem to put his request out of her mind.

"I'll be fine, I promise," he said silkily. "Though you still haven't given me your permission to paint you. For *either* work."

And suddenly it hit her—the solution to her problem with Samuel. She hadn't sent the sealed letter, fearful that no one would call for it at the Covent Garden post office as promised, but perhaps she could still right Samuel's wrong.

"I haven't, have I?" She stared him down. "Tell me something, Mr. Keane. Are you as willing to make a bargain with me for your painting as you were to make a bargain with Edwin for my portrait?"

His gaze turned wary. "It depends. What sort of bargain do you mean?"

Avoiding his gaze, she stirred the water in the fountain with one finger. "I will sit for you—clothed, of course. You may draw as many pictures of me as you please."

"And in exchange?" he prodded.

"You will find some way to get me inside a Covent Garden nunnery."

Three

Jeremy was shocked. Then intrigued. Then disturbed by the notion of Lady Yvette going anywhere near a den of iniquity.

Not that he would let her see it. He had a reputation to uphold, after all. "You don't need my help for that. Covent Garden is known for its enthusiastic acquisition of . . . er . . . nuns. Just walk in, and I'm sure they'll welcome you with open arms."

Her outraged gaze shot to him. "I'm not aiming to be a Covent Garden nun, you devil!"

He'd figured that, of course. He'd just wanted to spark that intoxicating fire in her eyes again. "Then why go in a nunnery?"

"I'm looking for a . . . a person."

"Ah," he said, as if he understood. Which he certainly did not. "A friend of yours?"

"Something like that." Her rosy cheeks showed she wasn't nearly as nonchalant about this as she let on.

"You have a friend in a whorehouse," he said bluntly.

She crossed her arms over her chest. "It doesn't matter why I want to go into one, just that I do. And since you enter them all the time, I figure you're the perfect person to sneak me in."

"I do have a bit of experience in that regard." Not as much as everyone assumed, but enough to know his way around. "Indeed, it would probably be safer for your reputation if I entered alone. If you'd just give me the name of the person—"

"I can't. I don't know for certain that my . . . er . . . friend is even there. This must be handled very discreetly. And it's essential that I go with you. I can't explain why."

This got more curious by the moment. "I assume that asking your brother to help you is out of the question?"

She paled. "He cannot know I'm doing this. He mustn't know."

"So if he finds out, he'll throttle me."

"Don't tell me you're afraid of my brother."

He bit back a smile. Her taunts were so transparent. "What can I say? I'm an artist, not a fighter. I've no great desire to have my nose bashed in."

"That would only happen if Edwin learned of it. Which he's not going to." She glanced away. "Our visits must be conducted in utter secrecy."

"You expect a notorious scoundrel like me to bring you into a brothel without having anyone remark upon it?"

"I can wear a disguise." She eyed him from beneath sooty lashes that made something tighten in his chest. And lower. "Or pretend to be your paramour, joining you for . . . whatever a paramour would do in a place like that."

Oh, he could think of several interesting things he could do with Lady Yvette in a whorehouse, none of them acceptable to a lady of her upbringing. Best to shove those ideas right out of his mind. "So how are we to visit a brothel when we're to be closeted out at your country estate for the next few weeks while I paint your portrait?"

She shrugged. "Preston isn't that far from London. We come into town often enough. All you and I need do is attend some other social affair, find a way to keep Edwin busy, and then dart off for a bit to make our Covent Garden visit."

"Really? That's 'all you and I need do,' is it?"

Ignoring his sarcasm, she tapped her chin with her finger. "We should go to the theater. It's already situated in Covent Garden. Of course we'd have to find a way to occupy Edwin . . ."

"A minor consideration," he said tersely.

This time his sarcasm registered, and he was rewarded with another lovely blush. "I'm sure we can manage it." She planted her hands on her hips. "Do you want to paint me or not? Because the only way I'll agree to sitting for either painting is if you do this for me."

If he had any sense, he would throw her bargain back in her face, and her brother's, too, for that matter. He didn't like being taken for a fool, especially by some secretive chit, no matter how clever and arresting.

But his mind was already leaping ahead to how

she would look robed in Roman white. Or maybe a knee-length Greek chiton. He already knew she'd have shapely calves to match the beautiful contours of her arms in those long, formfitting gloves she wore. And the image of her in something little better than a shift was rousing more than his artistic imagination.

He moved closer to the fountain, praying that the imposing marble bowl would hide his unwise attraction.

"Well?" she asked.

Her demanding tone wasn't helping his arousal any. He found imperious women intoxicating. They tended to be honest in bed. Nothing more erotic than a woman, even a saucy innocent, who asked for exactly what she wanted. Just the thought of this particular innocent asking for what she wanted, what she *needed*, had him hardening even more.

Damn her. He had no desire to wed anyone again, especially some earl's daughter harboring sordid secrets. And if he made advances toward her ladyship, that's exactly what would happen. He would find himself leg-shackled faster than his apprentice could mix paints.

So he was surprised to hear himself say, "All right. We'll visit the Covent Garden brothel as soon as I can figure out how to arrange it without ruining you." Then he paused. "You do know there's more than one, don't you?"

Her eyes widened. "You're joking."

"Not a bit. I believe there are at least three."

She began to pace. "Drat him, all he said was it was in Covent Garden!"

"He who? Blakeborough?"

"B-Blakeborough?" she repeated, clearly startled.

"Not your brother, then." A chill skated down his spine. Could it be her other brother, the criminal one? No, she would have involved Blakeborough if it were. Jeremy had enough experience with the English aristocracy to know that they closed ranks around their own. Or cut them off completely.

So this was clearly her own private affair. What had he gotten himself into?

She swallowed hard. "I was referring to my . . . er . . . source of information about the person I seek."

"And who is this source?" He fixed her with a hard look. "A friend? A secret lover? Before I agree to this insanity, I want to know who else is involved."

"You *already* agreed!"

"That was before I knew—"

Someone hailed them from the steps, and Jeremy looked up to find a scowling Blakeborough rapidly approaching.

"So this is where you two got off to," the earl said.

Pasting a bored expression to his face, Jeremy said, "We came out here to get some air. It was stifling in the ballroom."

Warily, the man glanced from Jeremy to his sister. But he must have seen nothing to give alarm, for his face cleared. "So? Did the two of you come to an agreement? Are you painting Yvette's portrait?"

Jeremy stared at Yvette, and the pleading look on her face punched him in the gut.

This was madness. She wanted him to help her with some secret scheme involving a brothel and an unknown gentleman. He barely knew her, wasn't even sure he could trust her.

Worse yet, she tempted him more powerfully than any woman had in years. Acting on such an attraction invariably led to something deeper, which invariably led to pain and guilt and shattering loss. As long as he confined himself to easy flirtations, he didn't end up with shards of a life to put back together.

And what would he gain if he agreed to her bargain, anyway, other than the hellish task of painting an insipid portrait of his bewitching Juno?

You'll get to do the work you really want. You'll have a chance to be a serious artist, not just a wealthy mill owner's son who succeeded at a few historical paintings. You'll get to show the world the potential in painting real life with its edges and heartbreak. What's a little trouble over some intrigue next to that?

He dragged in a deep breath. "Of course I'm painting it. As long as Lady Yvette agrees."

"Oh yes," she said quickly. "I can't wait to start."

Neither could he. But he was a glutton for punishment whenever a fetching female was involved.

"Well, then, Keane," Blakeborough began, "if you'd like to come round to our town house in Mayfair tomorrow—"

"Actually, Edwin," Lady Yvette cut in with a veiled glance at Jeremy, "Mr. Keane and I have discussed it, and we feel it would be best to paint the portrait at Stoke Towers."

The earl's gaze narrowed on her. "Why?"

"With Mr. Keane's reputation as a rogue, it wouldn't do to have people see him come and go regularly from our town house. It would almost certainly start tongues wagging. You don't want that, do you?"

"I suppose not," her brother muttered.

"Besides, you hate being in town when Parliament isn't in session. I could barely get you to stay tonight."

"That's true, but—"

"And we do have that charitable event in Preston for the boys' school you support—I can't sit in London being painted while the plans for that languish. Though if you want to put the portrait off for a few weeks, that could work. Of course, I don't know how long Mr. Keane intends to be in town . . ."

Jeremy resisted the urge to roll his eyes. Blakeborough seemed entirely unaware that he was being managed.

The earl glanced at Jeremy. "You agreed to this? Aren't you expecting your family to arrive soon?"

"My cousin wasn't sure exactly when. It could be weeks. And Zoe will send word the moment they do. Your sister tells me you don't live far from town. Is that correct?"

Blakeborough nodded. He surveyed the two of them as if trying to work out what plot might be afoot. But Jeremy had always been expert at hiding his feelings, and Lady Yvette seemed expert at hiding them from her brother, at least.

At last the earl sighed. "Oh, very well, Yvette, if you prefer it." He turned to Jeremy. "Do you play chess? Or any sort of cards?"

"Occasionally. Though I'm not particularly good at either."

"Even better," Blakeborough said with a rare smile.

Jeremy wondered if the earl possessed many friends. He didn't seem to. It was another thing they had in common.

"Well, then," Lady Yvette said, "we're agreed. Since I assume you're staying with your cousin, Mr. Keane, we'll fetch you in the morning before we leave for Stoke Towers."

Although he found her high-handedness amusing, even seductive, she was sometimes a bit presumptuous even for him. "I'm afraid that's too soon. I can start sketching right away, but the canvases must sit in your home for at least a week to acclimate to the temperature and humidity. So there's little point in my joining you before that's done."

"Canvases?" Blakeborough echoed suspiciously. "More than one?"

"Quite a few, actually, in case the work goes awry and I have to begin again. Or I change my mind about my approach, or I decide—"

"We understand," Lady Yvette said with a furtive look at her brother.

"So if you don't mind fetching my canvases in the morning," Jeremy went on, "I'll come out myself early next week."

"I see," she said. "Well, then, tell me the day you mean to arrive, and I'll send the carriage for you."

"I prefer to use my own equipage, so I may come and go as I please." He added, with a bit of sarcasm, "If that's acceptable."

She colored deeply. "Of course, but I assumed, that is—"

"That I would be happy to dance to your tune."

"Certainly not. I just thought perhaps you didn't have an equipage."

Right. He was no fool—she'd begun to consider him easy to manage, too. Well, she was in for a surprise. No one managed him—not his mother, not his sister, and definitely not some lofty lady of the realm.

"Actually, my lady," he said silkily, "I own a curricle for my use while I'm in England. Give me the direction to your estate, and I'll present myself at whatever time you see fit next Monday."

"I have a meeting that morning, but I'll be home around two," Blakeborough interrupted, sparing a sympathetic glance for his sister. "So any time after that will be fine."

"One more thing." Jeremy fixed his gaze on Lady Yvette. "I'll need to bring my apprentice. His aid will ensure I finish the portrait more quickly."

"Very well," she said. "Will he be staying with you? Or shall I find a room for him elsewhere?"

"He'll be comfortable enough in your servants' quarters, if you can accommodate him." He took another chance to provoke her. "*I'll* be fine in your servants' quarters if that's what your ladyship prefers."

"I'd prefer that you not be ridiculous," she muttered, eliciting a choked laugh from her brother.

Jeremy bowed. "I shall do my best to oblige your ladyship."

Apparently she caught that he was mocking her, for she cast him a hard look. He grinned. All right, this might be unwise for many reasons, not least of which was that he must spend part of his time on a formal portrait. But it had its advantages, as well.

He would definitely enjoy sparring with the prickly Lady Yvette.

~~~

The sun had set by the time the wedding celebration was over and the Barlow carriage headed across London for the town house.

"You're very quiet."

The sound of Edwin's voice made Yvette start. "So are you. What of it?"

"I'm always quiet. You, on the other hand, are a babbling brook after a social event. You like to tell me who said what and when. You like to either wax rhapsodic over the owner's collection of books or bemoan their lack."

"And describe the gowns," she said lightly. "Don't forget that."

"I see I should have kept quiet about your being quiet."

She let out a rueful laugh. Poor Edwin. She was such a trial to him. He liked his solitude, and she could only take solitude in small doses. Solitude gave one too much time to brood over the past.

"Very well, I won't bore you about the gowns. Although I did think that Lady Zoe's silver reticule was—"

"If you begin describing reticules, I swear I'll throw myself from the coach." Edwin paused. "But you *could* tell me what you and Keane were talking about in the gardens."

Uh-oh. Trying to keep things secret from her

brother always made her feel awful. "We were talking about the paintings, of course."

"Paintings? More than just the portrait?"

Oh, Lord, she couldn't believe she'd let that slip. "Not the portrait. We settled that immediately. His other paintings. The ones that have been exhibited."

"Ah, right. The ones you criticized."

"Gave an opinion of. That's different from criticizing."

"Hmm." Edwin stared out the window. "You do realize that by hiring Keane to paint you, I was not . . . I didn't mean to imply that you somehow *need* to be shown as—"

"It's all right, Edwin. I know what you think of me."

"I'm not sure that you do."

She banked as much irritation as she could. "You think I'm bent on thwarting your attempts at getting me married, so you wish to nudge me."

"Oh. Well, I suppose you're right about that." He sounded edgy. "I'm worried you're looking at past events as proof of why you should avoid finding a husband."

"What past events?" Samuel had sworn never to tell Edwin about her nearly ruinous association with Lieutenant Ruston. Had he lied?

"What happened toward the end of our parents' unfortunate marriage, of course."

"Oh. Right." She should have realized that Edwin didn't know about her and the lieutenant, or he would have said something ages ago. "And you? You're not letting Mama's unhappiness turn you cynical about marriage?"

"I may be cynical about romantic love, but I do *want* to marry. I need an heir. And you need someone to talk to other than your crotchety eldest brother."

Remembering what Mr. Keane had said about the deal with Edwin, she tensed. "Are you *that* sure I won't find a husband?"

"Damn it, don't twist my words again." He leaned forward to clasp her hands, startling her. "Any man would be lucky to have you. I am not trying to make you 'look attractive enough to convince some hapless fellow in search of a wife to ignore the evidence of his eyes' or whatever nonsense you think. I *know* you to be a beautiful, wonderful woman."

A lump stuck in her throat. "So why the portrait?"

"Keane pointed out that having you painted by a man as famous as he might increase your popularity in society."

That arrested her. What a clever devil Mr. Keane was. To get her to sit for his other painting, he'd convinced Edwin to commission a portrait he didn't want to do. How typical of a manipulative rogue.

Edwin squeezed her hands. "I only want you to be happy, you know." His voice held a soft affection she rarely heard. "If you really don't want Keane to paint you—"

"No, it's fine." She forced a smile. "I'm actually looking forward to it." Especially since it would enable her to get what *she* wanted.

"Are you?" With a speculative glance, he released her hands and sat back against the squabs. "Please tell me you're not interested in the man as a potential husband. I mean, he is quite wealthy, from what

I understand, but his reputation with women leaves something to be desired."

"Which is why I would never consider him as a suitor. I haven't forgotten the lessons I learned from Samuel." And his sly friend. She gazed out the window. "I know too well what havoc our brother wrought . . . what havoc that sort of feckless fellow always wreaks on anyone close to him."

A pall fell over the carriage. "You do understand why I'm not pursuing what Samuel told you."

She glared at him. "Not really, no. Somewhere in Covent Garden we have a young nephew living in a house of ill repute with his mother, Samuel's former mistress. And you're perfectly willing to leave the boy to that uncertain future?"

"First of all, we *may* have a young nephew. It's by no means certain. Indeed, I find it highly unlikely."

"Because Samuel never before sired an illegitimate child?" she said sarcastically. Just this year, Edwin had taken on the support of Samuel's last mistress, Meredith, and *her* child.

"You shouldn't have had to know about that." Edwin's voice hardened. "Indeed, the very fact that he told you about his mistress in a brothel shows how far he's sunk."

Samuel hadn't exactly volunteered the information. She'd forced him into it, in exchange for agreeing to post his letter to the woman. Once he'd told her about Peggy Moreton and her son, Samuel had hinted that the letter contained information to help his mistress financially.

But Yvette hadn't yet sent it. Once that letter was posted, she'd lose all control over the situation. Until

she determined for herself that her nephew was safe,
she wasn't giving the woman anything.

"I know how the world works," Yvette said gently.
"I'm quite used to hearing tales of woe from the
many charities I support."

"That I support at your behest, you mean."

She laughed. "That, too." She tried to make out
his expression in the dim light of the streetlamps.
"Admit it. You take some measure of enjoyment
from helping those who don't have what we do, or
you wouldn't support the school in Preston."

"That doesn't mean I'll provide for half the by-
blows in Christendom just because our brother
asked you to post some letter."

She'd better not tell him she still had the letter.
He might demand that she open it, which she'd
vowed to Samuel she wouldn't do.

"Besides," he went on, "what would we even do
with the child? Surely you don't have some fool idea
that you'd raise him yourself."

"Of course not. That wouldn't be wise for us *or*
the boy. But Meredith might be willing to raise him
with her son, as long as we pay for it. So far she's
been an exemplary mother to her own babe, and the
two children are half brothers, after all."

"Assuming this child genuinely is *his*."

"Why would Samuel lie about it?" Yvette asked.

"Because he heard that we're supporting Meredith and her babe, and he thought to take advantage
of that."

"I don't see how."

"He knows your tender heart. That you won't rest
until you find this child. So sending you on a wild-

goose chase into a bawdy house, at the risk to your reputation, might be his way of striking at me. He's quite aware that seeing you ruined would destroy me. He has never forgiven me for cutting all ties to him after Father disowned him."

Her heart faltered. This was the first time Edwin had advanced such an appalling theory. "You . . . you really think Samuel would do such a thing?" she said. "Use me to strike back at you?"

"I don't know. But I'd rather not take the chance."

That was precisely why she'd been desperate enough to involve Mr. Keane. And why she couldn't let Mr. Keane know the full story of what was going on, or that Edwin was aware of it all. Because then Mr. Keane would reveal her plan to her eldest brother, who'd nip it in the bud. Better to handle it herself.

Still, she couldn't keep from arguing with Edwin about his suppositions. "It sounds like a rather convoluted plan on Samuel's part. Why avenge himself on you when he wouldn't even be in England to witness your downfall? Surely he has worse enemies to strike at."

"So why do *you* think he alluded to his supposed child? Out of some goodness in his heart? Samuel's heart has been empty of such human feeling for quite a while."

"I can't believe that," she said, torn between her two brothers. If not for Samuel, she might have ended up . . .

With a shudder, she tucked that memory away. "You should have seen him in Newgate—full of remorse, wanting to make amends."

"He's always full of remorse once he gets caught. He forgets it soon enough the next time a pretty woman walks by." When they passed directly under a streetlamp, it briefly lit Edwin's tight lips and creased brow. "I hate to see you fretting over this. I don't trust a thing our brother says. You mustn't, either."

"So you truly won't do anything to find Peggy Moreton and her child?"

"I've already done all I could. I asked about an actress by that name and was told that none ever existed."

He'd actually pursued it to that extent? Perhaps he wasn't as heedless of the ties of family as he sometimes seemed.

He went on coldly, "And that means Samuel lied about his mistress's former profession."

"Or that he used her real name, not her stage name."

"Regardless, if I go asking after a woman and her son in the stews, I'll either look as profligate as he—which won't help your situation as a marriageable young lady—or I'll attract any number of impostors claiming to be the ones I seek."

"Then hire an investigator," she said.

"Yes, because they're all so discreet," he bit out.

"Edwin—"

"Perhaps you think I should ask my former fiancée's new husband to look into it. I'm sure he'd be eager for the task," he said bitterly.

They were back to where they'd started. The only investigators Edwin might trust were the very people who'd nearly been brought down by Samuel's latest scheme. She doubted that the Duke's Men would take part in what would probably appear to be another such scheme.

Yet the image of her four-year-old nephew in a bawdy house, seeing things no child should ever see . . .

"We cannot continue to clean up after Samuel," Edwin said curtly. "He's made his bed and now must lie in it."

Unfortunately, it would not be Samuel lying in that bed, but some little boy he'd sired in his usual cavalier fashion.

"Promise me you'll let yourself be guided by me in this," Edwin persisted.

Burying her hands in her skirts, she crossed her fingers and her ankles, too. "I promise."

There were times when one had to do what was right, even at some cost. And if the cost was sitting for a painting by a known scoundrel and acting the part of a loose woman in order to get into a house of ill repute, then so be it.

Four

The sun sank toward earth as Jeremy tooled his curricle up the drive to Stoke Towers. To him the place was just one more lavish English country house.

But to his young apprentice, it was apparently far more. "God strike me blind!" Damber said. "You sure have a lot of rich friends and family in England, sir."

After having been dragged through tumbledown hotels and inns for the past three months on the Continent, the lad had apparently forgotten that Jeremy wasn't just any artist. Sometimes even Jeremy forgot it. When he traveled, he preferred to live like the rest of the populace.

"Ah, but these are neither friends nor family," Jeremy said. "They're clients. And they'd best be rich if they're to afford me."

"From the size of the bowman ken they're living in, I'd say they're fat culls indeed."

"Language, Damber," Jeremy said sharply.

"Talking like you gentry coves is hard," the lad replied without a hint of repentance. "And what does it matter anyhow? You said I got the finest hand with a brush you ever saw. Ain't that enough?"

"No, it 'ain't.' If you sound like a coarse devil, it won't matter that you paint like a saint. No one with the money to buy your art will notice you if you don't seem at least moderately educated. And you do want to progress beyond apprentice, don't you?"

"I suppose," muttered the ungrateful devil.

"Then speak correctly. I know you're capable of it when you concentrate. I've heard you." He ran his gaze over the towering lad. For once, Damber's cravat was straight, his waistcoat buttoned, and his shirt tucked properly in his trousers. "You've finally begun to look like a gentleman, thank God. Now you must talk like one."

"I'll do my best, sir." Damber cast him a cheeky grin. "P'raps if you paid me more . . ."

Jeremy rolled his eyes. The lad already made twice what Jeremy's American apprentices had made. God, he was cocky. Which probably wasn't surprising, given the boy's rough upbringing. But despite the differences in their backgrounds, Damber reminded Jeremy of himself at that age—sure of his talent, passionate about painting, and thirsty for knowledge.

Which might not be a good thing, actually. If Jeremy had been a little *less* thirsty, his life might have been different. He wouldn't have pursued Hannah as a painting instructor. He wouldn't have tumbled into bed with her and ended up married too young.

He wouldn't have—

Thunderation, why was he brooding over that after all these years? Hannah and Theodore were dead, along with the man responsible. Time for him to move on. To stop dwelling on the past. To look toward the future.

His masterpiece.

As if Lady Yvette had somehow read his mind, she appeared on the steps of Stoke Towers, accompanied by a footman, and his blood quickened. Yes, his masterpiece, and his lady muse herself.

After nearly a week apart, he'd expected not to be so taken by her, but if anything, she was even more stunning in her ordinary gown of russet and gold stripes. And as before, her porcelain cheeks were faintly tinged with peach and the sun teased out the hint of red in her brown hair.

He should use burnt umber for that shade of chestnut. Perhaps with a little cream to capture the highlights and some black for the shadows. For *Art Sacrificed to Commerce* she'd have to wear her hair down, cascading over the edges of the marble slab.

Marble slab? Would Stoke Towers even have something that would prove adequate as an altar?

"Is that who you're painting?" Damber said breathlessly. "She don't look like some delicate gentry mort; she's a Long Meg, to be sure."

"Watch the vulgar language, Damber," Jeremy said mechanically. "She's not a Long Meg or—"

"But she is. She's almost as tall as me."

"That's not the point! You shouldn't call her that. Or 'gentry mort,' for that matter. She's a very fine lady, whom I intend to immortalize."

"What's 'immortalize'?" Damber asked.

"Look it up in that dictionary I gave you."

"And you complain about *my* language," Damber

grumbled. The boy hated looking things up. "You've got your own cant with all your fancy words. I'll wager 'immortalize' means something nasty like 'take a lady to bed.' It's got 'mort' in it, so it's got to be about ladies."

Jeremy stifled his laugh, not wanting to encourage the lad. "You'll have to find out for yourself in the dictionary." Frankly, it was a miracle the boy could even read, but someone somewhere had taught the young giant.

Damber shot him a sly look. "Wouldn't blame you, sir, if you wanted to take that one to bed. She's got a bosom on her that would float a ship. Though I bet she's as stiff-rumped as—"

"That's enough. A gentleman doesn't talk about ladies that way."

God, he couldn't believe he'd said that. Trying to educate his apprentice was turning him into a stuffed shirt.

Though the lad wasn't far off. Lady Yvette was indeed a bit stiff-rumped. And she did have an impressive bosom. Jeremy couldn't wait to see how it looked in that Grecian costume he'd acquired.

The image that rose in his head made his blood run hot. And *that* made him curse under his breath. He wasn't here to seduce her, as appealing as that might seem.

Annoyed with himself, he jerked the horses to a halt in front. But before he and Damber had even finished disembarking, Lady Yvette was marching down the steps.

"I expected you here earlier," she said coolly as the footman left her side to unload the curricle.

Damber nudged him, as if to say, *See? Stiff-rumped and proud.*

Jeremy ignored him. "Impatient to begin, are you? I do like enthusiasm in my women."

A telling blush rose up her beautiful neck to her cheeks. "I'm not one of your 'women.' And it wasn't enthusiasm. I just . . . We thought you'd be here sooner, that's all."

"Your brother said anytime after two. He didn't specify an hour."

"No, but I assumed . . . Oh, never mind." She faced Damber, who was giving her the once-over with an insolence she apparently chose to overlook. "You must be Mr. Keane's apprentice."

He gave a curt bow. "The name's Damber, my lady."

She cocked her head. "What an interesting name. Did you know that it's street cant for 'rascal'?"

"It is indeed, my lady," Damber said warily.

"Is it a nickname?" she went on with an air of fascination that surprised Jeremy.

Damber, too, apparently. "I suppose. Only name I ever had."

"I see." Compassion glinted in her eyes. "Well, then, it's a pleasure to meet you, Damber. I've informed the servants that you'll be staying in our extra room downstairs. I hope you'll be comfortable there."

"Long as it's no spring-ankle warehouse, I'll be fine," Damber mumbled. Then, as if realizing what he'd said, he added, "I mean—"

"I should hope it's better than a gaol," she said cheerily. "We have no catchpoles or caterpillars here, I assure you."

Damber perked up. "No, but I daresay you've plenty of country Harrys."

She laughed. "We do at that, sir. And high shoons, too."

Damber broke into a grin, then shot Jeremy an accusing look. "You said I wasn't to use cant around a gentry mort, and here she's using it more than me."

"Than *I*," Jeremy corrected him, then realized how ridiculous that sounded in light of the conversation.

How the devil did she understand Damber, anyway? Jeremy only did half the time. From his many trips to the stews, he thought "catchpoles and caterpillars" were sheriffs and soldiers. And he could guess what a country Harry was. But a high shoon?

"I'm afraid I'm not your typical gentry mort," Lady Yvette told Damber, with a twinkle in her eye.

To put it mildly. Come to think of it, she'd known quite a bit of coarse slang the night they'd met. Granted, her other brother had apparently been a criminal, but not the ill-mannered kind Damber had grown up among. So where had she learned it?

"I collect street cant for my dictionaries," she explained, as if she'd read his thoughts. "It's a hobby of sorts. Indeed, I would be delighted to have you add to my store, Damber, especially if you know any boxing terms."

Damber's mouth fell open. "I know more than anybody! You just tell me when, and I'll give you as many as you like."

"I shall take you up on that sometime." She glanced at the footman, who'd come up beside her to wait, having finished unlashing the men's bags from the back of the curricle. "But for now, you should probably get settled in."

"Aye, my lady," Damber said with a bob of his head.

She faced Jeremy. "Forgive me, Mr. Keane, but I'm not sure exactly what a painter's apprentice does. Will you need a valet, or will Damber—"

"My apprentice will do just fine for whatever I require," Jeremy said, ignoring Damber's groan. "If your man will show him to my room, he can start unpacking, retightening the canvases, and mixing my paints for the morning."

The lad had been getting too full of himself of late. It wouldn't hurt to remind him that talent was nurtured through hard work, and not all of it was as enjoyable as painting and sketching. Or, for that matter, trading slang terms with an unconventional earl's daughter.

"Very well." She turned to Damber. "Tom will show you to Mr. Keane's suite." She seemed to note the footman's stiff posture and added, "And your master is right. Perhaps you should save your use of street cant for me and Mr. Keane. I'm not sure my staff would . . . appreciate its colorful qualities."

"I'll be pleased to do whatever your ladyship wishes," Damber said in the King's own English, though the gleam in his eye and the tip of his hat were anything but gentlemanly.

She laughed as Damber walked off with Tom, cocky as ever. "He's a bit of a rogueling, isn't he? Clearly, you taught him well."

"Trust me, he was born knowing how to turn a woman up sweet. And what he wasn't born knowing, he learned in the stews."

Her smile faltered. "Is that where you met him?"

"God, no. I stumbled across him in Hyde Park, where the lad was sketching people for money."

"Lad?" she echoed.

"That hulking brute is only fifteen, believe it or not. If you'd seen him when I first met him, too scrawny for his frame, you'd have thought him younger still."

She searched his face. "You feed him well, I gather."

"He feeds himself well," Jeremy grumbled. "He's been eating me out of house and home ever since I hired him to be my painter's apprentice."

"So why did you?" She watched him with a veiled look. "Few people would take on a street urchin for a post."

"I regret the decision daily, every time I'm forced to wrestle with the lad over speech and manners. But . . ." He smiled, remembering the drawing of Damber's that had arrested him. "Then he'll show me one of his sketches, and I'm reminded of why I did it. Because he has a good eye and an amazing talent. That's rarer than you might think."

"Yet not many would try to nurture it."

Her eyes warmed, and he was once again struck by their lovely color. What a shame he wouldn't be able to capture those cat eyes sparkling from beneath dusky lashes. In his masterpiece they would be looking upward, only one of them visible, and that in profile.

Then again, there was the portrait. He'd get to paint her eyes for that. It was some solace for being forced to do the sort of work he detested. He could use the cobalt blue, tempered with Indian yellow and a trace of umber to get that emerald hue. But how would he capture the emotion within?

She had kind eyes, the sort a man could lose himself in, drowning in their soft sweetness while he—

Damn, there he went again. "Where's your brother?" he asked sharply as he realized they were entirely alone.

"Edwin had urgent business to attend to with our steward. But he will join us for dinner. In the meantime, I thought we could tour the house." She stepped closer and lowered her voice. "It will give us a chance to pick which room will suit your purposes for your secret work."

"Ah, yes," he said, surprised by the conspiratorial glee in her voice. She was apparently enjoying their subterfuge. "Lead on, madam."

As she walked inside and began to take him around, he found himself memorizing her movements: the turn of her head when she glanced back at him, the abbreviated wave she gave when indicating something he should notice, the lift of her imperious brow when he made some wry comment.

He should be focusing on the succession of rich rooms they passed through, but he'd rather study *her*. After all, he was to paint her.

That was the only reason he watched her obsessively. It wasn't because she fired his blood—oh no. He wasn't that foolish.

Right. Of *course* he was that foolish. He was a man, after all, faced with a lovely and remarkable young woman. He'd have to be carved of granite not to notice her attractions as she mounted the stairs ahead of him.

He wished she were already wearing that flimsy Grecian costume. Back in his wife's day, gowns had clung to a woman, showing every curve, but they'd grown stuffed of late—with petticoats and drawers and what all. It was hard to see the female figure beneath.

Oh, to see Lady Yvette's figure beneath. To run his fingers up those long legs to where her stockings ended and the bare flesh began. Odd that one buttoned-up English lady could so fire his imagination.

And his lust. Damn her.

"Does your apprentice know about the other painting?" she asked as they reached the next floor.

"He's aware that I'm working on a second project while I'm here, yes. I had to tell him that much so he'd understand why I'm having him mix extra paint, stretch extra canvases, etc. But for all he knows of the subject, I might be doing a private portrait of your brother's mistress or illustrating your diary." He grinned. "I could be up to any manner of shenanigans."

She flashed him an arch smile. "So he's been with you long enough to know your dissolute character."

"He knows enough," Jeremy said blandly.

"But once the painting is exhibited, won't he guess that I modeled for it?" She strolled down the hall.

"I create six or seven works a year. If this is chosen to be hung at the Royal Academy's exhibition next summer, he won't see it until then, much less be aware of when I painted it. It could be a work from before I hired him."

"Still—"

"Leave Damber to me." He caught her hand to halt her. "I promise to preserve your reputation, even with him."

Only after her eyes widened did he realize that her hand was bare. That the way he held it was intimate. That her skin was buttery soft, and her fingers more delicate than he'd expected.

That her breath had begun to quicken . . . as had his pulse. Thunderation.

He dropped her hand.

For a moment she stared at him with a look of unsettling intensity, as if trying to parse out his intentions. Then she released a ragged breath that clutched at him somewhere deep, and turned to walk briskly down the hall.

Fighting his lecherous urges, he strode after her. God, what devil possessed him? He ached to keep touching her. Which was absurd. He generally had better control over his desires.

She showed him into a spacious salon dominated by a large pianoforte. "Perhaps we could use the music room."

She sounded perfectly demure again. Obviously he wasn't quite the temptation to her that she was to him. That ought to relieve him.

But it didn't.

"Edwin rarely comes in here," she went on, "and it's wonderfully bright."

"It is indeed." He glanced around. "But aside from the fact that the earl will expect me to spend my days on the portrait, how will you keep the servants from noticing that you and I are disappearing for hours on end? Someone is bound to go looking for you and find us here. I don't see how you can keep it a secret as long as we are in the house. I'd hoped you might have some abandoned outbuilding—"

"No, that won't work." A frown creased her brow. "Everything is in use during the day. I suppose we could pretend to go riding and find a field somewhere . . ."

"Come now, your brother is sure to be suspicious if we say we're going riding alone together. He'll want to join us, especially when he sees me packing my canvases and sketch books, et cetera, to take along."

She released an exasperated breath. "What if we were to do it at night after everyone has gone to sleep? Can you paint at night, in dimmer light?"

"I can and have, though it's not my favorite." He eyed her askance. "But you're proposing that the two of us spend our evenings alone together."

Averting her gaze, she tipped up her chin. "Yes. What of it?"

"Didn't you characterize me as the sort of man who would as soon toss you down and have my way with you as look at you? You practically accused me of being as bad as your scurrilous brother Samuel."

"True, but I also said I know all his tricks. And yours." She crossed her arms over her chest defensively. "If we're in a room in the manor and you misbehave, I can always call for a servant."

"If you're naïve enough to think that threatening to call a servant would save you from seduction, then you don't know *any* man's tricks," he said dryly.

That seemed to give her pause. As well it should. "But if you try anything with me, you won't get your painting. And surely that's more important to you than attempting to bed one more woman in a long string of them."

"Of course," he said with a smooth smile.

She was right—it should be. Unfortunately, she didn't realize what a potent enchantress she was. The prospect of painting her while she was dressed in a flimsy costume had him fairly salivating.

Being alone with her at night for hours on end would be tempting fate. So of course, he must do it. He'd never been one to back down from a challenge.

"Very well," he said, "we'll work while everyone else sleeps. But this room won't do. It's fine for the portrait, but the thing that makes it perfect for painting in the daytime will make it disastrous for our evening trysts."

He gestured to the windows with their flimsy net curtains. "I'll need plenty of candles, lamps, and firelight to see by, and that will give away our presence to anyone who passes by below—servants, grooms, local populace. Not to mention your brother. Someone might come to investigate."

"That's true." Her brow furrowed. "We need something more secluded and private, but indoors. Perhaps down the hall?"

"It'll need to be far away from your brother's bedchamber or he'll hear us."

"True." Wandering out of the room, she looked around. "Edwin's suite is on this floor, as is yours. We can't use the library, because Edwin likes to go in there when he can't sleep. On the floor above, where my bedchamber and the others are, there might be a spare sitting room we could use."

"Too small." He peered up the open well of the staircase. "What's on the floor above that?"

She tensed. "Nothing, really. Just the old nursery and schoolroom."

"The schoolroom might do." Without waiting for her, he strode up the stairs.

"It isn't ever used," she protested as she hurried after him. "I can't even remember the last time a fire was laid in the hearth."

"As long as the fireplace still draws, it should be fine."

When they reached the top floor, he paused to look around, seeing only a series of closed doors. "Which room is it?"

Looking oddly reluctant, she meandered to the end of the carpeted hall and flung a door open. "Honestly, I don't think—"

But he was already stalking past her and into the room. A drugget covered the floor and Holland cloths draped the furniture, supporting her assertion that the room wasn't used. A globe sat bare and forgotten in a corner, a blackboard hung on the wall, and a few spindly chairs were scattered about.

Best of all, in the center of the room stood a massive oak table that had obviously been deemed too marred by scratches and stains to warrant protecting. It could serve as an altar if he covered it with white fabric.

He ran his hand over the dusty surface. A pity he couldn't use it as it was. The wood had stories to tell; he could practically hear it calling to him. But the altar's surface must be pale enough to show the blood that he would paint coursing down from his sacrifice.

His beautiful, provocative sacrifice, who remained frozen in the doorway, clearly uncertain of his choice. "Surely you don't think this will do."

"Actually, it's perfect."

He wandered the room in a fog of thought. He'd originally envisioned a wilderness scene, with Commerce as a stodgy fellow he meant to paint in later, looming over the lovely Art lying prone beneath his knife as her blood dripped onto the granite altar. But why should Commerce be outside? Better to use that classical frieze that spanned the schoolroom's ceiling. And the fretwork above the windows, like something out of a Grecian temple, or a bank.

Yes! The modern equivalent of the worship of money was the institution where all that money was kept! Banks often had Grecian architecture, some elements of which were in this very room.

Excitement coursing through him, he scanned the marble fireplace with its plaster medallion above, perfect for a bank. And the oak table could work as a counter, like those where clerks stood to serve the account holders.

He frowned. But the oak was still too dark to show the blood. Maybe if he—

"Mr. Keane!"

The voice startled him. Only after he turned to find Lady Yvette looking worried did he realize she'd spoken his name more than once. "Yes?"

"Where were you?"

He smiled ruefully. "Forgive me, my lady. When

I'm working I get a bit lost in the project, and my surroundings disappear."

She nodded. "Rather like Edwin when he's working on his automatons."

"Automatons?"

"Machines that you wind up and—"

"I know what an automaton is," Jeremy remarked. "I just wouldn't have expected your brother to have any."

"He does them for the boys' school we support. Says that they help the boys learn physics and mechanical skills and such. But I think he also does it because of Papa."

"Oh?"

"Papa collected dozens through the years. At first, Edwin fiddled with them only when they broke, since Samuel and I were so amused by them." Her face clouded over. "Then later he started making his own after Mama got sick, when he had to spend hours at her side because . . ."

Whirling on her heel, she walked into the hall. "We should go downstairs," she said in a remote tone. "I hear Edwin calling. And it wouldn't do for him to find us up here."

"No." Jeremy hadn't heard anyone calling, and he doubted she had, either. Something had spooked her, and he wanted to know what.

But now wasn't the time to raise the question. He'd wait until she was posing for him and couldn't easily run off. Then he'd find out exactly why his Juno was so skittish.

Five

Yvette sat across from Edwin in the drawing room, trying not to look at Mr. Keane. It was impossible. Tonight he wore a brilliant blue tailcoat that made his eyes shine so luminously, she could stare at him for hours.

Not that he gave her the chance. As she and Edwin played chess, he sat beside the fireplace and sketched.

She couldn't believe she'd agreed to meet with him alone at night. Was she out of her wits?

No. She was a grown woman in full control of her senses. She was older now, and far wiser. Surely she could handle the likes of Mr. Keane.

If you're naïve enough to think that threatening to call a servant would save you from seduction, then you don't know any man's tricks.

Oh, dear.

Still, he did want his painting. He would behave.

Look at him now, so intent on drawing her that he couldn't even make polite conversation. It was somewhat lowering that he saw her only as some object to sketch. If this was how he always worked, though, she would have nothing to worry about.

"Are you sure you don't want to take my place here?" She was determined to get *some* reaction from the man. "I'm no match for Edwin at chess."

He didn't answer. Edwin exchanged a glance with her.

"Mr. Keane?" she said sharply. "Would you like to play the next game with my brother?"

"Hmm?" The same vague expression he'd worn this afternoon crossed his face before it cleared. "Oh, sorry, no." He tore off a sheet, balled it up, and made as if to throw it into the fire.

"Don't!" She leapt up to take the paper from him. "Let me see."

"It's horrible," he said, though he let her have it.

She smoothed out the sketch, then gasped. With a minimal number of strokes he'd perfectly rendered her face in profile. "It's not horrible in the least. You made me pretty."

"You *are* pretty," Edwin interjected.

Mr. Keane ignored him. "I made you like every other chit in England." With a frown, he went to work again on his sketch pad. "You're better than that."

She didn't know whether to be flattered or insulted. "I would settle for pretty," she told him as she reverently slid the crumpled sketch into her nearby writing desk.

"Never settle for less than you deserve," he said. "It's always a bad idea."

The knife's edge of pain in his voice caught her

attention as she came back to where he sat slashing and shading with the pencil. "You sound as if you speak from experience."

Mr. Keane glanced up and blinked. Then his gaze shuttered before he pointed to her chair. "Go back there and stop moving about. I want to do more sketches. I have to figure out exactly how to pose you tomorrow, and for that I need studies."

She thrust out her chin. "Don't I get a say in the pose for my own portrait?"

"I should be the one with a say." Edwin hunched over the chessboard. "I'm the one paying for it."

This time they both ignored him. Mr. Keane settled back in his chair, his eyes roving her as if memorizing curves and lines. "Would you like a say? You didn't seem that enthusiastic about the portrait yesterday."

That was before she'd realized he could make her look pretty but still herself. "I'm not averse to it. And yes, I prefer to choose the pose."

He smiled faintly. "You don't choose the pose, my lady. It chooses you."

"Must you always speak in enigmas?"

"At least I don't speak in street cant." Crossing his arms over his chest, he broadened his smile. "Why do you, anyway?"

"I don't speak in it. I collect it for my dictionary."

"But why would a lady of the realm with any number of more appropriate pastimes open to her choose to 'collect' street cant?"

"Think of it as a scholarly pursuit."

He raked his gaze down her in a thorough assessment that made her cheeks burn and her stomach flip over. "You don't strike me as the scholarly type," he said huskily.

She glanced over to Edwin, then released a breath to see her brother still concentrating on deciding his next chess move. "You hardly know me well enough to determine that."

"True. So why don't you remedy that situation? Tell me why you collect vulgar slang instead of, say, butterflies."

"Samuel got her into it, the scoundrel," Edwin snapped.

Her heart faltered. She mustn't let Mr. Keane guess that her proposed bawdy house visit was connected to Samuel. She wasn't sure if she could trust the artist, and if he got even an inkling that Samuel was involved he might go to Edwin, who would quash everything. "But a long time ago, before Papa banished him from the family."

Mr. Keane glanced from her to Edwin in confusion. "Then why are you still gathering cant for your dictionary?"

"Because it no longer has anything to do with Samuel." *Or his friend, with whom I was infatuated. Until I realized that his interest in me was purely mercenary.* "Samuel was an aficionado of prizefighting and was always throwing terms around that I didn't comprehend. Wanting to understand him better, I started asking questions and taking notes. After a while, it became a bit of a hobby."

"An obsession, more like," Edwin said.

"But a purely academic one?" Mr. Keane searched her face. "I assume you've never actually been in those parts of London where it's spoken."

"I don't need to go into such parts to learn about it," she said defensively. "I've read all the dictionaries and Pierce Egan's books. Also, I work with several charities involving women of a lower station, and I hear their use of such slang."

"Besides," Edwin said, "it's not as if I would ever allow her to wander into Spitalfields or Wapping, even with an escort. It's not safe for her *or* her reputation."

Mr. Keane shot her a glance full of meaning.

"Edwin is always concerned about my safety," she said hastily, "even here at the estate. It's one of the disadvantages of having a much older brother."

Edwin settled back in his chair. "You could change me out for a husband. Then you could do as you please."

She snorted. "Do such indulgent men actually exist in society?"

"You'll never find out if you keep running them off," her brother said sourly.

Jane had accused her of much the same thing, and Yvette was sick of it. "I can't help it if all the men I meet are as stodgy as you."

"You mean, because they're shocked when you quiz them about vulgar terms?" Edwin glanced at Mr. Keane. "Every time she meets a sporting gentleman, she asks him about any slang he might know. It's one reason she can't acquire any respectable suitors: They decide she's either a bluestocking or rather lower than they thought."

She sniffed. "Gentlemen make no allowances for a woman having unusual hobbies."

"You could stop having them," Edwin pointed out.

"You could stop tinkering with little mechanical people and start tinkering with actual living ones," she snapped. "But I don't criticize *you*."

"I think you just did," Mr. Keane said gamely.

"Stay out of this!" She faced her brother. "Do you really want me to give up all my interests just to gain a husband? When you're not willing to give up yours to gain a wife?"

Mr. Keane laughed. "She's got you there, Blakeborough. What's sauce for the goose ought to be sauce for the gander."

"Ought to be, I agree." Edwin steepled his hands. "Sadly, in the rarefied atmosphere of our class, it is not. A man may be as eccentric as he pleases and still find a wife, especially if he has an estate and a title. But a woman, even an heiress, must be more careful if she doesn't want a man marrying her for her money alone."

His words fired her temper. "Yes, a woman must always be more careful. And more circumspect. And more *bland*." She glared at her brother, hands on her hips. "She must always sit just so and act just so, and never indicate one iota of what she really thinks or feels, because—"

"Stop right there!"

Mr. Keane's cry so startled her that she froze.

He leapt up to circle to the front of her. "Don't move. That's it. That's the pose." Dropping into the chair across from Edwin, he began sketching furiously. "Perfect. Absolutely perfect."

"Because she's being annoying as hell?" Edwin drawled.

"Because she's *fierce*." Mr. Keane's gaze met hers. "Gloriously, intoxicatingly fierce."

So was he, his eyes alight, his face wearing an artistic intensity as his pencil flew across the page.

Her pulse began to pound. "Oh, yes, paint me fierce. I like fierce."

"Then stop smiling," Mr. Keane chided. "Go back to how you looked before."

As she tried to do so, Edwin let out an oath. "This isn't the sort of image I had in mind for my sister."

Mr. Keane didn't even pause in his work. "I warned you there's a reason I don't do portraits. The sitters—or their families—never like how I portray them."

"But it's a fishwife's pose," Edwin complained, "with her hands on her hips like that. It's not the least bit feminine."

"It's the most feminine pose in the world. How often do you see a man stand like that?" Mr. Keane said. "It conveys strength of purpose."

"Yes, if the woman is an Amazon," Edwin snapped.

"I'm perfectly happy to be painted as an Amazon," Yvette got out through clenched teeth as she tried to maintain her pose. Amazons didn't let men make fools of them.

Mr. Keane smiled darkly at her. "Not an Amazon, my lady. Juno herself. You're a goddess of the first order. Amazons are soldiers in skirts, but goddesses can be both soft and fierce. That's what makes them goddesses."

Something shifted inside her chest. No man had ever called her a goddess. Certainly no man had ever captured the strange dichotomy of her character that so put off respectable gentlemen.

And though she tried to tell herself it was just Mr. Keane's roguery at work, she couldn't deny the heat in his eyes as he spoke. It sent an answering shiver of need down her spine.

Thank heaven Edwin couldn't see how Mr. Keane was looking at her. Though unfortunately her brother could probably see *her* reaction to it.

She tried to figure out what he was thinking, but Edwin was a master at hiding his feelings. Much better at it than she. He merely glanced from her to Mr. Keane with an unreadable gaze.

"You see?" Mr. Keane showed Edwin the sketch. "What do you think?"

Edwin's face softened slightly. "You're right," he said, a hint of awe in his voice. "She's magnificent."

"Much better than merely pretty," Mr. Keane said as he returned to sketching. "You're clearly a man of taste after all, Blakeborough."

A knot formed in her stomach. She wasn't quite ready to give up looking pretty. "Let *me* see."

"In a moment." Mr. Keane made a few more marks on his sketch pad, then rose to approach her. He paused just short of where she stood. "Can you look at this without changing your expression?" She lifted an eyebrow, and he chuckled. "Of course you can't. I know that just from spending half a day with you."

"Try me," she muttered.

"It doesn't matter. The light isn't that good anyway, and I've got enough of a drawing to work with. So memorize your position, and tomorrow we'll set you in the music room as we discussed. Then I'll start blocking out the portrait. Assuming you still approve of your pose in the sketch. Do you?"

The fact that he remembered her demand to choose the pose warmed her. "It depends. Let me see how it looks."

He turned the sketchbook toward her. It gave only the merest impression of her shape, with more detail about the face. But in a few strokes he'd managed to capture her fierce mood while somehow conveying the vulnerability beneath it.

And he hadn't made her pretty. He'd made her beautiful.

"All right?" he murmured, a gentleness in his tone.

"Yes." She was still trying to take in how he'd done it when he lifted the edge of the paper to reveal words written on the sheet beneath.

Will you meet me in the schoolroom at midnight to begin the other? If so, point to something on the sketch.

With her heart pounding, she touched her finger to the image of her dinner gown. "Shall I wear this tomorrow, too?" She hoped her voice didn't shake as badly as her finger.

"Whatever you wish to wear is fine."

The rasped words made her skin tingle. He stared at her with a look so pregnant with carnal possibilities that it sent her blood rushing feverishly through her veins. *Take care. You went down this road before, and it only led to heartache. He's a rogue. He's a rogue. He's a rogue.*

A pity that her body was deaf to her warning. Her body yearned to find out exactly how much of a rogue he was. What he might say to her in private, if he might kiss her . . . how he might touch her.

She scowled. Her body had best learn to listen. Because she didn't intend to make a fool of herself ever again.

And she certainly refused to end up used and discarded like one of Samuel's women.

Six

Jeremy arrived in the schoolroom an hour before the appointed time. He had to set his scene, arrange the tools of his trade . . . prepare himself for work with a woman who intoxicated him more with every passing moment.

He must gain control of himself. In the drawing room he'd made the mistake of showing how deep his attraction to Lady Yvette ran, and she'd registered it. He'd seen that in her eyes.

Maybe she even shared it, but it didn't matter. It could go no further.

Especially with some Englishwoman of high rank. Lady Yvette might collect slang and speak of charity work and show kindness to his apprentice, but she needed a certain kind of husband.

Not the kind who would trudge through the Alps to find a scenic view worth painting. Or the kind who was the subject of gossip about his sojourns in the brothels, where he went to search for whores to serve as models. Not the kind who was so incapable of love that he'd left his own wife to be—

No. He was perfectly capable of lust, but love was beyond him, as his short-lived marriage had proved. And a marital union without love on both sides was destined to end in a stultifying existence that crippled creativity. Or in heartbreak and suffering and death.

Silencing his memories, he concentrated on the task at hand—preparing the setting. First he had to stoke up the fire and light plenty of candles and lanterns. Unlike some artists, he didn't mind working at night if it suited the image he sought to create. The colors wouldn't be quite true—he'd have to review them by day to make sure he wasn't going awry—but this particular painting would benefit from some shrouding.

There was a bit of a moon and normally he could have used that, too, but not in this case. Regretfully, he closed the heavy curtains to keep anyone outside from noticing that they were working up here.

Then he peered at the curtain fabric—damask, in a pattern that could pass for wallpaper. He stretched out one panel until it formed a straight surface. With the frieze above it and the wooden table in front of it, it looked remarkably like bank décor. Better yet, it provided a lush backdrop that would make his subject's "sacrifice" more poignant.

Art, innocent and fresh and full of promise, being ravaged by the cold knife of Commerce. Yes. Excellent.

Next came the covering for the "altar." He'd figured out how to have his cake and eat it, too. Bank tables were sometimes littered with papers, so he'd had Damber working all evening on covering sheets of foolscap with inked words. Now he tossed those randomly across the oak surface. Yvette would lie upon them, and he could paint blood pouring over the white paper. He might even throw in some banknotes for good effect.

Growing more excited by the moment, he moved the chairs from around the table to a spot across the room. Then he put some cushions atop the papers for her to recline on. They would enable him to place her how he wanted. If he posed her right, the cushions wouldn't show.

With the scene set, he turned to erecting his easel, centering the sketch pad, and laying out his charcoals. Tonight he'd only be sketching.

Finally he opened the box he'd carried up the two flights of stairs. He drew out the floor-length Grecian chiton of white linen that he'd appropriated from Zoe's store of masquerade attire and shook it out. Silver clasps held the fabric at the shoulders, leaving the arms bare. He tried not to think of how provocative his Juno would look in it.

"Is that it?" came a voice from the doorway. "My costume?"

He tensed. She was here. "Yes." He glanced up at her, and his heart slammed to a halt.

Her hair was undone, frothing over her shoulders like a fine dark ale, and she wore what looked like a linen shift or nightdress with a muslin wrapper over it. She'd swaddled both in a voluminous brown shawl that was edged with a paisley design and finished with gold fringe.

The effect was stunning—like cream wrapped in a pastry shell and dotted with golden specks. He wanted to take a bite. He wanted to drink the ale and lick the cream. He wanted to peel away the layers—

God, at this rate he'd never survive the night. "You're early," he managed. "And more . . . er . . . informally dressed than I expected."

Her cheeks shone pink. "I had to allow my maid to undress me or she would have been suspicious." Lady Yvette stepped warily into the room, and the shawl's gold fringe sparkled about her in the lantern light. "Fortunately, everyone is generally abed by eleven here in the country."

"Then tomorrow we'll meet at eleven," he said. "I'll have little enough time to paint you as it is."

"At least you won't need to rise early. I sleep late most days, so Edwin won't find that the least bit suspicious. I've never been one to jump out of bed at dawn." Hugging her arms, she approached to look at the costume. "Shall I put this on?"

"Certainly."

"I suppose you want me to remove my nightdress underneath."

Yes. Oh hell, yes. "It would be best. I want the arms showing, and your nightdress is too fussy a design for a classical look."

Her cheeks were bright red now. "And my . . . other undergarments?"

"You can leave those on. I'll have you take off your stockings when I get to the feet, but that won't be anytime soon."

"All right." A few moments passed. When he simply stood there, she said, "Well? Are you going to turn around so I can change?"

"Sorry," he muttered as he put his back to her. "I'm not used to having a respectable female pose for me. Most of my models are . . . not the sort of women who care if I see them naked."

"Well, I *am* that sort," she said testily from behind him. "I'm afraid you'll have to get used to it."

The rustling of fabric that followed made him clench his hands. He wanted to watch. He wanted to touch. He wanted to run his fingers over that smooth, porcelain skin until she lost her stiffness and melted in his arms.

"All right," she said. "Where do you want me?"

In my bed.

Without looking at her, for fear he might combust, he stalked to the table. "Here. I need you to lie upon these papers."

She came up beside him. "The ink will ruin the costume."

"It doesn't matter. Zoe said she didn't need the chiton back. She has another she likes better, and in her present condition she can't wear it anyway."

Only then did he venture a look at her ladyship. The chiton was too short for her and showed a generous portion of her neat ankles and well-shaped calves. He skimmed his gaze up to where the silver thread rope belt cinched her waist, accentuating not only her lush hips but her ample bosom. To where her nipples, hard from the chill in the room, were imprinted on the linen.

His mouth went dry.

She must have noticed the direction of his gaze,

for she crossed her arms over her breasts self-consciously. "How am I to get up on there without dislodging the papers?"

Without a word, he scooped her up and laid her atop them. "Like this."

He stared down into her startled face, at the crescents of her dark brows, at her elegant nose . . . at her sweetly bowed lips. The urge to kiss her assailed him so powerfully that it was all he could do to let go of her.

Unfortunately, even releasing her did not relax her. She lay like a piece of furniture, stiff and unmoving, not at all like the symbol of Art that he'd envisioned.

"Not like that," he said tersely. "A bit more on your side. Use the cushions to support you if you must."

"Like this?" She shifted position, and so did her breasts.

"Yes," he gritted out, and jerked his gaze from them.

This was insanity. He'd sketched and painted naked women hundreds of times without really *seeing* them, and certainly without lusting after them. So, why, by all that was holy, must he really see and lust after *her*?

"Now," he went on, "cover your face with your arm as if to shield it."

"Like this?" She stared up at the ceiling with her arm fully over her face.

"No, looking forward."

"I thought you said my face would be in profile."

"I changed my mind. If you look toward me and

cover half your features with your arm, no one will recognize you. Especially if you angle it so your face is in shadow." Though he would leave her lips in the light. He had to capture that expressive mouth in full, which he couldn't do in profile.

She shifted so she was staring at him from beneath her arm. "More like this?"

"Better. Now pretend that I am above and behind you, coming down at you with a knife. You're taken by surprise."

She did as he ordered, but her stance was still awkward.

"Turn a bit more onto your side and crook one leg."

Once again she cooperated, but the entire tableau seemed posed and forced. Impatiently, he tugged at her limbs, trying to get a more relaxed look.

Then he let out an oath. "You look uncomfortable."

"And I will continue to do so, as long as you keep putting your hands all over me," she muttered, blushing furiously.

He lifted his gaze heavenward. "Very well, but you must at least attempt to look natural. Will it help if I rearrange the cushions?"

"I'm fine."

"Are you sure? We've got a few hours ahead of us, during which you'll have to hold that pose."

A note of panic flickered in her eyes before she masked it behind a wooden look once more. "Go start your painting. I'm perfectly comfortable."

No, she wasn't, but he was beginning to think it wasn't because of the pose. No doubt she was self-conscious about being so lightly garbed, but he couldn't help that. He wanted her to be Art personified, taken off guard and looking betrayed by Commerce's attack.

Had he been mad to think that a fine lady would make a good artist's model?

No. Lady Yvette was capable of being what he wanted. He'd seen it earlier, when she'd asserted her rights in the drawing room. He simply needed to bring out the real her. To take her out of herself, so she forgot who she was and how she was dressed.

"Now," he said as he walked back to his easel, "look tragic."

To his satisfaction, she lifted her imperious brow. "How does one 'look tragic'?"

"You tell me." He began to sketch.

"I'm sure I wouldn't know."

"Have you never experienced tragedy?"

The way she withdrew into her stony pose again told him that she had.

He followed his instincts and said the first thing that popped into his head. "Does it have something to do with this room?"

That startled her. "What makes you say that?"

"Because being in it clearly bothers you. Why?"

For a moment he'd thought he'd erred again, for she froze in place, a veritable ice sculpture. Then she muttered a curse. "Can't you just leave it be?"

"No. Unfortunately, although I've found the pose and setting I need, you aren't going to be comfortable with it until you are comfortable *here*. In this room."

"I *can't* be comfortable here."

He stared at her. "Why not?"

It took her a moment to answer. "This was where I spent all my time while Mama was . . . dying. It will forever be associated with her death for me."

The naked agony in her features was profound and genuine, and what he needed for his painting. But it also tugged at his heart. Because he knew what it was like to refuse to return to the scene of a tragic death.

That sort of connection between him and his subject rarely happened, and it made him feel almost guilty about rousing her pain.

Almost.

Ignoring his odd twinge of conscience, he sketched the play of emotion on her face while he had it. But she was already retreating into her safe, stiff cocoon, damn her. "How did your mother die?"

"I don't want to talk about it."

He fixed her with a hard look. "Then I will pack up my paints and return to London, and you won't get your trip to the brothel." When an expression of heartbreaking vulnerability crossed her features, he swore under his breath. "I'm sorry. That was cruel. But what I seek to show in my art is the depth of people's feelings. So if you can't—or won't—show them to me, I can't do my work."

Her throat moved convulsively. Then she gazed past him and sighed. "She . . . had consumption. It was awful. She lingered for months."

He'd never had to endure that—the wasting away of someone he cared about. It seemed somehow worse than Hannah's brutal but quick demise. "How old were you?" he asked as he resumed sketching.

"Ten. After Papa left, I helped care for her for a while. I didn't think she should lack for family to comfort her."

The thought of Lady Yvette feeling responsible for comforting her consumptive mother at ten chilled his soul. "Your father *left*? Where the hell did he go?"

Bitterness twisted her lips. "Oh, Papa was hardly ever here when I was growing up. He preferred the city. Mama was the one who ran the place. Even after the doctor said she had consumption, Papa hired a nurse for her and took himself off to London to sit Parliament. He said it was his duty." She glared past Jeremy. "Apparently being at his wife's side during her final months was *not* his duty."

Thunderation. Her father had been almost as much an ass as his.

"When Edwin heard of it," she went on, "he abandoned his studies at Oxford to ensconce himself here at Stoke Towers with me."

"Thank God someone in the family had sense. Though I'm surprised that your father allowed your brother to leave school."

"They had a mighty row about it when Papa briefly returned so he could order Edwin back to Oxford. I heard most of the argument before my governess caught me eavesdropping and took me away."

Her voice hardened. "Papa said it was a daughter's place to sit with a mother. That girls were good for little else, but his heir should be at school. Edwin refused to leave. He told Papa I was too young to watch Mama die and should be in the schoolroom instead. Edwin insisted upon staying at Mama's side."

A troubled look crossed her face. "Edwin won the argument. When Papa saw that Edwin wouldn't budge, he returned to London. Meanwhile I was relegated to the schoolroom until she died."

"And that bothers you?"

"I would have liked to stay with her. It's not as if I learned much anyway, sitting up here trying not to think about Mama coughing away downstairs."

"But your brother was right. It was no sight for a child of ten. And where was your brother Samuel in all this?"

"Still at school. Edwin and I were the only ones here. He spent his days in Mama's bedchamber, repairing automatons, and his nights trying to comfort me."

"Which your father should have been doing."

Anger flared in her eyes. "Papa said he hated sickrooms. So we didn't see him until the funeral."

Now she looked tragic. So tragic that he could hardly bear to put the image to paper. God rot her father. What sort of man abandoned his children at such a time?

"Edwin made excuses for him," she went on, "said that Papa couldn't handle the loss of Mama, but I always knew there was more to it than that. Because it seemed to me that he handled it perfectly well. He went off to London and never gave it another thought." She glanced at Jeremy. "Rather like you, abandoning your sister."

The attack took him off guard. He could understand how she might look at it that way, especially since it was uncomfortably close to the truth.

Unfortunately, defending his actions would mean

revealing some of *his* darkest secrets, and he wasn't about to do that. Not with her, not with anyone. He could barely stand to think about the past, much less talk of it.

Best just to let her believe him being as irresponsible as her father.

So, as always when the conversation veered out of his control, he changed the subject.

Seven

"Speaking of London," Mr. Keane said, "I've arranged for our brothel visit. I should have told you before, but I forgot."

"You *forgot?*" Yvette was cold and sore and growing more annoyed by the moment with sitting for the artist.

"If you'll recall, when you first came up here you were a bit . . . unsettled."

"Oh. True." Until this afternoon, she hadn't been in their schoolroom in years, and the idea of spending her nights in here with him had made her uncomfortable.

Little had she guessed it would end up being nothing to the discomfort of lying sideways on a hard wooden table, wearing hardly anything, with her arm resting across her face. No wonder he'd asked repeatedly about her well-being earlier. Her left foot was going to sleep. So was her right hand.

And he was *still* only sketching her. She hadn't

seen him pick up a paintbrush yet. For that matter, she didn't see any brushes or paints at all.

"Anyway," he said, "I'm telling you now."

Telling her what? Oh, yes. That he'd arranged for their brothel visit. "However did you manage it?"

"I engaged the help of my cousin Zoe."

Yvette stared at him in horror. "You told her I wanted to visit a bawdy house?"

"Don't be absurd." He chose another charcoal. "I told her I needed her to throw a masquerade ball as soon as possible. She was more than happy to oblige, since she owes me a favor."

"That must be some favor."

"You have no idea," he muttered. "In any case, the ball is at the end of next week. You and your brother should receive the invitation tomorrow."

"Oh, dear."

He shot her a sharp glance over the top of the canvas. "What?"

"Edwin hates masquerades."

"Your brother appears to hate everything."

She bit back a smile. "It does seem that way, doesn't it? But honestly, he can be very winning when I can coax him out of himself. He broods too much."

"I noticed."

"Don't worry—I'll talk him round to it. He knows that I enjoy masquerade balls, and I can point out that it would be rude of you not to attend your own cousin's affair."

Mr. Keane stared hard at her. "Do you do that often? 'Talk him round' to things?"

"Someone has to. Otherwise he'd spend his entire life alone in a room with his automatons. He doesn't like people much."

"Yes, I noticed that, too." Mr. Keane returned to sketching.

"Anyway, do you mean for us just to slip out of the ball together?"

"Yes. We'll be in costume, so as long as no one knows what we've come as, we'll be safe."

"Does Lady Zoe live near Covent Garden?"

"No, we'll have to take a hackney." He made a large sweeping motion with the charcoal over the sketch pad. "Mrs. Beard's establishment is on the near end of Covent Garden, so that's where we'll start."

"Good Lord, you certainly know your nunneries," she said acidly.

"If you'll recall, that *is* why you wanted me to help you." His eyes had gone a steely blue as he sketched.

"True." And his knowledge shouldn't irritate her so much, but the more she got to know him, the more it did. Perish the man.

A lock of his golden hair fell into his eyes and he swept it back, heedless of the black streak he left on his forehead. "When are you going to tell me exactly whom you're looking for in the nunneries?"

That put her on edge. "Soon." When he cast her a dark look, she added, "First, I need to be sure I can trust you."

"You mean, because I'm the sort of man who spends my time in brothels," he said in an oddly irritable tone. As if somehow he chafed at being characterized in such a way.

"Well, you do, don't you?"

His lips thinned into a line. "Yes, I do. Quite a bit, as a matter of fact." Now there was a certain defiance in his tone.

It roused her curiosity. She'd begun to wonder about his reputation as a whoremonger. Sometimes it didn't seem to fit him. Wouldn't a notorious seducer have at least tried to kiss her by now? Especially after the way he stared at her occasionally.

Of course, she might just be reading into that what she wanted to see. That he desired her. That he thought her worth seducing. Perhaps he didn't.

That was a lowering thought. How could she have any luck gaining a decent husband if the only men she ever attracted were fortune hunters and scoundrels? If she couldn't even tempt a rakehell while wearing a flimsy piece of linen and reclining atop a table?

Not that she wanted to tempt him. No, indeed. Though it might be nice—just once—to find out what it was like to be kissed with genuine passion. To be the object of a man's desire, not just his greed. Since Mr. Keane had no need of her fortune or rank, he might actually desire her for herself. Or her body, anyway. At this point, she wouldn't mind that so much.

She stiffened. Good Lord, this seductive pose was making her think the unthinkable. Which was probably his plan in the first place—to move slowly and subtly to seduce her. Although he was moving *really* slowly.

Once more, her curiosity about him and his habits was roused. "I've never understood why some men prefer frequenting bawdy houses to spending time with their wives."

He snorted. "You don't seriously expect me to enlighten you on that."

"Why not?"

"You're not even supposed to know brothels exist, much less what is done in them."

"Being respectable doesn't prevent me from being curious." When he merely kept sketching, she added, "It's not as if I'm like the average lady. I'm lying here half-naked at midnight so a rogue can paint me. That's hardly the behavior of a saint."

"It's hardly the behavior of a sinner, either." He shot her a hard glance. "To be a sinner, you have to do more with the rogue than be painted by him. You have to sin with him."

She swallowed. "And that would be unwise."

"It certainly would," he snapped, and returned to sketching.

Perversely, that peeved her. For a scoundrel, he was being awfully gentlemanly.

Or was she simply not attractive enough to tempt him? Perhaps she'd imagined all those heated looks. It wouldn't be the first time she'd misinterpreted a man's interest in her. "Don't you *want* to sin with me?"

Oh, Lord, she couldn't believe she'd blurted that out.

His face went stony. "The art of sinning isn't for novices, my lady. I have neither the time nor the inclination to teach it to an innocent."

She felt as if she'd been slapped in the face. She could tell a mere excuse when she heard one. "I should have realized you were just blathering non-sense earlier." She choked down her disappointment, struggling not to let him see it. "All those references to my 'magnificence' and being a 'goddess.' You didn't mean a word of it."

He strode up to glare at her. "I am not a man who lies, as a general rule."

"No, but you flatter well enough when you want something, don't you?"

He stepped nearer, a dangerous flicker in his icy eyes. "Oh? And what is it that you think I want, exactly?"

"This painting, of course. Though I still have no idea why you had to have *me* for it." She was worked up now, feeling hurt and betrayed and once again left out in the cold when it came to men. "No matter what you said about my 'attractions,' it clearly has nothing to do with that, or by now you would have—"

She halted, mortified by what she'd almost admitted.

The harsh lines in his face softened, and his gaze warmed. Then it dropped to her lips. "I would have what?" He tugged her arm down, then lifted his hand to smooth his thumb over her lower lip. "Done this?" He caressed her hot cheek. "Or maybe this?"

Her breath froze in her throat. She hadn't meant to provoke him to—

Well, of course she had, madwoman that she was. She should put an end to what he was doing; she knew quite well what it could lead to. But even as she opened her mouth to protest, he curved his hand behind her neck and bent toward her.

"No, you want more than that, don't you?" he murmured, within a breath of her lips. "Something decidedly more sinful, I would imagine."

Then he was kissing her, his lips molding hers, tasting hers. But before she'd even registered it, he drew back. "*That's* what you were hoping for, I suppose."

Hardly. It was the most chaste kiss she could imagine—which proved that his fervent need to paint her had naught to do with her and how she looked.

"Even the stodgiest of my suitors kisses better than that. So I think we've established that you don't—"

With a low oath, he kissed her again—harder, rougher. *Sinful.* This time she felt it to her toes. Then he hauled her up so he could clasp the back of her head and hold her still while his mouth covered hers more fully.

Every inch of her turned soft. Pliant. Yearning. She gripped his arms, meaning to push him back but clutching him closer instead. He groaned low in his throat, then pressed her lips apart so he could plunge his tongue inside her mouth.

Heavenly day. This kiss was intense and hot, the best she'd had in her life. He plundered her mouth in long, silky strokes that had her stomach doing somersaults and her blood pounding madly in her veins. Who knew that a mere kiss could turn one into a seething knot of sensation?

Some instinct made her entwine her tongue with his, and he froze, then kissed her more wildly, more deeply, with urgent, heady thrusts that had her straining up against him.

It was so thrilling and reckless. Unlike the lieutenant, he wasn't trying to steal her garter or some other token to use against her; he was too involved in the kiss for that. While his mouth ravished hers, he gripped her thighs as if to urge them apart, and she opened them to bring him closer, into the V of her legs. It was a far more intimate position than she'd intended, especially since it made the costume bunch up about her hips.

Now he was clasping her thighs. Good Lord! Even with her drawers between his flesh and hers, it felt so deliciously wicked.

He tore his mouth free to trail warm, open-mouthed kisses up her cheek to her ear. "Do you *really* not know how much you tempt me?"

"No." Having him flush against her down there was glorious. *This*, she'd never done before. "I . . . I'm not used to . . . tempting anyone, Mr. Keane."

"Jeremy." He nipped her earlobe, sending a frisson of sensation through her. "Call me Jeremy when we're alone."

Another intimacy. It banished her good sense entirely. "Jeremy?" she breathed.

"Yes, Yvette?"

"Kiss me again."

This time his kiss was leisurely, as if he wanted to savor it. *She* certainly wanted to savor it, and the feel of him against her, and the way his fingers flexed convulsively on her thighs as if he was trying to keep from caressing her . . . She wanted to savor it all.

And wouldn't it be wonderful to have him *touch* her somewhere naughty? Down there? Where no man had ever touched her? The very idea made her head swim and her knees wobble.

Cupping her head in his hands, he drew back to stare at her. "We have to stop this."

Her throat tightened. "Why?"

That was a silly question. She knew why. The last time a man had dallied with her, she'd nearly lost her pride, her reputation, and her future.

"Because I want to bed you—here, now. I've spent all evening thinking of how it would feel to have you." He swore under his breath. "Have I finally made you understand that I desire you?"

There was certainly no mistaking the heat in his eyes. "I'm . . . beginning to have some idea."

"But a gentleman doesn't act on his desires with a lady. Not unless he intends to court her." His gaze bored into hers. "And despite what you apparently think of me, I *am* a gentleman."

Her disappointment was as keen as it was absurd. "In other words, you do *not* intend to court me."

His face closed up. "I don't intend to court anyone, no matter how much I'm tempted."

She'd known that instinctively, yet she'd foolishly hoped . . . "And I don't intend to marry a rogue, so we're in perfect accord." Fighting for calm, she pushed at him.

He stepped back, and for the first time since she'd met him, he looked disconcerted. Shoving one hand through the beautiful hair she hadn't even had the chance to caress, he rasped, "It's not that I . . . God, I didn't mean—"

"You don't have to explain." She jerked the hem of the costume down. Lord, she couldn't believe she'd actually *invited* this . . . this humiliation. "I as

much as asked you to kiss me. You were merely . . .
obliging me."

His lips thinned. "What a very polite and English
way to put it."

"Well, it's true, isn't it? You gave me what I asked
for."

"I gave you more than you asked for." His heated
gaze drifted down to her mouth and lower, where
her breasts rose and fell with the urgency of her
breathing. "And more than I could afford."

"Yes, you made that perfectly clear." She turned
toward the table, wondering how she would ever
spend the rest of the evening lying on it while he
watched her and painted her and did nothing about it.

Because he didn't want her. Not for more than a
moment's dalliance.

Catching her by the arm, he hauled her around
to face him. "It was also far, far less than what I
desired."

"Because you're a gentleman—I know." She
tugged her arm free of his grip.

A look of frustration crossed his face.

He wasn't the only one frustrated. Experiencing
such passion and being told that one was good only
for *that* was mortifying. Especially since, in spite of
everything, a part of her *still* wished he had done
more. Gone further. Taught her . . .

Heavenly day.

"Perhaps we should stop for tonight," Jeremy
clipped out. "We can pick up again tomorrow night."

"An excellent idea." She snatched up her clothes
and headed for the door.

As she reached it, he called out, "Yvette?"

She halted. "Yes?"

"I promise not to overstep my bounds again. You needn't worry about that."

All she could manage was a nod before she fled. Because the truth was, she would much rather he overstep his bounds and sweep her back into his arms than play the gentleman.

And that was the cruelest turn of all.

Eight

Morning had barely dawned and Jeremy was already busy setting up for the formal portrait in the music room. He wished he could have risen later. But last night, even after "boxing the Jesuit," as Damber so crudely called self-pleasure, he'd been restless and aroused and incapable of doing more than sleeping in fits and starts.

He kept seeing Yvette in that chiton that left so little to the imagination. Kept hearing her ragged breaths, tasting her hot mouth, feeling her softness against his groin as he pressed into her.

Damn it to perdition!

How was it that none of his other models through the years, even the naked ones, had made him feel such intense need? Some had stirred his lust, but it had never lasted beyond a quick tumble if they were so inclined. Once they turned coy and flattering, they destroyed any lingering fantasy that painting them had aroused.

Not so with Yvette. She parried his barbs with a

clever wit that made him want to tease her more. Yet she could also be as sweet as forbidden candy.

Maybe that was why she tempted him. She was forbidden. That was all. It wasn't her soft smile. Or her kindness to Damber. Or the vulnerability beneath her prickly exterior that made him want—

Thunderation!

Work. He must work. That was preferable to driving himself insane.

"Not that color," he snapped as Damber stirred the paint in one of many clay pots set out on a tarpaulin they'd laid on the carpet. "I told you burnt umber, not burnt . . . whatever that is."

"Toast, mayhap. The kind I didn't get to eat." Scowling, Damber closed up the pot. Then, with a heedlessness that bordered on dangerous, he tossed it back into the box of paints. "I'd be happy with even burnt toast, but oh no, that ain't acceptable. Not when a certain gentry cove has taken the bloody notion in his head to rise before sunup and force me right to work."

Jeremy rolled his eyes. "Yes, you suffer so. Last night you probably dined like a king and slept on the softest bed you've ever—"

"Didn't matter, seeing as how you made me leave it so bloody early." Damber rooted around in the box for the burnt umber pigment. "And the gentry mort—" He caught himself. "The *lady* ain't even up yet!"

Thank God. Jeremy had to get his wits about him before she arrived. Last night he'd insulted her in every way possible—first by not kissing her, and then by kissing her too erotically. The way a man kisses a whore.

Or a lover.

No, never that. She couldn't be that to him, no matter how much she tempted him. And, God, but she tempted him. He itched to kiss her again, to run his hands up her thighs and touch what he'd stopped himself from touching last night. He ached to do *more* than touch.

How he would make it through the next several nights without trying to bed her was beyond him. But he must. Last night's activities couldn't be repeated.

"She'll be here soon enough," Jeremy told Damber, ignoring the leap in his pulse at the thought. "Then you can have all the breakfast you please down in the servant's quarters."

Damber shot him a sly look. "You want to be alone with her, is that it? Got the urge to give her a bit of the old rammer—"

"Don't talk about the lady like that, or I swear I'll turn you off."

Since Jeremy threatened that at least once a week, Damber didn't much react to that. Instead, he narrowed his gaze on his master. "You like her."

"Of course I like her. I wouldn't have taken a commission to paint her portrait if I hadn't thought I could endure her presence."

"I mean you *fancy* her."

Like a desert fancies rain. "Don't be a sapskull." Jeremy set up his easel with quick efficiency. "She's English, an aristocrat, stiff-rumped, as you put it. What would I do with her sort?" When Damber opened his mouth, Jeremy said, "Don't answer that. You know that's not what I meant."

"Wasn't it?" Heedless of the foul look Jeremy flashed him, Damber said, "You got up at dawn, which ain't like you, and you're trying to rid yourself of me so you can be alone with her. Seems pretty clear."

"Even if I wanted to be alone with her ladyship, her brother is coming in to chaperone, so it's impossible." Until tonight. When he would have her all to himself, displayed provocatively atop his makeshift altar. God help him. "Now stop flapping your jaws and do your job. Sharpen some pencils."

"Already sharpened them."

"You've restretched the canvases?"

"Aye." Damber crossed his arms over his chest. "Did them all last night. And what are you wanting with so many of them, anyway?"

Despite what Jeremy had said to Yvette, it wouldn't be that easy to keep their nighttime trysts secret from Damber. "I told you." Jeremy strode across the room to examine the mantelpiece so he could decide if he wanted it in the image. "I have some other works going."

"That keep you up into the wee hours of the morn?" When Jeremy shot him a surprised glance, Damber added, "Aye, I noticed. Came up to make sure you were done with me for the night, and you weren't in the room."

Jeremy fought to appear nonchalant. "You know perfectly well that when I can't sleep, I paint."

"Aye. But I usually see the results next morn." Damber glanced around. "So where is it? I don't see anything."

"Where it is doesn't concern you," Jeremy said

sternly. "What *does* concern you is this portrait. And since I may actually get to the painting of it this afternoon, you'd best have my materials ready. Have you set out my palette knife?"

"Done."

"And my brushes?"

"Done, done, done. Everything's done!"

Jeremy frowned at him. "So you've mixed all the colors I asked for—the Paris green, the bone black, the Naples yellow—"

Damber's face fell. "You said naught about mixing up Naples yellow."

"Yes, I did, last night. You were too busy flirting with the chambermaid to give me your full attention."

Damber thrust out his chest. "Well, you can't expect me to remember—"

"I can and I do." Jeremy quelled the impudent scapegrace with a look, then examined the canvas to be sure Damber had got it tight. "It's part of your position, lad. Best get used to it."

His shoulders slumped. "Yes, sir." As the boy turned for the paint pots, he mumbled, "S'pose I won't be getting breakfast until noon."

A light and lilting voice came from the doorway. "Why isn't Mr. Damber getting breakfast?"

Jeremy stiffened. It was her. "Because he hasn't finished his preparations. When he does, he can eat." He looked up from what he was doing, and her attire gave him pause.

Today she wore a day dress of moiré with a wide pelerine collar and slimmer sleeves than were currently fashionable. The fabric swished about her, and the touches of lace were interesting visually. But he didn't like the overall effect.

Was it the ivory hue, the color of unabashed innocence?

No. She'd worn white while he sketched her in the schoolroom, yet she still had looked as erotic as any soiled dove.

Was it the style?

He didn't think so. Though the neckline was slightly higher and the hem slightly lower than yesterday's gown, it was no less respectable.

So it must be the combination of the color and the staid cut and the lace. Taken altogether, they turned her into the personification of decency, a vestal virgin.

No doubt she was trying to remind him—and maybe even herself—that despite her curiosity about physical passion, she was still an upright female and not some round-heeled slattern. The problem was, her demure choice simply didn't work for the portrait. Now how in thunder was he to tell her that without insulting her?

"You're up early," he grumbled. "I thought you said you preferred to lie abed late most mornings."

Avoiding his gaze, she glided into the room. "I . . . um . . . couldn't sleep."

"Neither could the master," Damber said from where he stood stirring paint. "You're a daft pair, you are."

Ignoring Damber, she eyed Jeremy from beneath her lovely dark lashes. "I hope you found your bed comfortable enough."

"Perfectly so."

Except for its being too empty.

God, he needed to get hold of himself. "But I never sleep well in a new place."

Her pretty features froze. "Then you must get very little rest, given how often you sleep in new places in London."

The thinly veiled reference to his brothel visits gave him pause. Apparently he wasn't the only one regretting last night's intimacies. But she probably regretted them for vastly different reasons.

"Oh," Damber put in, "but the master ain't sleeping when he's out and about in town. He's too busy—"

"I'm sure Lady Yvette can guess what I'm up to, Damber, thank you," Jeremy said sharply.

Part of him burned to tell her the truth. That he generally spent his nights in the stews, painting. That he was more likely to sketch a whore than screw her.

But revealing that particular secret would be unwise. If the world knew that his models were primarily prostitutes, people would read meaning into that. Or be blinded to what he was trying to say because they were focusing on the outrage of his using a whore to model a respectable shopkeeper.

Besides, having Yvette think him a rank rogue might encourage her to keep her distance. Now that he'd assuaged her fears about her attractiveness, she had no reason to entice him. Just as he had no reason to tempt her.

And maybe if he said it a few hundred times, he would finally get it through his thick head. The one above *and* the one below. Both of which were painfully aware of her as she approached.

Then he noticed the white rose in her hand. "I hope you don't intend to hold that for the portrait," he said sourly.

She tipped up her chin. "And what if I do?"

"Don't mind the master, my lady," Damber cut in. "He's been grumpy ever since he put me to work without my breakfast."

"Oh, for God's sake," Jeremy growled. "Go eat! I'm tired of hearing about it."

"You see?" Damber said. "Grumpy as a shabbaroon."

A lively smile brightened Yvette's face. "*Shabbaroon?* I don't know that one."

Neither did Jeremy. He suspected he was better off not knowing.

Apparently she felt differently. Hurrying to a nearby writing desk, she took out some paper and exchanged her rose for a quill, which she dipped into an inkpot. "What does it mean?"

Jeremy scowled. "It means an apprentice who's a pain in the damned—" He caught himself when her quizzical gaze swung his way.

Her hand remained poised over the paper. "Is that really what it means?"

With a snort, Damber came to her side. "Of course not. I told you, he's a bear this morn." He gestured to the paper. "A *shabbaroon* is a mean sort of fellow. You know, 'mean' in both clothes and manners. Like *shabby*. Only grouchier."

"How colorful!" She jotted it down. "*Shabbaroon.* I'll have to use that one."

"Wonderful." Jeremy crossed his arms over his chest. "Any more 'colorful' terms you wish to add to

her ladyship's dictionary, Damber? Or are we actually going to start a portrait today?"

Yvette laughed, the tinkling sound tightening Jeremy's muscles in all the wrong places. "He *is* a shabbaroon this morning, Mr. Damber. You'd best flee to
have your breakfast while you can."

Warily, Damber glanced at Jeremy.

"Damn it, I already said you could go. I'll send for
you if I have need of you."

But as soon as Jeremy sent the lad off, he regretted it. It left him alone with Yvette. Which was
probably why, when she picked up the rose again, he
snapped, "No."

"What?"

"You're not posing with that flower." He gestured
to her ensemble. "And your clothes are wrong, too."
So much for telling her without insulting her.

With a look of cold contempt, she drew herself
up. "You said I could wear what I liked."

"I assumed you would choose something that
suited you. Like what you wore yesterday afternoon.
Or at dinner. Or even last week at the ball. Not
something so . . . so . . ."

"Elegant? Refined?"

"Innocent." The minute the words left his mouth,
he cursed his idiot tongue.

Shock tightened her features. Then she stepped
close enough to hiss, "I *am* an innocent, curse you."

"That's not what I—"

"Just because you and I shared a few kisses last
night doesn't mean that I'm a . . . a wanton. And it
certainly doesn't mean that you know me."

The reference to their kisses made every muscle in

his body bunch up. "I have eyes and ears, don't I? You may be chaste, but you're no innocent." When her gaze sparked fires, he added hastily, "I mean that as a compliment. Innocents are boring. The debutantes who do exactly as their mamas tell them are so bland as to make me retch. *You* are not bland. *You* are not boring. And you certainly don't make me retch."

"No, I just make you run in terror."

That startled him. "What do you mean?"

"Nothing." A shuttered look crossed her face. "So, what brought you to these conclusions about my character? The fact that I chose to wear white today?"

"Hardly. I assessed your character long before that. An innocent doesn't collect street cant. An innocent doesn't trade nights as an artist's model for the chance of searching a brothel to find God knows whom."

Mention of her secret plans seemed to take her aback. A blush stained her cheeks, and her throat worked convulsively.

He bent his head closer. "Your heart beats for something more than the insipid porridge that society feeds a lady of rank. You need fire and life and the thrill of the night. You want to get inside things and learn them, to feel everything and avoid nothing."

Her eyes suddenly shone luminous in the rich light of dawn. At last she seemed to understand what he'd been trying to say, albeit stupidly at first.

"The reason I know this," he went on, "is I have such needs, too. It's why I left home, why I won't go back. I want more. In that, we are very much alike."

They stood so close that he could smell her sweet scent, probably some ladylike decoction of hothouse flowers that he would despise on any other woman. Yet when she wore it, his every sense was aroused.

As if she knew what he was feeling, her translucent skin pinkened, and her expressive mouth parted slightly, a mere breath away.

His blood thundered in his ears. It would be so easy to close the distance and seal her lips with his. Or dip his mouth down to caress that spot on her throat where her pulse beat ever more quickly. Or even use his teeth to tug free the fichu that coyly hid the tops of her plump breasts—

"Good morning," said a steely voice from the doorway. "Am I interrupting something?"

Jeremy fought the urge to jerk back and give away what he'd been contemplating doing. Damn, damn, damn. Blakeborough had the most infernal timing.

It was probably just as well. Jeremy didn't need to be putting his lips and mouth and teeth anywhere near Yvette. He should be squelching this attraction between them, not encouraging it.

Straightening leisurely, he kept his gaze on her but infused his tone with boredom. "Your sister and I are merely having a dispute about her choice of attire."

With a quick, enigmatic glance at Jeremy, she pivoted to face her brother. "What do you think, Edwin?" She swept her hands down along her skirts. "Is this suitable for the portrait?"

Blakeborough still seemed suspicious as he looked

from Jeremy to her. "I'm surprised you're even awake. You don't usually venture from your room before noon."

She planted her hands on her hips, making Jeremy itch to start sketching her. "I was too excited about the portrait to sleep. So, what is your opinion? How do I look in this?"

The earl's suspicion faded as he scanned her attire. "You look exactly the way a debutante should—pretty and demure. A well-bred example of respectable womanhood. You're every decent gentleman's dream for his wife-to-be."

She blinked. Then she grumbled something that sounded like "Lord have mercy," before stalking off toward the door.

"Where are you going?" her brother asked.

"To change my clothes!" she called back as she disappeared into the hall.

As Jeremy struggled not to show his triumph, the earl shot him a confused look. "Am I missing something?"

So, so much. He forced a shrug. "You know women. They can be contrary."

"Yvette more than anyone." Blakeborough frowned. "I'm forever stepping awry with her."

"It's the same between me and my sister, trust me." Jeremy turned for the windows, still fighting to put out the fire Yvette had roused in his blood. "Perhaps it's the same between all brothers and sisters."

The earl took a seat on a nearby settee. "I don't know. She and Samuel got along quite well until Mother died. And then everything fell apart."

"Oh?" Jeremy pulled the curtains more fully open. "Your sister told me a bit about your mother's death. But she didn't say much about your brother, other than that he was a scoundrel."

"He didn't become one until after Mother died. That's when he began sliding further and further into degradation, until there was no going back. It was as if he blamed Mother for dying, and then took it out on every woman he met."

"Meanwhile, Yvette blames your father for not being at your mother's side."

A muscle worked in the earl's jaw. "Yes. And probably she blames me, too, for not making him stay."

"I don't think so. She's certainly said nothing of the kind to me."

Blakeborough's gaze narrowed on him. "I don't know when she would have. It's not as if the two of you have spent more than twenty minutes alone together all told, is it?"

"True," he said lightly. "Now, what do you think of having Yvette stand by the . . ."

Jeremy launched into a discussion of settings that he hoped would distract the earl from his suspicions.

But thunderation, these secret nights of theirs were already harder to hide than Jeremy had anticipated. He only hoped that he could get most of the work—for both paintings—done quickly. Because eventually Blakeborough was going to figure out that Jeremy and Yvette had another project on the side. And when he did, there would be hell to pay.

Which was why Jeremy had to put some distance

between him and Yvette, both physically and emotionally. If he wanted to get his masterpiece, he must be professional, even in their private evenings.

The earl mustn't ever guess that Jeremy had one iota of desire for his sister.

Nine

"Are we boring you, my lady?" a voice sounded from the nether reaches of Yvette's consciousness.

She jerked awake. Heavenly day. She couldn't believe she was standing with her hands on her hips in the middle of the music room and still managing to nod off. Someone should have warned her that modeling for an artist was tedious.

"I'm sorry, Mr. Keane." She glanced at Edwin, who watched her with a hooded stare. "As my brother said this morning, I'm not used to rising so early."

Jeremy, too, was watching her, but his gaze was clinical, removed. "It's all right. We've had a long day. The sun is setting and I'm losing the light anyway. Might as well stop for now."

"But—"

"I can keep working on the background." Jeremy smiled tightly. "Trust me, I have plenty to occupy me." He glanced at the clock. "Why don't you and your brother go on to dinner? Don't mind me."

She let her shoulders slump, and it felt so incredible, she wanted to do a little dance. Someone should also have warned her that modeling for an artist was extremely uncomfortable. Her spine felt as if someone had played piano on it for the past hour.

Then his words registered. She frowned. "You're not dining with us?"

He avoided her gaze. "No, I believe I'll keep working. But if you wouldn't mind, I'd appreciate having a tray sent in to me."

"Of course." She donned her role as mistress of the manor. "Perhaps we'll see you later this evening. In the drawing room."

Jeremy cast her a meaningful glance. "Yes, later. Maybe."

Her every sense went on high alert as she headed for the kitchen to order his tray. Somehow she'd managed to forget that they were to have a far more intimate sitting this evening.

You need fire and life and the thrill of the night.

What a devil. He thought he knew everything about her. And yes, he might be right about what she needed. But she wasn't willing to give up her future for it, or to watch as some scoundrel abandoned her for his mistress or other petty enjoyments. She needed a husband who wouldn't disappear at the first sign of trouble, and she was fairly certain Jeremy could never be that. Look at how he had run off to England to escape his family.

He claimed she was like him, but she wasn't. She would never shirk her responsibilities, just to have fire and life and the thrill of the night. She'd learned her lesson only too well with the lieutenant.

She had—truly she had. Even if Jeremy *was* the most fascinating man who'd ever kissed her.

Dinner proved an awkward affair. Edwin seemed even more melancholy than usual, especially with Jeremy not there. It didn't help that her thoughts were elsewhere, too. On what might transpire later. On whether Jeremy might attempt to kiss her again. On what she would do if he did.

"Take care, Yvette," Edwin murmured.

She practically jumped in her chair. Good Lord, her brother had begun reading minds.

She feigned a smile. "About what?"

"About Keane. The air fairly crackles between you. I don't know what happened this morning before I came in, but I couldn't help noticing that when you returned from changing your clothes, you were wearing that red silk evening gown I hate. I would have preferred that you wore something for your portrait that was less—"

"Interesting?"

"Yes, if by 'interesting,' you mean it shows too much of your . . . er . . . shoulders. That's the kind of 'interesting' a man can't help but notice. Especially a man like Keane."

"All he saw was that it was bright red and brought out the color of my hair." Sadly, that had seemed to be true.

"That's not what it looked like to me. I realize you find him an intriguing man of the world—"

"You have no idea how I find him." She was getting tired of men presuming to guess her thoughts. And then comment on them.

"I've seen the looks you give him," Edwin persisted.

"What looks? The exasperated ones? The annoyed ones?"

"Yes. Those. You don't take other rogues seriously, either laughing or flirting or mocking them. But you're nervous and cautious around Mr. Keane. Which is how I can tell you like him."

How startling that Edwin had surmised such a thing. He wasn't usually so astute about people's feelings. "That's preposterous." She forced herself to meet his gaze. "I wouldn't be so foolish as to like his sort."

His somber gaze saw right through her. "But you must admit that you—"

When he caught himself with a look of chagrin, she lifted one eyebrow. "That I what?"

"Nothing." He smoothed his features. "I must have misread your feelings."

"Yes, you must have." She placed her napkin on the table and stood. "I'm going to bed. Rising at dawn is clearly not for me."

He blinked. "What if Keane comes to the drawing room?"

"Then the two of you shall have a fine talk. You don't need me for that."

She could feel him watching her as she left. Was she really that transparent around Jeremy? If even Edwin could sense the simmering attraction between them, then it was dangerously obvious.

Once in her room, she told her maid she was ready to retire, then suffered through the motions of that preparation. But after her maid left her, she realized it was still too early to meet Jeremy in the schoolroom. So she lay down on the bed, meaning only to rest a moment.

She awoke to the sun streaming through the curtains at dawn.

Oh, Lord! She'd slept through their assignation!

Muttering every cant term for "ninny" that she knew, she called for her maid and dressed hastily. She ignored the poor girl's protestations that something must be amiss for her ladyship to be retiring and rising so early. It wasn't like her ladyship at all.

No, it wasn't. But at least she'd finally had a good night's sleep. Perhaps that would help her to endure a day of posing in public, followed by a night of posing in private.

A shiver shook her. It was the posing in private that she'd dreamed about all night. The kissing in private. The touching—

Heavenly day. She had to stop thinking about that!

Hoping to get a moment alone with Jeremy to explain last night's absence, she hurried toward the breakfast room, but before she could reach it, an arm snaked out to pull her into an alcove.

It was him, wearing that stormy look that both alarmed and excited her. "We had a deal. You're not holding up your end of it."

"I know, and I'm *so* sorry. I fell asleep. I'm not used to these hours."

"Really?" A faint sneer twisted his lips. "So it had nothing to do with what happened our first night together, nothing to do with the words we exchanged yesterday morning before your brother interrupted us?"

"Certainly not!" She glanced furtively beyond him into the hall, but no one seemed to be nearby, thank heaven. Still, just to be safe she lowered her voice. "I intended to show up last night. And I *promise* to show up tonight."

His hand still gripped her arm, holding her so close she could smell coffee on his breath. "Do you swear it?"

"Yes. I'll swear it on the Bible if you require it."

He searched her face, then released her with an oath. "That won't be necessary."

"Good. Because you don't seem the sort to carry around a Bible."

His lips twitched. "No." He scrubbed a hand over his face. "I suppose it was foolish of me to think you could spend all day and night posing."

"It was only my rising early yesterday that made it difficult, I assure you. But from now on—"

"From now on we should meet every other night, so you can get a good night's sleep in between."

"Don't be ridiculous. Then your painting would take forever!" She thrust out her chin. "I can keep up these hours if you can."

"I doubt that," he said in a lazy drawl. "Such hours are normal for me."

She winced. "Yes, I'm well aware of the dissolute life you lead."

"That's not what I meant." His gaze turned brittle. "And to quote your ladyship, just because you and I shared a few kisses doesn't mean that you know me. You have no idea what sort of life I lead."

She was beginning to think that might be true. "Very well," she said, assailed by an odd breathlessness, "why don't you explain it to me?"

That seemed to take him off guard. The seconds

stretched out as he stared at her, his eyes the vivid blue that had begun to haunt her dreams. His gaze drifted down to her lips and fixed there, making her heart flip over in her chest.

Then he jerked his gaze away. "No need. I won't be here long enough for that to become necessary."

The cold statement sliced through her, and she fought to hide her hurt. "Suit yourself. But then don't blame me for not understanding you. I can hardly help it if you don't *want* to be understood." Sliding away from him, she walked out of the alcove. "I'll see you in the music room after breakfast."

He didn't even try to stop her as she hurried off. And that annoyed her, though not nearly as much as his statement that he wouldn't be around long. She shouldn't expect anything more of him. Samuel had never stuck around with any of his mistresses. The lieutenant hadn't even stuck around after he'd kissed her.

Of course, that was because Samuel had nipped the scoundrel's plans in the bud—but still, men had a tendency to run off when things didn't go their way. Or after they got what they wanted from a woman.

But Jeremy *hadn't* gotten what he wanted. He hadn't bedded her. He'd barely even kissed her. Though perhaps seduction wasn't what he'd wanted at all.

An exasperated breath escaped her. She didn't really know *what* he wanted, other than to paint some odd work about Commerce and Art and seething emotions she didn't really understand. And to lecture her on who he thought she was.

Presumptuous fellow. She *knew* who she was. She just didn't know who *he* was. Not really.

Perhaps that was the problem. Perhaps if she could find out more about him she could better understand his situation. Why he'd left America. What he was running away from. Why he was so angry about his family trying to drag him back to his home.

Fortunately, at breakfast Edwin gave her the perfect opening for her questions as he thumbed through the mail. "Strange. I've received something from Lady Zoe."

"Mr. Keane's cousin?" She glanced at Jeremy. "Perhaps it's word of his family's arrival."

"Good God, I hope not," Jeremy muttered, and poured himself some coffee.

"Why?" she asked. "Surely your sister isn't such a dragon as all that. Or is it your mother who alarms you? She must be awful if you ran off to England to escape her."

His gaze narrowed on her. "She's not awful, and I'm not escaping anything. I'm merely attempting to broaden my knowledge of art, to view masterpieces I would never have the chance to see in America."

"So why do you care if your family comes to visit you? It's not as if they can force you to go back with them."

"Actually," Edwin interrupted, "the missive isn't about Keane's family. It's an invitation to a masquerade ball a week from Friday."

"Oh. How very . . . intriguing." She'd forgotten all about Jeremy's plan.

Jeremy glanced at Edwin. "Ah, yes, before I left

town, Lady Zoe mentioned that she was throwing one and wanted to invite the two of you. She asked if I thought it would be awkward for you to be around your former fiancée's relations. I told her that if you found it so, you would just refuse to attend."

When Edwin stiffened, Yvette bit back a smile. The best way to make sure her brother did as one wished was to challenge him not to. It got his back up. Edwin could be very proud sometimes.

"So what do you think?" she prodded her brother. "Shall we go? It sounds like fun."

"I see no reason to avoid it," Edwin said blandly.

She couldn't resist teasing him. "Really? I thought you hated masquerade balls."

"I'm not nearly the dullard you take me for. I know how to enjoy myself."

"But not by wearing a costume. Not by dancing with—"

"If you're trying to talk me out of attending, you're doing a good job of it," Edwin said.

Uh-oh. "Sorry. That was not my intention; I'd genuinely like to go. So you must take me."

He sighed. "I suppose I must."

She slanted a glance at Jeremy. "How else am I to find out from Lady Zoe everything I can about Mr. Keane and his frightening relations?"

The artist's face closed up. "There's nothing to find out, I assure you. Or at any rate, nothing terribly interesting."

"I seriously doubt that."

"Anyway," Edwin interrupted, "if we're all going, Yvette, I shall send an acceptance. I can do it while you're posing for Keane. I'll play secretary, and you can dictate my response." A sudden gleam in his eye put her on guard. "Perhaps it'll keep you from falling asleep. I don't know how you managed that while you were standing up. You'd think that your militant stance alone would have kept you on your feet."

She stuck her tongue out at him. "I defy anyone not to get bored while maintaining a fixed position for hours." She dipped her toast in her runny egg. "And I stayed awake much longer than I would have if I'd sat in a chair. Aren't you glad now that I chose my 'fishwife's pose'?"

"I'm not glad about anything," Edwin grumbled. "I begin to regret that I ever suggested this portrait."

She laughed outright. "Why? Because I've turned it to my advantage?"

He flashed her a rueful smile. "Because if you keep falling asleep, Keane will be camped here until doomsday trying to finish it."

"No, indeed." She ate a bite of toast. "He's got family coming any day now." She shot Jeremy a look of challenge. "If he's still working when they arrive, we can invite them to stay at Stoke Towers."

To her surprise, a laugh burst from the American. "Mother would never do that. This is her first trip to London. She isn't going to settle for moldering out at your country estate when she can be shopping on Bond Street."

Aha! That was one clue about his mother. "She enjoys shopping, does she?"

"Doesn't every woman?"

"Not your sister," Edwin put in. "Not according to what you told me at the wedding."

"He told you about his sister at the wedding?" Yvette said. "Why didn't you tell *me*?"

"Why would I?" Edwin looked truly bewildered. Sometimes he was too oblivious to be believed. "You didn't ask. And it had nothing to do with you."

"Perhaps I'm curious to know why Mr. Keane chose to abandon his sister to their family mills to come here."

"That's a tale for another time," Jeremy said smoothly. Pushing away from the table, he stood and laid down his napkin. "If I'm to get any work done, I'd better go make sure that Damber has everything ready for when her ladyship is done with her breakfast."

To her vast irritation, he gave a courteous bow and walked out, leaving her no more the wiser about why he was avoiding his family. It was so frustrating!

And Edwin was no help at all. That day, while she posed for her portrait, he chatted with Jeremy about everything except what she wanted to know. She didn't think he did it deliberately, but it was still vexing. Every time she broached the subject of Jeremy's mother and sister, Jeremy changed the subject to something that interested Edwin, and that was an end to her gaining any useful information about Jeremy's life outside his work as an artist.

So while they talked, she tried getting information from Damber. Unfortunately, she never got to be alone with the apprentice to really interrogate him about his master. Still, she was able to glean a few things from their long conversation about street cant and painting and such.

Apparently Jeremy's family was quite wealthy.

He'd received an excellent education at a boarding school in Massachusetts, then had left home to study painting in Philadelphia at the age of nineteen. He had only the one sister and was half heir to the family mills.

And he worked late most nights. How he managed that while also cutting a wide swath through London's stews and gaming hells was beyond her, but Damber wasn't forthcoming about *that*.

Later that evening, when she was posing privately for Jeremy, she came right out and asked him. He merely made some flippant remark and went on painting. Indeed, as the evening wore on and she quizzed him about his life in America, he continued to deflect her questions with jokes or facile tales of his travels, the sort she would imagine he used with any model.

Meanwhile, his formality chilled her to the bone. He called her "my lady" so often that she finally informed him acidly that only servants called her that. He refused to let her see the painting and threatened to expose her plans to her brother if she even attempted to look at it. And though he touched her sometimes to reposition her, his impersonal demeanor told her she was merely the model for his dratted work.

And that hurt. It was almost more than she could bear, to be alone with him with the reminder of their intimate kisses shimmering in the air while he treated her with cold professionalism.

He was a known rakehell, for pity's sake! Didn't they attempt to bed anything in skirts?

Not Jeremy, apparently. Over the next several

days, he and Edwin discussed art and America and society until she was sick of it. At night, Jeremy told her so many stories of his adventures she was sure she could publish an account of his travels.

Yet she learned from it only that he could be an amusing raconteur. Which perversely meant that when it came to his feelings or anything that really mattered, he was more impenetrable than the cockney slang of a Spitalfields doxy.

He sharpened his wit on her; she sharpened her wit on him. But it ended there. She saw nothing deeper of him. He might as well have been one of Edwin's well-crafted automatons, moving in carefully circumscribed ways, speaking of carefully circumscribed things in his brittle, removed manner. It was enough to make a half-dressed female scream.

Or cry. But she refused to cry over the likes of Jeremy Keane. She'd already told herself he was wrong for her. Why did she care if he agreed? She didn't. She wouldn't.

So on the morning of her ninth day of posing for the portrait, she'd decided to give up on trying to know him better. Tomorrow night was the masquerade ball and their visit to the bawdy house. Once that was done, she just had to suffer through his finishing the two paintings.

Clearly, whatever connection to him that she'd felt their first evening together had been imagined. Or else he was a master at keeping himself in check. And in her experience, that was never true of rogues.

Probably he'd kissed her to shut her up about her desirability so he could keep her compliant with his aims to paint her. Or something equally manipulative.

"Must you scowl?" Jeremy grumbled as he daubed and dabbed at his canvas. He seemed as out of sorts this morning as she.

"I didn't realize I was," she said coolly. "How unfeminine of me. God forbid I look like anything but a delicate flower for my portrait."

Her sharp tone must have caught Edwin's attention, for he glanced up from the accounting ledger he was going over. "You couldn't look like a delicate flower if you tried. And who wants a delicate flower, anyway?"

"No sensible man, that's for certain," said a voice from the doorway.

She glanced over and broke into a smile. "Warren!" Abandoning her pose, she hurried over to the Marquess of Knightford, who also happened to be Edwin's oldest friend. "It's been ages!"

"Indeed it has." With the usual twinkle in his eye, he bussed her on the cheek.

Warren Corry was the only man, other than Edwin and Samuel, allowed such familiarity. He was a flirt and a devil and notorious for breezing in and out of some of society's loftiest bedrooms, but to her he was part of the family.

Still, the impudent look he now gave her might make it difficult for an outsider to tell. "You're looking very lovely," he said with a wink and a grin. "I don't believe I've ever seen you in that gown, but it's most fetching. Brings out the bit of red in your hair."

She shot Edwin a triumphant look, and in the process caught Jeremy's gaze. He was staring daggers at Warren. It gave her pause, especially since it was the first hint of emotion he'd shown in days.

How odd. Could he be jealous? Oh, wouldn't that be delicious? She could finally vex him the way he'd been vexing her.

Though he didn't seem the sort to be jealous. Probably he was merely irritated that she'd broken her pose. Well, she wasn't a machine. He would just have to get used to it.

Deliberately, she turned her back on him. "What are you doing here, Warren? You can't be visiting your aunt and cousin." The estate of Warren's aunt lay quite close to Stoke Towers. "They're wintering in Bath."

"They *were*, but as of last night they're home. My aunt got bored and decided she and Clarissa would be better off in the country after all. So I was charged with accompanying them back." As guardian to his cousin Clarissa, he was often charged with such tasks. He sometimes even did them.

"You poor dear," she teased. "But that doesn't explain why you came right over to visit us the minute you arrived."

"Actually, Clarissa sent me to fetch you. She's still unpacking, but she hoped you might come help her and her mother pick her costume for tomorrow night's masquerade ball at the Keanes' in London. I assume you're going?"

"Of course! We all are." She cocked her head. "I didn't realize that you knew Lady Zoe."

"I don't, but my aunt went to school with Lady Zoe's aunt."

"You mean, Zoe's Aunt Floria?" Jeremy put in.

As if Warren's coronet of rank had suddenly dropped onto his head from on high, the marquess stiffened and turned to stare coldly at Jeremy. "I don't believe we've been introduced, sir."

A light glittered in Jeremy's eyes. "No. I don't believe we have."

"Forgive my bad manners." Edwin swiftly performed introductions, adding, by way of explanation, "Keane is painting Yvette's portrait."

"Is he?" Warren said in a surprisingly testy voice. "Did you know that he is often seen out and about in Covent Garden?"

"So are you," Jeremy countered. "I've seen you myself."

A flush crept up Warren's neck. "I happen to enjoy attending the theater."

"Among other . . . establishments." Jeremy shot Yvette a veiled glance.

How odd. Why was he was being so vulgar? Wait—did he think Warren had something to do with her trip to the bawdy house?

Oh, for pity's sake. She lifted an eyebrow at Warren. "As it happens, Edwin and I are quite aware of Mr. Keane's love of nunneries." She frowned at Jeremy. "We're equally aware of his lordship's preference for them. So why don't the two of you stop accusing each other of habits you'd probably congratulate each other for if I weren't around?"

Warren blinked. Edwin gave a choked sound that sounded something like a laugh. But Jeremy just watched Warren with a challenging gaze, as if ready to protect her should Warren assault her honor.

It was rather sweet. And utterly unexpected, given the way he'd been behaving lately.

"Now," she went on, "if you gentlemen will excuse me, I'm going upstairs to change into something more suitable for strolling over to Clarissa's with Warren. I shan't be long."

"What about your portrait?" Jeremy called as she walked away.

"Oh, let her have a few hours off," Edwin put in. "She's been a good sort about posing. I confess I didn't expect her to last *this* long."

She paused to look back at Jeremy with a blithe smile. "Why don't you work on the background? Or on one of those other paintings Mr. Damber says you work on at night?"

At her reminder that he owed her for doing him a favor, Jeremy stiffened, then gave her one of his mocking bows. "Whatever her ladyship wishes."

Edwin's chuckle followed her up the stairs.

Let Jeremy retreat into his cold fortress. If she didn't escape him for a few hours, she might do something reckless.

Like remind him she was a woman he supposedly desired. And that wouldn't be remotely wise.

Ten

It took all of Jeremy's will to hold his tongue after Yvette left the manor with the marquess. Not that she wasn't behaving entirely respectably; she did have her maid with her.

Still, she was wearing a fetching brown walking dress that accentuated her lush shape. While she'd paired it with an enormous pink-and-brown bonnet that would poke a man's eye out if he tried to kiss her, bonnets could be removed. Even a maid's presence might not prevent that if Knightford were the devious sort.

And he was bound to be. Jeremy didn't like the marquess. Or how the fellow looked at Yvette. Or the fact that the two had apparently known each other forever. She called him by his Christian name, for God's sake!

Thunderation, he was starting to sound like the English. Who cared what she called the ass? Who cared that "Warren" had salivated over her in that red evening gown she'd worn for the portrait?

No one could blame the man. Jeremy had spent the past several days staring at her in that gown and aching for her. Getting hard for her as he never had for any other model. It made their nights together unbearable, especially now that he knew what it was like to kiss her, caress her . . .

"Since Yvette's gone, I believe I'll get some estate work done with my steward." Blakeborough rose. "The servants will let me know when she returns."

Only with difficulty did Jeremy not ask when that was likely to be. He'd managed to put Blakeborough's suspicions about him and Yvette thoroughly to rest in the past week, and he wasn't about to ruin that by appearing overly concerned with her disappearance.

Still, that didn't keep him from spending the morning with one eye on the clock. Then doing the same thing all afternoon, while he worked on *Art Sacrificed to Commerce* without her. He should be glad of the chance to finish the Commerce figure—which he was modeling after himself using mirrors—but it merely kept her provocative image in front of him, making him wonder what in thunder she was doing over there with Knightford.

When she didn't return for dinner at six, Jeremy had to bite his tongue half off to keep from saying anything. By the time he and Blakeborough had dined without her and were making serious inroads into an excellent bottle of brandy, he could keep silent no longer.

"Does your sister mean to spend the night over there with her friends?" He knocked back the remainder of his third glass and poured himself a fourth, despite being well on his way to becoming foxed.

"Oh, I doubt it." Blakeborough swirled the liquor in his own glass. "Knightford will send her and her maid back in his coach before it gets too late. He always does."

Always? Jeremy frowned. "They see each other quite a bit, do they?"

"When he's visiting his aunt's estate, yes. Yvette is like a sister to him."

Jeremy had heard that one before. "Still, do you think it wise to let her spend time alone with the fellow?" He prided himself on the fact that he sounded unaffected. Unconcerned.

Or maybe not, because the earl eyed him closely. "Knightford has known Yvette since she was a babe. At eleven, he dandled her on his knee. At fifteen, he let her give him her lost teeth for safekeeping. He called her 'Pest' up until a year ago." He chuckled. "She said if he kept calling her that in public, she'd box his ears. He stopped."

That account of a friendship more familial than flirtatious didn't soothe Jeremy one bit. "Maybe he stopped because he started thinking of her as a desirable woman ripe for the plucking."

Blakeborough laughed outright. "I doubt it. Just a month ago, she tried to marry him off to one of her friends. He told Yvette he would wed after he got Clarissa situated with a husband." The earl snorted. "Whenever *that* magical day might arrive. The little witch keeps bedeviling him. And me. And any man foolish enough to take her on."

Jeremy eyed him closely. "Are you still talking about your sister? Or do you mean Clarissa?"

Blakeborough started. "*Lady* Clarissa." He swallowed some brandy. He looked as if he, too, might be growing foxed. "I mean, I'm talking about both. Peas in a pod, those two. Sure, they seem different at first glance. Clarissa's a bottle of champagne that explodes when you shake it, and Yvette's a pot coming to a slow boil. But if you ever see bubbles in either, you'd best take cover. Because trouble is brewing. Those two have a penchant for it."

Yvette sure did. She'd been coming to a boil for over a week now, getting more witty and effervescent the more annoyed she got with him. Which she'd been ever since the night they kissed.

How stupid he'd been to kiss her. That was why trouble was brewing, and he couldn't even regret it. Her supple mouth, so warm, so sweet . . . Oh, God, and those soft, silky thighs that Knightford might even now be—

Damn it. "You're saying you trust Knightford with her. Even though he's known for his flirting and his . . . women." Falling back against his chair, Jeremy cast the earl a belligerent look.

"So are you."

"Yes, and you keep me under a watchful eye. But not him."

The earl shrugged. "I know his character. He and I became good friends while getting Yvette and Clarissa out of scrapes." He waved his glass distractedly. "Warren might . . . flatter my sister, but she knows he doesn't mean it as anything. Plus, he only dallies with loose women, not respectable ones."

Jeremy scowled. He wasn't so sure. Any respectable woman who kissed like Yvette had been kissed before, and intimately, too. By Knightford? Or somebody else?

Knightford made the most sense. The man had apparently been allowed to see her whenever he pleased. And girlhood crushes sometimes *did* lead to more once the girl became a woman. Could the marquess be the one who'd prompted her to request that Jeremy sneak her into a brothel?

"Why do you care, anyway?" Blakeborough asked.

"Excellent question."

He didn't realize he'd said it aloud until the earl said, "I know. That's why I asked."

Thunderation. Jeremy couldn't admit the truth. That the idea of her being manipulated by Knightford into risking her reputation ignited something ugly in his chest.

Not jealousy. That'd be foolish. Very, very foolish.

"Because I like your sister." Avoiding the earl's gaze, he stared down into his brandy. "Admire her spirit. Hate to see it damaged by a man who didn't respect it."

"Me too."

The hard clip in Blakeborough's voice made Jeremy look up. Did the man suspect what had been going on in the evenings between him and Yvette?

How could he? Blakeborough would've already tossed him out on his ear.

"Well, then." Jeremy lifted his glass. "If you're not alarmed, neither am I." He set the glass down a bit harder than he'd intended, and some of the liquid sloshed over the edge. "I was just thinking of my own sister. How I'd react if some ass took advantage. If your sister's a boiling pot and Lady Clarissa's exploding champagne, then Amanda is a churning hot spring." He scowled. "And plenty of men are drawn to the heat."

"Too true." Blakeborough finished off his glass. "Haven't forgotten my promise to you, y'know. About finding your sister a husband. I made some inquiries. Haven't heard much yet, though."

"You haven't had a chance. You've been in the country ever since we first talked." Jeremy swigged more brandy. "But you can ask around at the masquerade tomorrow, right? Or go to your club after and ask there? I'll go with you. Yvette can stay with my cousin till we get back."

Blakeborough leaned forward unsteadily. "Can I tell you a secret?"

"Sure. Why not?" Jeremy bent forward, too, nearly oversetting his chair.

"I don't much go to my club. Don't like it."

"Oh, right. Yvette says you don't really like people."

Blakeborough drew himself up. "Now see here, I like people. Some of them. Just . . . not the ones in gentlemen's clubs."

"Don't blame you. I don't like 'em, either," Jeremy admitted.

"You've been in a club?"

The earl sounded so incredulous that Jeremy glared at him. "A few. As a guest. I'm a famous artist, y'know. Got relations in high places, too."

"True, true. I keep forgetting." Blakeborough poured himself more brandy. "Why don't you like the clubs?"

"I'm a solitary man. Prefer my own company."

"Or the company of whores."

Jeremy scowled into his glass. "At least whores aren't boring. Like the gentlemen in clubs."

"Club men *are* dull, aren't they?" The earl shook his head. "No one says anything interesting. It's all cards and bragging about mistresses and betting on which drop of water will reach the bottom of the window first."

"That really happened?" Jeremy snorted. "I thought that was a joke."

"Nope. Two fools made a bet on it."

"Stupid."

"Ridiculous. But that's the clubs. I only went to mine to drum up a husband for Yvette. That was pointless." He rolled his eyes. "Bunch of whoresons and doddering old fools and reckless gamesters." Sitting back against his chair, he gulped some brandy. "It did help me figure out who *not* to throw at her."

Jeremy blinked. "Did throwing men at her ever work? Haven't tried that with Amanda."

"Don't bother. The women don't like it. Talk about *trouble* . . ."

Blakeborough shuddered, and they both drank in a silent gesture of camaraderie.

"Honestly," the earl went on, "would you want a chap from the clubs to marry *your* sister?"

"Probably not."

"We need better suitors. Good ones. Steady ones. If we could find a club with those . . ."

"We should start our own club," Jeremy said with a sweep of his glass. "For gentlemen looking out for their sisters."

"Or their wards. Or daughters." The earl sat up. "We could compare notes on suitors. My brother was a scoundrel, and I didn't even know how bad. By the time I found out about the women he . . ." He lapsed into a long, brooding silence.

"The women he what?" Jeremy prodded.

"You don't want to know." He shivered. "But if anybody had told me what he was up to, I could have . . . I don't know . . ."

"Stopped him? Probably not. But you could have warned the women off."

"Exactly! Or their brothers. Or fathers. Or . . . whoever cared for them." Blakeborough set his glass down firmly. "We *should* start a club. To protect our women from bad suitors. Who better than us? Oh, and Knightford. We should bring him in."

"Knightford? He's got a reputation!"

Blakeborough's eyebrows shot up. "You do, too. That's why you'd both be good members. You could ferret out the scoundrels. And he knows dirt about everybody."

"Because he's down in the muck with 'em."

"Like *you*."

"Oh, for God's sake, I'm not in the—" Jeremy made a disgusted noise. "Anyway, why include him? He doesn't have a sister."

"But he has a cousin to marry off." The earl scowled. "*Someone* should find out about those fellows flirting with Clarissa."

"You seem awfully interested in Clarissa."

A dull flush colored Blakeborough's cheeks. "It's just a brotherly sort of concern."

Jeremy wasn't so sure, but he didn't want to

poke the bear. Not when they were getting along so well.

"So Knightford would *want* to join, because of Clarissa," Blakeborough went on. When Jeremy muttered a curse, Blakeborough added, "Better to have him close, where we can keep an eye on him. Right?"

Hmm. Good idea. They could make sure Knightford behaved. Didn't try to court Yvette.

Slumping in his chair, Jeremy scowled. What did he care who courted Yvette? Wasn't his concern. He had two paintings to finish.

And when the hell was she coming home, anyway? How could he paint her if she spent all her time with that ass Knightford?

"Excuse me, sir."

Jeremy glanced over to see his apprentice lurking in the doorway.

"Come in, come in, young Damber!" Blakeborough said with an expansive gesture. "We're just having a bit of brandy."

When Damber snorted, Jeremy rose to interrupt the young fool before he insulted the earl. "What is it?"

"I wondered if you were done with me for the evening, sir. I thought I'd go down to supper with the servants if you don't need nothing else."

The servants. Hmm. "Actually, I did want to speak to you about one matter." He dipped his head at Edwin. "That is, if your lordship doesn't mind my getting back to work."

"Do as you must," Blakeborough said genially, and poured himself another glass, clearly intent on finishing the bottle. "See you in the morning. We'll discuss our plans for our club more then."

"Certainly," Jeremy said, though he wondered if either of them would remember much of their conversation in the morning.

He'd better sober up. He still had to paint Yvette tonight, assuming that she returned.

Nodding Damber from the room, he waited until they were a short way down the hall before he halted the lad. "You and the earl's servants get along well, don't you?"

Damber eyed him warily. "I think so. Why?"

Yes, why? Oh, right. Yvette.

He bit back an oath. He really needed to clear his head. "I want you to try to learn what they know about her suitors or other male admirers. 'Specially Knightford, but anyone else they might mention, too."

After all, this was for her own good—to make sure this brothel visit wasn't the result of some devious fellow scheming to harm her.

With a scowl, Damber crossed his arms over his chest. "Why d'ye want to know? I like her ladyship. She's nice. Sounds to me like you want to stir up trouble for her."

Great. Damber actually had a notion to protect Yvette. Probably had an infatuation with her. Just what Jeremy needed.

Or maybe it *was*. "Actually, I'm trying to look out for her. I think a man is trying to . . . harm her, and I'm hoping to find out who so I can help her. But she won't tell me."

That was the truth. Perhaps not all of it, but still the truth.

Damber's face cleared. "Well, she does seem distracted of late. That's what the servants say." He lifted an eyebrow. "They blame it on you."

"It's not me. Her troubles began before we came here. I can't tell you more than that." He didn't *know* more than that.

His apprentice nodded. "I'll see what I can learn."

"Don't be too obvious. But try to find out something before tomorrow night." He would be armed with ammunition before he and Yvette headed off to that brothel if it killed him.

"What's tomorrow night?" Damber asked.

"A masquerade that the Barlows and I are going to." He grimaced. "And Knightford."

"Ah. Then I won't fail you in this, sir. You can be sure of it." Damber walked off.

"One more thing!" Jeremy called out.

The earl's words earlier about the younger Barlow brother nagged at him: *By the time I found out about the women he . . .* What exactly had Samuel Barlow done? The earl couldn't have meant the kidnapping that Manton had thwarted, because everybody already knew about that. But Jeremy couldn't see any other way that Barlow's shenanigans could relate to Yvette.

When Damber halted, Jeremy murmured, "See if you can also learn what got Samuel Barlow banished from the family."

Damber blinked, then nodded. "I'll do my best."

As Damber left, Jeremy headed for his bedchamber and an ice-cold pitcher of water. He meant to dunk his head in it a few dozen times, until he had better control of his senses. Because he needed to be sober by the time he saw Yvette.

He refused to head off to a brothel with her tomorrow night without having some idea of what he was getting into. And that meant acquiring information about her past however he must. Even if he had to coax it out of her himself.

Eleven

Yvette raced up the stairs to the schoolroom. She'd remembered to bring the costume that he called a *chiton*, but had forgotten to throw her shawl on over her wrapper and nightdress. Pray heaven no one caught her roaming the house like this. She was so flustered she'd never be able to lie her way out of it.

She wasn't late, but she had only minutes to spare. Jeremy was going to complain, the dratted grump. Well, let him. She wasn't his to order about.

Still, she hadn't meant to stay gone from home so long. But between Clarissa's amusing dithering over what to wear and Warren's dry remarks, she'd been having so much fun that dusk had turned into full dark and then dinner before she even knew it. Only her maid's remark about the advancing hours had prompted her to leave.

And now it was back to dealing with Jeremy. As amusing as he could be, he also exhausted her. She spent all her time trying to figure him out. For once, she'd rather be anywhere but here. But she'd made a bargain, and she meant to keep it.

She slipped into the schoolroom just as the hour struck eleven.

"Where have you been?" he barked from behind his easel.

Oh, Lord. "You know where I've been."

She headed for the coat rack to hang up her wrapper. Odd how she'd begun to feel perfectly comfortable half-dressed around him. No man had ever seen her in her nightdress, not even her brothers, yet here she was prancing about in front of a known rogue without a thought.

As she turned, he moved into the open space between them. His cravat and coat were missing and he was in his shirtsleeves, though the temperature in the room fell well below comfortable. His hair was disheveled, his features drawn.

In short, he looked rather wild. It did something disturbing to her insides, especially given how his gaze ate her up. He seemed somehow more dangerous than usual. She couldn't put her finger on why until he neared her and she smelled brandy.

"Why, Mr. Keane," she said uneasily, "I do believe you've been drinking."

"I was, yes." When she lifted her eyebrow, he added, "But I stopped a while ago. Long before your brother and I expected you home."

With a snort, she shook out the chiton. "I seriously doubt that Edwin was even remotely concerned about my return. Sometimes I stay over at Clarissa's as late as midnight. He's used to that. My maid always goes with me, and Warren always sends us back in his carriage with a footman for protection."

"Does he?"

When he crossed his arms over his chest, she realized with a jolt that his sleeves were rolled up to expose his forearms. How . . . titillating. His forearms were well corded with muscle, and she was reminded of how those arms had encircled her only last week.

He stepped closer. "You and *Warren* seem awfully chummy."

She fisted the chiton in her hands. He dared to behave like a jealous boor after practically ignoring her for over a week? Idiot. "Yes, we are chummy. What of it?"

"I don't like him."

"I don't care. He's not *your* friend." Somehow she managed to keep her tone light. "And you won't 'be around here long enough' for your feelings about him to matter, remember?"

The way he flinched was rather satisfying. About time she got some of her own back with him.

Then he smoothed his features. "My feelings will matter a great deal if your dalliance with him prevents me from finishing my paintings."

Oh, that really tore it. She marched up to him. "First of all, I'm here, on time, to pose for your dratted painting. Second of all, I'm not having a dalliance with Warren. Not that it's any of *your* concern."

He stared down at her, his expression unreadable, but she could see the pulse throb in his throat. Perversely, she wanted to touch it. It reminded her that he wasn't an automaton after all, but a flesh-and-blood man. A very *attractive* flesh-and-blood man, who made her quiver with anticipation.

Something flickered deep in his gaze. "So Knightford isn't the one asking you to go into a Covent Garden brothel?"

"What? No! Don't be ridiculous." When Jeremy's expression didn't alter, a chill coursed down her spine. "You don't believe me."

"I'm not sure what I believe." He circled her slowly. "Knightford just happens to come here the very night before the masquerade, and you just happen to go off eagerly with him. What am I supposed to think?"

"That I went to see my friend Clarissa? That I have things to do other than be at your beck and call night and day?"

"Maybe. Or maybe that the two of you wanted privacy so he could instruct you on whatever you had to do for him tomorrow night."

"What a ludicrous notion."

"Fine." He paused to lower his head to her ear. "If he's not the one prompting this mad escapade, then who? Because he's the only mysterious man I can see in your life just now."

Her pulse gave a panicky leap. She briefly considered telling him about Samuel, but then the stubborn side of her reared up. Why should she tell him anything? He wouldn't tell her a blessed thing about himself.

Besides, she dared not risk his blathering her family secrets to the world. Edwin deserved better than to see more scandal heaped on the family. And she highly resented Jeremy's acting as if this was an interrogation. She was not in the mood for his nonsense tonight.

"I shan't listen to this." Tossing the chiton down like a gauntlet, she turned for the door. "I'm going to bed."

"The hell you are!" He hurried to block her path, his face a stormy mask. "You promised to model for me, then ran off for the entire day. You owe me a session tonight, at the very least."

She crossed her arms over her breasts. "So I can lie there freezing and sore while you pepper me with ridiculous accusations about Warren?"

"They're not ridiculous," he said sullenly. "They're perfectly logical."

"To *you*. To me they sound like the product of a jealous mind, which has clearly—"

"Jealous! I'm not jealous."

"Oh? After the way you've been lately, I can think of no other reason for your erratic behavior tonight. *You* don't want me, but you don't want anyone else to have me, either."

"Now who's making ridiculous accusations?" His hard gaze locked with hers. "My 'erratic behavior' stems from my concern about this upcoming brothel visit. I want to know . . . I *deserve* to know the truth of why you're risking your reputation for it."

She squared her shoulders. "And *I* deserve to know what sort of man I'm entrusting my reputation to. If you expect to hear all my secrets, you must tell me some of yours."

That seemed to take him aback. With a sharp oath, he glanced away. "You don't want to know them, trust me."

"Oh, but I do."

"I don't want to tell them." He dragged a shaky hand through his already tumbled hair. "I *won't* tell them."

"Then you can't expect me to tell you mine."

When he swore under his breath, she slipped past him, headed for the door, but he snagged her about the waist from behind and pulled her up against him. "You can't go yet!"

"Look here," she said, digging her fingers into his arm, "I'm tired and cold and I don't feel like modeling."

"I know. You don't have to pose. That's not why I want you to stay. I just . . . don't want you to go, damn it."

"Why not? It isn't as if you actually wish to talk to me."

"The hell I don't. I talk to you every day."

She snorted. "If that's what you call it when you retreat behind your walls."

His arm tightened about her waist. "I don't retreat behind anything. I've been perfectly amiable, a consummate gentleman, and entertaining to boot. Why, you laughed at all my stories."

"I did. Yet they're still walls made up of practiced tales you've probably related a hundred times." Frustration made her tense. "When you tell them, you refuse to show one iota of your real self or acknowledge one iota of mine. You barely look at me, and when you do, you stare right through me. You ignore me."

"Ignore you! I don't ignore you. I *never* ignore you." His voice thickened. "The whole time you're lying on that table, I'm aware of your every gesture, every smile. I know where every part of your body is at any moment, because I watch them all. And not just so I can paint them. So I can fathom them. Understand how they're put together. How *you* are put together, inside and out."

She caught her breath, startled by the intensity of his words. The sudden fierce edge to them.

"I notice when you're angry or sullen or distracted." He flattened her against his body, his heat seeping through her flimsy nightdress. "I notice what you wear at dinner, how you move when you climb the stairs." His tone dropped low. "I notice *everything* about you."

Closing her eyes, she willed herself to ignore his words. But how could she when he was saying what she'd wanted to hear? When he was holding her so close that she could feel the imprint of his hardened flesh against her bottom?

Heavenly day. So *that* was what the ladies of the evening called a "cock-stand." She hadn't realized that a man's thing actually, well, *stood*.

At least she knew he wasn't lying about desiring her.

As if to prove it, he spread his hands over her thinly clad belly, starting a quivering lower down. Then he kissed a path to her ear. "Watching you lying there every night in that chiton drives me mad," he said in a rough rasp. "Watching you in your nightdress or your red gown drives me mad. Every gown you own drives me mad."

She swallowed hard. "I—I couldn't tell."

"I'm good at hiding it." His hot breaths warmed

her cheek. "I didn't want to end up on a dueling field with your brother."

"Edwin would never challenge you."

"I'm not so sure." He tugged at her earlobe with his teeth. "Yet here I am, risking it. For another taste of you, another chance to hold you, caress you. Even if only for a few moments."

Let it be more than a few moments.

"Tell me to leave and I'll go right now," he murmured. "But tell me to stay, and I swear I *will* taste and hold and caress you. As much or as little as you'll allow. I'm tired of fighting it."

So am I.

She caught her breath. Was she insane? Her choice was clear: Send him away. Never mind that he was saying such enticing things. She shouldn't fall prey to them.

But she couldn't help herself. For years, she'd hidden the wicked urges first ignited by the lieutenant. Even after he'd trampled on her heart, her wantonness had smoldered beneath the surface of her respectability. Whenever she flirted with a rogue, it was rekindled. And during the lonely nights in her bed, her wild imagination stoked the coals to a roaring blaze, which she attempted to soothe with her roaming hands.

For once, she wanted a *man's* hands roaming her. And not just any man's hands. *Jeremy's.*

"Yvette—"

"Stay," she said, before she could change her mind. "Stay."

A shuddering breath escaped him. "You won't regret it, I swear."

"I'm quite sure I will, but—"

He filled his hands with her breasts.

Heavenly day—how *delicious*!

His thumbs grazed her nipples, sending her arching up on her toes with a moan. Touching her own breasts furtively under the covers was nothing to this heady onslaught of feeling.

She pressed herself into his hands, and his breathing quickened against her cheek. "I ached to caress these beauties the first night I saw you, my Juno."

"I'm no goddess," she said, even as she exulted in his flatteries. "I'm a woman, with earthly needs and wants, not a creature of fantasy."

"How well I know. Because I'm a *man* with earthly needs and wants, all of which have been centered around you for days now. You have no idea how desperately I desire you."

Just not desperately enough to offer marriage.

No, she had too much pride to say that. Besides, if she spoke those words, he would turn skittish again and this amazing encounter would end. She couldn't bear it. She wouldn't.

He reached for the buttons of her nightdress. "May I?"

Without even thinking about it, she bobbed her head. Because she would give anything just now to feel his fingers on her bare nipples.

And he, being something of a scoundrel, was perfectly happy to oblige.

Expertly, he opened her nightdress to her waist, then reached inside to cup one breast. A trembling breath escaped her. How incredible! His hand kneaded her flesh, his fingers deftly plucking, rousing and soothing her cravings by turns, until she swayed against him.

"I want to look at you," he said.

There was no asking this time. He must have guessed she would go along, because he didn't even wait for an answer. He simply turned her in his arms and knelt on one knee to spread her nightdress open so he could stare at her breasts.

A blush heated her cheeks. What if he didn't like them? They always seemed too big and unwieldy and—

"I wish I could paint you just like this, half-naked in the lamplight," he said hoarsely. He brushed a finger over her nipple, and it hardened to an aching knot. His gaze darkened. "It would be only for me; no one else would ever see it."

"I hope that's not a request," she tried to joke. "You cannot paint me nude."

"I know." His eyelids lowered. "So I shall have to settle for tasting you." And his mouth covered her breast.

Lord help her. Even as she groaned a protest at that insanity, he licked and sucked and plundered her flesh with all the fire and life and thrill of the night that she craved. She craved the heat of his mouth and the slick swipes of his tongue as he teased and taunted and dragged her down into an ocean of feeling.

It frightened her how far she sank, how much more she longed for. Surely it wasn't normal to want something so much, to want to touch everything, *feel* everything. Surely this gnawing in her belly was unnatural.

But at least she could finally touch his beautiful hair. Spearing her fingers through the sun-drenched curls, she reveled in the feel of them sliding over her hands, engulfing her fingers the way he was engulfing her.

"You taste like cherries," he said against her breast.

"I doubt that," she said, choking back a laugh. "I don't rub . . . cherries on my bosom, I assure you."

"Then you *smell* like cherries."

"I drank ratafia at dinner. It h-has cherr—" She gasped when he tugged at her nipple with his teeth, sending her spiraling down into a dark, wild pleasure.

And when he offered the other nipple the same intoxicating treatment, letting his hand stroke the damp nipple he'd left behind, she thought her legs would crumple beneath her.

She clutched at his head to steady herself and he pulled her down astride his knee. Then he was kissing her with a carnal intensity that had her writhing upon his hard thigh.

Ohhhh. That felt astonishing, both too much and too little. One of his arms came around her waist to lock her close, and she looped hers about his shoulders to lock her even closer. He kept stroking her breast, silkily, sweetly, and she rocked against his leg. She wanted to fuse herself to him, to wring out every ounce of the aching pleasure.

"Ah, my pretty wanton, you inflame me," he breathed against her lips. "I could taste and touch you for hours. You're so damned lovely."

She *wanted* him to taste and touch her for hours, so badly that she didn't even care he'd called her "wanton."

Then she felt the dampness lower down and a tight little knot burning between her thighs, and panic startled to life in her. This was how seduction began. A woman fell in love with the feelings and forgot herself. It was dangerous, close to the edge . . . alarming.

She must stop this. Soon. Now. Before she found herself ruined.

Twelve

Jeremy had lost his wits, but he didn't care. Yvette was more sensual than he'd ever imagined. How could he stop caressing her soft breasts, kissing her soft mouth . . . wanting to bury himself between her soft thighs?

He ought to stop, yet he didn't.

She was his, damn it! *His* Juno, every lush inch of her, shining with vitality and humor and an unquenchable thirst for life. Her sweet warmth and dewy curls invited him in, and it took all his will not to jerk down his trousers and breach her. Even as he clasped her head to hold her still for his deepening kisses, he felt the pulse in her neck thrum hard against his hand.

Why did she do this to him? Women never had this powerful an effect on him. They never made him yearn for the impossible, want a life beyond what he could give. What he dared not give.

It was alarming how badly he wanted to keep her. He wanted to paint her a thousand times in a thousand ways, so he'd have her image to console him once he let her go.

As he must. As he would. In a moment or two.

But God, he didn't *want* to let her go. Not that he had a choice; he could already feel her slipping away. Her fingers were dragging on his shirt and her body stiffening.

She tugged her mouth free to stare at him with wild eyes. "I cannot," she said bluntly. "Not like this."

Disappointment slammed through him. For the briefest of moments he considered pressing the issue. If ever a woman was on the verge of seduction, it was Yvette. She wanted him. He wanted her. What else mattered?

You won't marry her. That's what matters.

"Damn it all to hell," he growled, scarcely realizing he'd said it aloud until she flinched. "I'm sorry. I told you I would taste and hold and caress you as much or as little as you would allow, and I meant it."

He should slide her off his knee, but he couldn't. Not yet. He bent his forehead to hers. "I just wish I were as much a rogue as you like to think. Because I *really* want to lay you down on this floor and have my way with you until the sun comes up."

"And then what?"

The words jerked him up short, and he moved back. "Exactly."

The look of hurt in her eyes made it easy this time to extricate himself from her body and set her on her knees beside him. But it didn't make it easy to extricate himself from the situation.

God rot it.

He rose to pace the room, hoping the movement

might subdue his rampant arousal, trying not to notice how erotic a figure she made as she remained kneeling on the floor while fastening up her buttons.

A foolish part of him whispered, *What if you were to offer marriage? Then you could have her to your heart's content.*

He fisted his hands at his sides. Yes, he could have her . . . until things went wrong. Until she realized he couldn't be the right sort of man for her. Couldn't love her as she deserved to be loved, couldn't give her a settled, normal life. Didn't *want* to give her a normal life.

Desire wasn't enough to make a solid marriage. Hannah had been fool enough to risk it with him anyway, but all she'd gotten for her trouble was an early death.

Guilt stung him, as always. With a scowl he strode to the easel. He wouldn't put another woman through that. Especially not one as tenderhearted as Yvette, who deserved better than an inadequate husband. Despite her prickly outside, she *was* tenderhearted. He'd figured that much out, at least.

"I can't stay," she said behind him.

With his back to her, he nodded. If he looked at her, he was liable to make the mistake of pulling her into his arms again. And if he did that a second time, he feared he wouldn't stop.

"I'm sorry that I—"

"Don't you *dare* apologize," he gritted out. "You did nothing wrong. It was my doing, all of it."

"I'm not apologizing for . . . what we did. I'm apologizing for not staying to pose for you. At this rate, you'll *never* finish your painting."

The hint of wry humor in her voice tugged at something deep in his belly, something he'd buried more years ago than he could count.

He shook his head ruefully. "I'll finish. I have to."

Even though he still hadn't figured out why this particular project consumed him, the burning need to paint it hadn't abated one whit. If anything, being here with her stoked it higher. He couldn't figure that out, either. He probably wouldn't until he completed the work.

"Don't worry about the painting," he said. "The parts that involve you won't take much more now."

"If you say so. But we have the masquerade tomorrow night. You won't get a chance to work on it then."

"That's fine," he said absently. Her mention of the masquerade reminded him that he still hadn't gleaned the information he wanted.

"Well, then. I'd better go."

"Wait!" He turned toward her, and his heart slammed in his chest.

She looked achingly beautiful, with her hair tossed wildly about her shoulders and her eyes glistening. Tears? Surely he hadn't made her cry.

God, this was precisely why he should never have touched her. "Just wait a moment."

"I can't stay," she said warily.

"I know. I merely wanted to ask you . . . concerning tomorrow night . . ."

If you expect to hear all my secrets, you must tell me some of yours.

Remembering her bitter words, he stifled an oath.

"Yes?" she asked. "What is it?"

"Never mind. I'll see you in the morning."

With a perplexed look, she shrugged and then left.

But he knew he would see her long before morning. In his thoughts, his fantasies. He would see her and want her, even as he knew how foolish it was to indulge the dream. Sometimes having a vivid imagination was more of a curse than a blessing.

Clearly, it would be yet another night of boxing the Jesuit.

The closer their coach rumbled toward London the following evening, the more nervous Yvette became. This was the night. She had Samuel's letter tucked inside her corset. Would she find his son? She hoped so. She didn't know how much longer she could play these mad games with Jeremy.

It didn't help that she fancied she could feel him staring at her again. The same way he'd been staring at her all day as she'd posed for him.

Their session had been entirely different from the last several. Oh, he'd been as reserved as ever around Edwin. But every time he'd looked at her, his words from last night had echoed in her ears: *I notice* everything *about you.*

Had she really not recognized it before? The way his gaze roamed her when Edwin wasn't looking? The rigid edge to his smile, the raw power of his eyes? She must have been blind. Or else he really had been as good at hiding it as he'd claimed.

She glanced his way now and caught her breath.

Yes, he *was* still staring at her. Or rather, absorbing her with his gaze, like a chunk of iron absorbs the sun's heat, then radiates it back.

Cursing how that made her heart flutter, she turned to look out the window at the full moon.

But he was having none of that. "So, Lady Yvette, whom exactly are you masquerading as tonight?"

The husky words strummed her senses, drat him, and when that made her hesitate, Edwin answered for her. "Can't you tell? She's a shepherdess."

"Ah. I wasn't sure. She could as easily be a dairymaid, a laundress, a linen draper—"

"Don't be ridiculous—women can't be linen drapers." Her anxiety over the coming evening lent sharpness to her tone. "And you would have recognized my costume at once if you hadn't been so tardy. You missed me handing my enormous shepherd's crook up to the groom."

"Once again," he drawled, "I apologize for my lateness. Damber had a bit of trouble with this hat." He blew at a feather that dipped down in front of his face. "The lad has never dealt with plumes before. Neither have I, for that matter."

Jeremy was dressed as a Cavalier, a costume he said he'd brought with him from London. She had to admit he looked quite dashing in his doublet and his coat trimmed in gold braid. Every lady at the ball would salivate at the sight of him.

She certainly was.

"It doesn't matter how late we arrive anyway," Edwin said with a dismissive gesture.

Edwin was dressed as himself. She had yet to see her brother don a costume for a masquerade. He always said there was no reason to do so when he intended to spend the entire evening in the card room anyway.

"I doubt anyone will even notice our entrance," Edwin went on. "Especially with Yvette dressed as she is."

"Why, thank you for the compliment," she said dryly.

"I only mean, dear girl, that for once you look like all the other young ladies." Edwin cocked his head at Jeremy. "She usually wears something more dramatic."

"Does she?" Jeremy's eyes gleamed at her in the darkness. "Like what?"

Curse him for that. Jeremy knew perfectly well why she wanted to blend in tonight—it would make it easier for her absence to go unnoticed. But if her brother started to wonder at her tepid choice of costume, his suspicions might be roused.

"Once," Edwin told Jeremy, "she went as Queen Elizabeth, complete with ruff and white painted face. She cowed every man she saw. But a shepherdess?" He grimaced. "There will be scores of them. Most young ladies aren't creative in their costume choices."

"Except for Clarissa," Yvette said quickly, hoping to change the subject. "She's going as a man."

Edwin scowled. "That's not creative. It's foolish. She couldn't pass for a man if she tried."

"I can't wait to meet this indomitable female," Jeremy said. "Between your description of her last night, and Yvette's clear admiration of the chit, I'm expecting nothing less than an Amazon."

"Edwin!" Yvette cried. "Surely you didn't describe delicate little Clarissa as an Amazon."

"I honestly have no idea," Edwin admitted. "Some of last night is a bit fuzzy." He glanced at Jeremy. "Though I do remember our talk of starting a club."

"A club?" Yvette sniffed. "What sort of club could the two of you possibly belong to? You're as different as chalk and cheese."

"Not as different as you think, eh, Keane?" Edwin said, elbowing Jeremy.

"Not when it comes to boiling pots and hot springs," Jeremy responded.

"And exploding champagne bottles," Edwin added.

They laughed heartily, bewildering her. What on earth was wrong with them? They'd been making enigmatic comments all day, punctuated by sly winks and nudges. She couldn't imagine what they'd done last night to turn them into such bosom companions.

Or perhaps she could. Jeremy had clearly been drunk in the schoolroom, and Edwin had dragged himself to the breakfast table at midday, looking like a piece of chewed-up gristle. If not for the fact that she'd never seen her brother overindulge, she would swear he'd been cropsick.

Bad enough that Jeremy was having a terrible influence on her. If he started turning Edwin into a mirror image of himself, the earth would fall off its axis.

"Well," she said, "I'm glad Clarissa is being daring, no matter how much stodgy old Warren complains."

"Knightford is stodgy?" Jeremy said incredulously.

"With her he is," Yvette said.

"I told you he'd make a good club member," Edwin told Jeremy. "We should add him to the list."

"We're making a list?" Jeremy said.

"We should. I've got half a dozen names I could add to it."

Yvette gaped at them. "You're not seriously starting a club."

Edwin crossed his arms over his chest. "We might. Why not? I have that property in Pall Mall we could use."

"We could call it St. George's," Jeremy offered. "Since we're fighting dragons."

"Or at least finding out their secrets so we *can* fight them."

"Dragons have secrets?" she quipped. "Next you'll be telling me you're hunting unicorns for their horns."

"Oh, we're hunting for horns, all right," Edwin said. "As many horns as we can lop off at the root before they impale someone precious to us."

When both men burst into laughter, she just shook her head. She'd long ago lost the gist of this conversation.

It was only after they'd arrived at the ball and Edwin was helping her down that she remembered what "horn" was slang for in the street.

A man's aroused penis.

Her blush flamed all the way into the Keane town house. Clearly she'd been collecting cant words far too long if she imagined they'd been talking about lopping off penises. That made no sense at all. No man wanted that.

She and Edwin and Jeremy were announced as

"a shepherdess, the Earl of Blakeborough, and the Earl of Rochester."

As they entered the ballroom, she said to Jeremy, "The Earl of Rochester? Why didn't you choose a famous artist instead of a Cavalier poet?"

"If I'm going to dress up, I prefer to pick something out of character. It's more fun."

She snorted. "Well, he's not *that* different from you in character. He did write a number of salacious poems."

"I know." He winked at her. "Why do you think I chose him?"

To her surprise, Edwin laughed. She shook her head, biting back a smile. Men could be such children, honestly.

The musicians struck up a reel.

With a glance at Edwin, Jeremy offered her his arm. "Shall we?"

"I would be honored, Lord Rochester."

He chuckled and led her away. But as soon as they were out of Edwin's hearing, he slowed his steps and made a pretense of looking for a safe spot to enter the floor.

"After our dance," he murmured, "I shall ask my cousin for the next. While Zoe and I are on the floor, you should find a way to escape to the garden." He craned his head, as if surveying the couples. "I'll meet you there as soon as I can. I have a key to the garden gate. We'll go out that way."

"My, my, you must have sneaked out of the Keane town house undetected before. Clearly you're a master at it."

He shot her a quick glance. "No more a master

than you are at sneaking about Stoke Towers late at night, my dear."

"Touché." She smiled ruefully and tugged on his arm. "We'd better dance, before Edwin gets suspicious."

With a nod, he swept her onto the floor.

⌒

It took Jeremy longer than he'd expected to get away, partly because Zoe had peppered him with questions about his stay with Yvette and her brother. And partly because he'd stopped to ask Zoe's husband, Tristan Bonnaud, co-owner of Manton's Investigations, about a gentleman whose name Damber had churned up during his spying—Lieutenant Ruston.

Bonnaud hadn't heard of the fellow, even in conjunction with Samuel Barlow. But the investigator *had* revealed more about Barlow than Damber had learned. So much so that Jeremy had been loath to leave the ballroom until he heard it all.

Which was why he was late. He only prayed Yvette hadn't grown tired of waiting for him and gone back inside, although that would certainly simplify matters. The closer he got to this meeting at the brothel, the worse he felt about going behind her brother's back to help her. It seemed disloyal, now that he and Blakeborough were a bit more chummy.

When he first hurried into the garden, he feared that she had indeed given up, for he didn't see her at all. The only person standing alone was a man in a domino costume—enveloping black cloak, a typical face mask, a pair of silver shoes peeking out from beneath—

Thunderation, it was her. No doubt if he removed that cloak, he'd find a shepherdess lurking underneath. And beneath that fetching angelic costume he'd find . . .

No, he mustn't think of what lay beneath. They had work to do.

He slid up next to Yvette and took her arm to guide her away from the few guests milling about. "The garden gate is back here."

With a nod, she let him lead her to the exit into the mews. "We will need to return through there, as well. I stowed my crook behind a tree out here."

"How did you smuggle in the domino?"

She shot him a winsome smile. "I didn't. Clarissa wore the cloak over her own costume to help me. I merely retrieved it from the coatroom. I already had the mask."

"Very clever." Had Clarissa helped her because Yvette was helping Knightford? Or was Yvette telling the truth when she'd claimed that the marquess hadn't had anything to do with her scheme?

Damber had said that if there was anything going on between Yvette and Knightford, the servants knew nothing about it. That was something, at least.

Still . . . "Does your friend know why you wanted her cloak?"

"Not entirely." That was all she said on the matter.

Very well, let her keep quiet for now. He meant to learn the whole of it tonight. Damber had given him some ammunition to use in coaxing the truth out of her.

They slipped through the garden gate and out to the street, where they hailed the nearest hackney. Plenty of them were about, hoping to catch a fare from the lofty folk at the ball.

Once he and Yvette were inside and the carriage rumbled off, he turned to her. "All right, we're about to enter a brothel where I'm well-known, so you have to tell me *something* about your plans. At the very least, I'll have to explain who you are to me and why you're there."

"Tell them the truth." She tipped up her chin. "That I'm there for the same reason I've given all along. I'm looking for a friend of mine."

"Does this 'friend' have a name?"

"Peggy Moreton."

He eyed her skeptically. "You just made that up."

"I did not." She drew her cloak more tightly about her. "Peggy used to be an actress, but she fell on hard times. I heard she landed in a bawdy house, so I'm trying to save her."

He stared hard at her. "*You* have a friend who's an actress."

She glanced out the window. "Well, she didn't *start* as an actress. Women rarely do."

That was certainly true, but . . . "You couldn't tell me this before?"

"And risk your revealing her shame to someone? No, I could not."

"Hmm." He wasn't quite sure he believed her, but at the moment he had no choice. "Your 'friend' isn't sufficient reason for why a lady of your rank would come to a brothel with a known scoundrel like me, instead of relying on an investigator or a brother to find the woman. Not to mention that if word got out—"

"It would be bandied about town and spark a scandal."

"So you'll have to be someone other than yourself if you want to preserve your reputation. The costume will only take you so far. These women aren't going to answer the questions of a masked female they don't know, or even answer my questions in your presence. They're a secretive lot."

"You ought to know," she said dryly.

He ignored the dig. "And they'll be particularly wary of a woman who speaks as well as you. They need an identity they can trust."

"Fine. Why don't we tell them I'm another actress? We're near the theater—we can say I just finished a performance, and I came with you to the bawdy house in search of my friend."

He stared at her. "That might work. They're comfortable with actresses and won't be too surprised if I bring one along. The role will also make it easier for you to be yourself. They'll just assume you're putting on airs. Actresses often learn how to mimic their betters for the stage, so no one will regard your fine speech as odd."

"I don't have to use 'fine speech,'" she pointed out. "I can speak street cant with the best of them."

A laugh erupted from him. "You *know* street cant, my lovely. That's not the same as speaking it. You say it with all the academic precision of a professor. Trust me, no one will take you for a street urchin or a dock whore by your language."

Glaring hotly at him, she slumped against the

seat. "You can be very annoying sometimes, you know that?"

"I'm merely speaking the truth. What's more, you *know* it's the truth. Not for nothing did your governess spend years schooling you on your speech."

"I suppose."

"Nonetheless, you should let me do most of the talking. The women will be more willing to answer my questions than yours."

"Whatever is best," she said irritably.

"Now that we have that settled—"

The hackney halted before the open doors and windows of Mrs. Beard's establishment, all blazing with light. Damn. They were here. His questions about Lieutenant Ruston and her connection to the fellow would have to wait.

Thirteen

Yvette watched as Jeremy climbed down and told the hackney driver to wait. Only then did she get a good look at the bawdy house.

Heavenly day.

It was one thing to study the language of fallen women or help them as part of her charity, where the soiled doves were on their best behavior and attempting to better themselves. It was another matter entirely to experience a bawdy house in all its sordid glory.

Hanging from every window was a woman in some state of dishabille. Bared breasts and hitched-up skirts abounded, probably to entice men inside. Through one window, Yvette could even see a couple engaged in a decidedly scandalous activity.

Good Lord.

With a smug smile, Jeremy held up his hand to help her out. "Are you all right?"

She snapped her gaping mouth shut. "Of course," she said, as if she visited bawdy houses all the time. "Why wouldn't I be?"

"It's not too late to give up this mad endeavor and return to the ball."

Firmly, she took his hand and stepped from the carriage. "No, indeed. I'm here for a reason, and that hasn't changed."

He eyed her closely but tucked her hand in the crook of his arm and led her up the walk.

Thank heaven she wore a mask. Otherwise, he would see the heat staining her cheeks and know just how difficult this was for her.

A shout came from nearby and she jumped, but it was only a couple of drunken louts calling to the whores in the windows, who waved cheerily back, trying to coax the men to come in.

Oh, dear. That fellow on the right even looked familiar!

She sincerely hoped she didn't know him. If she did, she'd never be able to look him in the eye again.

But that made her realize—there might be other men here whom she knew. Perhaps even women. Not all the reformed prostitutes at her charity remained reformed. This mask had better do its job, or she could find herself in deep, deep trouble.

Remembering her purpose, she scanned the women in the windows above, but she'd had only the most cursory description of Peggy Moreton from Samuel, and "a buxom chit with dark, curly hair" applied to half the women in the place.

Suddenly a blowsy female caught sight of Jeremy and cried, "Mr. Keane! I've got a hat for you!"

A hat? Was that street cant for a salacious act? Yvette wracked her brain for an alternate meaning to "hat," but for the life of her she couldn't think of one.

"What sort of hat?" Jeremy called up, seeming equally confused.

"You know, like the foreign musicians wear," said the female. "Now I can be in your picture!"

In his *picture*? Did the chit mean a painting?

His arm stiffened under Yvette's hand, and he avoided looking at her. "I told you, Sally, you're too blond for that role."

"I'll wear a wig! Wait there, I'll show you the hat."

As Sally disappeared from the window, an older and decidedly broader woman appeared to block the doorway. "Back to stir up my girls again, are you?"

Jeremy merely dipped his head. "Good evening, Mrs. Beard. You look to be in fine health."

So this was the famous abbess. Yvette couldn't stop staring. The woman had a bull neck, a half-exposed bosom the size of two cakes, and arms the width of small trees. A riding crop was tucked into the gold sash encircling her waist. She looked to be in fine health, all right—fine enough to beat a man twice her size into submission. No doubt she had, too, a time or two.

Mrs. Beard laid her hand on the crop. "Don't you try to turn me up sweet, Mr. Keane. I'm onto your tricks. And I ain't so sure that the money you pay for my girls' time makes up for the trouble you bring. They all fight for the chance to pose for your bloody pictures. Spoils 'em for doing their real jobs."

Yvette gaped at the woman. He was paying the soiled doves to model for him? *That* was why he spent so much time in the stews?

No, that couldn't be the only reason. Men didn't go to bawdy houses to work; they went to play.

Besides, if he'd merely been working, why hadn't he told her one of the times when she'd chided him for his debauchery?

I just wish I were as much a rogue as you like to think.

She let out a breath. He *had* told her, in myriad small ways. His gentlemanly courtesy. His protests over their meeting alone at night. His repeated concern for this bawdy-house visit. And in some larger ways, too—like by not bedding her the first chance he'd had. Yes, he'd kissed and caressed her, but he'd always restrained himself from going too far.

Still, he'd never corrected her assumptions about his character. Why not?

Then it dawned on her. He'd *wanted* her to believe him a big, bad scoundrel. He'd known she didn't approve of such men because she'd told him flat out. Perhaps he'd hoped that letting her think him one would provoke her into staying away, thus helping him keep his distance.

Or perhaps she was just seizing on this evidence that he sometimes painted or sketched at the bawdy house to prove what *she* wanted to believe—that he was a better man than she'd assumed. Well, whatever the truth, she'd unearth it tonight.

The big-bosomed Sally appeared in the doorway behind Mrs. Beard, waving a Spanish-style hat at Jeremy. "You see? I could pose as one of them foreign street musicians for you."

Jeremy winced, and Yvette could easily guess why. That well-fed chit could never look like a worn-down Spanish woman fighting for pennies for her children.

"If I put street musicians in the piece, Sally," Jeremy

pointed out, "I can pay one of *them* to pose." When the young woman frowned, he added soothingly, "I promise to find a place for you in a future work."

Sally pouted. "It ain't fair. Can't help it that I came back here after you'd picked all the girls for your big picture. I want to be in a painting, too." She glared daggers at Yvette. "I'm just as pretty as that Long Meg there, I daresay."

It took all Yvette's strength to resist a cutting retort.

"Sally!" Mrs. Beard barked. "Go take care of the gentleman in room eleven. I got no time for yer nonsense." As soon as Sally sashayed back down the hall, Mrs. Beard leveled a hard gaze on Jeremy. "I got no time for yers neither."

"I'm not staying long," he said smoothly. "I've got some questions for you, and once I have my answers, I'll be on my way."

"You'll get answers when *I* get answers." The abbess narrowed her gaze on Yvette. "Since when do you bring your own ladybirds to the brothel?"

"Miss Hardcastle isn't my ladybird," Jeremy said irritably. "She's a new actress at the theater down the road. We've just come from a masque performance."

Miss *Hardcastle*? Yvette dearly hoped Mrs. Beard had never seen *She Stoops to Conquer.*

"She came to London," he went on, "through the influence of an actress friend of hers, to try her hand at treading the boards. But when she arrived at the theater, her friend was nowhere to be found. She's been looking for the woman in her spare time ever since."

"And she stumbled over you instead?" Mrs. Beard asked.

Good Lord. Jeremy had certainly been right about the suspicious character of women in nunneries.

A crowd formed about them, made up of ladies of the evening, randy young gentlemen, and some passersby. Jeremy jerked his head to indicate the onlookers. "Could we go inside to your office? We'd like some privacy for this conversation."

Mrs. Beard nodded at Yvette. "Don't your actress friend have a voice?"

"Of course I have a voice," Yvette snapped. "But as Mr. Keane says, I'd prefer to discuss my friend more discreetly."

"Would you, now?" The woman's eyes shifted from Yvette to Jeremy and back. Then she turned back into the house, striding off down the hall.

"Come on," Jeremy murmured, and tugged Yvette into the bawdy house.

She struggled not to gape like some country Harry at everything she saw, but heavenly day, how did people live like this? The furnishings were garish, the carpets stained with who knew what, and the stench of human . . . fluids was barely covered by a pervasive and cheap perfume.

They passed a room where she glimpsed a man bent over with his trousers and drawers down and a giggling painted creature on the couch beneath him. Yvette could see his bare buttocks. She'd never seen a man's buttocks in her life!

She must have slowed to stare—how often did a woman get to see male buttocks in the flesh, after all?—but Jeremy jerked her forward. "I'll give you a tour later if you like," he said under his breath.

Though her cheeks flamed, she said lightly, "Oh,

good. Perhaps I can pick up some new words and learn how to speak more like a 'dock whore.'"

His smothered oath made her grin beneath her mask.

As soon as Mrs. Beard showed them into her office, Jeremy shut the door and got right to the point. "Miss Hardcastle is looking for a former actress named Peggy Moreton."

Mrs. Beard glanced at Yvette. "What makes you think the woman is here?"

Yvette avoided Jeremy's intent gaze. "I was told she resided here as . . . er . . . one of your girls. And if not here, then in another brothel in Covent Garden."

"Told by whom?" Mrs. Beard asked.

"Does it matter?"

"It do, indeed. I want to know who's flapping their jaws about my business."

The hint of threat in the woman's voice alarmed Yvette. "I—I cannot reveal who told me," she said, aware of Jeremy's eyes on her, "but I assure you I had to pry the information out of him."

Just mail the letter, damn you, and don't ask a lot of foolish questions. Better that you don't know too much about my son, anyway.

Too late. She'd just seen the sort of place where Samuel's son might be living. She would never give up the quest to find him now.

"If you can't tell me where you heard it from," Mrs. Beard said just as the door opened, "then I don't know no Peggy Moreton."

Sally breezed in. "Sure you do," she said, oblivious to her employer's frown. "She was the one who went by Peg Morris on the stage, remember?"

Was the one? Had the woman left the bawdy house? Or worse yet, died?

"This ain't none of yer concern, Sally," Mrs. Beard snapped. "Didn't I tell you to take care of the gentry cove in number eleven?"

"Already did. Got him off right quick."

Mrs. Beard scowled. "Ye daft cow, ye're not supposed to get him off right quick. Ye're supposed to make him wait. That's what they like. That's what makes 'em come back."

"Well, he must have liked it, because he paid me in ready blunt." With a sniff, Sally dropped some coins on the desk.

Mrs. Beard stuffed them into her apron pocket. "Then go out and get another chap, will you?"

Sally rolled her eyes and headed back for the door.

"Wait!" Yvette cried. "What happened to Peggy Moreton?"

"Why, she got a protector, lucky girl. Said he's going to marry her."

"That's enough, Sally," Mrs. Beard said. "Back to work now."

Yvette ignored the abbess to hurry out into the hall after Sally. "Where did she go? Do you know?"

Sally glanced from Yvette to Mrs. Beard, as if finally realizing she'd stumbled into something she shouldn't have. "I'm sorry, I don't. Not even sure I remember the man's name."

"Go on, Sally," Mrs. Beard ordered. "You've said enough."

Desperation gripped Yvette. Heedless of Mrs. Beard's threatening presence in the office behind her, she grabbed Sally's arm. "Just tell me one more thing—did Miss Moreton take the child with her?"

"The *child?*" Jeremy growled behind Yvette.

She ignored him. "The boy. Did she take the boy with her?"

Sally looked frightened now. "Please, miss," she murmured, tugging free of Yvette's hand. "I gotta go."

"It's time you leave, too," Mrs. Beard said to Yvette.

"No!" Yvette whirled on the abbess. "I have to know what happened to the boy. Did he go with Miss Moreton? Do you have *any* idea where they went? He'd be about four years old."

Mrs. Beard started out of the office, but Jeremy stepped into the doorway to block her.

She scowled. "I want yer friend gone."

"I'm not leaving until I find out what happened to Miss Moreton's boy!" Yvette cried.

People were coming out of the other rooms now, curious about the ruckus.

Mrs. Beard glared up at Jeremy. "Ye'd best get yer friend under control."

"Let me talk to her." Reaching inside his coat pocket, he pulled out a handful of guineas. "In private."

The woman's expression grew more speculative. "In private, eh?"

An argument erupted somewhere on the top floor, and she muttered a curse. Snatching the guineas, Mrs. Beard said, "Fine. I'd best go take care of that lot upstairs anyway. Use my office." A knowing glint shone in her eye. "Just don't get it too messy."

Messy? Oh, Lord, she thought they were going to do *that* in her office?

Before Yvette could protest her assumption, Jeremy nodded grimly and stepped aside to let the woman leave. With an amused glance, the abbess pushed past and swaggered down the hall, barking at people to mind their own business.

Yvette glowered at him. "You . . . you let her think that you and I—"

Jerking her into the office, he shut the door and locked it, then stared her down. "So that's what this was about. Finding a child."

All her indignation vanished. He knew the truth. And now he'd expect to know everything. "Yes." She pushed back the hood of her cloak and removed her mask. If she was going to explain herself, she wanted him to look her in the eye while she did it.

Swearing, he began to pace. "I heard this was how the English handled their by-blows, but I never thought to see it done so badly or callously. Didn't you bother to keep track of the boy's nurse? Didn't you pay her enough to take care of him on her own?"

That flummoxed her. "Pay her enough! What are you talking about?"

"The child you obviously handed over to someone else to raise." As he rounded on her, icy anger and betrayal glimmered in his gaze. "The son you obviously bore Lieutenant Ruston."

Fourteen

When Yvette gaped at him, Jeremy stared her down, unable to suppress his anger. No doubt she was surprised that he'd ferreted out her secret. All this time, she'd been chiding *him* for his presumed debauchery while she'd been hiding her own.

What a hypocrite! He *hated* hypocrites.

And true to form for hypocrites, she went on the offensive at once. "You think . . . You have the *audacity* to suggest that I bore an illegitimate child!"

"Do you deny it?"

"Of course I deny it! It's not true!"

Her certainty and the outrage in her voice gave him pause. But what other response could he expect of a respectable English lady? She certainly wasn't going to admit it flat out. That was why the Foundling Hospital in London was so well-funded—gently bred women who found themselves in the family way were happy to support the institution that secretly took their by-blows.

She marched up to him, eyes flashing fire. "And how did you hear of Lieutenant Ruston, anyway?"

You mean, the man who taught you to kiss? And more?

Damn it, he must uproot this jealousy spreading through him like a noxious weed. First Knightford, then Ruston. No woman had ever roused such possessiveness in him. "I heard of him from your servants, of course."

Horror suffused her features with crimson. "My *servants* told you this . . . this nonsense?"

"Not exactly," he said warily. "They told Damber."

"That I was intimate with Lieutenant Ruston."

"No! Not that. I mean . . ." Damn, this wasn't exactly how he'd intended to have this discussion—with her up in arms and him on the defensive. Determined not to let her brazen it out, he locked his gaze with hers. "They told Damber that there was talk of a possible marriage between you and the lieutenant."

"I see," she said frigidly. "And from that, you deduced that I let him get me with child."

Her genuine outrage threw him off-kilter. "It *has* been four years and some months since you knew the man, and you did say the child was four."

"So, based on that coincidence, you decided I was a lightskirt who secretly bore Lieutenant Ruston's love child. And then I what? Sent the babe off with an actress friend to raise, before completely losing track of the boy?"

"Something like that." When she put it that way it sounded far-fetched. And painted her in a light that seemed too harsh. Perhaps he'd been somewhat hasty. He would have expected her to have shown *some* embarrassment by now.

She crossed her arms over her chest. "And when was I supposed to have borne this child?" she demanded indignantly. "How did I hide that I was carrying it? Because I assure you, I haven't taken any months-long trips abroad in the last five years. You can have your spy Damber ask my servants about *that*, too, if you don't believe me."

Her sound logic—and the icy tone with which she delivered it—perversely reignited his temper. "If the boy isn't yours, why are you so desperate to find him? Why risk your reputation to come here for him? And why in God's name would you hide your plans from Blakeborough?"

"Because the child is my nephew, you dunderhead!"

He gaped at her as a knot tightened his gut. The boy was her *nephew*?

No, he couldn't believe it. Blakeborough wasn't the sort to sire—

As the truth hit him, he groaned. Not Blakeborough. *Samuel Barlow.* Her other brother, the criminal, who'd already sired one by-blow, according to Bonnaud.

Her eyes narrowed on him. "Yes," she said, as if she'd read his mind. "My brother's child. *Samuel's* child. I cannot believe you would think that *I*—"

"You can't blame me," he said defensively. "I assumed that if your secret mission involved Samuel, you'd have gone straight to your eldest brother for help." His reasons for his conclusions had been perfectly sound. He wasn't an idiot.

Though the look on her face said *she* certainly thought he was. "I did go to him. Edwin refused to help. He thinks our brother's claims about a son are part of some devious scheme to shame me or him or the family. Edwin ordered me to stay out of it."

Jeremy winced. That did sound like Blakeborough.

Dragging a hand over his face, Jeremy began to pace. All this time, he'd assumed she'd been involved with some blackmailing fiend, when she'd just been doing as she always did, following the lead of her too-kind heart.

"I can't believe you actually thought I was searching for my own child, whom I apparently abandoned to the dangers of the stews," she went on, hurt in her voice. "What kind of woman do you take me for?"

"The kind who has secrets involving brothels." He still chafed over being made to look the fool. But damn it, it had been a logical assumption. Mostly. "What did you expect me to think? You wouldn't tell me why you were coming here, and then I find out you're looking for a child, and given what I'd already learned about this Ruston fellow—"

"Because you sent Damber to question my servants," she accused. When he shot her a sharp look, she said, "That's what happened, isn't it? Our staff is normally very discreet."

"They'd have to be with a fellow like Samuel in the family, wouldn't they?" When she flinched, he cursed his quick tongue. "Sorry. I shouldn't have said that."

She glanced away, the emotions on her face showing she wasn't yet placated. "But you did send Damber to spy on me, didn't you?"

"I asked him to keep his ears open, yes." He stepped toward her. "It was strange that a lady would wish to visit a brothel for any reason, so I didn't want any surprises when we got here."

She gave a rueful shake of her head. "It appears that the joke is on you."

"And on you, too." He sighed. "Sorry that I . . . accused you . . . of bearing a child in secret. I wasn't thinking straight. Though it *is* odd that you'd be so adamant about coming here yourself. Most women would leave such matters to the men of the family."

"I know. And I did try." She rubbed her temples. "I just couldn't bear the thought of my nephew languishing in a bawdy house alone somewhere—not when I could make sure he was provided for. That's why I didn't want you to tell Edwin. Because he would put a stop to my plans."

"With good reason." Jeremy searched her face. "How can you be sure Samuel *isn't* scheming to hurt you? Given his past behavior—"

"You don't know anything about my brother," she said tersely. "He's not as awful as you think."

Jeremy arched an eyebrow. "So you deny that he kidnapped Jane's cousin. And got her maid with child."

She colored. "Well, yes, he did do *those* things. And I admit that he . . . has behaved very badly in the past. But though Edwin can't see it, there's still some good in him. The very fact that Samuel wanted to provide for his child proves it."

Jeremy eyed her closely. "What makes you think he ever intended to acknowledge his son, much less support him? The child *is* four years old, after all, and his mother has presumably been in a brothel for some time. He took no steps to get her out."

"That's because he didn't know until recently that she'd left the stage. He'd been living and working in York for the past few years. She was his mistress when he lived in London, but they parted before she bore his son. He told me he only later found out that she'd had a child by him."

"And you believed him," he said, highly skeptical.

"I did, and I do." Reaching into her cloak, she pulled out a letter. "Because of this: it contains something that will help Miss Moreton care for their son. That's why I'm here. To give her the letter and make sure my nephew is transferred to a better situation."

"He asked you to deliver his missive. To a brothel. Knowing it would ruin you to be seen in one."

"Well, no, not exactly." She dropped her gaze to the envelope cradled in her hands. "He told me to mail it to the Covent Garden post office. He said he heard that Miss Moreton regularly calls for her mail there. When I pressed him for a better address, threatening not to send the letter at all unless he gave me her direction, he admitted that she now worked in a Covent Garden bawdy house. Which is why he said I should merely post it."

"Well, at least the ass had *some* sense," Jeremy grumbled. "But of course, you couldn't leave it at that."

Her head shot up. "No, I could not. Nor could I worry about the possibility that Samuel might be scheming against us. If there was even the smallest chance that my nephew was out there suffering—"

She squared her shoulders. "And apparently, my

instincts were sound, too. Peggy Moreton has run off with Lord knows whom, and her child is now in another possibly perilous situation. So yes, I refused to abandon my nephew just because Edwin was being his usual cynical self."

Then it hit him why this was so important to her. Why the *child* meant so much. She'd essentially been abandoned by her own father, and that wound ran deep. It made her all the more determined not to see it happen to some poor lad.

He softened his tone. "Still, to come here looking for the boy yourself is extreme. Why not hire someone to find him?"

"I suggested that to Edwin. He said he didn't trust anyone to be discreet about it." She made a face. "He's worried that if more scandal erupts, it will keep me from gaining a decent husband."

Jeremy saw the earl's point. "Then *you* could have hired someone. You know the Duke's Men already, so you could—"

"Are you daft?" She seized his arm. "Promise me you won't say a word to your relations. They're sure to tell Edwin about it, and he will *kill* me."

"He's not as bad as all that," Jeremy said.

"Oh, right, I forgot." With a sniff, she released his arm. "You two have become quite chummy now that you're starting a club. I should have known you'd side with him."

"I'm not siding with anyone. I'm concerned about you, that's all. This search is unwise and bound to ruin you before it helps your nephew. For one thing, don't you think Mrs. Beard made note of your questions about the boy?"

She shot him a mutinous glance. "She'll just assume I'm interested because I was Peggy's friend."

"Yes, the friend who seems more concerned about the whereabouts of Peggy's son than about Peggy herself." When Yvette blanched, he added, "Mrs. Beard is sure to find that suspicious. She's probably also aware that the lad is your brother's by-blow. She's adept at ferreting out secrets to hold over her girls' heads."

"You should know," she said irritably, "given your friendly association with her."

He avoided her gaze. "I've never pretended to be anything I'm not."

"Right. All this time you let me believe you were the worst kind of whoremonger, when you were actually just using these women as your models. You and Mrs. Beard clearly have a very different sort of business arrangement than you led me to think."

Thunderation. He'd hoped Yvette might ignore the girls' chatter about his work. He should have known better. Every day she veered closer to knowing the real him. Every day she dug a little deeper, understood a little more.

It drew him in. It terrified him.

"Don't let Sally fool you," he said in a hard voice. "I'm no saint."

"So you also bed those women, do you?" She pierced him with her too-knowing gaze. "In between painting sessions?"

"Not necessarily," he prevaricated.

"But sometimes."

He swore under his breath. He considered lying, but he couldn't. Not to her. "Mrs. Beard's girls? No. Never."

That seemed to take her aback. "Yet you allow the entire world, even your own relations, to believe that you're this debauchee who wallows in the stews every night. Why?"

"It's none of their concern what I do."

She just lifted an eyebrow.

"Fine," he said. "I don't want people making assumptions about my works based on who poses for them. I don't want that to color the observers' perceptions of my paintings."

She let out an exasperated huff. "Then why choose soiled doves as models?"

"Because they have the right seedy appearance for the kind of images I paint. Because they're comfortable with their bodies. Because they're used to being looked at for hours." He scowled at her. "Because they don't ask annoying questions."

Apparently that hint was too subtle for Yvette. "So you *never* bed any of your models? Is that a general rule of yours?"

The question startled him. "Not a rule, no. I did it occasionally in my salad days, when I was randy." Until even that didn't drive the image of those two coffins from his mind. "I painted nudes then, so if the woman was willing . . ." He shrugged. "But as my abilities improved, I became more interested in the women as subjects. In how to transfer their sensuality, their characters . . . their humanity to the canvas."

Her expression saddened suddenly.

That set him on edge. "Why does it matter? Why are we even talking about this?"

"Because I've finally realized something important." Looking vulnerable, she swallowed hard. "To you, I'm just like them."

"Hardly," he clipped out, an instant and visceral reaction.

"I don't mean that you see me as a . . . a lady of the evening. But I'm still merely a model to you. A means to an end."

"That's not true." Every bit of him recoiled at the idea.

"The only difference is that you don't paint me naked, but—"

"I don't paint *them* naked." He bore down on her, unable to help himself. "But *you* I would paint naked in every conceivable position, if I had the chance."

She sucked in a ragged breath, her gaze locking with his.

Determined to banish her notion that she meant so little to him, he tugged her against him. "I do not lie in bed at night burning to possess *them.* I do not spend every modeling session enjoying *their* wit or being painfully aroused by it." He bent his head close. "And I assure you that I've never felt jealous of any man who looked at one of my models with lust. But I'm damned well jealous about you."

And as she stared up at him with those heart-breakingly beautiful eyes and that sweet mouth that tempted him every time he saw her, he gave in to his worst impulses and kissed her.

Fifteen

Much as Yvette knew she should resist him, she couldn't for the life of her. Certainly not in this place that reeked of sensual encounters, with its red velvets and its heavy perfumes and its half-naked rogues.

That in itself should have reminded her of what happened to women who gave in to men. But when he kissed her with such ardor, all she wanted was to kiss him back. Forever.

The forever part was a problem.

Breaking the kiss, she gazed up into his too-handsome face. "Yes, but why me? Why do *I* make you jealous?"

She knew he wasn't going to answer when his eyes glittered in the firelight . . . when his breathing grew hard and his body even harder as he backed her up against Mrs. Beard's desk. "You ask too many questions."

Then he kissed her again, with sweet, hot plunges of his tongue that tore down her walls and swept her into a maelstrom of conflicting urges. She'd wanted so much for so long. Why must he be the only one to knot all her wants into one giant need that had her flinging her arms about him, straining for more of him?

"My luscious lady." He untied her cloak and shoved it off her shoulders, then covered one of her breasts with his hand, fondling and kneading and thumbing her nipple to a fine point. "You don't know what you do to me."

She had some idea. She could feel the hard length of him through his Cavalier breeches and her flimsy shepherdess attire. She should have worn more petticoats.

But then she wouldn't feel the exquisite excitement of his hand sliding down her belly. And when he cupped her between her legs, she was definitely glad of her dearth of petticoats. "*Heavenly day!*"

"Yes," he said hoarsely. "A most heavenly day."

Somehow she doubted he meant the same thing as she. Because his eyes burned into her while he rubbed her down there, as if he knew what his touch did to her and roused those feelings deliberately.

Well, of course it was deliberate. He might not be quite the scoundrel she'd assumed, but he had experience that he put to good use. *Such* good use. Her blood fairly stampeded through her veins. Every sense was attuned to his clever, wicked fingers plucking and plundering with a deftness that made her moan.

"You like that, don't you, my pretty wanton?"

She couldn't deny that she liked it. And if a wanton was a woman who enjoyed being touched and caressed and kissed, then clearly she fit the bill.

Then he slid her skirt up her thighs.

"Jeremy!" she squeaked, and caught his hand.

His breathing warmed her cheek. "I want to look at you."

"T-there?"

"Yes, there. Just look. For now."

Why must that send a heady anticipation kicking through her? "All right. But only if you promise never to paint what you see."

He choked back a laugh. "You give me credit for more talent than I have. I wouldn't have to use models if I could paint from memory."

"Oh."

Apparently he took that for consent because he dropped to his knees and pushed up her skirts to expose her slitted drawers. With a gleaming gaze, he spread the split farther open, then gazed upon her. "What a fetching frame your drawers make for your lovely Garden of Eden."

She gulped. *That* cant term she knew.

When he lifted her leg to hook over his shoulder, she was mortified. It opened her up to his gaze most shamefully. Could he tell how it made her throb down there? Heat up? Dampen most embarrassingly?

"Have you . . . seen enough?" she whispered.

"Not quite. I need to get closer." So he did. But he didn't just look. He put his mouth on her. *There.*

Oh, dear, was it intentional?

His tongue licked her, and she gasped. Oh yes. Most definitely intentional. And shocking.

Not to mention thrilling. "Jeremy . . . ohh . . . This is . . . very naughty."

He chuckled but kept on what he was doing. Which was *amazing*.

As if fully aware of how her private parts ached, he stroked and soothed and laved them with his tongue so eloquently that her heart beat in places it never had before. What he was doing felt like . . . like . . .

"You taste like sin, my Juno," he murmured against her.

That was it. It felt like sin. Very good sin.

A wild laugh rumbled up from her throat. She was sinning in a nunnery that was really a bawdy house. And she wanted more, too. More of his devilish caresses. She wanted them harder. Deeper.

Deeper?

Heavens, his tongue had slipped *inside her.* She might just explode. Or faint. Or both. Could a person faint and explode at the same—

Ohhhh, good *Lord.* Her knees gave way and she gripped the desk for dear life. His lips were . . . and his teeth were . . . and . . . and . . . oh, *marvelous*! She pushed into him, greedy for more.

With a growl, he gripped her hips to lock her against his insolent, clever mouth. A drumbeat call to pleasure sounded in her ears, and, like a soldier blindly following, she marched toward it, faster, determined to catch the elusive sensation running just ahead of her.

"Jeremy . . . please . . . oh, *please*!"

He quickened his strokes, and she strained to capture that delicious feeling that was so very . . . very . . .

She hurtled over the edge and plunged right into bliss.

Oh yes . . . yes . . . *yes*!

A fractured cry escaped her, and her body shook and writhed with her enjoyment. What exquisite heaven!

It took some moments for her gasps to subside, and her body to settle into a luxurious contentment. So this was what it could be like with a man. She threaded her fingers through his thick hair, wanting to touch him, to be close to him.

His motions had already slowed. His mouth turned gentler, softer. Withdrawing. He kissed her thigh, wiped his mouth on her drawers, then slipped from beneath her leg and rose.

She leaned into him, unable to look at him. "That was . . . I didn't know . . . I never guessed—"

"I knew you would take your pleasure with the fierceness of a lioness." Enfolding her in his arms, he nuzzled her neck. "And I had to see it, at least once. Forgive me for that."

At least once. Why did he insist on building walls between them when there was no need? She didn't understand him. He wouldn't let her.

"Now *that* is something I wish I could capture on canvas," he said. "You in the throes of pleasure. But alas, I could never be that good an artist. No one could." He kissed the pulse at her temple. "That should tell you right there that you're more than a model to me."

"But not enough to be a wife." When he stilled, she wished she could take back the words. "I'm sorry."

"No, I'm the one who's sorry. I could never make you a good husband. I lack an essential—"

A loud knock came at the door, and they jerked

apart. Then they heard someone try the handle. Frantically, she sought to restore her clothing, to don her cloak and find her mask.

"I told you, my lord," Mrs. Beard said to someone else, "he's in there with his actress friend, Miss Hardcastle. He'll be out when he's ready."

"He'll be out *now*, if I have anything to say about it," growled a male voice.

Oh, Lord, it was *Warren*. How in heaven's name had he known to come *here*? Hastily she tied on her mask and worked at closing up the cloak's frog fastenings to hide her shepherd's costume.

A pounding began on the door. "Keane, you'd better open up! I want to talk to you!"

"Just stay calm, sweetheart," Jeremy breathed. "He thinks you're an actress. Keep quiet, and I'll get us out of this." Showing a remarkable presence of mind, he went to open the door. "What the devil, Knightford? You have no business—"

Warren pushed his way into the room, his gaze scanning it . . . and her. "*You*, Keane, have no business stealing . . . er . . . Miss Hardcastle from me. She and I have an agreement." Warren stared hard at her, and she could fancy he saw right through her mask. "Don't we, love?"

"You can't have her," Jeremy bit out. "Go back to your other wenches and leave her be."

"She's leaving with me, *right now*," Warren said with a meaningful glance in her direction.

Oh no, he obviously knew who she was. And he would tell Edwin, if she didn't stop him.

She headed for the door, but Jeremy caught her arm. "You're not going anywhere with him."

"Take it outside, gentlemen!" Mrs. Beard said. "I'm not having any disputes over a light-heeled wench who ain't even one of my girls. Out, the three of you!"

This time, Yvette was glad to be ordered out. Warren mustn't be allowed to talk to Edwin; she still hadn't learned where Samuel's boy was! But she didn't dare ask more questions of Mrs. Beard, not with each man gripping an arm as if he'd carry her out if necessary.

None of them said a word until they were in the street. Then Warren spoke in a low voice. "My rig is around the corner. Yvette's going with me, Keane."

"The hell she is! Everyone will see your crest when you drive up to the damned ball, and they'll know that you've been out alone with her. I'm not taking that chance." Jeremy waved to their hackney driver, who scurried to bring the horses round. "She and I already had a plan, and we'll stick to it."

That seemed to flummox Warren. "A plan? For what?"

"Let me explain—" Yvette began.

"No time for that," Jeremy said. "If Knightford has come after us, we've already lingered longer than we should have. Your brother will be looking for you." He opened the door to the hackney. "Get in."

"I'm going, too," Warren said firmly.

Jeremy glared at him. "Fine. It's better we have this discussion in private anyway, so we can get our stories straight."

Then Warren was half helping, half lifting her into the carriage. He sat next to her, as if to protect her from Jeremy, who jumped in and took the opposite seat with a glower that would have done Edwin proud.

As soon as the carriage set off, Jeremy snapped, "How did you find us?"

"How do you think?" Warren said. "I followed you to Mrs. Beard's."

"But that makes no sense," Yvette said. "I'm in disguise."

Warren snorted. "Some disguise—Clarissa's cloak."

"But any number of women tonight wore cloaks."

"True, but I didn't happen to see any of *them* leave with Keane."

"Thunderation," Jeremy said to Yvette. "Let's pray no one else recognized you."

"I don't think they did," Warren grudgingly admitted. "I only noticed when I headed out into the garden for a bit of air and saw you go off with a woman in a black cloak. At first I thought nothing of it. Although I knew Clarissa had worn one, she hasn't even been introduced to you. Then I spotted Yvette's crook behind a bush and put it together."

"Oh, Lord," she said.

"It took me a bit to figure out where you'd gone— I had to question the coachmen milling about—but I finally found one who'd overheard Keane giving the direction to the hackney driver, and I recognized the address."

"Of course you did," she said archly. "You're a frequent visitor to Covent Garden nunneries, as I recall."

Warren muttered a curse. "That's neither here nor there." He jerked his head toward Jeremy. "Besides, so is Keane. And he actually had the audacity to bring you *with* him!"

"Because I asked him to!" she cried. "He's doing me a favor."

That took the wind right out of Warren's sails. He sat back hard against the seat. "If this is about getting more words for those bloody dictionaries—"

"It's a serious private matter that's none of your concern. Mr. Keane was merely helping me learn the truth about . . . something."

"A truth that necessitated being locked up in a room with him?"

Thank heaven he couldn't see her crimson cheeks beneath the mask. "That was because I got into a dispute with Mrs. Beard. I became . . . rather hysterical, and Mr. Keane got me off alone to calm me down. And to discuss what to do next, since she refused to give me the information I required."

"What information?" Warren demanded.

"It's *none of your concern,*" Yvette repeated.

A muscle tightened in his jaw. "Why couldn't you ask *me* to help you?"

"You would have gone right to Edwin. And I didn't want him sticking his nose in it."

Warren blanched. "Bloody hell, girl—"

"I am not a girl! I am a full-grown woman with a mind of her own."

"More than you could possibly know," Jeremy muttered.

"Damn it, Keane," Warren said, "couldn't you stop her from whatever her scheme is? Why didn't you refuse to help her?"

"We *are* talking about the same female, aren't we?" Jeremy drawled. "The Lady Yvette *I* know is rather bullheaded."

Warren swore again. He was swearing an awful lot for a respectable gentleman.

"We're nearing our destination," Jeremy said. "So here's what I propose. The three of us will enter the garden by the same gate we left through. Once there, Lady Yvette will remove her cloak and give it to you. Then she'll retrieve her crook, and we'll return to the ballroom. If anyone asks, you say you were retrieving Clarissa's cloak, and found us talking in the garden."

Warren crossed his arms over his chest. "Here's what *I* propose. I march her straight inside to Edwin, and tell him you've been squiring her to a brothel and God knows where else."

"Warren!" she protested.

"You would see her publicly ruined, is that it?" Jeremy said icily.

"No, not publicly. But I think he should know—"

"If you tell him," Jeremy said, "he will either challenge me to some idiotic duel—which I won't fight—and word of the challenge will get around and she'll be ruined. Or he'll demand that I marry her—which I'll agree to do—and then her *life* will be ruined on account of being forced to marry me. Which do you want? Neither sounds like a particularly good choice to me."

Yvette gaped at him. He would *marry* her? To protect her reputation? Or just to pacify Edwin?

"Damn it," Warren said. "When you put it that way . . ."

"My plan is better," Jeremy said.

"God rot it." Warren rubbed his chin. "Very well. But what if someone sees us enter the garden and recognizes her? Or if Edwin is outside, checking every equipage? Or if anything else goes wrong? What then?"

"If the choice is taken from us, I'll offer marriage right then and there. I won't have her life destroyed." Jeremy's gaze met hers, veiled and enigmatic. "I never intended that."

Though his manner was cold, the words were so sweet, she wanted to cherish them. Except they were drowned out by *Neither sounds like a particularly good choice to me.*

Why was Jeremy so hell-bent on avoiding marriage? If he really wasn't a rogue, then there was no need for him to remain a bachelor.

Curse Warren for showing up and interrupting what Jeremy had been about to tell her. She was almost sure he would have explained his reluctance to marry. Tomorrow night, when they were alone in the schoolroom, she would demand an answer.

"Is all of that acceptable to you, my lady?" Jeremy asked.

Her throat tightened to see him pulling away from her, returning to his earlier formality. Didn't he see that she couldn't do it after sharing such intimacies?

"That's fine," she said wearily.

But none of it was fine. She was rapidly coming to care for him, and like every man she'd known—with the possible exception of Edwin—when things got too difficult, he ran.

At least he'd offered to marry her if she were ruined. But she could never let him go through with it—because the last thing she wanted was a husband who'd married her out of duty, who'd abandoned his family for Lord knew what reasons, and who kept his cards always close to his chest.

So she'd better pray they were not caught. Because she also refused to end up a social outcast.

❧

Jeremy was in a panic the entire way back to his cousin's town house, though he didn't dare show it in front of that ass Knightford, who would blast his way through any chink in Jeremy's armor.

But looking at Yvette, so still and pensive across from him, made Jeremy want to pummel something. She deserved better. And he'd nearly ruined her entirely in Mrs. Beard's office, all because he'd wanted to pleasure her, to see her reach her ecstasy at his hands. If Knightford hadn't shown up when he had, God only knew how far Jeremy might have gone.

What a selfish devil he was. Which was precisely why he shouldn't marry her. He couldn't give her what she needed.

But he *could* protect her from disaster. Since Yvette clearly mustn't keep running off to brothels with him in search of her nephew—they'd be lucky if they got her through tonight unscathed—he'd have to help her another way.

That meant involving Bonnaud and the Duke's Men. Though she'd begged him not to, there was something she didn't know. Bonnaud and Zoe owed him quite a bit. Last year Bonnaud had uncovered the fact that Zoe wasn't the legitimate heir and countess in her own right that the world had assumed. Which meant that Jeremy *was* the legitimate heir to his cousin, the Earl of Olivier. He'd agreed to keep their secret because he had no desire to be an English lord.

That hadn't changed, but his relations were aware that they were indebted to him for their entire future. Bonnaud would be utterly discreet, would even be willing to investigate on behalf of the son of his brother's enemy, Samuel, if Jeremy asked it.

So he would ask it. It was the least he could do for Yvette. It was vastly superior to her risking her reputation searching the city for her nephew. And it was better than his marrying her.

He glanced out the window. Was it? She'd make a wonderful wife. He could easily imagine her in his bed, easily imagine her joining him on every adventure.

The image of her gawking at that bare-assed fellow in the brothel leapt into his mind, and he bit back a smile. Oh yes, his curious and clever lady might be eager for any exploit. And once they headed into the logical next adventure—having children—she'd make a wonderful mother.

His smile faltered. If she survived childbirth. If she even survived *marriage* to the reckless and wild Mr. Jeremy Keane, whose very presence in her life would provoke more scandal.

Yet, God help him, he was tempted to risk it. How dangerous was that?

"We're here," she said in her low, melodic voice, tightening something deep in his chest.

Not his heart. He had no heart. He couldn't risk

having one, because hearts always ended up broken. And he'd spent too long protecting his to offer it to her just because he wanted to bed her.

The three of them got out, slipped through the garden gate unseen, and put their plan into action with surprisingly little trouble.

Until they reached the doors into the house and Blakeborough walked through them. "Where the devil have you been?" he barked, directing the question to Yvette.

"In the garden," she said without missing a beat. "Why? Were you looking for me?"

"You haven't been in the garden *all* this time. I went over the entirety of it a while ago." Blakeborough fixed his gaze on Knightford. "Tell me the truth, Warren. Where has she been?"

Jeremy held his breath.

Then Knightford smiled. "With me and Keane, of course. They encountered me while I was fetching Clarissa her cloak. We stood a while talking. Then Keane wanted to get some air, so we moved outside."

"I went past the coatroom as well," Blakeborough said tersely.

"Oh, that must have been when we went to get refreshments," Yvette said shakily.

Jeremy could tell that Blakeborough had noted her nervousness, so it was best to distract him. "Knightford and I were discussing our club," he said boldly.

Knightford blinked. "Er . . . yes. Your club."

Blakeborough's whole manner softened. "Not just my club and Keane's, old chap. We want you to join, too."

"I told him," Jeremy cut in. "I made it clear that we couldn't do it without him. But he's still hesitant."

"I'm surprised," Blakeborough told Knightford. "Given all your trouble with Clarissa and her antics, I'd think you would make good use of a club where men compared notes concerning suitors for their womenfolk."

A stranger's voice sounded from beyond Blakeborough. "Is there such a club?" asked a fellow Jeremy didn't recognize, accompanied by another gentleman Jeremy didn't know.

"Not yet," Blakeborough said. "But we mean to start one, Mr. Keane and I. And Knightford, if he agrees."

"The idea is growing on me," Knightford assured him. "Keane has only given me the sketchiest of details, however. Perhaps we should have a drink and discuss it."

"Can I join you?" said the other fellow, and his friend echoed the request.

Blakeborough frowned. "Actually, gentlemen, I was looking for my sister so we could return home. But I'll call on both of you when next I'm in town, and we can discuss how to go about forming such a club." He nodded to Knightford. "I'll call on you tomorrow. We can talk about it more then, if that's all right."

"I look forward to it," Knightford said. "Actually, I believe Clarissa is ready to leave, too. That's why I was fetching her cloak."

Jeremy had no doubt that Clarissa would support her guardian's story, since she'd obviously been allowed into Yvette's confidence to some extent.

"Well, then," Blakeborough said, any suspicions he'd had about what Yvette had been up to seemingly having vanished. "Are you ready to leave, Yvette?"

"Yes," she said quickly. "Quite ready."

Taking her arm to head into the ballroom, Blakeborough asked, "Are you coming, too, Keane?"

"Actually, no."

Yvette tensed, and Blakeborough stared at him questioningly. "No?"

"Not tonight." He couldn't spend another evening with her alone and control himself. He needed time to think, to figure out how to go on. His work was becoming entangled with her, with his feelings for her. He had to sort things out.

"I need some additional pigment for the portrait," he went on. "I also want to take care of a few business matters, and to find out if there's been any word about my mother's ship. I'll return to Stoke Towers in a day or two." He met Yvette's gaze. "You're not rid of me yet."

Her face fell, and the sight of it cut him to the bone. But it was for the best. Even if it hurt her temporarily, they needed to cool their friendship. Then maybe when he saw her again, they could keep a more professional distance. A safer distance.

It took everything in his power to walk into the ballroom away from her, knowing that her feelings were probably wounded. And that such wounds would harden into anger by the time he saw her again. Or, worse yet, indifference.

But at least he hadn't compromised her.

"Hold up, Keane!" called a voice behind him.

Knightford, damn him.

Jeremy faced the ass. "What?"

The marquess grabbed him by the arm and steered him back out into the garden. Blakeborough and Yvette had already disappeared, probably headed for the entrance to call for their carriage, so it was just the two of them in the corner as Knightford released his arm with a little shove.

"You are not to go near her again, is that understood?"

With a nonchalance borne of the armor he'd developed through the years, Jeremy examined his fingernails. "It will be rather difficult for me to avoid her while painting her portrait."

"You know precisely what I mean, you arse. I'd better not hear of any more private rendezvous in locked rooms."

Jeremy cast him a bored look. "I'd better not hear of you speaking one word about them to anyone, her brother included."

"Why? Because you care about what happens to her? I have trouble believing that."

And Jeremy wasn't about to contradict it. Knightford mustn't suspect how deeply he *did* care, or the man would surely go to her brother. "Because Blakeborough has commissioned her portrait from me, and I mean the painting to be my ticket into the Royal Academy. You understand."

Knightford cocked his head, as if uncertain whether to believe him. "I understand that you have a reputation."

"A well-deserved one, I assure you. So if you think I would settle down with some English chit who probably dresses in the dark, you're mad."

"But you'd seduce one, I daresay," Knightford said grimly.

"And be caught in a parson's mousetrap? Not I. Besides, she put me in my place very effectively."

Knightford relaxed his stance. "She does have a way of doing that." His gaze turned speculative. "Tell me what she was looking for at the brothel."

"No."

"Why not?"

"She asked me not to. I may be a scoundrel, but I'm no tattletale."

"But Edwin should know of it."

"Then she'll tell him. In her own good time."

Knightford scowled. "You're an arse, do you know that?"

"It's a popular opinion," Jeremy said dryly. "I live down to it as often as possible."

But he grew weary of playing that role. Once, it had suited him to assume the mantle of Byronic artist. It kept people from getting too close. Ever since he'd met Zoe and Bonnaud, however, he'd begun to see that family could be pleasant to have around sometimes. Lately he'd been less inclined to hold people at arm's length, which was probably why he'd foolishly allowed Yvette beneath his guard.

"Are we finished here?" he asked Knightford.

"For now. I may still call you out."

"Go ahead. But you'll be proclaiming me a coward the next day. Because I will not fight you."

Knightford's eyes narrowed. "That wouldn't help your aspirations to be part of the Royal Academy."

"But it would keep my neck intact, wouldn't it?"

He headed away from Knightford, toward the ballroom. But it was only as he entered that he remembered something disturbing.

He still didn't know who Lieutenant Ruston had been to Yvette.

Sixteen

Three days after the ball, Yvette sat at a table in the drawing room at Stoke Towers, putting together kits of sewing materials for the women at her favorite charity and trying not to think of Jeremy. But when her distraction led her to drop yet another needle on the rug, she cursed under her breath.

"How many of those kits have you put together?" Edwin asked from his usual post, working on his account ledgers. "A hundred?"

"It seems like it, but it's only been fifty. I promised them seventy-five."

"Then I suppose it's good that Keane hasn't been here. Though God only knows when he intends to finish that portrait I'm paying him for."

Yes, God only knew, because Yvette certainly didn't. She hadn't heard anything from the dratted man. Not. One. Word. The portrait didn't worry her; it was the search for Samuel's son that concerned her. She needed Jeremy for that.

Though that was *all* she needed him for. She'd had

time to settle her emotions, to think through everything that had happened, and a marriage between them would never work. It simply wouldn't. He was too . . . too . . .

Oh, what a liar she was! She missed him.

She still wanted him. And if she couldn't have him as a husband, she might even settle for having him as a lover.

A blush heated her cheeks. Would she? She'd always sworn to steer clear of rogues, but he was no rogue. And he was the most exciting man she'd ever met. The most stimulating, and certainly the most intriguing. Why *not* share his bed? It wasn't as if she had any impending proposals on the horizon. And the idea of never having a chance to be with him intimately—

Drat him. Surely he had to come back sometime. He had his other painting to finish.

She would have broken his rule and peeked at it, but not trusting her *or* the servants, he'd hidden it somewhere. Or more likely had handed it to Damber for safekeeping. Since the servant had rushed to London as soon as his master wrote to summon him, she had no idea where the painting was. For all she knew, Damber might have dropped it into the pond.

"Lady Clarissa Lindsey!" announced a footman.

Before Yvette could do more than blink, Clarissa breezed into the drawing room and threw herself onto a chair next to Yvette with wild abandon. The woman did everything with wild abandon—rode, sang, told outrageous stories that got people laughing. Despite her blond, green-eyed china-doll exterior, she was a hellcat in skirts, which was precisely why Yvette liked her.

And if sometimes a haunted look crossed her face, well, that was Clarissa, too. Yvette only wished she knew what caused it.

"Good afternoon, Clarissa," Edwin said without looking up from his account books. His shoulders had gone rigid the moment she entered the room. They generally did. "To what do we owe the honor of this visit?"

"I'm not visiting *you*," Clarissa said blithely. "I'm visiting Yvette."

Edwin lifted his head, then his eyebrow. "I don't see the distinction. The house belongs to me."

Clarissa flashed him an arch smile. "That's like saying that the palace belongs to the king, so no one can visit the princesses without visiting him, too."

His gaze sharpened, and he lounged back against his chair. "Are you comparing me to the king?"

"Only if you're bloated and red-faced and an aging debauchee. Which you clearly are not."

"Goodness, no," Yvette cut in, before Edwin could chide her friend for her rash words about His Majesty. "Edwin is the opposite of all those things."

"Indeed. It's his particular charm." Clarissa turned to Yvette. "But I'm not here to talk about your brother."

"Then I hope you're here to help me put together sewing kits for the poor ladies at the charity." Yvette pointed to a jar of needles. "Those have to be stuck through placards that we place in the kits."

"Oh, very well." Clarissa went to work on the needles. "And while I help you, you can tell me all about that artist fellow who's doing your portrait. When you visited us the other day, you neglected to mention that he is so very good-looking."

With a snort, Edwin returned to perusing his account books. But Yvette now noticed him rubbing the back of his neck. He did that when he was agitated. No doubt he was still worried about Yvette's association with Jeremy.

As Yvette opened canvas bags, she weighed her words. "I suppose *some* would find Mr. Keane attractive. Assuming that one liked that sort of thing."

"Oh, come now, he was handsome as sin in that costume, admit it."

Yes, if Sin had an angel's golden locks and glorious blue eyes. Jeremy certainly made Yvette feel like sinning. Recklessly. Thoroughly.

Often.

"It's only because he has that American way of seeming carefree and wild. That can sometimes be appealing."

"Sometimes!" Clarissa snorted. "I doubt he's anything less than gorgeous at any time. I can only imagine how divine he must look in dinner attire."

Divine, indeed. Yvette hoped she got to see him in it again. Or out of it. The sight of Jeremy in shirtsleeves had quite heated her blood. Just imagine if he were wearing nothing but—

"Don't be vulgar," Edwin said through clenched teeth.

Yvette nearly jumped before she realized her brother was speaking to Clarissa.

Her friend tipped up her chin. "Pray tell me, why is it vulgar for a woman to admire a man's looks? Men admire women's looks all the time."

"Ah, yes, I forgot," he said. "You aspire to be a man these days, complete with trousers and waistcoat."

"Don't tell me you're angry that I didn't consult you about my costume at the ball," Clarissa said, an odd gleam in her eyes. "Really, Edwin, I didn't know it mattered so much to you."

Edwin scowled. "Don't be ridiculous. I don't give a farthing what costume you wear. You can dress yourself as a Turk, for all I care."

"I'd much prefer to be the Turk's harem slave," Clarissa said sweetly. "Only think how much fun that costume would be. All those flowing, nearly transparent fabrics and flimsy pantaloons. I could wear some kohl around my eyes and show my belly, and practically ensure that I'm asked to stand up for every set."

A curious flush rose over Edwin's face. He stood abruptly, gathered up his account ledgers, and headed for the door. "Forgive me, ladies, I have work to do. You'll enjoy your chatter more without me here anyway."

As he walked out, Clarissa cast him a speculative look and said softly, "I sincerely doubt that."

When he was gone, Yvette turned to her friend. "Why do you persist in taunting him so?"

A strange expression crossed Clarissa's face before she shrugged. "It's good for him. He's too sure of his opinions and his place and his rules. Someone has to shake him up, and you don't do it nearly as much as you should." She leaned over. "Now, enough about your rigid brother. Tell me more about your Mr. Keane."

"He's hardly *my* Mr. Keane. He's been in London ever since the ball."

"He's probably working up the courage to offer for you."

"Not a chance. The man has sworn off marriage, though I don't know why."

"He's an artist. *And* an American." Clarissa stabbed a needle through a placard. "They're mad, all of them. But handsome, I'll grant you. You could have a flirtation with him. That would be such *fun*. As long as you're careful, of course."

"You mean, the way you were in Bath?"

Clarissa's face darkened. "That was all Mama's fault. She tried to turn it into something more despite my wishes."

That had been the real reason for Clarissa's abrupt return home. Some fellow in Bath had fallen madly in love with her, and Clarissa had apparently *not* returned the feeling.

"Anyway," Clarissa went on, "according to Warren, you and Mr. Keane are already rather friendly."

Yvette's heart dropped. "What did Warren tell you?"

"It wasn't what he told me, but what he asked me. He quizzed me about what you'd been up to lately, and how close you were to Mr. Keane, and whether I thought you could get into trouble with the man. He wouldn't ask such things if he had no suspicions." Clarissa cast her a knowing look. "He was *very* interested in your well-being."

Yvette recognized that look. "For the last time, I am never marrying Warren, even if he would have me, which he wouldn't."

With a sigh, Clarissa poured more needles out of the bottle. "You can't blame me for trying. My cousin desperately needs a wife, whether he acknowledges it or not, and if it were you, I'd have an ally whenever he becomes draconian in his restrictions."

"I do sympathize. I'd hoped for the same thing with Jane. But she ran off and married Lord Rathmoor instead."

"Silly woman. Edwin is miles more handsome than Lord Rathmoor." When Yvette shot her a sharp glance, Clarissa added hastily, "Well, he is. But don't tell him I said that. It will swell his head. And the last thing that man needs is more arrogance. Why, he couldn't even lower himself to wear a costume at the ball!"

"He never does. Not even a domino." Yvette shoved a folded piece of linen into a canvas bag. "And speaking of dominos, Warren didn't ask you about how I came to be wearing your cloak, did he?"

"He did, but I told him what we agreed upon—that I had no idea. He assumes that you stole it for your own purposes." She slanted a sly glance at Yvette. "Did you have your secret rendezvous with your secret friend whom you won't tell me anything about?"

"I did. But it proved pointless."

Clarissa turned serious. "Do take care, Yvette. For all my teasing about flirtations, this smacks of Lieutenant Ruston all over again." Clarissa was the only person in the world, other than Samuel, who knew the details of that disaster.

"It's nothing like that, I assure you." Yvette focused her attention on folding a yard of wool. "My secret meeting was perfectly respectable. Besides, I'm much older and wiser now. I would never fall for the likes of such a rogue again."

Clarissa looked skeptical. "If you say so."

"I do." Time to get Clarissa off dangerous subjects.

Setting down the wool, Yvette stood and held out her hand to her friend. "Now, how would you like to see my unfinished portrait?"

~❧~

It was after midnight when Jeremy carried a wooden box up the stairs and down the hall to his room at Stoke Towers, accompanied by the footman who was hauling his empty trunk up from storage. Jeremy had given the servant some story about why he'd come in the middle of the night to pack up his belongings, but it didn't matter what the fellow thought. No footman would be fool enough to wake the family when they were all abed. So Jeremy ought to be safe until morning.

He meant to have his trunk ready to be brought down for when the servants rose, and then be waiting for the earl in the breakfast room early. That way he could explain his hasty departure without having to see Yvette, since she would undoubtedly rise later.

Coward.

Yes, he was. But he couldn't face her one more time alone. And if she learned he was back, she would do her utmost to see him privately before he could escape.

The servant carried the trunk inside Jeremy's bedchamber and accepted with a nod Jeremy's overly generous vail. Once the footman left, Jeremy shut the door and set the wooden box down by the bed. He'd returned for two reasons—to retrieve his masterpiece, on the slim chance that he could complete it one day, and to tell the earl that he'd finished enough of Yvette's portrait that he could put the final touches on it elsewhere.

Because he had to leave Stoke Towers. He'd thought it over the entire time he'd been in the city—engaging the Duke's Men in Yvette's search, visiting the exhibit . . . trying not to think of the woman who'd seized his cursed imagination.

The idea of being with her intimately consumed him. That little taste of her at the brothel hadn't been nearly enough. He wanted to taste her again, to tease her and take her and school her in all the ways of pleasure he'd learned through the years. If he stayed here, he would almost certainly indulge those urges.

He would almost certainly ruin her.

Damn it, why had he no self-control around her? The last time he'd been unable to curb his prick, he'd been eighteen and in the throes of his first infatuation. Although, to be fair, as a young widow, Hannah had been as eager for their joining as he.

Indeed, she'd blamed herself for their first swiving once it had forced him into an untenable position. It was true that their affair might have ended then, if not for her becoming pregnant . . .

Thrusting the dark memory from his head, he strode over to the dressing table, dragged its stool to the large seventeenth-century oak bed, and climbed up to feel around atop the oak tester. His painting remained there, where he'd left it the night before they'd ridden off to the ball. He'd been storing it there every evening after he was done working.

He let out a breath. No one had discovered it, thank God. He'd figured they wouldn't; he couldn't imagine the servants cleaning atop the tester every single day, but it never hurt to be sure.

Dragging the canvas down, he propped it against the bed and examined it to assess his progress. He could make do with what he'd painted so far, since the Commerce figure was done, but if he left now, the Art figure would never be as good as he wanted.

Yvette had an elusive air he still hadn't managed to capture, a blend of naïveté and sensuality that was the very essence of allegorical Art at its best. His depiction of her face just wasn't right. It wasn't entirely . . . her. And he wanted it to be her. It *had* to be her, whether it was recognizable to anyone else or not.

He slammed his fist against the bedpost. He didn't want to leave his work undone. But neither did he want to leave *her* undone. And if he spent even one more night alone with her . . .

No, he couldn't risk that. He wouldn't risk *her*. Which meant he must go.

But not without his work. The difficult part would be getting it out before dawn, unnoticed. As long as he removed it before anyone saw it, they could never tie it to her. He'd painted her face in enough shadow that he was fairly certain she wouldn't be recognized if he ever exhibited the work.

That was what the deep wooden box, made to the proper dimensions, was for. Since the paint was still wet, he couldn't wrap the canvas up, so he'd needed the box to transport it in. He and Damber would have to carry it out very carefully.

Right now his apprentice was packing up the paints and other materials in the music room downstairs, which would take him a couple of hours. Then they'd figure out how to get the box outside without damaging the painting inside or being questioned about it. After all this, Jeremy wasn't going to lose his masterpiece. One day he *would* finish it, damn it.

A knock came at the door that led to the servants' passages. It had to be Damber, who occasionally enjoyed using the servants' door to take him by surprise. The stupid boy thought that was a lark.

The lad probably just had a question, but on the off chance that some other servant was in the passageway, Jeremy grabbed his painting and climbed up on the stool to stow it back in its hiding place.

Then he returned the stool to the dressing table on his way to the door. "Damber, I told you—" he began as he swung it open.

The sight of Yvette waiting nervously in the passageway made his heart falter. Damn it all to hell. The one woman he'd planned to avoid.

Without waiting for an invitation, she slipped inside and shut the door, then had the good sense to latch it, since she wore her night rail and wrapper as she had during all their secret sessions.

It had been one thing for her to dress that way upstairs, but if she was found in his bedchamber dressed like that . . .

Oh, God. "You shouldn't be here."

"Don't you think I know that?" When she spotted his trunk, she paled. "Thank heaven I retire late and my bedchamber window overlooks the drive. Because if I hadn't heard the carriage pull up, I wouldn't have come. And you would have left without a farewell."

He forced himself to ignore her wounded tone. "I intended to speak to your brother in the morning before I headed off."

"But not to me." When he glanced away, unsure how to answer that, she added, "That's what I thought. As usual, you're running away."

His gaze snapped back to hers. "I'm doing what's best for us both. Surely you realize we're playing with fire. The only way to stop it is to end our mad bargain."

She edged closer, and her bedclothes swished about her like the veil of a bride, meant to tantalize, to tempt . . . to torment. Unfortunately, now that he knew what lay beneath them, it did exactly that. His prick strained against his trousers, making him swear under his breath and pray the dim light would mask his arousal.

"So you mean to abandon our bargain as well as abandoning us." Her eyes accused him. "You mean to scurry off with your half-done paintings and leave me wondering about my nephew with no way to do anything about it."

"I'm already making discreet inquiries on your behalf. When and if I learn something about the boy, I will visit and give you my report. During the daytime. Well chaperoned."

That didn't seem to satisfy her. Not that he'd thought it would. "And the paintings? What of those?"

"I'll make do with what I've done so far in the case of *Art Sacrificed to Commerce*. The portrait is far enough along that I can complete it elsewhere."

She clutched at the bedpost, as if to steady herself. "Am I that much of a trial to you that you can't even bear to stay here long enough to finish them?"

"Yes," he said bluntly. "I can't control myself around you. I am used to doing what I want, taking what I want. But if I take what I want from you, it will be the ruin of you. And me."

"Of you?" Her throat moved convulsively. "Why?"

"Because if I take your innocence, I *will* marry you, and I'm not made for marriage, sweetheart."

She stepped closer. "Why?"

Thunderation, this was precisely what he'd wanted to avoid. "It doesn't matter why. Just trust me when I say what I am. And what I am not."

"How can I? You let me believe you a rogue because of some idea about what people would say concerning your art. You let me believe you didn't care about me, when you did." She planted her hands on her hips. "I think it's time I stopped trusting the impression you give of yourself and start demanding that you tell me the truth. Since you're breaking our agreement by running off in the dead of night, the least I deserve is an explanation about why you are so determined to avoid marriage."

He gritted his teeth. "Fine. The truth is, I would make any woman miserable."

"Why?"

"Damn it, stop asking that!"

A steely glint appeared in her lovely eyes. "Why?"

"Oh, for God's sake," he muttered.

"I'm not leaving until I get answers," she said stoutly, and to his horror, she sat down on his bed. "I'm not going to let you run away from here, as you've run away from your family and your responsibilities. I want to know *why*, if you find me attractive and you enjoy my company, you are so afraid to—"

"I refuse to be the ruin of another wife, damn you!"

As shock lit her face, he cursed his quick tongue. But it was out now, and he couldn't take it back. *"That* is why."

Seventeen

For several moments, Yvette could only gape at Jeremy. Then she wrapped her arms over her stomach in a futile attempt to stop its roiling. "You're . . . you're *married?*"

"Not anymore." Raking one hand through his already disheveled hair, he dropped onto the stool near the dressing table. "But I was, years ago."

She couldn't breathe, couldn't think. He'd had a wife. A *wife*! Heavenly day, she'd never guessed. He hadn't even hinted at it! "Why have none of your friends and relations mentioned it? Lady Zoe or Jane or—"

"They don't know about it. The marriage was so brief—only six months' duration—that my parents never even told distant relations like the Keanes in England. And I prefer not to speak of it."

"Clearly," she muttered.

That gained her a dark look. "It was long ago, in a time far removed from my present life. I married at the age of eighteen, and she was dead by the time I reached nineteen."

Dead. Not divorced or missing.

Yvette was glad of that, then chided herself for being glad. "What happened to your poor wife that she passed away so young?"

The pain that slashed over his face tugged at her heart. "She died in childbirth. Along with my son."

She sucked in a ragged breath. No wonder he painted melancholy subjects and looked bleakly upon domestic life. How could he not, after experiencing such a tragedy so young? To lose his wife and son after a marriage of only six months—

Oh, dear. Wanting to clarify his meaning, she fumbled for how to ask. "I suppose difficulties are to be expected in childbirth when a babe is born so early."

He lifted an eyebrow at her. "Don't be coy, Yvette. The child was born after the requisite number of months. I'm sure you can guess why." Glancing away to stare grimly into the fire, he added, "Although his death did make it easier for my parents to *claim* that a too-early birth was what caused the tragedy."

A veil passed over his face. "God forbid that the Keanes of Montague have a grandson rumored to have been sired on the wrong side of the blanket. That wouldn't do. Especially when no one but their black sheep of a son approved of the mother."

So *that* was why he'd been so quick to assume that Yvette had borne an illegitimate child. He'd had to face that possibility with another woman.

An intense curiosity welled up in her—to know about his wife, about his family, about all the things he'd refused to discuss in the past. But she must tread carefully to avoid spooking him. This was a weighty secret indeed, one he'd apparently kept quiet for some years.

She began with what she considered an innocuous question. "How did you and your wife meet?"

His stiff stance made her wonder if he would unbend to reveal even that much. Then, with a shuddering breath, he locked his gaze with hers. "You want to know it all, I suppose."

"If you'll tell me." She let her compassion show in her face. "I promise not to judge."

A bitter laugh escaped him. "You mean, you won't judge me as unfairly as I judged *you* that night at the brothel."

"I don't blame you for leaping to conclusions. You were unaware of the facts. Once you heard them, you understood my reasons quite well." She tipped up her chin. "I should hope I'm just as capable of being open-minded."

"Touché." He bent forward to prop his elbows on his knees and gaze once more into the fire. "Very well, what was it you asked?"

"How you met your wife."

"Ah, yes." He threaded his fingers together between his knees. "We met because of our mutual interest in art. I'd sketched and painted for years, mostly just to amuse myself and my family, but the closer I got to eighteen and my departure for college, the more I wanted to make art my profession. Hoping to convince my father to let me study painting, I sought a teacher in our nearby town who could help me improve enough to show Father that I had real talent."

A faint smile crossed his lips. "That's how I stumbled across the Widow Miller, who was only twenty-two. Her late husband had been an engraver and she had some talent herself, but because he'd left her virtually penniless, she'd been forced to take on students in order to support herself."

"And support her children?"

Again, pain twisted his features. "No. They'd had none."

After that sent him into a long silence, she prompted him to go on. "So you became her pupil."

He roused, as if from a dream. "I paid for the tutoring myself out of my generous monthly allowance. While my parents assumed I was drinking in taverns like most men my age, I was actually having secret lessons with Mrs. Miller."

"My, my, you certainly are good at secret meetings with ladies."

"I am that," he drawled. "Though it probably didn't hurt that she had her own cottage. It made it easy to spend enough time with her to really learn something."

A lump stuck in her throat. "And for you to fall in love with her."

He shot her a sharp look. "More like lust. It's not the same. Or so I'm told, although romantic love isn't a feeling I've ever experienced myself."

Well. Nothing like being blatantly warned that he didn't love her. That perhaps he *couldn't* love her.

Not that it mattered. She didn't love him, either.

Or rather, she *hoped* she didn't. The last time she'd fancied herself in love with a man who kept secrets, it had ended so awfully that she no longer trusted herself when it came to men.

Still, she hadn't given up hope that one day a gentleman would sweep away all her fears and she would know he was the one she could marry. Recently she'd even begun to hope it might be Jeremy. But he seemed bent on dashing that hope.

Fighting to hide her tumultuous emotions, she asked, "What about the Widow Miller? Was she in love with you?"

He shook his head. "She was still mourning her late husband. But we shared common interests and were both young and lonely and randy as hell. So it was probably inevitable that we ended up in bed together."

Inevitable? Yvette snorted. If the woman had possessed a pair of eyes and Jeremy had been even a tenth as handsome as he was now, it had definitely been inevitable. Especially for a widow, who needn't worry about losing her innocence. Widows were notoriously wanton, she'd heard.

And having spent time in Jeremy's arms, Yvette began to understand why.

He stared down at his hands. "When I learned Hannah was bearing my child, I wasn't exactly overjoyed. I had big plans—to go away to Philadelphia, about three hours from Montague, and study painting at the Pennsylvania Academy of the Fine Arts. Then I'd planned to travel and view the world's masterpieces."

A sad smile twisted his lips. "Hannah knew of my

dreams and didn't want me to give them up for her. When I proposed marriage, as I knew I must, she said she would only marry me if I continued with my plans. She suggested that we go to Philadelphia together as husband and wife."

His voice hardened. "We were so naïve. We thought we would merely march into my father's study, announce we were getting married, and he would happily send us off to Philadelphia with his blessing. And my usual allowance."

The bleak look in his eyes made her want to cry. "It didn't happen that way."

"Hardly." He straightened on the stool. "My father wasn't about to permit his only son to run off and become an artist. He'd always meant for me to manage the family mills, as he'd done from the day he'd married my mother."

Jeremy clenched his hands into fists on his knees. "The branch of the Keanes that moved to America hadn't been wealthy. He'd always craved what his rich relations had, so he was eager to marry Mother and get his hands on her mills, since she was her father's only child and heir. After Father and Mother inherited the company, he was determined I would be his successor."

"But you didn't want that."

"I *never* wanted that. I respected the work it took for him to keep them running, but I didn't see why I had to do it, too. By the time I'd turned eighteen, he already had competent managers. He didn't need me. Or so I thought."

A muscle worked in his jaw. "But when I told him I wanted to marry Hannah and go study painting in

Philadelphia, he made it quite clear that he wouldn't countenance that. He said he'd cut me off if I pursued art as a profession; everything would go to Amanda."

"That's awful!" She was irate on his behalf. "In England a father can't cut off his son like that, you know. Or not easily, anyway."

"Well, then, I suppose there are some advantages to the English system of inheritance." Anger flared in his eyes. "I wanted to tell him to give my inheritance to someone who gave a damn, but I couldn't. I'd soon have a wife and baby to support. So Father had me where he wanted. He said he'd give his blessing to the match if I agreed to stay at Montague and learn how to run the mills."

His voice grew choked. "Hannah told me I should refuse his conditions. We would go to Philadelphia without his money. She would give lessons and I'd find a position somewhere until we could save enough for me to attend the academy."

He paused, as if fighting for composure, and Yvette choked down tears of sympathy. She could see how much it cost him to tell her this. Should she even have asked him to speak of it?

Yes, she'd been right in that. Any man who kept such torment bottled up inevitably found himself dragged down by it. She'd seen it happen to both Edwin and Samuel after Mama's death. Neither of her brothers had ever fully faced their grief, as she had. They'd simply twisted it into something else. For Edwin, it had been cynicism and melancholy. For Samuel, it had been recklessness.

But Jeremy's tragedy had run far deeper than

theirs. To lose a wife and child in one fell swoop! How had he borne it?

He drew in a long breath as if to steady himself. "But I feared that Hannah and I striking off together on our own was beyond my abilities. I had no experience at anything but being a rich man's son. How was I to find a position that paid well enough to take care of a family?"

A fierce expression crossed his face. "I refused to have my pregnant wife attempting to support me while I tried futilely to find a post. No child of mine would grow up eating gruel because I was too proud and stubborn to be the man my father wanted. So I gave in to Father's demands."

"You had no choice," she said softly. "No matter what your late wife said, following your dreams would have meant enormous sacrifices for her and your child. She must have been a very fine woman to consider living a harder life just so you could one day pursue schooling in art."

"She was a fine woman indeed." He rose, his face a mask of regret. "Yet despite knowing that, I couldn't . . . I never did . . . love her. I *liked* her, mind you. I enjoyed her company. I even convinced myself that I could be happy married to her and running the mills, if that was to be my whole life. But deep down, I knew that would never satisfy me. I already resented giving up my dreams, settling into a life that didn't suit me."

He walked up to the bed to stare at her. "Don't you see? A lovely woman of character—one carrying my son, for God's sake—still couldn't engage my heart, couldn't change my innate selfishness. We lived together as husband and wife for *six months*, and that never changed." His voice grew choked. "That's when I knew."

"Knew what?" she asked, her own heart in her throat.

"I'm not the kind of man who falls in love. Mother always said I would learn to love Hannah eventually, as she had learned to love Father, but I knew that would never happen for me. And when Hannah went into labor, and I wasn't—"

He scrubbed a hand over his face. "Let's just say that I had already become the same sort of selfish being my father always was. Like him, I was clearly not the sort to feel deeply. And what woman wants a man with no heart for a husband?"

"But you *have* a heart!" Yvette jumped up. "I've seen it countless times—your kindness to Damber, your kindness to me in what you saw as a foolish quest. Those do not speak of a heartless man. Or a selfish one who can't love."

"That's not love. That's basic human decency. But from everything I've been told, a woman wants more than that. She wants a man who will happily sacrifice for her, give up his future and hopes and dreams if that's what it takes to secure her. I was incapable of that sort of selflessness then, and I doubt I'm capable of it now."

"You're basing your opinion of who you are on what you did and felt when you were *eighteen*. Good Lord, you were barely grown. You were thrust into a marriage before you fully knew what you wanted out of life. How you reacted to the weight of such responsibility then says nothing about the man you've become."

"You don't understand—"

"I do! I, too, had an early experience with someone who made me wary of marriage. But at least you had the good sense to recognize the true nature of your feelings for your late wife. I was more foolish— I let myself be blinded by infatuation and flattery into fancying myself in love. Looking back on it, I know I had no idea what being in love truly meant."

His gaze narrowed on her. "You're talking about Lieutenant Ruston."

She sighed. Of course he would recognize that. "It's neither here nor there who it was. My point is—"

"Oh no, you're not going to escape that easily." He bore down on her. "You said you wouldn't tell me your secrets unless I told you mine. Well, I have. Now it's your turn."

"But we're not finished with your story! I still don't know how you ended up at art school after your wife's death or why you're at odds with your mother."

"There was no reason to stay after my wife and child died," he said blandly, "and definitely no reason to run Father's mills. He realized that and agreed to let me leave, so I did. And I'm not at odds with my mother."

"Liar."

A shutter came down over his features. "Don't read more into it than there is."

"But Jeremy—"

"Enough." He urged Yvette to sit on the bed, then sat beside her. "Tell me about Lieutenant Ruston."

A pox upon it. "You'll think me a peagoose."

He smiled faintly. "I doubt that."

"*You* were not the one who fell for the blandishments of a practiced scoundrel. I assume that your late wife didn't set out to seduce you to gain your hand in marriage?"

"No, she did not. If anything, I seduced her. Why do you think I proposed marriage? I knew I was at fault. And we're not talking about me, anyway."

She sighed. He wasn't going to let it go, was he? She should never have brought it up. This was what came of sharing confidences—all of one's flaws were unveiled. "It was long ago. I've practically forgotten it."

"Yes, I can see that," he said with some sarcasm. "Here, I'll make it easier for you. I know that the man proposed marriage when you were twenty, and I know that he was found afterward to be a fortune hunter. I also know he left Stoke Towers with his tail between his legs. I assume that your father or Blakeborough discovered his mercenary aims and had him packed off."

"My, my, your spy Damber is quite the chatterbox, isn't he?"

"Yvette—"

"Oh, all right." She steadied her shoulders. "It wasn't Papa *or* Edwin who sent the lieutenant away. It was Samuel. He was the one who saved me." She lifted her gaze to Jeremy. "Why do you think I want so desperately to find his child? Because it's the least I owe him for thwarting Lieutenant Ruston's attempt to blackmail me."

Eighteen

A roaring filled Jeremy's ears. "Blackmail! That ass *blackmailed* you? How? Why?" He frowned. "Never mind that—I know why. To force you into marriage."

She bobbed her head. "You think *you* were naïve at eighteen? I was a veritable idiot at twenty, I assure you."

"I don't believe that." He seized her hands. "Some men are bastards who take advantage of everyone they meet, even clever young women."

And the thought of some fellow trying to force her into marriage for his own mercenary purposes made Jeremy want to hit something. Or someone, preferably the lieutenant.

He fed that rage to keep from dwelling on the fact that he'd revealed so much of his past to her. Not all of it, though. Never all of it. If she knew how truly selfish he'd been, she would never speak to him again. And as wise as that might be, he couldn't bear it.

So he focused on her association with Ruston instead. "But how did the man blackmail you, exactly?"

Her cheeks blushed a bright crimson. "This is so embarrassing."

Fear of what she might say seized him by the throat. "He didn't hurt you, did he? Because if that ass harmed anything but your pride, I swear I will hunt him down and lop off his 'horn' myself." When she looked startled by his vehemence, he added hastily, "I mean, just so I could make sure he never used it against any other innocent female."

She looked skeptical of that reasoning, but murmured, "Well, he didn't even use it against me, so you've no need to worry on that score." Even as relief coursed through Jeremy, she added, "But he taught me to doubt myself. My instincts." She squeezed Jeremy's hands. "For that, I can never forgive him."

"Understandably." He gazed at her lovely face and wondered how any man could want her just for her money. "So, what exactly did he do? How did he even end up here at Stoke Towers?"

She blinked, then said tartly, "What? Your spy couldn't unearth that?"

He ignored her sarcasm. "Apparently not. All he said was that the man visited here for a few weeks one holiday."

Pulling her hands free, she nodded. "He came here with Samuel, who was his shipmate. They were given leave for Christmastide, and the lieutenant was an orphan with no family, so my brother invited him home."

Jeremy choked down the impulse to point out that the brother she credited with saving her had also brought the snake into Eden in the first place. "Did your father agree to the invitation?"

"Papa didn't know or care. He was off in London as usual, doing whatever he always did there. After Mother died, we almost never saw him. Edwin had already reached his majority years before, so Papa left him in charge since Edwin, who never really liked society, was content to run things."

"So Blakeborough was the man of the house while Ruston was here paying court to you." And still just as oblivious to how deeply his sister felt.

"Yes." She rose to walk over to the fire. "I'd met Lieutenant Ruston a few times before, when Samuel was on leave. Samuel had mentioned him in letters often, and the lieutenant would send me words for my dictionary through my brother. I had come to consider him a friend."

Crossing his arms over his chest, Jeremy saw the stiffness of her back, heard the unsteadiness of her voice. Her sense of betrayal was evident in every line of her body. "But he was not."

"He seemed to be, at first." She turned halfway toward Jeremy, putting her in profile. "He was gentlemanly and courteous and said lovely things that made my heart go pitter-patter." A chill froze her voice. "I was so stupid."

He wanted to jump up and go hold her. Out of sheer self-preservation, he stayed seated. "It isn't stupid to take someone at their word. Scoundrels are convincing liars."

He waited for her to make one of her usual observations about how he ought to know, being a scoundrel himself. When she didn't, it tightened his chest the same way her words had earlier.

But you have *a heart!*

God, he hoped she was wrong. Hearts got trampled on. He'd been through enough pain without the crushing agony of a broken heart. Yet he didn't want her thinking him a scoundrel, either. As usual, he wanted to have his cake and eat it, too.

Exactly like Samuel and the lieutenant. He winced. "Besides, your brother vouched for him. And you probably trusted your brother."

"At that point, I was still naïve enough that I did. Though truthfully, I don't think he realized Lieutenant Ruston's real motives."

Jeremy kept his doubts about that to himself.

"Nor can I blame my brother for my weakness for handsome men." She shot Jeremy a rueful glance. "In his navy uniform, Lieutenant Ruston fairly blinded a silly young girl like me."

"I can't imagine that you were any more a silly girl then than you are now."

A furrow appeared between her eyebrows. "Oh, but I clearly was, or I'd have known better than to believe his flatteries. I should have been on my guard from the moment he called me 'a delicate flower.' I haven't been delicate from the day I was born."

Out of nowhere, he remembered what she'd said the day Knightford had shown up: *God forbid I look like anything but a delicate flower for my portrait.*

Like Shakespeare's famous heroine, the lady clearly protested too much. Ruston had succeeded with her because he'd found her weakness—her secret desire to be considered as dainty and delicate as other English ladies. That was why she'd initially chosen such boring clothes for her portrait, why she'd melted when she thought Jeremy had made her look pretty in his first sketch.

She might be fierce and bold, but even Yvette desperately wanted to be seen as feminine. Unfortunately, in her society the feminine ideal was dainty and delicate. It made him want to shake her, then kiss her until she was left in no doubt about her femininity.

He chose his words carefully. "You aren't remotely delicate, that's true." When her gaze shot to him, vulnerable, uncertain, he added softly, "Because delicate things break. They don't withstand the blows of life. You are made of stronger stuff, made to persevere, and thank God for it. The world needs more women like you."

Hannah had been delicately made. Perhaps that was one reason he'd always found it so difficult to be close to her. Even though she possessed ample strength of character and conviction, he'd always been afraid he might hurt her physically somehow.

Odd how he never feared hurting Yvette physically. What he feared was that he wouldn't get enough of her. That he wouldn't assuage his need hard enough, fast enough, deeply enough—

Oh, God, don't think of her like that, or you'll soon be doing more than just sitting on this bed.

He cleared his throat and bent forward, hoping to mask his wayward prick. "And just because the lieutenant proved to be a devil in the end doesn't mean that what he said about your charms was a lie."

A snort was her only answer.

"So," he said, to prod her on, "he pretended to be your friend."

"And more." She played with the ties of her wrapper. "He persuaded me to go with him unchaperoned on long walks through the woods. He persuaded me to let him steal a kiss here and there."

Jeremy's arousal vanished, replaced by a jealous anger that he dared not show—that he didn't even approve of, for God's sake. "More than one kiss, then," he said, hoping he sounded nonchalant.

"Yes. Toward the end of his stay, he mentioned marriage. I told him I'd be honored to marry him, and I would wait for him to ask permission of my father in London." With her head bent, her hair veiled her face, but he could hear the consternation in her voice. "That's when he became . . . a bit strange."

"Strange?"

"He said that given his lack of connections, he knew my father would never approve a marriage. So it was best that we take matters into our own hands and elope."

"And you told him to jump off the nearest cliff, I hope," Jeremy growled.

She shot him an exasperated look. "Have you forgotten that I fancied myself in love? At that point I was incapable of cold-blooded logic. When I was with him, his proposal seemed perfectly acceptable. The problem was, when I was away from him—"

"You came to your senses."

"Somewhat." She shook her head. "The funny thing is that Papa probably wouldn't have stood in the way if Lieutenant Ruston had gone the usual route to marriage. By that point he'd begun to realize that I wouldn't easily find a husband. I'm sure he would have considered a naval lieutenant to be perfectly acceptable."

Jeremy mused on that. "Perhaps your father would have. But I'm sure Blakeborough would have had a say in it, and *he* would have put his foot down. He would have had the man's prospects investigated, and when he found what the lieutenant was apparently trying to hide, your brother would have put a quick end to that courtship."

"Do you really think so?" she asked wistfully.

"I do. And apparently so did the lieutenant, which is why he pressed the elopement."

"I suppose." She fell into a long silence, clearly musing over this new way of looking at things.

"In any case, you obviously didn't elope." *That* would have gotten out somehow. Elopements were hard to keep secret.

"No, but not for any lack of his trying." She let out an enormous sigh. "When I expressed concern over the idea of running away together, the lieutenant became more, shall we say, aggressive physically."

Jeremy rose, his blood roaring in his ears once more. "What does that mean, exactly?"

His temper must have showed in his voice, for she cast him a startled look. "Not what you're clearly thinking, and nothing even as devilish as what you did. I always squelched his attempts to . . . er . . . caress me." She added archly, "He wasn't as sly at it as you are. Or as good."

Out of habit, he said flippantly, "No one is."

She raised an eyebrow. "Don't play the rogue with me, Jeremy. I know you better now."

So she did. "You still haven't told me how he managed to blackmail you."

"Oh yes. The truly embarrassing part." A blush rose up her neck to her cheeks. "Remember, I truly believed he respected me and would never do anything beyond kissing."

His heart began to pound. "But he did."

"Sort of. But it was my fault. On his last full day with us, I didn't protest as I should have when he pulled the door of the music room nearly closed and sat down beside me to kiss me."

"It was *not* your fault. He knew what he planned. You did not."

She rubbed her arms. "But I was also desperate to be alone with him. I knew I wouldn't see him again for some time. And he'd already told me he intended to consult with Edwin about our marriage after dinner, and then go on to London to speak to Papa."

"In other words, he said whatever it took to put your guard down so he could attempt to compromise you."

"I suppose you could look at it that way, yes."

"That is *not* the act of an honorable man. At least I warned you what I wanted from you, and gave you the chance to refuse before I even touched you."

A softness touched her face. "You did, indeed."

"So what exactly did Ruston do?"

"He . . . slid his hands up my calves beneath my skirts . . . and I let him." Her gaze turned steely. "When he got to my garters and I protested his actions, he untied one and slipped it into his pocket, saying that surely I wouldn't mind if he kept a token of my affection for all his lonely nights without me.

I was still sitting there with his hand on my stocking, wavering on whether to ask for my garter back, when we were discovered."

"By Edwin."

"Actually, no. Although I later learned that the lieutenant *had* arranged for Edwin to meet us in the music room, my brother had been delayed by some estate business. So we were discovered by the footman who came to inform him of Edwin's delay."

"That was a stroke of luck."

She smiled wanly. "Not exactly. The footman was newly hired. I couldn't count on him to keep silent, though I asked him to. His arrival spooked me so that I fled, thus thwarting the lieutenant's scheme to have Edwin find us together doing something naughty. Only later did I remember that the lieutenant still had my garter."

Her voice hardened. "And my noble swain used it to his advantage. Before dinner, he drew me aside and said that if I didn't meet him secretly that very night and elope, he would go to Edwin with the garter, demand that my brother call forth the footman to corroborate his story, and then force Edwin and Papa to accept the match by implying that the lieutenant and I . . . that we . . ."

Jeremy bit back a vile oath. He *would* hunt Ruston down, by God, and he *would* lop off the bastard's horn. Damned devious whoreson.

She shuddered. "It was an excellent plan. If a gentleman has had access to a woman's garter, people assume he's had access to . . . well, you know. It put me in the most dreadful quandary. Neither Papa nor Edwin would have called his bluff, knowing that the lieutenant could destroy my reputation. Either way, the lieutenant would gain my hand in marriage."

Her voice caught. "But in the latter case, my family would believe the worst of me."

The thickness in Jeremy's throat threatened to choke him. "So what did you do?"

"I begged him to show himself the gentleman I thought him to be and just ask Papa for my hand as he'd originally intended. I was still clinging to the hope that he really did love me. If he had gone through everything properly even then, I probably would have married him."

"And been miserable for it."

"No doubt." She scowled. "But as you say, he must have known that an investigation would turn up something to scotch any wedding, because my pleas only made him protest his great love for me and hold fast to his plans. So when I couldn't convince him to relent, I went to Samuel with my plight. The lieutenant was his friend, after all."

"Ah, yes." Once again, Jeremy wondered about Samuel's motives for bringing home such a snake in the grass. But perhaps Samuel *hadn't* known what his friend was capable of.

Right. And pebbles turned into pearls when the moon was high, too. "So Samuel saved you. How, exactly?"

"At first he said he didn't think it could be done. He had no idea where his friend might keep the garter, or if the footman could be silenced." She shook her head. "It was a hopeless case."

"Yet he somehow managed it," Jeremy said dryly.

She flashed him a bright smile. "He did. Shortly before the time I was to meet with the lieutenant or else be humiliated before my brother, Samuel turned up in my bedchamber with the garter in hand and a promise he'd extracted from the footman not to say anything to anyone."

"Did your brother say how he accomplished this miracle?" The story grew more suspicious by the moment. Jeremy was almost certain something else had occurred to put an end to Ruston's scheme.

"He told me he had prevailed upon Ruston to behave like a gentleman, and that the man had come to his senses and given back the garter before Samuel sent him packing."

"And you believed that?"

Her face clouded over. "Well, no. Especially not after I heard through gossip a short while later that the lieutenant had eloped with some other heiress. Clearly he was a rogue through and through. And to my knowledge, fortune-hunting rogues don't have consciences."

"Not generally, no."

"But I never heard a word about it, so Samuel must have done something. I suspect he threatened to call the man out."

Jeremy suspected something else. "How do you know Blakeborough had no hand in it?"

"Edwin? He would have said something to me, I'm sure. At the very least, he would have plagued me about it for all eternity."

"Perhaps." It was odd, though. Something rang false in her recitation of events, and given that Samuel's heroic act was the basis for her risking her reputation looking for the man's by-blow, it would be good to know the truth.

But he could think of no way to find it out without damaging her reputation.

There was something else he wanted to know, too. "Tell me, Yvette, if Samuel hadn't successfully interceded on your behalf, what decision would you have made? Would you have eloped? Or taken your chances with your father?"

"I certainly wouldn't have eloped. At least if I called the lieutenant's bluff and he went to Edwin first, there was *some* hope that Edwin might find a way out of it, be able to meet the man's price or something before Papa heard of it. By that point, I would have taken any chance to prevent having to join myself forever to a man who I began to fear only wanted me for my money."

"You can't be sure that was the only reason Ruston wanted you."

She eyed him askance. "I haven't had any better offers of marriage in my nearly seven years on the marriage mart. There's been lots of flirting, but very little courting by respectable gentlemen who weren't after my fortune. It doesn't exactly speak well for my ability to attract suitors. Why, even you would rather run off than risk being trapped in a marriage with me."

His throat tightened. "It's not like that."

Crossing her arms over her chest, she stared him down. "Then why are you packing a trunk and fleeing in the dead of night?"

"I'm trying to protect you."

"From what? A life of ruin?"

"Or marriage to a selfish fellow who can't be what you need."

She stared mulishly at him. "It couldn't be worse than a life of lonely spinsterhood."

"You'd be surprised." He stayed rooted in place, afraid that if he walked any closer, he would abandon all caution and seize her as his. "You *will* find someone one day, and you'll be glad that I left."

"No. I shall never be glad of that."

The husky denial pierced his chest. "Ah, but you will. Just as you eventually came to be relieved that you didn't find yourself trapped in a marriage with Ruston."

Anger flushed her cheeks as she closed the distance between them, coming near enough that he could smell her sweet scent and see the trembling of her throat.

She thrust her face up to his. "Don't compare yourself to him. You aren't remotely alike."

"No? I took advantage of you, as he did."

"Hardly. I made my choice at every juncture. You gave me full warning of your intentions, and I accepted your advances. And whenever I protested, you let me go. You didn't try to wheedle further or come back later to blackmail me with my own wantonness." She grabbed his arms. "So don't tell me you and he are the same. You are *nothing* like him. He wanted only my money, whereas you—"

"Want only your body." If it took being cruel to make her stop this madness while he could still think, then he would be cruel.

But his words didn't have the intended effect.

"Really?" Her eyes gleamed at him in the lamplight. "Then why are you running away to avoid sharing a bed with me?"

With *sharing a bed* ringing in his ears, he scowled at her. "Damn it, you have no idea what you're about."

"I know that you desire me for my body *and* more, which isn't something I've had with any other man." Her breathing quickened. "Do you realize how rare it is for a woman to find someone who understands her, who accepts her as she is?" With a heartbreaking catch in her voice, she murmured, "Don't leave. I can't bear it."

Neither could he. "It doesn't matter." He pulled free of her grip. "Without me, you have a future."

"As what? Edwin's hostess? Clarissa's friend?"

"You're young still."

"As are you!" She fisted her hands at her sides. "Do you really expect me to believe that you're perfectly happy being alone, flitting from place to place, never settling, never knowing the joy of steady companionship?"

That she had delved beneath everything to find the hard knot of loneliness inside him struck terror in his soul. "Not happy, no, but content. It's better than making another wife miserable."

Frustration lit her features. "Then don't marry me. Give me what we both want. You want me in your bed, and I want one blessed night with a man who likes what he sees when he looks at me, who doesn't think me shrewish or ungainly or too bold."

Thunderation. "You're being too bold now," he pointed out, though it fired his blood as nothing else could.

She moved so close that her mouth was a breath from his. "That's what happens when a woman craves fire and life and the thrill of the night for too long. She gets tired of waiting for it to come to her, and she goes out to grab it for herself. I've followed the rules my whole life, and what has it gained me? For once, I want to know what I'm missing. And you're the only man I want to show me."

The words stiffened his prick to pain. "If I show you any more than I have, I'll ruin you."

"I know. And I don't care."

He caught her head in his hands, needing to touch her, if only to shake some sense into her. "You'll care a great deal if you find yourself big with my child."

Though that seemed to give her pause, she didn't pull away. "It's a risk I'm willing to take."

"But not one *I'm* willing to take. I won't leave you with a babe on the way. Which means I'll have to marry you, and I—"

"Don't want to marry, yes, I know." She raised an eyebrow. "So much for your claim to selfishness. A selfish man wouldn't care if he ruined me. A selfish man wouldn't care if I were left enceinte."

"You don't know a damned thing about what a selfish man wants."

It was time to demonstrate exactly how unwise this was. He hauled her against his fully aroused body. "You want to see what a selfish man does when confronted with a woman he desires? Fine. I'll show you." Then he took her mouth with all the savage hunger roiling up inside him.

He wasn't gentle or tender or kind. He manacled

her to him with one arm while gripping her chin with the other, so he could plunder and devour to his heart's content. He gave her no time to breathe, allowed her no space to retreat.

But she didn't seem to want to retreat. She rose to his rough kiss like an eagle to the sky. It was heaven.

It was hell.

He told himself that once she saw the fierceness of his need, she would balk. Then when she withdrew, he'd finally be able to let her go, before he took what he wanted.

The trouble was, he wanted so very much. He wanted her mouth opening and her clothes opening and her lush body opening to let his raging prick inside . . .

With a growl, he tore off her wrapper and tossed it aside, then filled his hands with her breasts. As long as she kept her night rail on, he might be safe. And he could touch and caress and still enjoy some part of her.

But then she uttered a soft mew of satisfaction that sent his blood into wild riot, and she began working to loosen *his* clothes, too. God help him. He would destroy every painting he'd ever created just to have her hands on his naked body.

Before he could even make a conscious choice, he was shedding his coat and waistcoat and helping her untie his cravat.

Angry with himself for his easy acquiescence, he stopped her when she reached for the buttons of his shirt. "You first," he ordered. "Take off your night rail."

If there was one thing his Juno didn't like, it was being ordered about.

So the minute she began to unbutton her frilly linen gown, he groaned. She wasn't retreating or balking, damn it.

At least he would get to see those lovely full breasts hanging free, so one day he could paint them from memory and have them forever, just for him. Besides, surely she still had on her drawers and he would still be safe.

Although *she* wouldn't, if anyone stumbled in on them.

Keeping his eyes on her shaky fingers and the flesh exposed with each undone button, he strode to the main door into the hall and latched it, then leaned back against it to watch her. And to steady himself. Because just the sight of her unfastening her clothing was getting him hard as a pike.

By the time she finished, her cheeks were the pink of peonies. But being the stubborn minx she was, she soldiered on, pulling the night rail off over her head and dropping it on the floor.

She wore no drawers beneath it. She wore nothing at all.

His pulse jumped into a stampede.

Almighty God in heaven, never had he seen a woman with such curves. It wasn't just her ample breasts with their velvety, carmine-tinged nipples, though he did enjoy those. It was also the lush hips that he couldn't wait to grab hold of and the creamy thighs that would put Titian's Venuses to shame. It was the thick thatch of umber curls that hid the delicate flesh he'd tasted only nights ago.

When he saw the beauty of her nude form, more enticing than that of any model he'd ever painted, he grew even more desperate to show her how dangerous this was, how dangerous *he* was. He had to bring her to her senses before he lost control entirely. He must drag her down into the depths with him, as he'd nearly done at the brothel, and show her just how coarse he could be. That ought to send her running for the door before she lost her virtue.

And if it didn't?

Then God help them both.

Nineteen

If there'd been any doubt in Yvette's mind that Jeremy wanted her in his bed, it was laid to rest. His eyes smoldered with an unholy heat that made her yearn and burn and want things she'd never dreamed she could have.

She'd expected to feel shy in front of him, even embarrassed. But what woman in her right mind could feel ashamed when the man whose touch she craved was looking at her like *that*?

And sporting such a large bulge in his trousers. She'd heard it was considered good for a man to be . . . prominent there. Though she didn't understand why, she was certainly willing to find out.

"I had it wrong," he said in a low growl, his gaze eating her alive. "You're not Juno—you're Circe, the witch who turns men into beasts."

Circe, the seductress. Yvette rather liked that.

Trying out her seduction skills, she cast him what she hoped was an alluring smile. "Are you turning into a beast?"

"See for yourself." Pushing away from the door, he unbuttoned his shirt and dragged it off. As he went to work on his trouser buttons, she let her eyes feast on the glory of his bare chest.

As with every other aspect of his appearance, it would put a Greek god's to shame. It was chiseled and broad, with a dusting of dark blond hair that tempted her gaze lower to where his lean stomach looked firm enough to sustain a pile of bricks, and his hips . . .

Well. No woman in her right mind would complain about that man's hips.

Then he slid off his trousers and drawers in one fluid motion, and her every sense went on high alert. *Oh my word.*

The rod of flesh rising from a bed of bronze curls was monstrous. No wonder the slang dictionaries jocularly called it a "yard"; it was massive. She couldn't *imagine* taking it inside her, no matter how long it actually measured.

Fighting for calm, she said, "I assume that sculptors are terrible students of anatomy."

"What?" he asked, clearly startled.

"On statues, the men's privates are . . . well . . . small and demure."

"Demure." He uttered a choked laugh. "That's because the men aren't aroused, sweetheart. An aroused man looks very different from a man with his prick at rest."

Prick. Such a vulgar word. Even Grose's entry for it spelled it with dashes.

"Your . . . er . . ."

"Prick," he supplied in a coarse voice. "Surely that

shows up in your cant dictionaries. You can't even say the word, can you?"

He was daring her, and she never backed away from a dare. "Of course I can say it." She tore her gaze from its impressive size to look him in the eye. "Your *prick* is clearly not at rest."

Somehow, just speaking the naughty word aloud excited her, made her want to be wicked and wanton and all the things a lady should never be.

As if he could tell, his face grew shadowed, and he said, with a hitch in his voice, "Come here, Circe. I'm eager to feel your hands on my prick."

She moved closer. "I can see how eager you are."

Both of his eyebrows shot high. "Clearly you spent entirely too much time at the brothel the other night."

"I didn't spend enough, or I'd know where exactly to put my hands."

Fire leapt in his features. "Anywhere you damned well please. Because I intend to do the same."

But when he reached for her, she stepped back. "Not yet. You've had several chances to caress me already, and I've had none, so I need a few moments to explore before—"

"I start mauling you?" he finished, his guttural tone thrumming her senses.

"You start turning me into mush. You owe me that."

Some unreadable emotion gleamed in the gaze that bore into hers. "I suppose I do." He let his arms fall to his sides. "Go ahead then, if you feel you have to . . . have to . . ."

He stuttered to a halt as she put her hands on his

chest, eager to touch, stroke . . . enjoy. He was so firm, so supple. So deliciously hers. She thumbed the flat nipples, echoes of her own, and was delighted by his sharp, indrawn breath. It encouraged her to investigate further, to sweep her fingers over his flexing muscles, to slide her hands over his abdomen.

"Yes," he hissed, "lower. Touch my prick, damn it."

The harsh command made something carnal uncurl in her belly. Any other man telling her what to do would have sparked her ire, but this was Jeremy. Everything he said or did seemed to arouse her.

She closed her hand about his jutting flesh.

"Oh, God," he breathed, then barked, "Grip it tight. Stroke it up and down." When she did as he bade, he growled, "Like that, yes." Then he caught her about the waist. "I've waited long enough for my turn."

That was all the warning she got before he slid a hand between her thighs. She let out a squeak of surprise, then a moan as his fingers delved through her damp curls to find the tight kernel of flesh that was so eager for his caress. And when he began to rub it, deftly, roughly, she shuddered with the thrill of it.

Oh my *Lord*. He did that quite well. It was so sensual, so . . . oh, heavenly day!

"God, you feel like silk," he said, as if the words were torn from him. "I can never show in a painting how something feels. I'd give anything to capture the slick velvet of your skin. Nothing is as soft as you are here."

Breathing heavily now, she gave his prick a long, sensuous pull. "And nothing is as hard as you are here."

Heat flared in his face. "Not for long, if you keep doing that."

Before she could wonder what he meant he was pulling her toward the bed, where he tumbled her down upon it with little ceremony. As she rolled onto her back, he stretched out beside her and threw one leg over hers as if to trap her.

He braced himself up on one elbow, his eyes raking her body shamelessly. "You would drive a man into Bedlam." He cupped a breast, then pinched the nipple erect. "These lovelies of yours make me insane."

The compliment made her arch them up toward him, which had him sliding down to take them in his mouth in turn. As he sucked and teased, she drank up every sensation his lashing tongue sent through her body. Who was being driven to Bedlam now?

He smoothed his hand down her abdomen, past her navel, and then settled it between her thighs. Craving a firmer touch, she squirmed against it. But when he thrust a finger deep inside her it startled her, and instinctively she jerked her legs together.

He withdrew his finger at once and lifted his head from her breasts. "Having second thoughts, are you?"

Triumph sounded in his voice. But why? Then it dawned on her. The devil was deliberately trying to demonstrate how "selfish" he was.

She wouldn't let him get away with that. "No second thoughts." Forcing herself to relax, she let her legs fall open. "Just taken by surprise."

He stared at her. "You really are a wanton, aren't you?"

If he'd intended to wound her with the words, he shouldn't have said them in such a husky voice. Determined to make her point, she seized his rampant prick. "And you really are a scoundrel. What of it?"

With a shuddering breath, he closed his eyes, though he didn't pull his prick from her hand. "Damn it, Yvette, you know this is wrong."

She took that for an admission of what he'd been trying to do. "It doesn't feel wrong to me." She drew his hand back to the spot between her legs that ached for him. "It feels marvelous, actually."

His eyes shot open, hot and hungry. "I give up." This time when he slid his finger inside her, it was slow and smooth and utterly delicious. "You win."

"Oh?" She shimmied beneath the clever stroking of his finger. "What do I . . . win?"

"Probably a lifetime of misery." He nipped her earlobe. "But I don't care anymore. I need to be inside you . . . I need . . . I need . . ."

"I know." She wrapped her arms about his neck. "So do I."

He uttered a choked laugh. And that's when the seduction truly began. His hands were all over her; her mouth was all over him. She wanted to taste him, smell him, absorb him into her skin. She'd never imagined it could be like this with a man, so profound, so exhilarating.

She no longer even cared if he married her. She just wanted to experience him in all his glory. Just once.

Then, with a shock, she realized that his . . . prick . . . was pressing inside her. Her surprise must have shown on her face, for he drew back with a hooded expression. "I can stop if you want. Even now."

She stared into his eyes and saw beneath the carefully manufactured exterior to the suffering man. The one who didn't believe he had anything to offer. She knew better.

Brushing her lips over his, she whispered, "Don't stop. Never stop."

And with a groan of pure relief, he buried himself inside her.

She tensed. There was a burning sensation and a feeling of fullness that wasn't exactly pleasant. He hesitated, breathing hard, his eyes dark and fathomless in the dim light of the dying fire as he waited. For what, she wasn't sure.

Until he murmured, "Relax. It will be all right if you relax."

That remained to be seen. "Have you ever deflowered a virgin?"

He hesitated. "No."

"Wonderful," she grumbled. "My innocence is being taken by a novice."

With a fractured laugh, he nuzzled her forehead. "A bit better than a novice, I should hope. And regardless of your state of innocence, relaxing always improves matters."

No harm in trying. She forced herself to loosen her muscles and allow him to seat himself more fully inside her.

"Better?" he asked.

"A little." A very little. The pressure was uncomfortable and the position awkward. But at least it hadn't hurt as much as she'd been told to expect.

"I'll make it better. I swear it, my Juno."

"I thought I was Circe now."

One corner of his mouth curved up. "You're both." His gaze bored into her. "And both are mine."

She might have protested the sheer possessiveness of that statement if he hadn't begun to move, in and out, with stealthy strokes that made her squirm beneath him, wanting to find some more comfortable position.

This was so very . . . personal. His skin rubbed hers everywhere. His harsh breaths surrounded her. His mouth played with her ear. "My sweet . . . tight . . . Circe . . ." he whispered as he slid into her like a bold Odysseus. "You are . . . you are my . . ."

"Ladybird?" she prodded, to take her mind off the intrusion of his flesh into a place it should never have gone.

"My muse." Sweat beaded up on his forehead. "My muse and thus my soul."

The words, so close to a declaration of love, melted her, making her cling to him and press a kiss into his shoulder. Then he tugged her knees up about those masterful hips of his, and the shift in position made him thrum the part of her that had only somewhat been engaged up till now, and she forgot what he'd said.

She forgot her name, her place, her rank. All she knew was the thundering glory of Jeremy driving in and out of her in the most intimate act she could have imagined. The burning became a lovely warmth, and the pressure became wonderful, and her heart began to pound in time to his thrusts.

His body took command of hers like a general

stealing a march on Napoleon, and she was truly conquered. He made her feel like a woman. *His* woman.

"Ah, sweetheart," he choked out, "my fantasies of you . . . fell short of the . . . mark. You feel like . . . This feels like . . ."

"A dream," she whispered.

"Yes. A dream."

One where he was hers forever. Where they could do this forever. Where he could love her forever.

Love her? She feared that would never be. If he'd balked at marrying her unless he was forced into it, then . . .

No, she wouldn't dwell on that. For the moment, she would live in this dream of having him over her, around her, *with* her. Besides, he'd called her his "soul." That meant something, didn't it?

Now the pleasure humming down low had started to keen, then wail inside her, echoing through the hall of her body, which had felt silent and lonely for so . . . very . . . long. A decadent music now filled her, spurred her, made her reach for something just . . . beyond . . .

Yes! *There!*

An ecstatic cry tore from her, provoking him into a lunge so deep, she fancied she could feel it in *her* soul. And as he gave a throttled groan and spilled himself inside her, she held him fiercely close and prayed to never wake up.

Because once the dream ended, she feared what might happen to her heart.

Twenty

As Jeremy descended to earth and the explosion in his brain subsided, he collapsed atop Yvette. His heart beat a wild rhythm in his ears, and his blood was on fire.

It had been so good, better than he'd ever dreamed it could be. It felt so right to be with her that it terrified him. Because he ought to be raging against the madness that had possessed him. He ought to be chiding himself for letting his iron control slip.

But he couldn't. It had brought him to this point, this woman. A woman he still wanted. A woman he feared he'd never stop wanting.

"Jeremy?" she whispered.

"Yes, sweetheart?" He brushed his lips over her hair, reveling in its satiny texture and flowery scent.

"You're . . . rather heavy. I'm having trouble breathing."

He rolled off her with a laugh, an echo of the giddy joy he'd known in his childhood before everything had gone to shit. She'd brought him that, too. "Sorry, didn't mean to smother you." He tugged her into his arms. "I wanted you to feel 'the little death,' not the big one."

She snuggled close. "What's the little death?"

He drew back. "Don't tell me that the Queen of Cant has never heard of *la petite mort*."

"I only know English cant, not French," she said with a pretty pout.

"Well, *la petite mort* is what you and I just experienced—that culmination of our . . . activities." He thumbed through his limited store of street cant gained from Damber, and added, "Perhaps you know it better as the term 'to come.'"

She blinked. "Oh! I have heard of that. I always wondered what the definition meant, but the one time I asked a lexicographer, he blushed and ran out of the room, so I never asked again."

Jeremy threw his head back against the pillow and laughed heartily. "I would dearly love to have seen you questioning a man about *that*."

"Stay around, and you may get to see it again," she said lightly.

Just like that, everything turned more serious. Nothing like blunt honesty to sober a man up.

He shifted to face her. "I fully intend to stay around. Now that I've taken your innocence, I intend to marry you."

"That's not what I meant," she said hastily. "I told you I don't expect that." She cupped his cheek. "I just don't want you to leave quite yet. Stay. Finish your paintings." Her voice turned halting, ragged. "And then, when you're ready to go—"

"I won't leave you ruined. It's unacceptable."

A frown knit her brow as she pushed up onto one elbow. "And it's unacceptable to me to have a half-hearted husband."

"I suppose you're waiting for an ardent profession of my love," he said, unable to keep the bitter note from his voice.

Something flickered deep in her gaze. Anger? Disappointment? He wasn't sure, since it vanished almost as soon as it appeared. "I'm not waiting for anything from you," she said. "You've told me often enough that you have no intention of taking a wife—a second wife, that is—and I took you at your word."

Her seemingly blithe disregard for what he'd viewed as a certainty unsettled him. "I also said that if I ruined you I knew I'd have to marry you. Did you think I lied?"

"Of course not. But I made it quite clear that you didn't have to, and I assumed that you accepted what I said. Because I meant it. I still do."

This was starting to annoy him. "Yvette—"

"Has it occurred to you that you aren't the only one who can be selfish?" She left the bed to pull on her night rail, her back to him. "That perhaps I merely wanted to experience pleasure at your expense?"

That had *not* occurred to him. It was preposterous. The blood smearing his prick showed that, for God's sake. They were lucky it hadn't been enough to stain the covers, but that didn't change the reality: She'd been a virgin. And virgins didn't blithely go about seducing men for pleasure.

Did they?

Apparently he'd hesitated too long, which she took as an answer to her question. "So you see, it's settled. No one need marry anyone. You'll remain here to complete your paintings, and then—"

"Yvette. Nothing is settled. It's true that I wouldn't have chosen to marry, but now we must. It's as simple as that."

"It is not!" She whirled on him. "If we marry, it will be because we *want* to, not because you feel duty-bound to. I won't be part of your repeating what happened twelve years ago."

"You won't be," he said tightly. "It's an entirely different situation. This time I'm secure in my profession. This time I'm not giving up any plans for you."

"Oh? So you will continue going to brothels for your models?"

He blinked. "Well . . . obviously that would have to end. But—"

"And you intend to stop doing whatever you please whenever you want because you now have a wife whose needs must also be considered?"

Even though Yvette was unaware of all the circumstances, her remark was so uncomfortably close to what had happened with Hannah that it made him scowl. "I know how to be a husband, damn you. Just because I act like a bachelor doesn't mean I don't realize—"

A knock came at the door into the hall. They both froze.

"Who the devil is *that*?" Panic in her face, she searched for her wrapper. "Oh, heavenly day, could Edwin have figured out that I'm in here?"

"It's probably Damber," he murmured. "The

damned lad got done sooner downstairs than I thought. He can wait."

"You can't be sure it's him." She dragged on her wrapper. "Even if it is, you have to get dressed or he'll suspect something."

"He'll suspect something when he finds you in here in your nightclothes," he grumbled, but got out of bed to pull on his drawers and trousers.

A knock sounded again, this time louder. "Master?" came Damber's voice through the door. "I'm done packing up downstairs."

The infernal fool spoke in what he thought was a low volume, but a low volume in the streets where Damber had grown up was a high volume in the quiet halls of Stoke Towers. And Blakeborough's room was on the same floor, damn it.

"I'm coming," he growled at the door.

He turned to Yvette, only to find her heading for the servants' door. "Wait! We're not done talking about this."

A shutter came down over her face. "There's nothing to talk about. I'll see you tomorrow."

"Damn it, Yvette," he began, but she was already out the door.

He considered going after her, but then Damber would really be suspicious. And since he hadn't secured her hand in marriage yet, he dared not do anything that might compromise her reputation. Given her story about Ruston, Jeremy feared that Edwin trying to force her into marriage would only get her back up and make her refuse outright.

She mustn't refuse to marry him. Even though he would be all wrong for her. Even though she could find better. None of that mattered any longer. He'd taken her innocence, so he *would* marry her.

Muttering a curse, he strode to the door and swung it open. Only after Damber stood there gaping at him did Jeremy remember he was shirtless.

"What are you staring at?" he barked. Standing aside to let the boy pass, he cast a quick glance about the room, but there was no trace of Yvette. Except for a hint of her perfume.

But maybe he was imagining that.

Damber fixed him with an accusing glance. "Why is the bed all mussed?"

Jeremy thought quickly. "I sat down to rest for a moment and fell asleep. I had just roused and was changing my clothes when you knocked. So I'm afraid I haven't gotten any packing done yet."

God, he sounded like an idiot.

"I suppose you want me to do *your* packing, too," Damber grumbled. "It's nearly two a.m. I thought you wanted everything done by now so we could head off first thing."

He couldn't leave now. Everything had changed. "Actually, I've decided to delay my departure a few days."

"What?" Damber crossed his arms over his chest. "After I already packed up the paints and canvases and the—"

"Yes, yes, unpack it all."

"Tonight?"

Jeremy took pity on the lad. "It can wait until morning. But early, mind you. By the time the family is up I want everything back in place, before anyone can wonder what's going on."

"The servants are still going to wonder. They already knew we were leaving. What do you want me to tell *them* is the reason for staying?"

Damn, he'd forgotten that. After he offered for Yvette, which he intended to do first thing in the morning, they might very well speculate about what had happened in the wee hours to change his mind.

He couldn't have anyone gossiping about his future wife. "Tell them I got a good look at the portrait in the light of day and realized I wasn't as far along as I thought."

That would also serve as an excuse for remaining if Yvette turned down his first offer. Because, damn it, he wasn't going to leave here without securing her hand in marriage. If he had to work on that bloody portrait for a month to have time to convince her, then he would.

"So you want I should tell the grooms to stable the curricle?"

"Yes, then you may go on to bed."

"Are you sure?"

Jeremy glanced sharply at him. "Why wouldn't I be sure?"

The hulking fellow shoved his hands in his pockets. "I dunno. You're acting peculiar is all. One minute we're sneaking about the house to pack up and slip away in the dark of night, and the next you're having a nap. Not to mention that the room smells like . . . like . . ." He sniffed.

"Like what?"

"Like you been tupping one of the maids."

Oh, God. Jeremy laughed, hoping it didn't sound

as false to his apprentice as it sounded to him. "Have you ever known me to tup a maid?"

"Well, no. But there's always a first time."

"You're imagining things," Jeremy said irritably. "Now, out with you. I can't go to bed as long as you're lounging about in my room."

Damber sniffed. "Just trying to help. But I'll make myself scarce, I will." He headed out the door, muttering, "I swear, sometimes I think you mad as a hatter. Or p'raps a little . . ."

The boy's mumbling trailed off down the hall. With a roll of his eyes, Jeremy closed the door and headed straight for the brandy flask he kept on his dressing table.

Only a few hours until dawn. No point in going to bed now; he wouldn't get any sleep. Besides, Blakeborough was an early riser, so if Jeremy wanted to catch him and offer for Yvette before she got up, he'd better stay up.

All right, he supposed he should wait until she agreed to marry him. But it wasn't unusual for a suitor to first ask a woman's male guardian for her hand. And it couldn't hurt to get her brother on his side. Especially with Yvette surprisingly reluctant.

Cursing, Jeremy drank from his flask. He *had* handled it badly, damn it. He should have made it sound less as if it were a "duty" and more as if he were in love with her. Though that probably wouldn't have worked. Yvette could read him too well for that. And he would have been lying.

He scowled. Yes, lying. Just because he thought about her too much, wanted her too much . . . craved her too much didn't mean he loved her. Love was about putting someone first. Clearly he didn't know the first thing about that. If he'd loved her, he wouldn't have tumbled her with no heed for the consequences. Or risked her reputation by letting her talk him into taking her to a brothel. Or done any number of the things he'd done in the last few weeks with her.

And clearly she knew he was a bad bargain. She hadn't agreed to marry him, had she? She hadn't made any grand professions of love herself.

I'm not waiting for anything from you. You've told me often enough that you have no intention of taking a wife— a second wife, that is—and I took you at your word.

He winced. He hadn't exactly made it easy for her to say anything. With a flash, he remembered her expression after he'd dictated their need to marry with all the subtlety of an ox.

She'd been hurt. She'd hoped for more, and he'd hurt her.

As guilt clutched at his throat, he took a longer swig from the flask. Damn it, this was why he'd wanted to stay away from her in the first place! He wasn't the right sort of man for her.

Not that it mattered; he had to marry her. No other man would take her after this, or if he did unwittingly, he would make her life hell when he learned the truth. And she deserved to have a decent husband, to have a home of her own and children.

An image leapt into his head, of Yvette happy and content with a babe on her knee. *His* babe on her knee. Some fat and sassy cherub of a girl or a rest- less, sweet-faced boy crawling along the floor to his father . . .

No! He'd been that route before, only to have it all turn to shit in his hands. He wasn't going to throw himself into that dream again.

He would offer marriage because he must, because it was the right thing to do. But he would not indulge his sudden inexplicable urge for a romantic entanglement. That way lay madness.

❦

It was a miracle that Yvette made it back to her room without crying. Once she was there tears boiled out of her, born as much of anger and frustration as of hurt feelings. She resisted the childish urge to tromp about her room and throw things that made a lot of noise. That wouldn't do a bit of good, and it would call attention to her secret activities, besides.

But blast it all, she wanted to scream! Him and his pity proposal. What had she been thinking? Had she really believed that sharing a bed with the blasted man would magically make him swoon with love for her? Say he would die if he couldn't have her?

She dropped onto the bed. Yes. She *had* believed it. Not consciously, of course. But the fierceness of his desire had convinced her that he really cared, that he wanted her for more than just a bed partner.

That he might actually love her.

She snorted. What a fool she was. Hadn't she learned long ago that rogues only wanted to get beneath a woman's skirts?

No, that wasn't fair. A rogue would have taken

her to bed and then said a merry farewell. Jeremy had resisted her, tried to run away from her. And when she hadn't taken no for an answer, he'd made love to her and proposed marriage.

Rogues didn't propose marriage.

She threw herself back on the bed. So now what was she to do? Obviously, if she *did* find herself breeding, she would have to marry him. But barring that possibility, she didn't want a husband who saw marriage to her as a supreme sacrifice. Though neither did she want to be left ruined and alone.

She *hated* conundrums. Especially the kind that involved a certain aloof artist who became a pillar of fire whenever he touched her or kissed her or bedded her.

A sigh wafted out of her. Every part of her ached, yet she would do it again in a heartbeat—not just for the amazing pleasure at the end, but for the wonderful feeling of closeness she'd felt with him.

The feeling had been building for days, but it had blossomed into something more when he'd listened to her tale about the lieutenant without criticizing her behavior. He'd been irate on her behalf, ready to slay dragons and lop off horns for her.

She sat up. Yes, he had been, hadn't he? Not exactly the behavior of a dispassionate admirer of her body. Perhaps the dratted idiot really *did* have feelings for her. Perhaps he even really wanted to marry her.

Or perhaps she was spinning dreams again that could never come true.

Well, if something more than a guilty conscience and a rampant prick was guiding his determination to marry her, he'd have to tell her. Or show her. Or somehow reassure her that wedding him wouldn't be a huge mistake.

Because she wasn't about to risk marrying a man who could make her life a misery. She'd rather be ruined and alone than suffer that.

Twenty-One

"You want to *what?*"

Standing in the midst of Blakeborough's study the next morning, Jeremy winced at the man's incredulous tone. Perhaps he shouldn't have sprung the matter so abruptly, but it was too late to go back now. "I said, I want to marry Yvette. If she'll have me."

For the first time since Jeremy had met him, the earl looked completely confounded. "Marry her. You want to marry my sister." Blakeborough excelled at stating the obvious.

"Surely you've noticed that she and I get along very well."

The earl, who'd taken a seat behind his desk when they'd first entered, now leaned forward to stare at him over it. "Yes, but well enough to *marry*? Have you even asked her?"

Thunderation. He could hardly admit he'd asked her more than once after he'd made love to her like a randy hound with no self-control. Or an ounce of sense.

"Not exactly." Under the circumstances, he figured it was all right to shade the truth. "We've discussed the idea, but—"

"Have you? That comes as a surprise." Blakeborough cast him a considering glance. "Is that why you've been gone these past few days? Trying to drum up the courage to ask her for her hand?"

Jeremy scowled. "Certainly not."

"Hoping that absence would make her heart grow fonder, and she would agree to your proposal immediately upon your return?"

"Not that either," he grumbled. "Damn it, Blakeborough, will you accept my offer or not? Assuming that she does, too."

The earl snorted. "That's an enormous assumption, old chap. She's turned down three other suitors before you."

"But I thought she'd never had . . ."

Her words last night came to him. *I haven't had any decent offers of marriage . . . very little courting by respectable gentlemen who weren't after my fortune.*

Damn her. She'd *had* offers, just not "decent" ones from "respectable gentlemen." His blood ran cold. What kind of proposals had she had?

"Were these other offers viable?" Jeremy asked.

"They were from gentlemen of good family and connections, if that's what you mean."

"That is *not* what I mean, and you know it."

Blakeborough sighed. "Then no. Not viable. I probably would have refused them myself if matters had gone that far." His tone hardened. "No fortune hunter or roué with a roving eye is going to marry *my* sister."

Jeremy gritted his teeth. "I do hope you're not including me in that description."

"Should I?"

Bad enough he'd had to bare his soul to Yvette. Must he do it to Blakeborough, too? "No. I have a substantial fortune of my own, and I don't have a roving eye."

"Just a penchant for frequenting brothels."

"Only because I use the women as models for my paintings." That much he felt safe in revealing.

It gave him the satisfaction of seeing the earl flummoxed again. "Truly?"

"Yes. Ask Mrs. Beard herself if you don't believe me."

Blakeborough stiffened. "I hardly think that will be necessary. Although if I learn you're lying to me, I will put an end to any talk of marriage at once, no matter what Yvette thinks about it."

That gave Jeremy pause. "And have you done that before, put an end to talk of marriage heedless of her wishes? Or perhaps to save her from a particularly nasty suitor?"

The sudden guilty flush in the earl's cheeks gave him away. "I have no idea what you're talking about."

"The hell you don't. You knew about Ruston, didn't you? You're the one who sent him packing."

Blakeborough jumped up in alarm. "How do *you* know of Ruston?"

"She told me."

With a stunned look, the earl sank back into his chair. "Yvette told you about Ruston."

"As I said, we get along very well."

"It must be extremely well if she told you about

that arse. I'm not sure even Knightford is aware of what Ruston attempted."

That rather pleased Jeremy.

Blakeborough steepled his fingers in front of him. "What exactly did she tell you?"

"Everything, I think." Jeremy eyed the man nervously. "Why, what do *you* know?"

"More than she realizes."

"Aha, I was right! I told her you must have had a hand in putting an end to the ass's blackmail, but she didn't believe me."

"No, she wouldn't—not with the way things have always been between us." Blakeborough's expression darkened. "My sister sees me as the enforcer of rules, the petty dictator of Stoke Towers. She doesn't understand that, thanks to our absent father and rogue of a brother, *someone* had to be in charge. And it fell to me."

"She does realize that."

"I don't think so, or she would come to me with these things. She's afraid I might restrict her freedom too much. Afraid of what I might do." The earl's voice turned regretful. "She's afraid of *me*."

"She's not afraid of you. She's afraid of disappointing you. It's not the same."

"She could *never* disappoint me."

The fierce certainty in those words took Jeremy by surprise. He'd never seen Blakeborough show that much depth of feeling. "Then tell her that. She needs to hear it. For that matter, tell her the truth about your part in saving her from Ruston. Because right now, she thinks Samuel was her savior." *And that's why she's doing fool things like going to brothels looking for your nephew.*

The earl cast him a pained glance. "Better that she think him her savior than that she know the truth. It would destroy her. They were close in their youth, so if she knew how he'd betrayed her . . ." He uttered a shuddering breath. "I couldn't do that to her."

An icy chill wracked Jeremy. "How *did* he betray her?"

Abruptly Blakeborough stood and stalked to the window, then back. "I only know what Samuel was willing to admit after I caught him attempting to arrange a hired chaise to carry Ruston and Yvette to Gretna Green. It was sheer luck that I was in Preston an hour before Ruston meant to run off with her."

"Oh, God. That must have been after Samuel claimed he could do nothing to help Yvette, before he turned around and 'saved' the day."

Edwin's gaze grew murderous. "Probably. Fortunately, the chaise owner admitted the truth when I warned him I would report his participation to my father if he didn't. He wasn't fool enough to cross the earl's heir. Everyone in Preston knew I ran things at the estate. So when Samuel wouldn't say a word at first, the chaise owner admitted what Samuel and Ruston were planning."

"To carry Yvette off . . . with her consent, of course, assuming she would have given in to the blackmail."

"Ah, yes, the blackmail." The earl's face clouded over. "When pushed to the wall and threatened with a visit from our father, who'd already had enough of Samuel's irresponsible behavior, my brother revealed that Ruston had sworn to destroy Yvette's reputation if we didn't let him marry her." Blakeborough paused to shoot him an uncertain glance. "That *is* what you're talking about, isn't it?"

"I told you—she revealed everything to me."

Reassured, Edwin went on. "My damned fool of a brother actually thought he could bully *me*, too. Said we had to let the elopement go on, or the family would be shamed. He even tried to weasel out of his own responsibility for the situation. He claimed he'd had no idea about Ruston's intentions when inviting the man to Stoke Towers."

"But you didn't believe him."

"Certainly not. The very fact that Samuel was arranging transportation for an elopement instead of coming to me to consult about the situation showed he was part of it."

"So how did you put an end to it without involving Yvette?"

He clenched his hands at his sides. "I called his bluff. I told him I wasn't letting her go anywhere with that arse. And if Samuel didn't fix the problem, I'd tell Father my suspicions about his part in it. Since Father had already threatened to cut Samuel off entirely if the idiot took another wrong step, I gave Samuel a choice—regain Yvette's garter and silence the footman, or lose everything."

"And he agreed to set matters straight."

"Oh, yes. He knew I was as good as my word. Once he'd done his part, I called Ruston in and informed him that my friends on the Navy Board would be appalled to learn that a naval officer was attempting to elope with a respectable female against her family's wishes. I told him I could have him cashiered and make sure he never worked again."

Jeremy blinked. "Remind me never to get on your bad side. You have connections I had no idea about."

"I may have slightly exaggerated," Blakeborough admitted with a smug smile. "But Ruston couldn't know that. And in the process of defending himself, he blamed everything on Samuel. Said that Samuel had promised to encourage the match if Ruston promised to be generous to Samuel with Yvette's money."

"Did you believe Ruston?"

"Sadly, yes."

"You truly think Samuel tried to sell her to his friend for a piece of the profits." Jeremy gritted his teeth. "I hate this ass more and more by the day."

"Which one?"

"Both, to be honest."

Blakeborough nodded grimly. "I blame myself for Samuel's behavior. I knew he was in debt to a number of fellows in the prizefighting set. I should have seen the signs, should have realized he was desperate."

"How could you? Sometimes people can be very good at hiding what's in their hearts." He should know. "Besides, it was your father's responsibility."

"Of course." As if realizing he'd already revealed more than he wished, he pasted a cool expression to his face. "If Father had been here, I'm sure he would have acted. And he did cut Samuel off eventually."

"You could have told Yvette about Samuel's perfidy then."

A scowl knit Blakeborough's brow. "You've heard how she talks about herself. If she'd known her own brother had sold her to his friend, all it would have

done was make her feel even worse about her ability
to attract men. At least after it was over, she was able
to believe that the courtship part was real, even if
the end result was bad."

"Sadly, even that was denied her. She found out
later that Ruston was a fortune hunter and put two
and two together."

The earl blinked. "She did? How?"

"Oh, for God's sake, you can't protect her from
everything. She hears gossip like anyone else."

Blakeborough dropped into a chair. "She never
said anything."

"Of course not. She was embarrassed and humiliated. And she didn't know that you knew. She
wanted to preserve her pride."

He nodded absently. "That was another reason
I didn't reveal my part in it. So that she could preserve her pride."

Jeremy rolled his eyes. Thanks to Blakeborough's
careful consideration of her feelings, she'd risked her
reputation to find Samuel's son. Perhaps he should
tell the earl about that.

And have Blakeborough find out that Jeremy
had been squiring her about town to brothels? That
would hardly help the situation.

"You still haven't answered my offer of marriage,"
Jeremy said bluntly. He had to get over that hurdle
first. Then he could persuade Yvette.

"Do you love her?" Blakeborough asked.

Thunderation, leave it to the earl to ask the one
question he'd been dreading. He'd planned on
lying, but faced with the man's somber expression,
he couldn't. Because he knew it would get back to

Yvette, and it would give her hope for things he couldn't give her.

When Jeremy didn't answer right away, Blakeborough added, "Look, I am the last person to say that marriage requires love. I'm not even sure I believe in the word—I rather suspect that it's nothing more than a sly term for good old-fashioned lust. But I know my sister. And she expects to have some semblance of . . . whatever it is."

"And I can give her that," Jeremy said, relieved by Blakeborough's practical approach. "Because I do feel a deep affection for her, I assure you. As long as that's enough—"

A knock came at the study door, and Jeremy tensed.

"Excuse me a moment," the earl murmured, then called out, "Come in."

A footman entered. "My lord, there's a woman here to see Mr. Keane." The servant's posture was rigid, and he wouldn't look at Jeremy. "She *claims* that she's his sister."

Amanda was *here*? Oh, God, just what he didn't need. Time had run out.

And why had the servant said that she'd *claimed* to be his sister?

Oh, right. Except for her blue eyes she looked nothing like Jeremy, who was the spitting image of their father. Amanda looked like their Irish mother, short and small, with a head of auburn hair and a dusting of freckles over her lightly tanned skin. No doubt the fellow thought Amanda was his mistress.

Of all the times for his sister to show up, why

must it be now? The last thing he needed was Amanda reminding Yvette of all his shortcomings. Perhaps if he could whisk her away before Yvette awoke—

"Thank you," Jeremy said to the footman, and headed for the door. "Is my mother with her?"

The footman's expression faltered as he realized he'd stepped wrong. "Er . . . no. Miss Keane has come from town with a man who claims . . . who *is* another relation of yours. A Mr. Bonnaud?"

Oh, damn. Bonnaud was here, too. And that could mean only one thing—he'd learned something about Samuel's by-blow. Otherwise, he would have waited until he saw Jeremy in London again to speak to him about it.

All the more reason to get to his relations before they got to Yvette. "Blakeborough, if you don't mind . . ."

"No, of course not. I confess I'm rather eager to meet this ladder-climbing sister of yours."

God help him. Jeremy hurried into the hall. At least he could count on Bonnaud to be discreet in front of the earl. He wasn't so sure about Amanda.

"Jeremy!" she cried as he entered the foyer.

"It's good to have you here," he said as he bent to receive her kiss.

Despite the complications she presented, he was genuinely glad to see his little sister. It had been far too long. Which was why he pretended not to notice that she wore a typically unfashionable gray wool dress.

"Why didn't Mother come with you?" he asked. When it dawned on him that their trip might not have gone well, his stomach flipped over. "She's all right, isn't she?"

"She has a cold and is exhausted from the trip, which is why we left her with Lady Zoe. Not that you care." Amanda sniffed as she removed her anti-quated bonnet and handed it to the footman. "We haven't heard a word from you in months."

He relaxed. If Mother had been seriously unwell, Amanda wouldn't be chiding him. She'd be braining him with the nearest fire poker.

"Yes, I've been such a bad boy," he teased her. "Traveling about and seeing the world and behaving as if I were a *grown man*. Fancy that." He turned to Bonnaud. "Good to see you, too, sir."

They shook hands, Bonnaud gazing at him with a meaningful look. But before Jeremy could figure out how to get the man alone, Blakeborough cleared his throat.

"Ah, yes," Jeremy said. "Lord Blakeborough, may I present my sister, Miss Amanda Keane. Amanda, this is my friend, the Earl of Blakeborough."

"Friend?" Amanda looked the earl over skeptically. "I thought he commissioned a portrait from you. That's what Mr. Bonnaud said."

Blakeborough blinked at her forthright words. "I . . . er . . . did indeed commission a portrait from your brother, but we've become friends in the mean-time, haven't we, Keane?"

"I hope so." Because that would make the man more likely to accept Jeremy's suit. Which he *still* hadn't done.

"In fact," Blakeborough added, "Keane and I are starting a gentlemen's club together."

"I thought you were returning to America any day now, Keane," Bonnaud said warily.

"He *is*," Amanda put in.

Assaulted from all sides, Jeremy stifled a groan.

The earl smoothly said, "I believe that my friend's plans aren't entirely settled. Eh, Keane?"

"Not entirely, no," Jeremy said noncommittally.

"Well, regardless, I need to speak to you alone." Bonnaud turned to the earl. "Is there a place where Keane and I can be private, my lord?"

"You may use my study," Blakeborough said, though his eyes burned with curiosity. He smiled at Amanda. "Miss Keane, I'm sure you're famished after your journey. I was just going in to breakfast myself, so if you'd care to join me . . ."

"I'd be honored, sir." With a thin smile, Amanda took the arm he offered.

As she left, she cast a glance back at Jeremy. He knew that glance. It said, *You're in big trouble, mister. And handing me off to a handsome earl is not going to get you out of it.*

One crisis at a time.

He gestured down the hall. "Shall we, Bonnaud?"

"Certainly."

If Yvette slept as late as she usually did, perhaps he could settle everything before she even arose. Otherwise, between his irate sister, Samuel's missing son, and an offer of marriage that *still* hadn't been made properly, this had the potential to turn into quite the Shakespearean drama.

Twenty-Two

Yvette awakened slowly, deliciously. She'd been having the most extraordinary dream. Jeremy had been lying naked between her legs, doing exquisitely shameless things to her that made her feel like a woman. His woman. Even now, thinking about it, her legs fell open—

She froze. She was sore. As if . . . as if . . .

Heavenly day! She sat bolt upright as she remembered it wasn't a dream. It wasn't a fantasy or a hope that she one day might experience the melting joys of marital bliss. She'd experienced them. Or at least some of them.

More memories surfaced, and she remembered *why* she'd fallen into Jeremy's arms with no restraint.

Flying from her bed, she hastened to the window to see if his equipage still sat out front. Not that its absence would tell her much—she wouldn't know whether that meant he'd left or if his curricle was safely stowed in the carriage house.

But looking out, she found a different carriage

entirely in the drive. It wasn't Jeremy's or Warren's or anyone's that she recognized. It had a crest, but try as she might, she couldn't make it out from here.

She rang for her maid, then began her ablutions. Within moments, the girl rushed inside as if she'd merely been awaiting the call. "Oh, milady, thank heaven you're awake! You'll never guess what's going on."

Her heart faltered. He was leaving after all. But in a different carriage? That made no sense.

"Mr. Keane's *sister* has arrived. Did you know he had a sister?"

"Yes," she said, with a sinking in her stomach. A sister who meant to carry him back to America. Curse it all!

Rushing to her bureau, she jerked out her corset and petticoat. "We have to hurry," she told her maid, who was already rushing over to help her into her undergarments. "He can't leave before I talk to him."

"Yes, milady."

It took far too long to get her laced up, and the whole time it was being done, she was barking orders. "I need my best silk stockings. And the simplest coiffeur you can manage. And for a gown . . ." She paused to think.

"The white day dress with the pink flowers?" her maid supplied helpfully.

"No, definitely not the white. His sister is supposed to be quite the energetic sort, so something more sporting. My red redingote dress with the purple sash."

Today of all days, she mustn't look insipid. She

had to convince Jeremy to stay in England, at least long enough for her to . . . to . . .

To what?

As her maid helped her into her clothes, Yvette tried to think. She hadn't accepted his offer last night, and honestly, she wasn't sure he'd even meant it. He might turn out to be like plenty of other men who bedded a woman and ran. If so, then keeping him here was pointless.

And if he renewed his attentions? Offered her marriage again?

Her heart pounded at the very thought. It would mean he hadn't just been spouting nonsense last night.

Still, she didn't want to marry him if he was only offering out of a sense of duty. He'd done that before and it had ended badly. But neither could she bear the idea of his leaving her here to live without him.

As a hollow feeling of panic rose in her chest, she blinked back tears. He couldn't leave. He mustn't!

You're in love with him, you fool.

"God strike me blind!" Yvette swore.

"Excuse me, milady?" her maid squeaked.

Heavens, she shouldn't have said it aloud. What was wrong with her? "Forgive me. I was just trying out one of the new oaths for my dictionary."

Her maid said nothing, and Yvette ignored her scandalized silence. Meanwhile, ten other street oaths played a refrain through Yvette's head.

She *was* in love with him. How on earth had she done that?

By watching him struggle with his guilt over the deaths of his wife and son. By glimpsing the man beneath the mask, and realizing he was a man she could care for deeply. A man she could love.

That was why she couldn't stand the idea of his leaving. Because deep down, she hoped that if he stayed, she could persuade him to be in love with her, too.

She winced. Of course that never worked. One fell in love or one did not. One was never persuaded into it by another person.

"Milady?" her maid asked, dragging her from her thoughts.

She glanced around to see the servant offering her a choice of shoes. "The ones with the purple embroidery. And I've changed my mind about my hair. Just tie a ribbon about it and leave it at that."

"Milady, you're a grown woman!" her maid said, scandalized yet again. "Do you want to shock his family?"

"Oh, all right, but make it quick." At the moment, his family was lucky she wasn't going down in her night rail and wrapper.

When her maid was *finally* done, Yvette forced herself to descend the stairs with some decorum. But her composure faltered when she reached the foyer to find no one was there.

Hearing sounds from the breakfast room, she went there first. As she entered, she spotted Edwin at his usual spot at the table. He wore a forced smile as he spoke to the diminutive woman seated next to him, who looked like a sprite from the forest. Or from Ireland, given her red hair.

It had to be Miss Keane. Despite the woman's entirely different coloring and size, she had Jeremy's gorgeous blue eyes. And there was something in her smile that reminded Yvette of him, even though Miss Keane's fashion choices were utterly different.

Edwin rose. "Ah, there's my sister now."

As Yvette walked forward to greet them Edwin seemed to watch her with more intensity than usual, as if assessing her mood or something. It alarmed her exceedingly. Could he tell what she'd spent half her night doing? Did it show in her face? What if he knew? Oh, *Lord*!

Beside him, Miss Keane smiled affably. "So you're the woman my brother has been painting."

And swiving.

She swallowed hard. She had to get hold of herself, before she gave everything away. Edwin was now wearing his polite endurance-of-strangers face, and clearly he wouldn't be wearing that if he suspected anything. He'd be wearing an I'm-going-to-kill-Keane face.

Yvette held out her hand to Jeremy's sister. "Yes, I'm the subject of your brother's latest portrait. We're delighted to have you here. Mr. Keane has told us so much about you and your family."

The woman's smile faltered as she took Yvette's hand and released it. "Has he? I do hope it wasn't all bad."

"No, not bad at all." Yvette flashed the woman a reassuring look, though he really hadn't said much about his sister. She sifted through their conversations to find something complimentary. "He told me you're very capable of taking care of yourself."

"That sounds like something he'd say. It's his way

of rationalizing the fact that he refuses to come home to Montague and help me with the mills."

Because his wife and child died at Montague.

Yvette bit back the words, though the sudden realization settled hard in her chest. Time to change the subject. "So when was the last time you saw him?"

"The week he set sail for England, earlier this year. He met me and Mama for the day in Philadelphia, as he often does." Miss Keane sighed. "That's when he told us he was making this trip. He said he'd be gone a few months . . . but . . ." She forced a game smile that barely masked the worry in her eyes. "A few months turned into eight. As he likes to say, he blows with the wind."

A painful pressure squeezed Yvette's heart. "Yes, I gathered." And men who blew with the wind didn't marry earl's daughters and settle into comfortable existences on country estates.

"Lady Yvette," said a rumbling voice from behind her.

She whirled around to find Mr. Bonnaud standing there. Why was Jane's brother-in-law here? Oh, right. He was also cousin to the Keanes by marriage. He must have accompanied Miss Keane to Stoke Towers.

"Good morning, Mr. Bonnaud," she said brightly. "I hope you had good weather for your journey."

"Yes." The word was clipped. "Actually . . . er . . . Mr. Keane is in your brother's study and sent me to fetch you. There's a matter he wishes to discuss with you privately."

Panic gripped her. What was wrong with Jeremy?

Didn't he know that her brother would suspect something if he was setting up private meetings with her?

But oddly, Edwin didn't look upset. He wore a fond expression that was utterly unlike him. "Go on, then," he said. "Don't keep the man waiting."

This was strange. Since when was he pushing her toward Jeremy?

Then her stomach sank as she realized why. Jeremy wanted a moment alone to say his farewells before he left with his sister. And Edwin was so ecstatic over the man's leaving that he couldn't wait for it to be done.

Her temper rose the closer she got to the study. She refused to let Jeremy go without a fight. She had a trick or two up her sleeve.

Breezing into the study, she said, "You can't leave yet. You still owe me a portrait."

With a startled expression, Jeremy turned to face her. Then a sly smile kicked up one corner of his mouth. "I thought I owed your *brother* a portrait. As I recall, you weren't that keen on it."

"Well, I'm keen on it now. You have to finish it." She crossed her arms over her chest. "And you also still owe me a chance to find my brother's son. So you see, you can't leave yet. You haven't done what you promised."

A shadow crossed his face, and his smile vanished. "Not the first part, no. But I have done what I promised regarding your brother."

That knocked the breath from her. "Wh-what do you mean?"

He glanced down at the desk and tapped his fingers restlessly on what looked like a small stack of papers. Then he came around to face her, his gaze steady. "Bonnaud has found your nephew."

Not expecting that, she swayed a little on her feet. He darted forward to catch her around the waist. "Sorry," he murmured. "I should have given you more warning."

Her mind stuttered into a gallop, putting things together. The appearance of Mr. Bonnaud here. The odd way Jeremy had looked at her when he'd called her in. "But how . . . When . . ." She narrowed an accusing gaze on him. "I asked you not to involve your relations!"

"Because you feared that they would be indiscreet. But I knew otherwise."

She pulled away from him. "Oh, you did, did you?"

"Yes. And you'll have to trust my judgment in that because I cannot tell you why. But I had good reason to believe in their discretion. So I hired them. It was better than your risking your reputation to find the lad." He smiled faintly. "And I knew you'd never stop looking."

The warmth in his eyes spread a soothing heat through her jangled nerves. "When did you arrange—"

"The day after the masquerade ball. They've been working on it ever since."

Oh, Lord. All this time. And he'd engineered it for her. How very sweet. Surely it showed a level of caring beyond the ever-present desire simmering between them. "So . . . so that's why Mr. Bonnaud is here."

"Yes. To consult with you and your brother. Bonnaud cannot continue to pursue this without the earl's consent."

Her heart sank. "No, no, no, no . . . Edwin mustn't be involved. He will never forgive me!"

Jeremy stepped up to steady her with a hand under her elbow. "First of all, Blakeborough isn't your enemy. He is perfectly capable of listening to reason."

"That's what *you* think. When he hears about the brothel visit and our bargain and—"

"We don't need to tell him any of that, sweetheart. We'll say that you confided your concerns to me, and I decided to find the boy on my own. I enlisted the help of the Duke's Men because I knew that, as my family, they would keep the secrets of me and my friends. Your brother need never hear the whole truth."

When she just stood there, trembling, he added softly, "But you *must* tell him what's going on. Otherwise, the child will be sent to the Foundling Hospital."

Her mouth fell open. "*What?*"

"The lad's mother wants to marry, and her would-be husband doesn't want her by-blow hanging about. So if Blakeborough doesn't step in to help, she means to place the boy elsewhere. And you'll lose all chance of overseeing his care."

Her heart flipped over in her chest. "She can't do that. He deserves a home, a family."

"Well, he's not going to get one unless you involve your brother. Only Blakeborough has the kind of connections—and the motivation to use them—to find a deserving family for the lad."

After a moment's hesitation, she admitted, "That's probably true."

"So you're willing to bring your brother into it?"

With a sigh, she nodded. She couldn't let the poor child go to the Foundling Hospital. He deserved to have a loving adoptive mother.

"Good." Jeremy squeezed her elbow reassuringly. "First, I think we should send for your brother, so the two of us can explain everything. Then we can bring Bonnaud in to present the details of his report, which is on the desk. I haven't had time to read the whole thing, but he gave me the gist of it. I'm sure he will be happy to answer your questions. All right?"

She released a shaky breath. "Yes."

As Jeremy stepped into the hall to have a servant summon Edwin, she wandered to the desk to look at the papers. A name caught her eye: Elias Samuel. Miss Moreton had named her child after his father.

Unexpectedly, tears burned Yvette's eyes. It was nearly over. All that was left was to prove, to Edwin's satisfaction, that Elias was Samuel's boy. Then Yvette could deliver the letter to Miss Moreton—or Edwin could—and could arrange for Meredith to take care of their nephew. Her obligation to Samuel would be fulfilled.

And Jeremy's obligation to *her* would be fulfilled, as well. If he chose to leave, she had no way to compel him to stay, the paintings notwithstanding.

"Are you all right?" Jeremy asked softly as he re-entered the room.

She blinked back her tears. She would die before she let him see how upset she'd become over his leaving. "I'm fine. I just . . . can't believe they were able to find him."

He came over to place his hand comfortingly on her waist. "Yes, well—"

The door opened and Edwin entered. "Don't let me interrupt," her brother said in an unusually jovial voice. "I see that you've told her, Keane. And I assume that since you've called me in, she has accepted your offer."

"What offer?" Yvette stared at Jeremy, whose hand was still on her waist, and the answer hit her. "You've already asked my brother for permission to marry me?"

"Yes." His eyes locked with hers. "This morning before anyone arrived. He said that his answer is dependent upon yours." He took her hand. "And so is my future. So I do hope you'll say yes."

She noticed he hadn't mentioned love or any great yearning for her company, or anything else to indicate that his feelings about her had changed since last night. Before she leapt willy-nilly into his arms, she had to determine if he was still just offering for her out of duty.

"Why do you wish to marry me?" she asked.

With a furtive glance at Edwin, he murmured, "You know why."

"Actually, I don't. Pray enlighten me."

Would he reveal what they'd done together? Or drum up some other reason they ought to wed?

He just stared at her, looking frustrated. It *was* as she'd feared. He was marrying her because it was the right thing to do.

She drew her hand from his. "I'm sorry, Mr. Keane, but—"

"No, don't refuse me yet. At least think about it." His eyes burned into hers, full of feeling. Why couldn't he express it?

But he was right. She should not refuse him out of hand. "Very well. I shall take some time to consider the offer."

"Wait a minute, Yvette," Edwin said. "If he wasn't asking you to marry him when I came in, what the devil *was* he doing?"

Oh, dear. Time to be honest with Edwin.

Forcing a smile, she turned to her brother. "It turns out that Mr. Keane has managed to locate Miss Peggy Moreton and her child." As she saw the shock spreading over Edwin's face, she gulped down apprehension. "You'll be pleased to hear that Samuel's son has been found at last."

Twenty-Three

Jeremy tensed. Blakeborough didn't *look* pleased. He wore an expression of betrayal, as if he'd just been kicked in the ballocks.

An unfamiliar sort of guilt settled in Jeremy's chest. He'd had few close friends in his life, and he'd certainly never betrayed one.

Then Blakeborough turned his anger on Yvette. "You told Keane about Samuel's supposed by-blow. And about that . . . that *woman.*"

Jeremy's guilt vanished, replaced by an instinctual need to protect Yvette. "Yes, she told me." He moved in front of her. "She needed to confide in someone who could help her decide how to act. And as I explained this morning, she and I grew quite close during our time together doing her portrait."

"Really?" the earl snapped. "I was there, too, and I don't recall talking about my damned brother and the damned request he made of my sister."

"Edwin—" Yvette began.

"You forget that she and I didn't work all the

time." Jeremy fumbled for an explanation of how they'd grown so intimate. "We danced together at the masquerade ball. Occasionally, you left us alone with Damber so you could attend to estate work."

"So now your insolent apprentice knows my family's business as well?" Blakeborough roared.

"Stop it, Edwin!" Yvette cried. "I told Mr. Keane about Samuel the first night I met him, when we danced. I said the only way I would agree to sit for a portrait was if he found my nephew for me."

That halted the earl's fury right well.

Jeremy wished he'd thought of that explanation himself. It made perfect sense, and was nearly the truth, too.

Blakeborough scowled at her. "You were that desperate—"

"Yes!" She pushed past Jeremy, headed for her brother. "I told you how upset I was." When she reached Blakeborough, she softened her voice into the same understanding murmur that had made Jeremy spill his own secrets to her last night. "But it's all right. The Duke's Men are very discreet. And Mr. Keane made it clear to them that he regarded the investigation as a personal favor. They will not betray *his* secrets, even if they're not too fond of Samuel."

Jeremy watched as the anger in the earl's face slowly subsided. And she thought she had no influence over him? Her brother might have a bit of a temper and a rigid code of behavior and a pride stiff enough to hoist a mountain, but clearly he cared about his sister.

The earl drew into himself. "So I suppose that's why Bonnaud is here."

"Yes," she said. "He brought his report. Shall I call him in so he can give it? We need to decide what to do."

Though Blakeborough set his shoulders like a man preparing for battle, he grumbled, "Might as well. The cat's out of the bag now, isn't it?"

"Out and apparently on a rampage," Yvette muttered as she went into the hall.

The earl rounded on Jeremy. "You knew about Samuel all this time. And you agreed to go behind my back to find out—"

"Forgive me. The friendlier you and I became, the worse I felt about it. But honestly, your sister would have done something foolish if no one had helped her with the matter. I figured it was better that Manton's Investigations, with their vast experience, do the looking than that she do it on her own, which is what she proposed."

All right, so he was heaping lies upon lies. But Yvette deserved to be shielded. Because while the earl clearly wasn't as critical of her as she thought, he still wouldn't look kindly upon her activities the night of the masquerade ball.

"Now you understand why I thought you should tell her about Samuel," Jeremy went on. "I hoped it might keep her from behaving rashly."

Blakeborough drew himself up as if to retort, but before he could, Bonnaud and Yvette returned.

"So," the earl told Bonnaud, "I understand that Mr. Keane engaged you for an assignment involving my feckless brother's trail of mistresses. I'm surprised you even agreed to take it on, given how he injured your family."

Bonnaud shrugged. "My family—my brother—injured you by stealing your fiancée. So I figure we're even."

For a long moment, Blakeborough just stared at the man. Then he gave a grudging smile. "Stole her *back*, one might say. But I suppose you're right. And I do appreciate your help in the matter." He cast a glance at Jeremy. "Even if I don't appreciate that it was requested without my knowledge."

"To be fair," Bonnaud said, "Mr. Keane didn't feel we should bother you with it until we could be sure there was something to your brother's claim."

"Ah," the earl said, as if that settled everything, which they all knew it did not. "I take it that you've decided there *was* something to Samuel's claim."

"Yes." And with that, Bonnaud launched into a dispassionate recital of everything he'd found.

Jeremy had heard most of it already. How Bonnaud had tracked Miss Moreton down. Where he'd learned she was staying. What had been done to determine if the boy Elias was truly Samuel's son.

Though Jeremy tried to pay attention to the conversation, he couldn't help being distracted by Yvette. She'd been on the verge of refusing his offer, and the fact that she wouldn't even look at him worried him. What if she *did* refuse him? How would he live with himself, knowing that he'd ruined her for any other man?

Not that he wanted to see her with another man. The very idea made him surprisingly hot under the collar.

"What do you think I should do, Keane?"

"Hmm?" Jeremy jerked his gaze from Yvette.

"Sorry, Blakeborough. I'm afraid I was woolgathering."

The earl glanced from him to Yvette. "Bonnaud says that Miss Moreton is eager to give up all claim to the boy. But I don't want to be tricked into supporting a child that isn't my brother's, all because a soiled dove wants to marry some gentleman."

Jeremy could understand why. From what Bonnaud had said, Blakeborough was already supporting Samuel's last mistress and babe. "Then meet with Miss Moreton yourself. Ask her your questions, and see how she responds."

The earl's lips thinned. "That's all well and good for you to say, but I'm not adept at assessing people's reactions and figuring out whether they're lying."

"Mr. Keane is," Yvette put in. "So take him with you. The two of you ought to be able to figure it out together. Or I could go—"

"No," Blakeborough said firmly. "You are not going. That would be entirely unwise."

"I agree with your brother," Jeremy told her. "Involving you is unacceptable." When she blinked at him, clearly startled by his vehemence, Jeremy softened his tone. "But I promise to act as your representative in this matter. It would be my honor."

The sudden softness in her gaze started an unfamiliar fluttering in his belly. "Very well," she said. "But if I am not to go, I want to know one thing." She turned an anxious gaze on Bonnaud. "When you met with Miss Moreton, was the boy there?"

"Elias? Yes."

She folded her hands together at her waist as if to hold her emotions in. "How did he seem?"

"He wasn't suffering, if that's what you're worried about. But he was also very quiet. Too quiet for a four-year-old, if you ask me." When worry crossed her face, Bonnaud added hastily, "But then, I don't know much about children."

She nodded, but her concerned expression didn't abate.

Jeremy hated seeing it. "We'll set things right, sweetheart. I promise you."

The endearment made Yvette glance nervously at Bonnaud, but the investigator took a sudden interest in straightening the papers of his report.

Meanwhile, her brother was watching her with a wary expression. "I assume you still think we should have Meredith raise the boy with her own son."

"I think it would be best, yes."

"At my expense, I suppose," Blakeborough grumbled.

"Well, not entirely," she said. "I . . . um . . . probably should have mentioned this before, but I never posted that letter Samuel gave me. I held on to it in case we found her. What's more, he implied that the contents would secure the future of Miss Moreton and her child."

"What?" the earl said. "Why didn't you reveal this before?"

She steadied her shoulders. "You were determined to believe the worst of Samuel. I hardly thought hearing about any financial help for her would change anything. And we couldn't know what it was anyway until we found Miss Moreton and gave her the letter."

"The devil we couldn't." Blakeborough held out his hand. "Give me the damned envelope."

"Not if you intend to open it."

"You haven't even looked inside?" the earl said incredulously, echoing Jeremy's own surprise.

"I have not. He made me swear not to."

"*I* didn't make any such promise," Blakeborough said, "so give it to me, and I'll open it."

"No." She clutched the missive to her breast. "Samuel did me a great service once, and I shan't betray his trust."

Realizing what she meant, Jeremy scowled at the earl. "Tell her. She deserves to know."

"Tell me what?" she asked.

With a furtive glance at Bonnaud, who was listening intently, Blakeborough muttered, "Nothing. But I'll need the letter, if only to bring it to Miss Moreton."

Yvette tipped up her chin. "I shall give it to Mr. Keane once we reach London. I know I can trust *him* to follow my wishes."

Jeremy stared hard at the earl, willing him to finally tell her the entire truth about Samuel.

But Blakeborough merely grimaced. "Fine. Do as you please. Keane and Bonnaud and I will go today to meet the damned woman."

"We'll go tomorrow," Jeremy cut in without stopping to consider. When all eyes turned to him, he said, "I'm nearly finished with the portrait. I can be done today if I can have a few more hours with Lady Yvette."

"There's no need to finish the portrait, now that you and my sister—" The earl halted, quelled by another hard glance from Jeremy. Understanding finally dawned. "Oh. Right."

Jeremy continued. "Meanwhile, Bonnaud can return to the city with Amanda. Then his lordship and I can leave for London first thing tomorrow. If that's all right with everyone."

He still needed to convince Yvette to marry him. If he left for London today he'd be caught up in the snare of dealing with his family, and Yvette would remain here, firming her objections to his suit with every passing moment.

That wasn't to be borne. He had to make another try.

"I did ask Miss Moreton to wait a few days before packing her son off," Bonnaud mused aloud. "So if his lordship wishes to delay a night, it won't hurt anything."

Yet again, Jeremy was grateful that Zoe had married Bonnaud. The man had an uncanny ability to sense when his interference was welcome.

"All right." Blakeborough glanced anxiously at his sister. "Yvette? Do you mind if we delay our visit to Miss Moreton for a day?"

Jeremy held his breath when she hesitated. Then she said softly, "No, it's fine."

But he noticed the convulsive movement of her throat, the furtive glance she shot him. Had she guessed why he wished to remain?

All the better if she had. Because he wasn't going to let her throw away her future out of some misplaced idea of what a marriage should be.

"So this is where you've all gone off to," came a voice from the doorway.

Jeremy groaned. His sister wasn't going to like any of this. "Yes, but we're done now." He walked over to her. "Bonnaud had some personal news to convey to his lordship, which is one of the reasons he chose to accompany you here."

"So now that he's conveyed it, he and you and I can go to London." Her expression challenged him to gainsay her.

Thunderation. He glanced over at his companions. "Would you mind giving me a moment alone with my sister?"

Mumbling their acquiescence, they all left the room.

He shut the door. When he faced Amanda, she wore her most mulish expression. "How long will it take you to be ready?" she asked.

"I'm not going with you today."

"Then when?"

"Tomorrow." When she bristled, he added, "I have a commissioned portrait to complete, so I'm staying here until then to make sure it's done. You can go back with Bonnaud and tell Mother that I will be there in the morning. I'll squire the two of you about as much as you like for the duration of your stay, but I need to finish here first."

"And then you'll return to America with us?"

He dragged in a shaky breath. "No."

"The hell you won't."

He forced a smile to his lips. "When did you start cussing, sis?"

His teasing didn't pacify her one bit. "A long time ago. Not that you would realize it, since you've barely paid us any heed for the past twelve years."

Thunderation. "You know why."

Her stance softened. "Yes. I suppose I do. But now

that Papa's dead, you need not stay away just to punish him."

"I wasn't . . . That's not why . . ." But he supposed that *had* been part of it. Punishing Father for his lies, for what he'd brought about at the end. Except that even after Father's death, Jeremy had still found it impossible to breathe every time he thought about returning to Montague.

Amanda didn't understand that. Montague was everything to her. She couldn't grasp why he just wanted to forget. And now she was here, insisting on his dwelling on the past.

"If it wasn't Papa keeping you away," she asked, "then why not come home?"

The plaintive note in her voice was almost too much to bear. He leaned back against the door. "You don't need me to. You run everything quite well without me, you and Mother."

"Blast it, Jeremy, it will take both owners to get loans, to expand, to make the necessary improvements to the mills that Papa was never willing to approve."

Old duties tugged at him. He ignored them. "I'll sell you my half. That's the best I can do."

She huffed out a breath. "But Mama has to allow it, and she won't."

"I'm *not* going back, damn it! I'm staying in England." *With Yvette, assuming she will have me.* "Mother will just have to accept it."

"You don't know Mama very well if you think she's giving up on her only son."

The words drove an arrow through his heart. He dug his fingers into his arms, fighting the urge to run, hard and fast, away from the pain. He'd begun to realize that he couldn't run far enough to escape it. "I can't discuss this now, Amanda. Not here. But I will come first thing in the morning and speak to Mother, and we'll settle the matter once and for all. All right?"

She stared at him warily. "Do you *swear* to come to London tomorrow?"

"Yes. You'll see me as soon as I can get there in the morning."

"I'll hold you to it." She crossed her arms over her chest. "Now that I know our relations run an investigative concern, if you run away, I'll hire them to find you wherever you go."

He let out a long breath. He'd managed to postpone dealing with his family for another day, thank God. "I promise not to run this time." But he would also not give in on the subject of returning.

He'd simply make that clear to Mother in a way she could finally accept.

Twenty-Four

It was well past noon by the time Yvette stood on the front steps with Edwin and Jeremy, watching as the visitors left. How had Jeremy managed to convince his sister to return to London without him? Whatever he'd said, when Miss Keane had walked out of Edwin's study with her brother, she'd looked entirely different from when she'd gone in. Deflated. Worried.

Jeremy, meanwhile, had vanished behind a wall of wry remarks and teasing. Since his sister had only participated halfheartedly, he'd turned them on Yvette, who'd been in no mood to suffer them, either.

And now he apparently thought to go back to working on the portrait as if nothing had happened. No doubt he meant to spend hours giving her his smoldering looks and tempting her into thinking wicked thoughts. He expected to get her so eager for him that she would agree to anything he asked.

Not a chance.

The dratted devil wanted to marry her without making any effort at all. Without saying why he wished to or telling her he loved her or even explaining why he refused to return to America. And all because she'd fallen into his bed.

Well, she might have been deplorably easy to seduce, but he would soon find she wasn't so easy to marry. Getting her assent would require more than kisses and facile flatteries. He would have to prove he actually cared about her. If he could.

"About your painting—" she began.

"Actually, I was thinking we might go for a walk," Jeremy said. "It's too lovely a day to be cooped up inside."

She gaped at him. "I thought you wanted to finish the portrait."

"We've got enough time for that later on. I feel the need for some exercise first. I'm sure you do, too."

She didn't know how to answer. They'd never been on a walk together. Strolling about the grounds sounded delicious.

So delicious that it raised her suspicions. Jeremy was proposing it precisely because he knew it would tempt her.

"I'd be delighted to go for a walk," she said blithely. "And I'm sure Edwin could use one, too."

When Jeremy glowered at her brother, Edwin blanched. "A walk? Why in God's name would I go for a walk with the two of you?"

She looped her arm through Edwin's. "As Mr. Keane says, it's a lovely day. And I know how much you enjoy walking with companions."

"No, I don't," Edwin protested. "Everyone moves

too slowly and stops too often. I prefer a solitary walk. You *know* that."

Sometimes she could throttle her brother for his absolute inability to play along.

She frowned meaningfully at him. "But surely on a day like this . . ."

Edwin caught sight of her expression, and apparently the truth *finally* dawned on him. "Ah, yes. A day like this. That . . . changes everything. So, I suppose we're off for a walk."

She shot Jeremy a triumphant smile. If he wanted her, he would have to work for it. And if he didn't work for it, it would prove he didn't *really* want her as a wife.

"Let me just fetch my bonnet," she said.

"No need for that," Jeremy said. "I thought we'd merely tour your deer park, since I haven't seen it."

With a shrug, she let the two men usher her down the steps so they could stroll along the path leading into the woods. Although the men flanked her, it was Jeremy she was conscious of. She fancied she could feel his gaze scrutinizing her, feel his heat emanating toward her. Perhaps this hadn't been such a good idea.

Unless . . . "So," she said brightly, "if I'm to marry you, Mr. Keane, how would we live? For that matter, *where* would we live?"

Edwin stiffened. "Perhaps it would be better if I went over to—"

"No, indeed," she cut in. "These are questions *you* as my guardian should have asked."

To her surprise, Jeremy laughed. "She's got you there, Blakeborough." He stared warmly down at her.

"We'll live in London or somewhere close. You can choose the house. I don't really care where."

"As long as it's near the bawdy houses, right?" she quipped.

"Yvette," Edwin ventured, "he says he only goes to the brothels to find models."

She ignored her brother, her eyes fixed on Jeremy. "I know what he says. But they're still brothels."

Jeremy's eyes gleamed at her. "Once we marry, the only female model I'll need is you."

The words were so unexpectedly sweet that her throat tightened. "So all your paintings will be of dark-haired Amazonian females?" she said archly.

"Junoesque," he corrected her. "Beautiful, Junoesque females with clover-green eyes and porcelain skin and imperious posture." He punctuated the husky words by gliding his gaze down her in a slow perusal that set every part of her on fire.

Curse him. He was too good at this. "And what about your family?" she asked, to put the shoe on the other foot.

"Oh," he said blandly, "I don't think they'd enjoy modeling for my paintings at all."

She eyed him askance. "I mean, what about the fact that they live in America? Surely you'll want to visit from time to time. Will you take me with you?"

A shadow crossed his face. "We'll cross that bridge when we come to it," he said noncommittally.

"Because if you ever intend to return there to live—"

"I don't." His expression was cold. "I can't."

Why? she wanted to ask. If he hadn't loved his wife, why was seeing the site of the woman's death so painful? But she couldn't ask that in front of Edwin. She didn't feel right revealing the intimate details of Jeremy's past without his permission.

She took another tack. "You still haven't said *how* you intend for us to live."

That made him smile. "Are you fishing for information regarding my finances, Lady Yvette? Because that is usually handled in the settlement arrangements. But if you insist upon discussing it here, I can assure you—"

"Ah, look!" Edwin cried, pointing to a speck at the top of the hill opposite the woods. "It's our gamekeeper. I've been meaning to speak to him regarding the . . . the . . ."

"Snipe?" Jeremy supplied helpfully.

"The snipe, yes." And before Yvette could stop him, her brother was stalking away from them toward the speck he claimed was their gamekeeper.

The moment he was out of hearing, Jeremy chuckled and offered her his arm. "You should have known better than to involve Blakeborough in our quarrel, sweetheart. He doesn't like quarrels. Or being in the middle. Or parrying your dizzying array of thrusts."

She glared at his arm. "We'll see about that."

When she started after her brother, Jeremy caught her about the waist and tugged her back onto the path. "Leave him be. This is between us, and you know it." He challenged her with a thin smile. "Unless you're afraid you can't handle me by yourself."

Drat the man. He was daring her again. She should tell him to go to the devil.

She didn't. "Fine," she said, and marched into the park.

For a short while, he just followed at a leisurely pace as she barreled along the graveled path in an attempt to vent her temper. But when they came to the picturesque bridge over the stream that separated their land from that of Clarissa's family, Jeremy put a hand on her arm to halt her.

"This looks like a nice spot for our discussion," he said quietly.

It was, actually. The summer sun barely penetrated the overhanging trees, but where it did, it danced on the stream's surface like fairy lights. The warble of the water twined with the croak of the toads to soothe her agitation and settle her nerves. And because of the bends in the shallow stream on either end, they were entirely private so long as no one else came along the path.

Propping his elbows on the stone parapet, he gazed out over the water. They both stood there, silent, before she drummed up the courage to ask the most crucial question. "Why do you wish to marry me?"

He hissed out a breath. "Because I ru—"

"Do *not* say it's because you ruined me. I've already warned you of the insufficiency of that argument. And if that's your only reason, I see no sense in our marrying."

There. She'd laid her cards on the table. It was his turn.

As the silence stretched out between them, she looked expectantly at him. In profile, he wasn't just handsome but beautiful, like a marble bust of some unknown Greek youth contemplating his future.

"The truth?" He angled his body toward her, one elbow still propped on the parapet.

"Always."

His eyes glinted diamond-bright in the shadows. "I've never wanted a woman as much as I want you."

"In your bed, you mean."

A fiercely tender expression lit his face. "Not just in my bed. Everywhere, doing anything. Presiding over dinner, driving my curricle, accompanying me on my trips to wherever. You stimulate me, body and soul, as no woman ever has. Surely that counts for something."

It did. It counted for quite a lot. Indeed, she was so surprised that she couldn't swallow past the thickness in her throat.

When he continued, his voice held a fervent certainty. "You make me feel things I don't want to feel, make me yearn for things I don't want to yearn for, hope for things that seem impossible." He pushed away from the parapet to loom over her. "You're annoying as hell, yet every time I'm near you, I want more. Does that make any sense? Because it damned well makes no sense to me."

There was a certain belligerence in his tone and stance, as if he were sure of being tossed aside after that odd little speech. As if he *feared* being tossed aside.

Perversely, that convinced her of his sincerity . . . and of the depth of his feelings. It might not be love, but it was something to build a marriage upon. At least she could hope that one day his feelings *might* blossom into love.

"So if that answers your question—"

She stretched up to give him a soft kiss.

He froze. And when she drew back, he stood there motionless, seemingly stunned.

Then hunger lit his face and he swept her into his arms.

His kiss was a sweet and fiery answer to all her fears, reminding her that he stimulated her, too. That he, too, made her want and yearn and hope for the impossible. That he made her love.

With her heart in her throat, she threaded her fingers through his dappled golden hair, glorying in the soft silk of it as she clasped him close. He delved deep with his tongue to probe and caress and seduce. The kiss went on and on, until they were both forced to break it in a desperate bid for air.

He shifted her so she was sandwiched between his body and the wide stone parapet, then planted his hands on either side of her, making a little thrill flash through her. "I've thought of nothing but this since last night," he murmured. "Hell, I've thought of nothing but this since the day I met you."

Then he returned to kissing her as if his life would end if he stopped, and she wrapped her arms about his waist. She knew it was unwise. They hadn't by any means settled things. But the way he was holding her, touching her, was too intoxicating to resist.

Only after he dragged his mouth from hers to kiss a path down her neck did she summon the will to chide, "What do you think you're doing?"

He tongued the hollow of her throat. "Answering the question of why *you* should marry *me*. Aside from the argument that I took your innocence."

When his hand swept up to cover her breast, she gasped. "And I suppose you think . . . seducing me is the answer."

"One answer." His palm kneaded her through the fabric with a deftness that made her mouth dry and other parts of her wet. "But there are others."

She found it hard to breathe, much less speak. "Such as?"

"I'm willing to put you into any number of my famous paintings."

"What if I don't . . . want to be in your famous paintings?"

With a smug smile, he bent to nip her ear. "I could tell how much you hated it by how eagerly you posed for them and how readily you dressed for them."

Beast. "I had a reason for complying. We had a bargain."

"Right. Your brother. And that's another reason you should marry me. How many of your English gentlemen would bring you to a brothel if you requested it, no questions asked?" His free hand slid tantalizingly down her ribs to her waist.

She shivered deliciously. "You did ask questions."

"And you didn't answer them. Yet I took you there, anyway. Wasn't that sporting of me?" He undid her sash with one hand and dropped it onto the bridge.

Oh, Lord. "Y-yes. Very sporting. But not a situation likely to be repeated in . . . the future."

"So you say. From what I've heard of him, your brother could have fifty by-blows. We might have to visit any number of brothels in the future."

When he began to unfasten the front buttons of her redingote dress, she made a feeble attempt to stop him, ignoring the wild anticipation pulsing through her. "Are you mad? Edwin could be back any minute."

With a snort, Jeremy continued what he was doing. "I'll be much surprised if your brother shows up again before dinner. He was itching to get away from us."

Grudgingly, she admitted the truth of that. Apparently, Jeremy had begun to know her brother almost as well as she.

"And besides," he went on as he undid the last of her buttons, "if he did find us together, what could he do? Make us marry? That's an even better reason to risk it."

He lifted her onto the parapet, and her gown fell open to reveal her corset and petticoats shamelessly exposed to the air. His gaze drifted down to where her breasts were pushed high within their corset cups, and his voice turned guttural. "I can think of several excellent reasons to risk it."

The idea that he would make love to her here, in the outdoors, was so tempting . . . *so* outrageous! "But *anyone* could stumble upon us."

"Yes. Anyone could." Piercing her with a dark glance, he bent close. "Tell the truth—that excites you, doesn't it? The idea that we could be caught any minute."

She gulped. It did excite her. She really *was* a wanton.

Keeping his heated gaze locked with hers, he pushed down the cup of her corset to fill his hand with her breast. "That's another reason you should marry me," he said silkily. "Because how many men would make love to you in a forest, no matter the risk?"

Her breath quickened as he thumbed her nipple. Delicately. Seductively "Mr. Ruston attempted . . . something similar, if you'll recall. I—it didn't work for him."

"Yes, I remember your saying that you parried his advances quite well." With his other hand, he began to drag up her petticoats. "But you've barely even tried to parry mine. So I suspect I'll have more success."

She was gathering breath to protest that arrogant statement when he took her mouth with his once more.

Twenty-Five

Jeremy reveled in Yvette's eager response to his kiss. She was his again. He might be half-drunk from lack of sleep and reeling from his wildly swinging emotions, but he still had the presence of mind to seduce Yvette.

Thank God. Because right now the need to be inside her was eating him alive.

Merely seeing her expression when he'd suggested doing this *here* had been enough to spur him on. Curiosity had warred with propriety in her face, and, as always with his Juno, curiosity had won. That was one of her most entrancing qualities.

Even as he ravaged her mouth, he undid the buttons of his long frock coat and drew it open so it could better shield them. Then he pushed up the layers of her frothy undergarments to get to the sweet flesh at her core. But before he could plunder that, too, he felt her fumbling to unfasten his trousers.

He couldn't resist teasing her. "I see I've quelled all your fears about making love in the outdoors."

"Not all of them." Her eyes sparkled up at him as she flicked open the buttons of his trousers, causing his prick to strain against the fabric. "I'm still not sure I want to be found in my altogether by anyone wandering the woods."

"You won't. If I lift your skirts and lower my trousers and drawers, my frock coat and your gown will protect your modesty."

"Will they?" Her fingers froze on the still-fastened buttons of his drawers as she looked up at him. Her eyes shone the deep green of the forest above and around them. "Are you sure?

"Sure enough." Covering her hand with his, he urged her to continue her unbuttoning, and when she did, his blood thundered in his ears. "Here, I'll show you."

He hoisted her legs so he could press in between them and tuck her knees against his waist on either side, inside his frock coat.

She blinked. "My, that is rather . . . intriguing."

To say the least. He fought to control his arousal as she finished undoing his drawers. "Lock your heels behind my thighs."

With color suffusing her cheeks, she did so. That brought her so tight against him that his prick practically jumped out of his open clothing, like a compass needle seeking north.

When she felt the impudent devil swelling against her, her eyes widened. "Good Lord, I had no idea that people did this in this fashion."

He choked back a laugh. "People are rather creative when it comes to doing 'this' in any fashion. You'd be surprised."

Working his finger into her thatch of curls, he stroked her delicate pearl, then gloried in her moans and sighs. He was so intent on inciting her to madness that he almost missed her halting whisper, "This doesn't mean . . . that I'll marry you . . . you know."

Oh, he did know. Only too well. He rubbed the full length of his erection up and down against her soft, damp flesh. "It doesn't mean that you won't, either."

Her expression was a mix of vulnerability and a heartbreaking yearning that stole the breath from his lungs and spiked his need to be inside her to painful heights. Breathing hard, he felt for the entrance to her quim and drove himself deep.

Exhaling on a sigh, she squirmed against him. "Ohh, Jeremy . . . that's so very . . . *oh* . . ."

"Yes, it is." With his prick firmly seated inside her, he thought he'd died and gone to heaven. "You're like hot velvet, my fierce Juno. My lovely wife-to-be."

"Not your wife-to-be . . . yet . . ." she managed, though her eyes slid closed, and her face wore a look of such rapture that it made it impossible for him not to move.

"You will be." Gripping her waist to anchor her against him, he began to thrust into her, first with easy plunges, then harder and deeper ones that dragged moans of pleasure up from her throat. And his, too, as she leapt to meet each stroke, her fingers digging into his waist.

With her head arched back he could see the pulse beat in her neck, and it fed his own frantic pulse. There was nothing lovelier than Yvette in the throes of passion. He would never tire of the sight.

Which was why he meant to make sure he got to see it again and again and again, to have her in his bed . . . in his life.

She slammed hard against him. "Oh . . . heavens . . . you . . . you . . ."

"Marry me, sweetheart." He brushed kisses over her chin, her lips, her cheeks, whatever he could reach. "Don't say no."

"Jeremy . . . please . . . more . . ."

The word inflamed him. He drove into her, reveling in how she clung to him, undulated against him. Reveling in the hot flesh that enveloped him and welcomed him and made him feel something beyond mere desire. "Say yes . . . to me. To us."

Somehow he would persuade her with this, their joining. He would make it good for her. He would make it so she never wanted to let him go, so they were as tightly bound together as man and woman could be.

Because he knew that was what he wanted. Her and him together. "Marry me. God, just marry me . . . and I swear I'll make you happy." It was a promise he'd always been terrified to make. Yet somehow it seemed right with her. And he'd do anything, promise anything, to keep her.

Within reason. But it wasn't reason that drove him to please her, to drive hard against her where he knew it would most arouse her. To kiss her and pet her and make her his. *His*, damn it.

"Ohh . . . like that," she whispered. "That is . . . It feels so . . ."

"I need you." The urge to come rose in him, inflaming him, making him pound into her, making him say things he shouldn't, things that showed just how strong a hold she had on him. "I need you, Yvette . . . God, I need you . . ."

Her body clamped tight about his prick as she neared her climax. "Yes," she whispered. "I need you, too. Yes . . . oh, Lord, yes . . . Jeremy . . . *Jeremy* . . ."

And as she gave the keening cry that heralded her release, he drove into her and came . . . hard, violently, with all the force of his roiling, raw emotions.

The contractions of her body milked him dry, turning him weak-kneed as a green lad with his first woman. God, that was incredible. *She* was incredible.

As they drifted down into normalcy, their bodies still straining against each other, she pressed her lips to his ear and murmured, "Yes, Jeremy. Yes."

And he had his answer at last.

❧

When they emerged from the woods sometime later, Yvette was relieved to see that no one else was about. She was certain she looked exactly like she felt: as if she'd just been thoroughly—and most pleasurably—seduced.

I need you.

His sweet words rang in her ears. That was all she'd ever wanted. For Jeremy to need her. If he couldn't love her, she could live with at least being needed. It was enough for now.

"So we're agreed?" Jeremy entwined his fingers with hers, then lifted her hand to press a kiss against her bare skin. "You'll marry me?"

The tenderness of the gesture sent a delightful

shiver echoing down her spine. "I suppose. Though I did give my answer under duress."

"That explains why you screamed at the end."

"Jeremy!" she chided in mock outrage. "You're the most wicked man I know."

"I'm the most wicked man *I* know." He grinned. "And you like that about me. Admit it."

"Sometimes." She shot him a coy look. "Under certain circumstances."

"The ones where you scream?" he teased.

She merely arched an eyebrow, eliciting a laugh from him.

"Wait up!" a voice hailed them.

Yvette froze. Edwin. Heavenly day. She tried to pull her hand from Jeremy's but he wouldn't allow it, gripping it tightly as if it were his own personal treasure.

The moment Edwin reached them, his gaze arrowed in on their joined hands. "So the offer has been accepted, I take it."

Jeremy's whole body seemed to tense, as if he still wasn't entirely sure of her.

She squeezed his hand. "Yes. It has been accepted."

Edwin broke into a rare smile and clapped Jeremy on the back. "It's about damned time." He walked with them back to the house, chattering about wedding plans in a manner most uncharacteristic of her cynical brother.

After that, everything moved at a dizzying pace. Edwin wanted to celebrate, and the household had to be informed. Her maid went into raptures over the prospect of a wedding, but when Damber was told, he seemed remarkably unsurprised.

Had he guessed what she and his master had been doing behind his back? If so, he thankfully kept it to himself, merely offering them his heartiest good wishes for their future.

For her, the most encouraging reaction to the whirlwind of congratulations and teasing and winking suggestions was Jeremy's. He didn't act like a man trapped into wedding the woman he'd deflowered. He looked happier than she'd ever seen him. Perhaps he did care as deeply for her as his words had implied. Perhaps a marriage between them really could work.

But she had no more time to dwell on it once Jeremy pointed out that she might as well go with them to London in the morning. As he put it, since a wedding had to be planned, it made more sense for her to decamp to the Blakeborough town house than to try to manage it from Stoke Towers.

He was right, which sent her into a flurry of preparations for travel. There was no time to waste! There was packing to be done and arrangements to be made with the staff and a million and one things that had to be handled before she could leave.

By the next morning, when Jeremy handed her into Edwin's traveling carriage, she was exhausted. Fortunately, the coach was roomy and comfortable, and the trip to London wouldn't be long, especially with both her brother and her fiancé in good moods.

Fiancé. A secret smile crossed her lips as she took in Jeremy's finely tailored coat of oxblood wool with gold buttons and satin-trimmed lapels. She had a fiancé, and quite a handsome, well-dressed one at that.

As the coach lumbered down the drive, with Jeremy's rig taking up the rear, driven by Damber, Edwin glanced at Jeremy. "So what's in that enormous box in your curricle? I know it wasn't the portrait, since that's still sitting in my drawing room. Though I don't suppose there's any need for *that* to be finished now, eh, Yvette?" He winked at her, startling her. Edwin never winked.

Jeremy cast her a knowing glance. "It's something I worked on when I wasn't painting the portrait. I fear it's nothing that would interest you, but your sister might find it intriguing."

"I doubt it," Edwin said bluntly. "She doesn't like your darker pictures." He caught himself. "No offense, old chap."

Her fiancé merely laughed. "None taken."

When Jeremy then winked at her, she had to suppress a snort. Good Lord, who knew that getting married would start a veritable onslaught of winking among all in her sphere?

"So what's the subject of this other painting?" Edwin asked.

Oh, dear. Time to get him off *that* topic. "Heavens, Edwin, do allow the man to have *some* secrets." She smoothed her skirts. "And speaking of secrets, now that I'm engaged to be married, I see no reason why I can't go with you and Jeremy to meet Miss Moreton."

That did the trick. Edwin scowled. "You're not going."

"But Edwin—"

"She lives in Spitalfields with her new . . . paramour," he said. "It won't be a fit place for a lady."

"You'll tell me everything that happens, won't you?"

"Of course," Jeremy said with a tender smile. "I'll give you a complete report."

"Are you going there straightaway, as soon as we arrive in London?"

"I must stop in at my cousin's to speak to my mother and sister," Jeremy said. "I promised Amanda I would do so first thing. So Blakeborough and I will leave you at your town house, and then go on to Zoe's."

"Nonsense," she said. "I should like to meet your mother. And it makes sense that I be there for the announcement of our engagement."

Jeremy's smile grew forced. "Of course."

"Do you not want me to meet her?"

"Don't be ridiculous," Edwin cut in. "You have to meet his mother. I'm sure he's just nervous about it, eh, Keane?"

"Yes."

His short response told her that whatever had transpired between him and his sister had not been happy. More than ever, Yvette was determined to find out the circumstances of the rift, though she was also apprehensive. What if his mother was a harridan? What if she didn't like her son's new betrothed?

Yvette stared out the window and tried not to worry. The little he'd said about his mother didn't give her much to go on. Her imagination conjured up all sorts of horrible possibilities—that his mother didn't fancy English ladies, that his family were against the aristocracy in general. By the time they reached the Keane town house, Yvette was a bundle of nerves.

So she was caught entirely off guard when a tiny, birdlike woman with graying auburn hair came tripping down the steps to greet them, wreathed in smiles.

"Jeremy!" she cried. "My dear boy!"

As he caught her up in a hug, a strange mix of affection and worry suffused his features. "I'm so glad you're here, Mother."

The sentiment sounded genuine, which perplexed Yvette even more. Was he at odds with his family or not?

At the moment, she would say "not," since his eyes misted over as he squeezed his mother tight. It was a very sweet scene. Even Mr. Bonnaud, who'd come out to join them, wore a smile, and Miss Keane, who stood up the steps a short distance, was wiping her eyes.

It dawned on Yvette how long eight months must have felt like to Jeremy's family. She couldn't imagine being away from Edwin for so long. It had been hard enough to cut Samuel from her life.

Unlike Jeremy's sister yesterday, his mother didn't chide him when he finally released her. She just patted his cheek fondly, then pulled back to look over Yvette and Edwin, who'd instinctively drawn nearer each other.

"And this must be Lord Blakeborough and his sister." Mrs. Keane's blue eyes were keen and quick as she stared at them. "Amanda told me all about you both, about how courteous you were to her yesterday. And it's most kind of you, my lord, to hire my son to paint for you."

The way she spoke of her son's work as if he were

some sort of housepainter made even Mr. Bonnaud blink. Yvette cast a furtive glance at Jeremy, but he merely rolled his eyes. Undoubtedly he was used to his mother's remarks.

His sister came to her mother's side. "Mama, he was commissioned to do a portrait of Lady Yvette. It's rather more important than you make it sound."

"Oh! A commission, is it? I suppose that *is* quite grand." Her gaze narrowed on her son. "And he only had to travel to England to get it. Fancy that."

Yvette choked down a laugh. Ah, *now* came the chiding.

"Mama, please," Miss Keane murmured. "Don't be rude."

"Is it rude to ask why my only son is gadding about the world without a word to his mother for months at a time?"

"It isn't rude," Jeremy drawled, "but I would prefer that you wait to flay me with your tongue until after I introduce you to my new fiancée." He reached back to take Yvette's hand and draw her forward. "Mother, may I present Lady Yvette, the woman who just yesterday afternoon consented to be my wife."

Though Mr. Bonnaud appeared to take the announcement in stride, Miss Keane and her mother looked utterly shocked. The reactions of the two women worried Yvette until his mother murmured, "Does she know about—"

"Hannah? Yes."

Yvette released a pent-up breath. That explained their reactions. If even Jeremy's London relations were unaware he was a widower, then his family would be justified in thinking he'd told no one else.

"Who's Hannah?" Edwin hissed beside her.

Yvette groaned. She'd forgotten to tell her brother, and apparently it hadn't come up in his discussion with Jeremy yesterday. "I'll explain later," she whispered as his mother came toward her.

The tiny creature fixed her with a steely gaze reminiscent of her son's. "So you're going to marry my rascal son, are you? Do you know what you're getting into, my lady?"

"I think so, yes," she said warily. "My other brother is a rascal, so I've had some experience in dealing with the breed. Indeed, I would venture to say that half the men in the *ton* are rascals, yet I manage to annoy them more than they annoy me."

Mrs. Keane blinked, then burst into laughter. "I see. Then it appears my son has found a woman who can keep up with him for once." She held out her hands. "Welcome to the family, my dear."

Relief coursed through Yvette as she took the woman's hands and squeezed them. "Thank you, Mrs. Keane. I hope we can be friends."

"I have no doubt of that. I can use an ally in my fight to tame my son."

"God, Mother, I'm not that bad," he grumbled.

"You're worse, usually." Drawing Yvette from Jeremy's side with surprising strength for one so small, Mrs. Keane tucked Yvette's hand in the crook of her arm. "Now, come inside and let's have some refreshments while you and Jeremy tell me all about how you came to be engaged."

Oh, dear. That would be quite an interesting conversation. So much to say. So much to leave out.

But before they could go more than two steps up,

Jeremy stalked ahead to block their path. "Yvette hasn't had a moment to herself since yesterday, Mother, so we're carrying her to the earl's town house to rest while he and I and Bonnaud head off to attend to a business matter. But we'll all join you for dinner. Assuming that Bonnaud doesn't mind having two more guests thrust upon him."

"Zoe is always delighted to show off her hostess skills, I assure you," Mr. Bonnaud said with a smile.

"Actually," Yvette put in, "I don't mind just staying here while the three of you go take care of matters." She patted Mrs. Keane's arm. "I'd like to become better acquainted with my future relations."

The look of alarm that crossed Jeremy's face gave her pause, but it vanished quickly, making her wonder if she'd imagined it.

"Of course," he said coolly. "I merely thought you might like to nap since you were run ragged yesterday."

"I can nap later." With a smile, Yvette teased, "Your mother and sister and I have to plot a wedding. That will require all three of us."

"And several shopping trips to Bond Street, though we won't tackle those today." His mother made a shooing motion. "So go handle your business affairs. But don't be too long, unless you want to have no voice in the plans. If you keep avoiding your family, you may find yourself with a wedding full of all the sentimental nonsense you've mocked for years."

"Horrors," Edwin mumbled. "Come, gentlemen, we'd better go. Knowing my sister, she'll be plotting an extravagant affair in St. Paul's Cathedral, which will cost me a pretty penny. The sooner we head that off, the better."

Jeremy hesitated, but he clearly knew when he was outnumbered. Muttering something that sounded remarkably like "Shit and damn," he marched down the steps and got into the carriage with Edwin and Mr. Bonnaud.

Yvette certainly hoped his mother's ears weren't as good as hers.

"I don't know about you," Mrs. Keane said, gesturing up the steps, "but I'm ready for a cup of tea. And Zoe is dying to question you about my son's behavior when he's a guest at others' houses. Besides, she'll want to be part of the wedding plans. Judging from what I've seen so far, she'll know exactly how to host a breakfast that isn't as insipid and dull as most English affairs."

Yvette bit back a smile. She was beginning to see where Jeremy got his opinionated nature.

The next three hours flew by, with Lady Zoe and Mrs. Keane arguing amiably about when Jeremy and Yvette should wed, where they should wed, how Yvette should dress, and how many dishes should be served at the breakfast. Yvette tried to interject her opinions, but with two women as strong-minded as Lady Zoe and Mrs. Keane, it was pointless. Besides, she enjoyed watching the skirmishes.

The only thing that bothered her was how quiet Miss Keane was. The woman hadn't appeared to be shy yesterday. What was making her reticent, even aloof, today?

When after a while Miss Keane said she needed to finish some unpacking and excused herself, Yvette told the other two ladies she needed to visit the necessary and hastened out after the woman.

She caught up to her near the staircase, relieved to see that no one was around. "Miss Keane, may I have a moment?"

With a nervous glance back at the drawing room they'd just left, Miss Keane said, rather sharply, "What is it, my lady?"

"Please, there's no need to stand on ceremony with me. Call me Yvette. We're soon to be sisters, after all."

The words seemed to hit Miss Keane like a blow, for her face crumpled and her eyes filled with pain.

"Oh, dear, what's wrong?" Yvette asked. "I do so want us to be friends, and I feel as if somehow I've insulted you. I assure you it was unintentional. Sometimes my tongue just runs away with me, and—"

"It's not you, my la—Yvette. And please, do call me Amanda." She hesitated, then drew Yvette down the hall to where it was a bit more private. "I don't mean to be rude, but how much did my brother tell you about his marriage to Hannah Miller?"

Yvette suddenly found it hard to breathe. "I believe he told me everything. That his wife died in childbirth after they'd been married only six months."

"Yes, but did he tell you how it devastated him? Especially given my father's part in causing her death—"

"What do you mean?" A chill froze her spine. "If she died in childbirth, it was no one's fault."

"It was a bit more complicated than that. And

Jeremy has never gotten over it." Amanda searched Yvette's face. "That's the only thing that worries me about his sudden decision to marry you after you've only known each other, what, a month or two?"

"A little less than that." The bottom dropped out of her stomach. "But I believe that he's sincere in his wish to marry."

"I'm sure he is. But—" The woman cast Yvette a pitying look. "Well, the thing is, you're the very image of his late wife. She too was tall, dark-haired, green-eyed, and sweet-faced. I fear that—forgive me for being blunt—he's marrying you simply because he can't get past what happened. He's trying to re-create his first marriage so he can do it right this time."

Good Lord. Could that really be? Yvette couldn't bear to believe it. "While I know that his wife's death was difficult for him, I—"

"It's why he won't return home, why he hasn't remarried. Why I have to fight to get him even to talk about the future of the mills. He hates them, you know. He blames them and their hold on Papa for Hannah's death. I thought once Papa died he would get past it at last, but I don't know if he can, given *how* she died."

Yvette couldn't speak, couldn't move. Until that moment, she hadn't realized just how much she'd been ignoring his secretiveness regarding his past. But now she realized it was even worse than she'd feared. "Why are you telling me this?"

"Because I like you, and I hate to see you head blindly into a marriage with a man who has been shattered—may always be shattered—by the past."

When Yvette made some inarticulate sound, remorse flooded Amanda's face. "Oh, I shouldn't have said anything. It was wrong of me to interfere. If the two of you are in love—"

"To use your words, it's a bit more . . . complicated than that," Yvette choked out.

Amanda looked alarmed, then guilty. Taking Yvette by the arm, she led her into the dining room nearby. "Here, sit down. I'll go fetch you some wine."

Before the woman could leave, Yvette caught her sleeve. "No, I'm fine." Or she would be. In a couple of decades, perhaps. She fought for calm, fought to steady herself. "Please. I've asked your brother a number of times to tell me the source of his conflict with your parents, but he won't answer. Will you tell me?"

Miss Keane turned ashen. "I've really gone and done it, haven't I? He'll never forgive me for saying anything in the first place."

"I'm glad you did." Though her heart was fracturing into little pieces, Yvette forced some steel into her spine and patted the chair beside her. "I have to know what I'm getting myself into, and he won't tell me. So please, I beg you, will *you*?"

The woman stared at her bleakly a long moment.

Then at last she gave a terse nod and dropped into the chair. "What exactly is it you wish to know?"

Twenty-Six

Jeremy was surprised that the earl didn't ask for Samuel's letter the moment they set off, but apparently Bonnaud's presence kept him in check. Meanwhile, Bonnaud spent the ride congratulating Jeremy on his impending marriage, while Jeremy spent it trying not to think about what his mother and sister might be saying to Yvette.

One thing he could count on. Though he wasn't so sure about Amanda, Mother would never tell Yvette the details of Hannah's death. She'd always resisted discussing Father's actions. Someday he'd have to tell Yvette everything himself, but not yet. He still couldn't bear the idea of her knowing how his selfishness had cost Hannah her life.

As soon as they arrived, Bonnaud introduced Blakeborough to Miss Moreton. From the moment she brought her son forward, everything changed. Even Jeremy could see that the lad resembled the earl to an astonishing degree. Indeed, Blakeborough was visibly shaken, then let out a long-suffering sigh, as if already realizing he was doomed to take on another dependent.

But what really settled the matter was when Jeremy gave Miss Moreton the letter. She opened it warily. After reading it, however, she looked a bit dazed as she sat turning the pages over in her hand.

"I should like to see what my brother wrote," Blakeborough said, more a command than a request.

A sudden anxious look crossed her face. "My lord, I want you to know that I had no idea of what he was planning, and no involvement whatsoever in—"

"The letter, Miss Moreton."

Swallowing hard, she handed it to Blakeborough, who read it aloud so Jeremy and Bonnaud could hear it, too:

Dearest Peg,

If you're reading this, then my sister succeeded in posting it. I'm sure you've heard of my trial and sentence of transportation. It was only after I was in Newgate that I learned you had left the stage. One of my boxing associates saw you at Mrs. Beard's some months ago. He made inquiries and learned of our son.

So Samuel hadn't lied about not knowing of his son until he was already in gaol. That was rather surprising.

I know we parted on bad terms, but I don't like to think of any child of mine being raised in such a place. I'm enclosing documents that should help you get money in another way to keep you and little Elias in a better situation. They prove we were married at the time of his birth.

Blakeborough raised his head to gape at Miss Moreton. "You were married?"

She looked grim. "Keep reading, my lord."

The forger who made up the papers said they should hold up well enough to convince my brother, and I'm sure your acting abilities are up to the task of playing the long-suffering wife. Forgive me for resorting to such a subterfuge, but Edwin is hard-hearted and unlikely to give you any aid unless he thinks the child is legitimate.

Blakeborough's voice faltered at that. After a few moments, he set down the letter. "Everything else is personal." He leafed through the other sheets. "And these must be the supposed documents of a runaway marriage in Scotland."

"Good God," Bonnaud muttered. "Your brother is quite a piece of work."

"Yes, that's Samuel for you," Blakeborough said tonelessly.

"But Elias *is* his?" Jeremy asked Miss Moreton. "Or you believe him to be?"

"I know him to be," she said stoutly. "I was a faithful mistress to Samuel when we were together."

"So you admit you weren't married to my brother," the earl said.

Paling a little, she shook her head. "I wrote to him concerning his son a couple of times, but got no answer. I heard later that he'd been cut off by your father, so I suspect he didn't get the letters. I didn't know how or where else to find him, and I didn't want to incur your father's wrath by presenting myself there. I wasn't sure he would help anyway. Then once I heard Samuel was in gaol . . ." She shrugged. "There seemed no point in pursuing anything."

Jeremy felt compelled to champion the child, if only for Yvette's sake. "Blakeborough, your brother couldn't have known Yvette would try delivering the letter in person rather than posting it. So whatever he wrote about the child is probably true. Unless you think he's playing some double game."

"I wouldn't put it past him," Bonnaud said.

"Nor would I." Blakeborough glanced over to where a grubby Elias sat on the floor, stacking up a set of worn wooden blocks. "But I have eyes. And, despite what my brother thinks, a heart. I believe he was being honest about his paternity."

He looked at Miss Moreton and steadied his shoulders. "So, madam, I understand you wish to marry soon."

And that was that. From there, nothing was left but to negotiate the handing over of the boy. They were done and out the door in a matter of moments, with Blakeborough promising to send a servant to fetch the lad the next morning. He said he needed time to prepare for placing the boy.

On the way home, they were a rather somber threesome. Or rather, the earl was somber; Jeremy and Bonnaud were merely reluctant to intrude upon his silent reflection.

But as they neared the Keane town house, Blakeborough roused himself. "I need to go on to Meredith's and settle with her if she will take Elias."

"Do you think she will?" Jeremy asked.

"I believe so. She was grateful when we agreed to provide for her and her babe, and this will be no financial imposition. It will also give her son an older brother. If you wouldn't mind, I'd like Yvette to go with me. She's better with Meredith than I am. But we'll be back in time for dinner."

"That's fine." Jeremy gazed at the man, wondering how he'd endured his brother's shenanigans for so long. "It was good of you to take the child. Yvette will be relieved."

"Which is why I'm doing it. The *only* reason I'm doing it."

Jeremy didn't believe that one whit. He'd seen Blakeborough's haunted expression when the man had seen Elias. It made him wonder about the earl's relationship to his own father. Given what Yvette had said, she probably hadn't been the only one to feel neglected.

When they stopped, Jeremy told the earl he'd go in and fetch Yvette. Then he and Bonnaud climbed the steps together.

"I can't believe you're getting married," Bonnaud said. "Does this mean no more trips to the stews?"

"I don't know what it means." That was the God's honest truth. "But I suspect that in future my choice of subjects may . . . er . . . shift a bit."

Bonnaud laughed. "No doubt."

As they entered, it struck Jeremy that the place was unusually quiet. The chatter of four women planning a wedding ought to have raised the rafters, but he heard nothing. Just as he wondered if they'd gone to do some shopping, Yvette appeared in the hall.

He walked toward her. "You'll be pleased to know that everything went well. Your brother is waiting outside. He wants you to go with him to Meredith's to arrange for—" He halted as he noticed her swollen eyes and red nose. Alarms clamored in his head. "What's wrong?"

Instead of answering, she flashed Bonnaud a stiff smile. "Your wife said to tell you she's in the nursery and could use your advice on furniture."

That sounded like a trumped-up tale if Jeremy had ever heard one, but Bonnaud merely headed up the stairs.

Only then did Jeremy ask, "Where are Mother and Amanda? Are they all right?"

When he tried to take her arm, she shied away. "They're fine," she said, not meeting his gaze. "But you and I need to talk."

The words curdled his stomach. He managed a nod, then followed her into the drawing room. When she shut the door, dread spread through him like a noxious weed.

"What's this about?" he demanded.

She faced him, a hollow look in her eyes. "Why did you never tell me that I resemble your late wife?"

That threw him off guard. "Because you don't." If that was her only concern, he could clear this up right now. "Why? Did my mother tell you that you did?"

"According to your sister, Hannah was a tall, green-eyed, dark-haired—"

"Oh, for God's sake, you're listening to Amanda? My sister has no visual sense; haven't you noticed her poor taste in clothing? She's bad with faces and colors. She only notices such things in broad terms."

Yvette fixed him with an unrelenting stare that made him desperate to convince her.

"Hannah was tall, yes," he went on, "and dark-haired and green-eyed. But she was also thin and frail, a delicate woman whose features bore no resemblance to yours. You're nothing alike, either in temperament or in appearance. If you give me a moment, I'll go find the miniature of her that's somewhere in my belongings and show you."

That made her pale. "You keep a miniature of her?"

"She was only my wife briefly, I'll grant you, but still my wife. Would you have wanted me to forget her entirely after what she suffered?"

"You mean what she suffered in childbirth. When your father told the physician attending her that he should save the babe at all costs. Even if it meant the loss of your wife."

His heart dropped into his stomach. Oh, God, no. No, no, no. "Amanda told you," he choked out.

"Yes." She continued in a halting voice. "She said the physician informed your parents that the babe's head was too large and he could only be removed if your wife were cut open, or if the child was . . . destroyed. Your father gave the order to save the boy. But they'd delayed too long, and the child was stillborn. Your wife died a few hours later."

Hearing the events described in Yvette's heart-wrenching tones was bad enough, and she hadn't even touched upon the worst part—that Jeremy hadn't been there to stop it.

"Amanda had no right to tell you," he said hoarsely.

"*You* should have told me." Concern filled Yvette's face. "She's worried about you. And now *I'm* worried about you. About us."

He could hardly breathe. His worst fears had been realized, and it hurt even more than he'd expected. "It has nothing to do with us."

"It has everything to do with us, if you can't get past the death of your wife and son!"

He fought to sound reasonable, normal. "That's absurd. It's been twelve years. Of course I've gotten past it."

"Really? I don't think you realize how little you have." Her cheeks ashen, she stalked over to a sofa and pulled something from behind it, then set it in front of him.

Art Sacrificed to Commerce.

"What in thunder? You broke into my luggage? Took out my unfinished work, which I expressly forbade you to view before it was done?"

"I impressed upon Damber the importance of the situation, and he pried open the box."

"The 'importance of the situation,'" he said, mocking her serious tone. "I can't see what my painting has to do with anything."

"For one thing, the woman doesn't resemble me in the least."

"I know! I keep working to get her face right, but I can't. I think it's the shadows or . . . Damn it, I don't know. But I don't understand why my incompetence as an artist has anything to do with us."

"It's not—" She huffed out a breath. "*Look* at it! For once, Jeremy, really *look* at your painting. The woman doesn't resemble me because your subject *isn't* Art sacrificed to Commerce. It's Hannah being sacrificed on the altar of your father's obsession with his mills."

He froze, gaping at the picture. "That's not . . . It was never meant to . . ."

Horror swept through him. She was right.

He'd made Commerce older, as would be appropriate. But in so doing, he'd actually painted an image of his father as he'd looked years ago.

Jeremy's chest tightened, his ribs feeling as if they were closing in on him, crushing him, making it hard to breathe. The painting he'd been driven to do was not what he'd thought at all.

And now that he could see it, everything fit. Commerce was his father, a man so consumed by his legacy that he'd sentenced his daughter-in-law to death rather than lose the possible future of that legacy. Even the work's background had elements of the bank where Father had done business. And though Jeremy had painted a wound in Art's chest, the knife dripping with blood was actually poised over Art's belly.

"Oh, God . . . oh, God . . . oh, God . . ."

Yvette stepped nearer, tears trickling down her cheeks. "You said you didn't know why you were compelled to use me as your model. But I know why. Because I look enough like your wife to play the role you needed."

"No," he whispered. "That's not true!" He didn't want it to be true. There was something deeper between him and Yvette, something real and sweet and pure, something beyond Hannah's death.

"It *is* true. You know it in your heart. You're trying to purge your grief, and you're using me to do it. Because you can't get past the horrific choice your father made."

"Not just *his* horrific choice."

She blinked. "Wh-what do you mean?"

"It was mine, too." Bile rose in his throat. No point in not telling her all of it now. "I chose not to be there when I should have been. If I had been—"

"Then *you* would have had to make the horrific choice."

"Yes! And I would have chosen my wife. Not a babe who might end up dying anyway. She deserved better than that." He clenched his fists at his sides. "Especially after she was forced into marriage to a man who couldn't love her."

Sympathy softened her features. "She wasn't forced," she said gently. "She knew the possible consequences when she shared your bed."

"She didn't know we would end up enslaved in a life we didn't choose. She didn't know I'd be wed to the mills as much as to her."

"That wasn't your fault."

"Maybe not, but her death . . ." Unable to bear Yvette's pity, he faced the fireplace. "I failed her, don't you see? I failed her by not being there."

She came over to place her hand on his arm. "Jeremy—"

"No!" He shook off her hand. "You don't understand. Father never wanted her to be my wife. Yet even knowing that, even realizing that her time was near, I still left her to his care. I *trusted* him. Because the work of the mills had to go on. So instead of staying with her, I let him convince me to go to a damned meeting in Philadelphia where everything was about money and how to make it!"

About commerce. He cringed. Oh, God, the painting fit that, too. How had he not seen it before?

"So I suppose you're right," he continued in a low voice. "*Art Sacrificed to Commerce* probably is about her and him."

"Or perhaps her and you," she said in an aching voice. "It's you as the model, isn't it? Your mother said you looked like your father, but it goes beyond that. You blame him . . . and you blame yourself. So both of you wield the knife."

"Enough," he said in a ragged whisper. He felt bludgeoned by the truth, bludgeoned by the past.

"I'm sorry, Jeremy. I didn't say all that to make you feel worse. I just wanted to explain why you and I shouldn't—"

"Damn it, Yvette, you might be right about the painting's true purpose, but you're wrong about you and me." He fixed her with his gaze. "I didn't use you to purge my grief. You've been the first real light in my life in years. The moment I saw you, I knew I wanted you. The painting was just an excuse to have you."

Her eyes warmed, and she seized his hand. "Then prove it."

That stopped him cold. "How the hell am I supposed to do that?"

"Mend the rift with your family. Return to Montague and settle your affairs. Stop running." When he tried to jerk his hand from hers, she clung tight to it, refusing to release it. "Because the only reason I can see for your not going home is your inability to get past the deaths of your wife and son. Unless you can do that, you're not ready to begin again with a new wife."

His throat worked convulsively. "You don't know what you're asking of me."

"I do. Facing the past is hard. But your father is dead now, and your mother and sister need you. They suffered along with you back then, though you probably couldn't see it. Let them help you grieve now and put it behind you at last. So you can go on."

Struggling for breath, he slipped his hand from hers. "Is this a new requirement for our marriage?" he said curtly. "Even though you've already accepted my offer, you're imposing some new condition—"

"I didn't know all the facts then. And yes, now that I do, this is what I require." A flash of pain darkened her gaze before she steadied her shoulders. "Because the truth is, Jeremy, I've fallen in love with you."

The words stunned him, then crept through him like ivy seeking out cracks in the bricks he'd used to wall up his heart. She loved him. Even after everything she'd learned about his past, she *loved* him?

Her eyes filled with tears. "I thought I could marry you despite your not feeling the same, but I find that I cannot. If we're to have a life together, you can't always be running—from love, from the past . . . from me. My father ran from all the hard parts of marriage." Her voice cracked. "I can't watch my husband do it, too. I just . . . can't."

"I'm not sure if I can do what you ask," he choked out.

"Then I don't see any way for us to wed," she said mournfully. "Because marriage only works if the husband and wife can both look forward."

A knock came at the door. Neither of them responded, but the door opened anyway to reveal his mother. "Oh. Forgive me. A servant came in to say that Lord Blakeborough is still waiting in his carriage for his sister."

Yvette gave her a forced smile. "Thank you, Mrs. Keane. Please tell the servant I'll be there in a moment."

His mother glanced from her to him and frowned, but she left.

"I have to go," Yvette murmured.

"Don't." He caught her hand. "I don't want you to go. Please don't go."

Her expression conflicted, she kissed him on the cheek. "Take care of yourself. You know where to find me if you should change your mind."

Then she walked out.

He stood there numb. Disbelieving. After all they'd meant to each other, all they'd shared, she'd broken their engagement. Or rather, she'd put a condition upon it that he could not meet.

Or could he? Was Yvette right? *Was* he running away from everything and everyone? If they married, would he eventually run away from her, too?

Art Sacrificed to Commerce caught his eye, and he felt that horrible lurch again as he stared at the work. After all these years, what had pressed him to paint it?

Father's death, obviously. Jeremy had started

thinking about the painting shortly after the funeral. Working on it the past few weeks had obsessed him. Yet although he was generally a quick painter, this one hadn't come quickly.

He hadn't been able to get Yvette right, no matter how much he reworked her image. Was it because he'd wanted to make her into Hannah and hadn't yet succeeded?

No, he didn't think so.

"My, my, that is . . . very . . ."

He whirled to find his mother staring at the painting with widened eyes. She managed a weak smile. "I guess that answers the question that Lady Yvette kept avoiding—how you ended up engaged. Did her brother actually allow—"

"No." Although Mother would never hurt Yvette's reputation, he ought to try to explain away the re-semblance to Yvette, or otherwise hide the truth from her.

He just didn't have the heart for it anymore.

She cocked her head. "Is that your father?"

"No." Jeremy speared a hand through his hair. "Yes. Well, both of us, really."

His mother stood in silence, taking in the image. "It's not finished, I take it."

"Not yet." And he seemed to have lost all desire to complete it. What would be the point, now that he knew why it had consumed him so?

"What do you call it?"

"*Art Sacrificed to Commerce.*" He held his breath, waiting for her to make the inevitable connection.

"Ah. So it's about your father not letting you go to art school when you wanted."

A maniacal urge to laugh rose up in him. Mother had never been very deep. "That's not what Yvette says. She says it's about Hannah, about my guilt over her death. Amanda told her some nonsense about how she looks like my late wife."

"Well, that's absurd. Your fiancée looks nothing like your late wife." She snorted. "Amanda never was very observant when it came to people. I hope she didn't upset Lady Yvette too much."

A lump stuck in his throat. "As a matter of fact, my fiancée doesn't want to *be* my fiancée anymore. She's convinced that I haven't let go of the past. She says that marriage isn't for those who are still living past tragedies."

"Ah."

When she said nothing more, he slanted a glance at her. For the first time, he realized how old his mother was getting. She was still in her late fifties, but gray had finally begun to overtake the auburn in her hair, and time had etched lines in her face where there had been none before. Had all this happened in just eight months?

Your mother and sister need you. They suffered along with you back then, though you probably couldn't see it. Let them help you grieve now and put it behind you at last. So you can go on.

"Why didn't you stop him?" The question he'd always wanted to ask burst out, and he realized that if there had been any rift between Mother and him, it was this. That she hadn't prevented Hannah's death.

When Mother paled, he said, "Forgive me. I know you don't like to speak of it, but surely *you* didn't think Father's choice was right—to save the babe over my wife."

She began to tremble. "Must we talk about this?"

"I think we must. If I'm to lose the woman I love over it, then let me at least—"

He halted as he heard himself. The woman he loved.

God, he was such a fool. He loved Yvette.

Of course he loved her. How could he not? She was his lodestone, drawing him in. Anchoring him to the world, to a reality outside his past. He'd been so convinced he couldn't or shouldn't or wouldn't fall in love that he'd refused to see the truth slapping him in the face.

He loved her. And if he wanted to get her back, if he wanted to make a life with her, he would have to change things.

His mother looked as if she might faint. Hastily he went to her side and urged her to sit on the settee opposite the sofa.

He sat next to her and took her hand, noting the blue veins that grew more prominent with each passing year. "I don't mean to upset you, Mother, and I don't ask this to accuse you of anything or blame you for anything. I just need to understand why you let him do it. Why you didn't stop it."

She gripped his hand in hers. "Because I agreed with his choice."

He gaped at her. Surely she hadn't said what he thought.

"You weren't there, Jeremy. She was in agony. Even at nine months along, she was such a frail thing, and pale as death besides. The doctor said she probably wouldn't survive the birth anyway, even if we destroyed the child. He said that if he opened her up, we might still save the babe." She thrust out her chin. "Your father gave the order, but I agreed with it. Perhaps I was wrong, but—"

"Why did you never tell me this?" he asked in a hollow voice.

"So you could cut *me* out of your life, too?" She swiped a tear angrily away. "You were both so stubborn, you and your father. He wanted to force you to his will, and you fought that with every ounce of your being. And after Hannah died, he blamed the doctor, you blamed him, and I knew better than to take a side." Her words grew choked. "I didn't want to lose my only son. But I suppose I lost you anyway."

"No," he said earnestly. "Never. I love you, Mother. I just . . . couldn't bear to go back to Montague, to face the truth. That I should have been there. *I* should have made the choice."

"If you had, it wouldn't have ended any differently, my dear boy. I never was able to make you accept it, but sometimes people just die, and there's not a damned thing we can do about it."

She pulled his head down and kissed the top, as she'd done so many times when he was a boy, and he clutched her to him, fighting the tears stinging his eyes.

"I know your father was a hard man," she whispered into his hair. "He never understood you, and he didn't know a blasted thing about how to talk to people without getting their backs up. But he didn't want Hannah dead, I swear. He just saw a chance to save his grandchild, and he took it."

Jeremy's control crumbled. Gripping his mother tight, he gave way to his grief—for the wife no one had been able to save, for the baby that had never had a chance, for the years he had lost with the hard man who'd been his father.

Mother held him and murmured soothing nonsense, as if he were her little boy again. And he didn't care. There was something freeing about losing himself in the comfort of his mother's arms.

After a while he pulled away to find Mother crying, but she was smiling through her tears. She cupped his cheek tenderly. "Oh, my poor lad. You must leave it behind."

"Yes."

It was time to forget and forgive. He saw that now. Yvette was right: going on in the way he'd been was impossible. He wasn't even sure he was capable of it anymore. These past few weeks had changed him. *She* had changed him.

Mother sniffled, and he drew out a handkerchief for her. With a tremulous smile, she took it. "What will you do about your Yvette?"

His Yvette. He liked the sound of that. "Whatever I must to get her back. Because I can't bear to be without her."

Then prove it.

He brushed a kiss to his mother's cheek, then rose to stare critically at his painting. Maybe it was time to head in a new direction. And how better to start than with this?

Twenty-Seven

Ever since Yvette and Edwin had driven away from the town house, she'd struggled to hide her feelings. But it was hard not to keep thinking about the shock on Jeremy's face when she'd interpreted his painting the way she saw it.

How could he have been so blind to it? Had he been entirely unaware of the stake he kept twisting in his heart? He had to have known it was there.

Well, thanks to her, he couldn't ignore it now. And she wasn't sure that pointing it out to him had been a kindness. Sometimes one had to lie to oneself in order to endure pain.

Except that he'd been lying to himself, or hiding from himself, for years and years. Wasn't it time to put that aside? Or had she been asking too much to expect that? It was fine for her to say he should get past the deaths of his wife and son, but it couldn't be easy.

"You look upset," Edwin said.

Lord. She really wasn't hiding her own pain very well if even Edwin had noticed it.

Although she couldn't bear the idea of exposing her torn-open heart to Edwin's critical perusal, she supposed she had to tell him what had happened. "Mr. Keane and I aren't getting married," she said, trying to sound nonchalant. "I decided that we wouldn't suit after all."

He drew in a heavy breath, his face unreadable. "I see."

"That's all you have to say?"

"Yes. Ultimately it's your choice, isn't it?"

"It is."

Except that she could still hear Jeremy's words in her heart. *I don't want you to go. Please don't go.*

It might be her choice, but she wasn't sure she'd made the right one. And judging from her brother's expression, he wondered the same thing. "You think it's the wrong choice," she accused him.

"Don't put words in my mouth," he said stiffly.

With her confrontation of Jeremy still ringing in her ears, that got her dander up. "You think I'm too particular."

"Certainly not."

"Well, then, you think I'm too contentious to find a husband."

"I think you're too afraid."

She froze. "Of what?"

"Of making the wrong choice again. The way you did with Ruston."

Her heart faltered. Edwin was supposed to be unaware that she'd *ever* made a choice about the lieutenant. Unless . . .

Oh, Lord, Jeremy had been closeted alone with Edwin for some time yesterday morning, according to the servants. "Jeremy told you about Lieutenant Ruston."

"No." He drummed his fingers nervously on his knee. "I knew all along."

She caught her breath. "About the blackmail? About my garter?"

"All of it. From the beginning."

The soft words fell into the stillness of the carriage like a stone into a pond, rippling the surface of their relationship in ever-widening waves.

Remembering that Jeremy had suggested something of the sort, she clenched her hands together in her lap. "How?"

He glanced away. "The day it happened, I caught . . . Ruston in town preparing for your elopement."

She raised an eyebrow. He was lying. She could tell because he was awful at it. Always had been. "I see. And Lieutenant Ruston simply told you all about the blackmail when you encountered him?"

Her brother began to rub the back of his neck. "I . . . um . . . well . . ."

Wait a minute. "*Samuel* was the one who told you, wasn't he?" She should have realized Samuel wouldn't have been able to handle the matter alone. "He told you so you would fix things."

Edwin's startled glance sent a chill down her spine. "Right. Exactly. Samuel told me, and I stepped in to fix things."

Her eyes narrowed. If that were the case, why not tell her about it all those years ago? Why let Samuel get the credit for saving her? For that matter, why make up some nonsense about catching the lieutenant in town?

A pounding began in her temples. "It wasn't Lieutenant Ruston you encountered, was it? It was Samuel. He was in on the lieutenant's plan from the beginning."

Edwin muttered a curse under his breath, and her heart clenched inside her chest. All this time she'd clung to the memory of Samuel as he'd been in his youth—her wild and fun brother—but that brother also didn't care about anyone but himself. He certainly hadn't cared about her. Not the way she'd cared about him.

She choked down tears. "Oh, Edwin," she said sadly. What a fool she'd been to believe Samuel. She should have realized that Edwin had caught Ruston and taken care of the situation. Then hidden it from her. "Why not just tell me?"

His eyes were solemn. "I didn't want you to know that he would betray you like that. Bad enough that Ruston had broken your heart. I couldn't stand to let Samuel break it, too."

Touched to the depths of her soul, she reached across the carriage to clasp his hands. "That is quite possibly the dearest thing you've ever said to me. Or done for me." She fought back her tears, knowing they would only upset him more. "I know it's long overdue, but thank you. For looking after me, and trying to protect me from being hurt."

He flushed a deep scarlet. "What are brothers for?"

Clearly not *all* brothers, but *he* certainly was. Thinking of Samuel reminded her of where they were headed. "And thank you for stepping in to save little Elias, too. I know you didn't have to."

His expression hardened a bit. "You're damned right I didn't have to," he grumbled, but now she knew that his gruff manner was mostly for show.

She should have realized it before. He'd always been a decent sort; she'd just been too busy balancing the chip on her shoulder to notice.

With another squeeze of his hands, she sat back. "Why did you decide to tell me about Samuel's betrayal today, of all days? Did something happen at Miss Moreton's?"

"Yes. But that's not why. Keane has been urging me to do so ever since I told him the truth yesterday." He fixed her with an earnest gaze. "I don't want you fearing that Keane is just another Ruston. Because I honestly think he's not. I believed the rumors at first, but now I don't think they're entirely true. He's a better man than he's willing to let anyone know."

"I'm fully aware of that. And that has nothing to do with why I broke with him."

When he looked expectantly at her, she realized how very much he cared about her. And how little faith she'd put in him heretofore. She'd been as bad with Edwin as Jeremy had been with his family—closing him out, not revealing the doubts of her heart.

Perhaps it was time she told him what she could. If nothing else came of her two-day engagement to Jeremy, at least she could make sure she held on to the one good thing to come out of it: a better relationship with her brother.

With that decision made, she began to explain about Jeremy.

The rest of the day passed in a daze for Yvette. The meeting with Meredith, who'd readily agreed to take Elias. The interminable trip home to Stoke Towers. The lonely dinner with Edwin that reminded her she was supposed to have been celebrating her engagement tonight with Jeremy and his family. All of it felt otherworldly, as if it existed on one plane and she on another.

How would she go on if he couldn't change? Was it even right of her to ask him to?

Yes. She knew herself too well to believe she could marry a man who still had one foot in his old pain. Who, as his sister had put it, had "been shattered—may always be shattered—by the past."

But oh, how it hurt. Going to bed was a pointless ritual; it wasn't as if she could sleep. She still smelled him on her nightdress. Though it wasn't their lovemaking that she kept dwelling on.

It was the other things—how he'd listened to her tale about the lieutenant without judging, how he'd persisted in wanting to marry her because he'd ruined her . . . how he'd held her and complimented her and confirmed what she'd wanted to believe—that she was a woman worthy of a decent husband. One who genuinely cared about her.

By the time she fell into a fitful sleep, it was nearly dawn. When she awoke, the noonday sun was streaming through her windows.

For a moment, she considered just lying there all day. She couldn't cry any more; there were no tears left. But she could wallow in her misery, in the pain of having a blade lodged in her heart.

Like the blade in Jeremy's cursed painting, it held untold torment. She stared sullenly at the ceiling. Perhaps *that* was why he'd painted the image, as a prediction of how he was plotting to stab her through the heart.

She sighed. A self-pitying bit of nonsense if she'd ever heard one.

What was she doing? Trying to turn herself into Edwin? That would accomplish nothing. Better to keep busy, to do something useful to keep her mind off the pain.

She got up.

Some hours later, she was dutifully putting sewing kits together in the drawing room when her butler entered. "Mr. Keane is here to see you, my lady."

Just like that, the blade she'd been fighting to ignore sliced deep once again.

Curse him. No doubt he had come to try to convince her that none of it mattered. That they should marry anyway, because she was ruined. She couldn't go through this again. She would put an end to the agony once and for all.

"Show him in," she said in her loftiest voice. Rising from her chair, she fought the urge to look in the mirror over the fireplace. She knew what she'd see—a haggard woman in an old gown, whose hair barely looked presentable.

She didn't even care. Especially once she caught sight of *him*.

Jeremy looked even worse than she. Although his

unruly tumble of blond curls somewhat enhanced his appeal, his bloodshot eyes and drawn face did not. Had he spent the night drinking? He certainly looked it.

She fought a twinge of sympathy until she saw the large box he held in his right hand. Oh no. Not the painting. If he was here to explain away what he'd depicted, she would toss him out on his ear, and his dratted canvas, too.

Better yet, she would tromp on it.

"Good afternoon, Mr. Keane," she said, hoping she sounded calmer than she felt. "What brings you back to the wilds of Hertfordshire?"

"So formal already, sweetheart? I would have thought you'd take at least a week to revert to calling me Mr. Keane."

The word *sweetheart* was all it took to crumble her defenses. "Please, Jeremy, don't toy with me. I can't bear it."

He looked stricken. "I understand. Because I couldn't bear being away from you, not for one night, even knowing it was necessary."

Her throat felt tight and raw. "Necessary?"

"You asked me to prove that I had gotten past the deaths of my wife and son. So that's why I'm here. To offer my proofs."

All she could do was gape at him.

He laid a sheaf of papers on the table. "Here's my contract with Amanda, selling her my half of the mills. We practically had to beat the lawyers about the head and shoulders to get them to write it up so quickly, but they managed it."

She stared at the contract. "That only proves you've got out from under the mills at last, which is exactly what you wanted anyway." She lifted a bewildered gaze to him. "Although Amanda said your mother had some say in it and had refused to sign the papers unless you came back to Montague to settle other affairs."

"Yes." He moved closer. "Which is why my mother and sister and I are leaving for Philadelphia in a few months." His gaze burned into hers. "After you and I wed."

Her blood began to pound in spite of her caution. "Assuming that we do."

He flinched. "Yes."

"And you're really planning to return to America."

"For a visit, yes. And I'd like you to go with me." His voice turned husky. "I want to welcome you to my home. To introduce you to the other members of my family. I want you to see that I truly *have* put the past behind me."

Hope had begun to replace the blade in her heart, but she was afraid to embrace it entirely. "Is it safe to assume that you've mended the rift with your mother?"

A soft smile crossed his features. "Considering that she ordered me to carry you triumphantly back to London, I think it's safe to assume that I have." His eyes turned serious once more. "I have much to tell you, my love, but before I do, I have to show you something."

She was still reeling from the words *my love* when he set the box on the table and opened it.

As he lifted it, she began, "Jeremy, I don't want to . . ."

Then she saw the painting, and her mouth dropped open.

He'd repainted whole parts of it. It had clearly been hastily done, but the changes were still quite obvious. He'd turned the figure of his father back into himself, and instead of holding aloft a knife dripping blood, he gripped the post of a tester bed, which was what he'd turned the banker's counter into.

The background still worked, with its columns and lush curtains, but he'd altered her clothing to make it a nightdress by adding lace around the edges and changing the top half. And he'd not only painted over the wound but had given her a lower neckline to show a generous portion of bosom.

Heavenly day.

And those weren't the only changes he'd made to her figure. He'd painted over the arm that shielded her features and had made her face more prominent. This time the woman *was* clearly her. She looked sensual and erotic. Where before she'd been gazing up at her attacker in fear, now she looked up at him adoringly.

Like a woman in love. With a man who also looked to be in love.

She checked the impulse to leap into his arms with all the joy filling her heart. She had to be sure first. "What does it mean?"

"It means I love you. I probably have for some time. But I was so busy trying not to love you that I couldn't hear the cry of my heart. Because although you were mostly right about *Art Sacrificed to Commerce*, you were wrong about one thing."

His intent gaze speared her. "Perhaps it did start out as a work about my past, about my guilt over

Hannah's final hours. Father's death had dragged me back into my anger, and that anger needed an outlet. So I felt compelled to paint this. Or rather, this as it was."

He stared down at it. "After I met you, however, things began to change. No matter how I tried, I could never get your face right. I worked on it and worked on it, and somehow it came out wrong every time."

Her blood chilled. "Because you were trying to paint Hannah."

"No." He smiled. "I considered that, but no. It was always you I wished to paint. But I was trying to fit you into an old paradigm where you didn't belong. And the more I tried to make you fit, to turn you into the victim necessary for my lofty image of what the work was to be, the less it worked."

He caught her hands in his. "Because you, my Juno, have never been a victim. You've always chosen your own path, even when Ruston threatened blackmail. Hannah let my father and me push her into what we wanted; you would never do that. Hell, you wouldn't even let me marry you after I ruined you."

As her heart began to soar, his voice thickened with emotion. "That's why I couldn't get your face right. Because somewhere in the depths of my artist's soul, I realized that you would never fit. That if I ever got your face right, the rest of it wouldn't fit. Nothing would fit anymore. And I wasn't ready to face that—ready to have a new purpose."

He drew her into his arms. "But I'm ready now. Ready to look forward and not back. With a new wife. With my only love. So, are you ready, too?"

If nothing else had convinced her, the heartbreaking sincerity in his face would have done so.

"I've been ready for a very long time," she whispered.

Relief flooded his features. Then he was kissing her with the sweetness of a lover newly born, a man who had finally found his purpose. Found his Juno.

After he'd lightened her heart and curled her toes and done any number of things to the rest of her parts, she pulled back to cast the painting a regretful look. "You can never exhibit it, you know. Edwin would shoot you."

He flashed her one of those smoldering looks she adored. "I don't intend to exhibit it. It's mine. And yours. Our private painting, if you will, depicting our passion. And our love."

"I like the sound of that. Though it definitely needs a new title. The old one won't suit."

"It certainly won't."

She viewed it carefully, enraptured by it. Lord only knew where they would hang it. Perhaps in their bedchamber?

Then inspiration struck. "I know what the title should be."

"Oh?"

She grinned at him. "*Lessons in the Art of Sinning.*"

He burst into laughter. "Sounds perfect." He slid his arm about her waist to draw her close. "Because I intend for us to have a great many of those."

Epilogue

Hertfordshire, England
December 1829

Jeremy headed for the drawing room of the brand-new home he'd purchased in Hertfordshire with the proceeds from selling his share of the mills. Walton Hall was located close enough to Stoke Towers that Yvette could visit regularly, but far enough to give them their privacy. It also put them a bit nearer London, a distinct advantage given his growing status as a prominent artist.

How strange that only a few months ago the idea of owning a sprawling estate would have sent him fleeing. Now, he took pride in it. Because of her. She'd utterly changed his life. By lancing the wound in his soul, she'd settled the restlessness that had made him blow with the wind.

Every day with her was an adventure. Every night with her was an erotic exploration. He liked adventures. He enjoyed erotic explorations. And he *loved* her. What more could a man ask for?

He quickened his stride, eager to catch her alone. Though this was the first day of their holiday house party, the other gentlemen were out shooting and the other ladies in town shopping. He'd been trying to get a bit of painting done when a footman told him that his wife had returned without the others and wanted a private moment with him in the drawing room.

He sincerely hoped she had something wicked in mind.

But the minute he entered, thunderous applause put paid to that hope—not to mention startling him out of his wits. "What the—"

He choked off the word *hell*. His mother and sister were both here, along with the rest of their houseguests.

"Surprise!" Yvette gestured to the wall with a bright smile. "The shopping jaunt was a ruse to pick this up in town. We had it put up while you were in your studio."

He turned to see the portrait of her in all its glory, hung in the beautiful frame he'd picked out himself. "That is the most excellent portrait I've ever seen," he said. "By a very talented artist, too."

When everyone burst into laughter, Yvette approached to kiss him on the cheek. "No one will ever accuse you of being modest about your abilities, darling."

That got another laugh. He laid his hand on the small of her back. "Ah, but it isn't my abilities that make the portrait excellent, my love. It's you. You're amazing."

"You flatterer, you," Yvette said with a teasing smile. "Do go on."

"Here, here!" Blakeborough raised his glass of champagne. "To my amazing sister."

She blew her brother a kiss as everyone joined him in the toast. Then their guests began to chatter among themselves, some of them heading over to examine the portrait more closely.

Jeremy slipped his arm more firmly about her waist. "You do like it, don't you?"

"I like everything you paint."

"No, you don't. I seem to recall a rather insulting comment about looking at dead deer at the breakfast table."

"Oh, right. I forgot about that. But I do like *most* things you paint." She lowered her voice. "Especially the picture on our bedchamber wall that scandalizes the servants."

He chuckled. "At least you're not naked in it. I still have to paint that one."

She eyed him askance. "That will have to wait until after our trip to America with your mother and sister. Can you imagine Amanda bursting in on us to tell us about some new piece of mill equipment and finding me nude?"

"I daresay she wouldn't even blink. My mother, on the other hand—"

"Good Lord, don't even think it!" She glanced over to where his mother was regaling a gentleman with the tale of her arrival in England. "I'm looking forward to our trip. To seeing where you grew up." She slanted a wary look at him. "Do you mind?"

"Why would I mind? I'm the one who invited you."

"I know, but . . . it's been years, and—"

"I don't mind, and I know what you mean. But I'm fine, really." He squeezed her waist. "Besides, I can't wait to see what you make of our quaint American customs."

She arched an eyebrow. "Probably the same thing you and your sister make of our quaint English customs. Especially the Christmas ones. Like Stir-up Sunday, which you mocked exceedingly because we English have a whole day to celebrate 'mixing up a dessert,' as you call it."

"That one is odd, but I do like others of your Christmas customs. I'm already rather fond of the mistletoe kissing idea."

"Yes, I know," she said, eyes gleaming. "Last night, when you asked me to explain what was hanging in the hall, I had no idea that this morning I'd find mistletoe in every available room in the house, you wicked rogue, you."

"Is my brother being wicked again?" Amanda asked as she approached them. "Haven't you cured him of that yet?"

"Certainly not." Yvette grinned. "Why would I?"

"Well, he's not the only wicked man around here," Amanda grumbled. "Some stranger just came up to me in the hall and kissed me right on the lips."

When Jeremy laughed, Yvette said, "Oh, dear, I probably should have explained mistletoe to your sister, too."

"How did you respond?" Jeremy asked Amanda.

"I kissed him back, of course. It's not every day a handsome gentleman kisses me."

"That's because it's not every day that you dress

so well." When his wife elbowed him, Jeremy said, "What? It's true. Amanda looks unusually well-attired tonight."

Yvette had been advising his sister on her clothing choices. Sometimes his sister even listened.

"Be that as it may," Amanda said, "after I found out who he was, I wished I'd slapped him for his impertinence."

"Why? Who is he?" Jeremy asked. "Point him out and I'll go defend your honor." Then he ruined that statement by laughing.

"You're such a child." Amanda pointed to a man engaged in a heated conversation with Knightford. "That's him. I don't even know his name."

"Uh-oh," Yvette said. "That's Lord Stephen."

"Knightford's youngest brother?" Jeremy said incredulously. "Is he one of our guests?"

"He is now. Clarissa spotted him in the village today and asked me if she could invite him. I was happy to do so. Edwin and I know him well."

"Yes, but Knightford doesn't seem pleased about it. The reason I haven't met the man is the marquess wouldn't even let him join St. George's," Jeremy said.

"Probably because he'd bore all of you with his heated opinions. I would brain him in under a minute, myself." Amanda scrutinized the man with a more than cursory interest and colored oddly before snapping her gaze back to them. "Well, I think I'll go look at the portrait. People have been crowding around it so much I haven't yet had the chance." And off she went.

For the next few moments, as Yvette's attention

was commanded by another guest, Jeremy watched Amanda and Lord Stephen. When his sister wasn't sneaking looks at Lord Stephen, the man was staring brazenly at her.

Jeremy recognized that look. It was how he'd stared at Yvette the first night they'd met.

And given what Knightford had said about his brother, it worried him. Lord Stephen had no money, he'd burned every bridge to every connection, and he had no useful profession other than causing trouble. He'd probably kissed Amanda because he'd heard she was an heiress.

Thunderation.

The guest Yvette was speaking to walked off, and she caught the direction of Jeremy's gaze. "What do you think?" Yvette whispered. "Aren't they perfect for each other?"

"No. He's probably hunting a fortune."

"Oh, I doubt that. And even if he were, she would see right through it."

He frowned. "I'm not so sure. My sister isn't good with managing men the way you are, sweetheart."

She burst into laughter.

"What?"

Tucking her hand in the crook of his elbow, she leaned up to kiss his cheek. "You are absolutely the only person who sees me that way. And I love you for it."

When she then cast him a sparkling smile, he forgot all about his sister. He forgot all about the guests and the portrait and the fact that it had been accepted for exhibit at the Royal Academy.

All he could see was his wife. Yvette had been so

frantic with making sure their new house was ready for guests, and then settling them in yesterday, that it had been three long nights since he'd made love to her.

"Tell me, sweetheart, as my guide to all things English: just how improper is it for a hostess to leave her guests and disappear for, say, an hour or two before dinner?"

"Very improper." Her gaze turned sultry. "Why? What did you have in mind?"

"I thought we might take a walk in our new gardens. Find a wooded area. Or maybe even an ornamental bridge."

"It's rather cold outside," she pointed out.

"Ah, right." He bent to whisper, "Then I suppose we'll have to settle for our own bed."

And as she laughed, he drew her from the room. There were definitely some compensations to being a man who no longer blew with the wind.

Want even more sizzling romance from
New York Times bestselling author
Sabrina Jeffries?

Don't miss

THE STUDY OF
SEDUCTION

the second book in her sexy Sinful Suitors series.

Coming soon from Headline Eternal.

One

London, England
April 1830

"Clearly, you have lost your bloody mind."

When every member present in the reading room of St. George's Club turned to look at Edwin Barlow, Earl of Blakeborough, he realized how loudly he'd spoken.

With a quelling glance that sent them scrambling to mind their own business, Edwin returned his attention to Warren Corry, the Marquess of Knightford. "This plan of yours can't possibly work."

Warren was Edwin's closest friend. Really, his only friend, aside from his sister's new husband, Jeremy Keane. Edwin didn't make friends easily, probably because he didn't suffer fools easily. And society was full of fools.

That was precisely why Edwin, Jeremy, and Warren had started this club—so they could separate the fools from the fine men. So they could protect the women in their lives from fortune hunters, gamblers, rakehells, and every other variety of scoundrel in London.

Warren was clearly taking that mission very seriously. Perhaps too seriously.

"Clarissa will never agree," Edwin said.

"She has no choice."

Edwin narrowed his gaze on Warren. "You actually believe you can convince your sharp-tongued ward to let me squire her about town during the season."

"Only until I return. And why not?" Warren said, though he took a long swig of brandy as if to fortify himself for the fight. "It isn't as if she hates you."

"No, indeed," Edwin said sarcastically. "She only challenges my every remark, ignores any advice I offer, and tweaks my nose incessantly. The last time I saw her, she called me the Blakeborough Bear and said I belonged in the Tower of London menagerie, where ordinary people could be spared my growls. "

Warren burst into laughter. When Edwin lifted an eyebrow at him, Warren's laugh petered out into a cough. "Er, sorry, old boy. But you have to admit that's amusing."

"Not nearly as amusing as it will be to watch you try to talk her into this," Edwin drawled as he settled back in his chair. "She's not going to agree."

"Don't be too sure. You mustn't take her pokes at you as anything more than her usual mischief-making. You let her exaggerations get under your skin, which only tempts her to tease you more. You should just ignore her when she starts plaguing you."

Ignore Clarissa? Impossible. He'd spent half his life trying unsuccessfully to unwrap the mystery that was Lady Clarissa Lindsey. Her barbed wit fired his temper, her provocative smile inflamed him, and her shadowed eyes haunted his sleep. He could no more ignore her than he could ignore a rainbowed sunset . . . or a savage storm.

For three months now, she'd been isolated at Warren's estate, Hatton Hall, and Edwin had felt every second of her absence. That was why the very notion of spending time with her sent his blood pumping.

Not with anticipation. Certainly not. Couldn't be.

"What do you say, old boy?" Warren held Edwin's gaze. "I need you. *She* needs you."

Edwin ignored the leap in his pulse. Clarissa didn't need *anyone*, least of all him. Thanks to the fortune left to her by her late father, the Earl of Margrave, she didn't have to marry for love or anything else. She'd reportedly refused dozens of marriage proposals since her debut seven years ago.

But it wasn't her fortune that had men falling all over themselves trying to catch her eye. It was her quick wit. Her effervescent personality. Her astonishing beauty. She was the fair-haired, green-eyed, porcelain-skinned darling of society, and she almost certainly knew it.

Which was why he rather enjoyed the idea of watching Warren attempt to convince her that she should go about town with a gruff curmudgeon like himself. "Assuming that she and I both agree to this insanity—how long would I have her on my hands?"

"It shouldn't be more than a few weeks," Warren said. "However long it takes me to deal with her brother in Portugal. I can't leave Niall stranded on the Continent with all the unrest there right now."

"I assume she knows that's the reason for your trip."

"Actually, no. She doesn't yet even know about his letter, which was waiting for me when we arrived from Shropshire for the season. I wanted to be sure you would agree to keep an eye on her before I told her. But once she learns that this involves Niall, she'll want me to go after him, and she'll realize I won't do that unless I'm sure she's safe."

"Safe from this Durand fellow." The reason for this charade Warren was proposing.

Warren's jaw hardened. "Count Geraud Durand, yes."

Settling back into his chair, Edwin drummed his fingers on his thigh. "If I'm to do this, you'd better tell me everything you know about this Frenchman."

"He's the French ambassador's first secretary. And because the ambassador had to return to France right after Christmas, Durand is now running the embassy as the *charge d'affaires*. The position gives him a great deal of power."

"And what the devil does he want with Clarissa?"

"A wife. He asked her to marry him in Bath some months ago."

That stunned Edwin. Men in the field of diplomacy generally preferred wives who were not inclined to speak their minds.

"She turned him down," Warren went on. "That's why we had to return to London. Unfortunately, he followed us here. He seemed to have made it his mission to gain her no matter what. He was at every public event we attended after our return from Bath. Twice, he tried to accost her on the street."

His lips thinned into a grim line. "The bastard frightened her enough that she started avoiding going out in public, and you know that's not like her. So after we spent Christmas at your brother-in-law's, I whisked her and her mother off to Shropshire where I knew he dared not follow, since he had to serve as *charge d'affaires* here. I'd hoped our absence would give his ardor time to cool."

"And has it?"

"I don't know. We've only just returned, so I've not had time to assess the situation. But I'm not taking any chances. She has to be protected while I'm trying to sort out her brother's situation. He can't continue abroad like this indefinitely. And I can't continue to manage my properties *and* his, even with Clarissa's help."

Edwin snorted. "Clarissa helps?"

"There's more to her than you realize."

Ah, but Edwin did realize it. Granted, he wouldn't have expected her to have any skill at estate management, but despite her outrageous manner, he sometimes glimpsed a seriousness in her that reminded him of his own.

Or perhaps she just had dyspepsia. Hard to know with Clarissa. She was entirely unpredictable. Which was why she always threw him out of sorts.

Warren waved over a servant and ordered another brandy. "Honestly, accompanying her won't be as trying as you think. Don't you need to go out into society this season anyway? Aren't you bent on marrying?"

"Yes." Well, he was bent on siring an heir, anyway, which required wedding *someone*. Though God only knew who that might be.

"You see? It's perfect. You have to go on the marriage mart. Clarissa wants to enjoy the season, and I want her to find a husband. It's an ideal situation."

"If you say so." How he could successfully court anyone with Clarissa hanging about was anyone's guess, but he supposed it might improve his stern reputation if he had a beautiful woman on his arm at the usual balls. Assuming she would even agree to take his arm. That was by no means certain with Clarissa.

Warren eyed him closely. "You were still recovering from the loss of Jane last season, so this will be your first real attempt to secure a wife since Jane jilted you. Do you have any particular lady in mind?"

"No. I know what I want. But God only knows if I can find a *who* to go with it."

"And what exactly are your requirements for a wife? Other than that she be of breeding age, I suppose."

"I would prefer a woman who's responsible and uncomplicated. One who's quiet and sensible."

"In other words, someone you can keep under your thumb. The way your father kept your mother under his thumb."

A swell of painful memories made acid burn his throat. "Father didn't keep her under his thumb; he ignored her. I will never do that to my wife."

"You will if she's as dull as what you describe." Warren leaned back in his chair. "When I get around to choosing a wife, I want a lively wench who will keep me well entertained." He winked. "If you know what I mean."

Edwin rolled his eyes. "Remind me again why we asked you to join St. George's? You're as bad as the men we're guarding our women against."

"Ah, but I don't prey on innocents. Any woman who lands in my bed jumped there of her own accord. And I dare say that's true of any number of fellows here."

It probably was. Even Edwin had taken a mistress in his twenties when his loneliness had grown too acute to endure. That hadn't, however, been a very satisfying experience. Knowing that a woman was with you only for your rank and money was somehow more lonely than not having a woman with you at all.

Although with his sister Yvette now married and out of the house, he'd started to feel the disadvantages of a solitary way of life. So once more he'd be looking for a wife, always a singularly awkward experience.

Especially since he didn't know how to please a woman. Or even how to talk civilly to one. He couldn't spin a clever yarn, or hide an opinion beneath a facile compliment. Sadly, most women seemed to prefer facile compliments to blunt truths. Hence, his difficulty finding a suitable wife. "When will you broach this with Clarissa?"

He looked at his pocket watch. "At dinner, in about half an hour. I was hoping you'd come."

"*Now?*"

"Why not? Might as well get it over with, eh? And I *am* leaving for Portugal in the morning."

Devil take it. Edwin would have liked more time to prepare. He was not the spontaneous sort. "Planning to have us join forces against her, are you?"

"That wasn't my intention initially, no." Warren gulped some brandy. "When we left Hatton Hall for London, I'd hoped that by now Yvette and Jeremy would have returned from America. And you know that Yvette can talk Clarissa into just about anything."

Edwin smiled. His sister could talk anyone into just about anything, even him.

"But I gather they're still abroad," Warren continued.

"It may be a few more weeks before they return. Sorry."

"Well, it can't be helped. At least my aunt will be there to help persuade her."

Edwin suppressed a snort. Lady Margrave, Clarissa's mother, was a flighty female who rarely offered sound advice, so Clarissa rarely heeded her. He doubted that this time would be any different.

Warren rose. "I'm truly sorry that I have to run off. So, are you coming or not?" The casual words were belied by his tight expression.

They both knew that Edwin hadn't yet agreed to the plan. And why not? Because the thought of spending weeks in Clarissa's company put him on edge as nothing else could.

But it didn't matter. Warren was his friend, and wouldn't hesitate to help if the shoe was on the other foot. So neither would Edwin.

He stood. "I'm coming."

* * *

Clarissa's mother turned to her in a panic. "I cannot believe your cousin did this! Warren knows better than to invite a man for dinner with no warning. What was he thinking?"

Clarissa raised an eyebrow at her mother's reflection in the bedchamber's looking glass. "He was thinking that it's just Edwin, whom we've known for ages. And who comes regularly to dine."

"I don't know if pigeon pie is quite suitable for guests," Mama said as if Clarissa hadn't spoken. "Oh, and Madeira! Edwin loves his Madeira, you know, and we are fresh out!"

"Mama—"

"And the pickled onions were too sour the last time we ate them. I was hoping to use them up tonight, but if Edwin is coming—"

"Mama, calm down! It's not as if we're expecting the Tsar of Russia, you know." She smiled into the mirror. "Although Edwin *would* make a fine tsar. All he'd have to do is be his usual autocratic and dictatorial self."

Thankfully that observation broke her mother out of her fretting. "And he would look quite the part, too, wouldn't he? All that dark hair and that chiseled jaw."

And broad shoulders and regal bearing and slate-gray eyes as coldly beautiful as a Russian night spangled with stars.

Clarissa scowled at herself. She must be addled to be thinking of Edwin like that. Though he *was* sinfully handsome. In a sort of standoffish way.

"Why, I can almost imagine him in an ermine cape and one of those tall, furry hats," Mama said.

Clarissa laughed. "Edwin would only wear such a pretentious thing to a coronation, and then only because he had to."

His manner of dress was always correct, but terribly sober.

Unlike hers. She examined her gown in the mirror and smiled. Edwin would probably look sternly upon the confection of lace and lavender bows. But she would never change her gown for *him*. Let him give her one of his ruthlessly critical glances; she would not be cowed by them.

Indeed, it was merely force of habit that had her

pinching her cheeks until they glowed nicely pink. It was not because she wanted to look pretty for Edwin. No, indeed.

"You know, my girl," Mama said, "if you were a bit nicer to that man, you could probably have him wrapped about your finger in a matter of weeks."

"Oh, I doubt that. Edwin is far too inflexible to be wrapped about anything. More's the pity." Clarissa would dearly love to see the woman who could manage *that*.

But it wouldn't be her. Edwin, of all people, would never accept her as she was, especially once he knew the full extent of her youthful mistakes. And she wasn't bending to anyone's demands of what a wife should be—not his, not Mama's, not Warren's. She'd allowed a man to bully her once, and it had shattered her life.

Never again.

Pasting a brilliant smile to her lips, she whirled to face her mother. "Shall we go down?"

"Not yet, my angel. The servant said the gentlemen are already here. So we should keep them waiting. You must never let a man be too sure of you."

"It's *Edwin*, Mama," she said tightly. "He's sure of everything and everyone, no matter what I do." She offered her arm to her mother with her usual coaxing smile. "Come now, I know you're positively dying for a glass of wine. I certainly am."

"Oh, all right." Leaning on Clarissa's arm, Mama let herself be led to the door. "But you must promise to give him a compliment first thing. Men like that."

"Right," Clarissa said noncommittally.

"And don't contradict him all the time. Men despise fractious women."

"Mm-hmm."

"And do *not* spout your witticisms incessantly. It's very mannish. Not to mention . . ."

As they made their slow way down the stairs, Clarissa let her mother drone on, only half-listening to the usual recitation of little tricks designed to hook a man and reel him in. Those might have enabled her mere cit of a mother to snag an earl, but they smacked of deception to Clarissa.

If a man couldn't like her as she was, what was the point? Clarissa could barely hide her true opinions from Mama. How was she to do it with a husband?

Not that she ever intended to *have* a husband. At the very thought of taking a man into her bed, her hands grew clammy and her throat closed up.

No. Marriage was not for her.

". . . and do be sure to save the biggest slice of cake for him," Mama was saying as they reached the bottom of the stairs.

"Nonsense. I'm not saving *anything* for Edwin."

"That's only fair," drawled Edwin from somewhere in the shadows to the right of the staircase. "I'm not saving anything for you, either."

Striving to hide her surprise, she halted as he came into the light.

"Edwin!" Mama cried. "My dear boy!" She held out her hand.

Dutifully, he came forward to take it. "You're looking well, Lady Margrave," he murmured as he bent to brush a kiss over Mama's cheek.

"You're looking rather fine yourself," Mama chirped as she drew back to survey him.

And Lord, he was, in his tailcoat of dark blue wool and his waistcoat and trousers of plain white poplin. Even his cravat was simply tied, which only accentuated the masculine lines of his jaw and sharp planes of his features, so starkly handsome.

How had he managed to grow only more attractive in a mere three months? And why on earth was she gawking at him? This was *Edwin*, for pity's sake. It would swell his head even more if he knew what she was thinking.

Instead, she teased him. "Don't tell me—you were so impatient for us to come down that you've been pacing the foyer in anticipation."

The idea was ludicrous, of course. *Impatient* wasn't even in Edwin's vocabulary. If ever a man believed that slow and steady won the race, it was him.

And he clearly recognized the irony, for he flashed her one of his rare smiles. "Actually, I was fetching this from the library. Warren told me he was done with it." His eyes gleamed in the lamplight as he held out a book. "Of course, if you wish to read it yourself . . ."

"Doubtful," she said. "If it's a book *you* loaned him, then it's deadly dull."

"Clarissa," Mama chided beneath her breath.

But Edwin merely laughed, as she'd hoped he would. She took great pride in the fact that she could sometimes make him laugh. No other woman seemed able to. No other woman dared try.

"Well, it *is* about mechanical engineering, which I would imagine isn't your favorite subject," he said. "However did you guess?"

"Because I know you so well, Lord Blakeborough."

He sobered, his gaze turning oddly intense even for him. "Do you? I'm not so sure."

The words hung in the air for a moment in frozen silence before that was shattered by her cousin's approach.

"I found another book you might enjoy, old boy," Warren said as he bent to kiss first his aunt, then Clarissa. "It's about automatons."

As Warren handed him the book, keen interest leapt in Edwin's eyes. "I haven't read this title. Thank you. I'll get it back to you as soon as I'm done."

"No hurry." Warren shot Clarissa a veiled glance. "As you well know, I won't need it anytime soon."

Whatever was that about?

Before she could ponder it, Warren offered Mama his arm. "Come, Aunt, let's get you off your feet while we have our wine before dinner."

"Thank you, my lad," she cooed, and let him lead her to the breakfast room. "That is ever so thoughtful of you! But then you always were a dear. Why, I remember when . . ."

As Mama prattled on, Edwin was left to come behind with Clarissa. "So," he murmured, "exactly what were you refusing to save for me?"

It took her a moment to remember that he'd overheard her earlier. "The biggest slice of cake."

"I don't like cake."

"I know. That's why I'm not wasting it on you. You won't appreciate it, and you'd probably eat it just to be polite."

He slanted a serious glance at her. "Perhaps I'd give it to you, instead."

"I doubt that, but we'll never know, shall we?" she said lightly. "I'm saving it for myself, regardless."

"So I heard."

"Because you were eavesdropping." Mischief seized her. "How rude of you."

They passed into the breakfast room, and he shrugged. "If you don't want people hearing your pronouncements, you shouldn't talk as loud as a dockworker."

Mama paused while settling onto the settee. "A dockworker! For shame, Edwin—what a thing to say to a lady! Have you no pretty compliments to offer?"

When he stood blatantly unrepentant, Clarissa said, "If Edwin knew how to compliment ladies, Mama, he would be too popular in society to settle for having dinner with the mere likes of *us*."

"There's no settling involved, I assure you," he said irritably.

She was still congratulating herself on getting beneath his cool reserve again when Warren stepped in. "Play nice now, cousin. We need him."

"For what?" Clarissa asked.

Instead of answering, her guardian gestured to the settee. "You'd better sit down. I've got something to tell you and your mother."

headline ETERNAL

FIND YOUR HEART'S DESIRE...

VISIT OUR WEBSITE: www.headlineeternal.com
FIND US ON FACEBOOK: facebook.com/eternalromance
FOLLOW US ON TWITTER: @eternal_books
EMAIL US: eternalromance@headline.co.uk